A Debt to the Stars

A Story of the Metaspacial Blockchain

Kevin Hincker

Skylake Media

$$* \quad * \quad *$$

*"On Earth or in the stars, the bankers get f*ing rich and the rest of us suffer. I wish someone would do something about it."*
    - The Pirate Cetus

CONTENT WARNING

A lot of f*bombs.

The Cover

Many readers ask about the cover, which was created by a truly brilliant artist named Thea Magerand, to whom I owe my own debt.

Discover her here: https://www.ikaruna.eu/

1

There are ten million cultures in the Known Economy, all recorded on a tiny fraction of a single link of the endless Metaspacial Blockchain.

—From *The Book of* Ω64, of the Swandeen Pracis

Diana's eyes flicked left again, to the red countdown timer blinking *T-minus 3 hours 02 minutes*, which meant ten minutes had already passed since she'd wedged behind the podium to face this cabin full of bored science writers. She'd come down so her anxiety wouldn't affect the launch team, hoping reporter questions would numb her like they typically did. But ten minutes at the mic had only seen her anxiety grow. It wasn't that she was superstitious. Experience had simply taught her the unwritten rule; a project as complex as Namaka was guaranteed a snag, a last-minute, mission critical Problem, just before launch.

So what would it be—a valve? Sonar calibration? Exterior antennas?

She fingered her collar, felt hot sweat behind her ears, felt the room tightening like a coffin full of folding chairs. It had probably been a mistake to come. She glanced back to the reporters and pointed to one she recognized.

"So *Diana*," he started, "you and Greg Dantly looked more than a little *starry-eyed* on deck yesterday, and I think what *everybody's* wondering is, are you and Greg romantically involved?"

"Well, here's the thing *Dan*," she said, and gestured to the pseudoscreens floating at her sides, tracking ocean floor temps, weather metrics, sensor data. "The subject of this briefing is historic deep water bioprospecting, not my romantic life or my *not*-romantic life. Those are pictures of the bottom of the ocean, see them? Let's stay on topic." She resisted the impulse to pull at her collar again.

"Is it true that you, Greg Dantly, and Liz Mustang all roomed together at MIT?" Dan pressed.

"We were in the dorms with everyone else," she said, "next question. Not Dan. In the back?"

"What's the one thing you're most worried will go wrong today?" someone shouted.

"Nothing will go wrong at all," Diana said. "We won't have any problems. Another question?"

"Any seasickness for you Diana?" a woman wondered.

"No. Does it feel hot in here to anyone?"

"Diana," a man called from the back, "you're 30 now, since your father died in 2029 you've been CEO of Roark Pharmaceuticals. What do you think Atticus Roark would make of the way you've run his company?"

"My god, you people," Diana meant to whisper, but instead semi-shouted into the mic, though the journalists hardly noticed. She pointed at the pseudos again, at the graphs and mission goals. She flipped damp red hair off her neck and took a breath.

"For one thing," she started, "what does my age have to do with anything? And look, yes, fifteen years ago my father did a great thing for the world and we're all in his debt, but what we're doing *now* is what really matters. Does anyone have—"

The clank of the cabin door interrupted her as it swung in, and the reporters turned. Diana watched as one of Liz's sailor-technicians stumbled through. And just from the look in his eyes she knew—they had their Problem. Hydraulics? Chip failure? They had backup hardware. It would be fine.

She watched the tech sidle through the chairs, reporters craning to watch. Then he reached her, and leaned in to whisper, "He's…"

"Say it," she insisted, "what?"

"It's Marcus, Ms. Roark. His hand is broken."

It took a second. The Problem was… "His *hand?*"

The tech nodded. "Just a freak accident, he crushed it in the retrieval harness. They're having him airlifted to the mainland for surgery." The tech was staring. Shocked. "The reserve pilot's still delayed on shore… Liz says we lose satellite access in twelve hours… Greg's in Spear One, but there's one pilot for Spear Two, so Liz says… the mission's off. We have to scrub the mission."

Diana shot another look to the timer—now impossibly frozen at 2 *hours 58 minutes 21 seconds*—and cursed herself for not simply building Namaka its own constellation of micro-sats. Instead they'd flown this super-array from fifteen separate providers. Missing their window could set them back a year—maybe years. Her eyes strayed from the timer to the newly stirring reporters. Drug bioprospecting bored them but they loved a shipwreck, and they sensed a sudden storm on the horizon. She deflected one question while she sent the tech back to Liz, mentally unspooling dive data.

The Problem wasn't what she'd expected: Marcus injured, Greg the only pilot, and they needed *both* subs in the trench to sync the array. But the solution was obvious. To her at any rate. She broke from the podium toward the door, and as she slipped through she heard the reporters behind her finally begin shouting better questions.

FIFTEEN MINUTES later she emerged from a stairwell onto the deck of the Stalwart wearing the yellow pilot jumpsuit she had grabbed from Marcus's locker. It ballooned around her small frame. She had it cinched with a cargo strap. The air was cold up here; the waves had swelled, chop rattled them sideways. On the horizon off the stern was a pencil smudge—the Northern Marianas Islands, almost underwater now, after decades of rising seas.

She saw the Spears at the stern in their launch cradles, and just for a moment she paused to appreciate them. Each soared thirty feet, taller than the ship's con, a pair of crimson, PressureGlass torpedoes, their wide thruster housings tapering to transparent pilot capsules. The crew called them The Blenders.

Greg stood exactly where she'd expected him, by the flank of Spear One, counseling a group from the launch team. The team looked crestfallen but riveted. People liked being consoled by Greg Dantly. Greg was telling a joke and they were tolerating his humor like everyone did, because of the cheekbones and the sympathetic diamond eyes.

One of the launch crew saw her and started in surprise, tapped another, then they were all looking, and finally Greg turned, squinting in the cold wind. He wore the same industrial lemon pilot suit she did, although on him it looked primped in place, like cherubs had dressed him. He was the clothesiest astrobiologist on the planet.

He jogged to meet her at the rail, sorrow dashed, and stepped close to embrace her, but she stopped him. He gave her suit a confused look. He had to know what it meant, he was resisting the admission. This would be a challenge, she knew, but she also knew the buttons to push.

"Why the suit?" he asked. She saw his admission dawn. "Are you... no. You've got to be kidding."

"I'll take Spear One down myself."

Negotiation begun, she thought. She knew how this idea would play with Greg. All the reasoned arguments were on his side. The reasonable course was take a loss, come back in a year, but Atticus

Roark wouldn't have surrendered because of a broken hand, so she needed a lever to use on Greg that was stronger than reason. She checked her watch, hoping the tech had found Liz. Liz was the lever.

"You're taking Spear One..." Greg wondered, like he was missing important facts.

"We finally get to dive together," she told him, giving him a smile neither of them trusted. "Look, getting to this point was too complicated. It'll be too costly to put it back together, the shareholders will kill me."

"Wait, *shareholders?* Since when do you care about shareholders?"

"That is my job, Greg. Shareholders. So. We're going to drop, deploy beacons, log the perimeter—just the essentials—and come back. I am a qualified pilot you know."

"What do you mean *qualified?*" he sputtered.

"I own you when the Spears are ambulatory. *All* of you."

Greg closed one eye, peered at the darkening, wind-blunted ocean, and said, "Yeah Diana, in the *tank* you beat us, but that's *sims* and this is *seven miles underwater.*"

"I'm going, and someone needs to tell the crew. You or me."

It took him a moment. Then he began peeling off his suit. Like she'd known he would.

"No way," he said. "Too risky, a risk for you, it's crazy... believe me, there'll be other chances, and please don't, don't hold this against me, I mean you're a *CEO*, you're a *blockchain theorist* for god sake not a sub jockey..."

Diana finally heard steps on the deck behind her, saw Greg's eyes narrow as he focused, and then Liz Mustang stood between them, ocean wind yanking Medusa-hair over Pharaoh-dark eyes. She wore waterproof rubber pants tucked into rubber boots and a thin white tank top, tattoos spiraling up brown arms and around her neck. Reptile ink, mostly snakes and geckos, with serpentine strings of text.

"Liz," Greg nodded, his tone careful.

"Hey bitches," Liz observed, "we have to scrub, is this a wet bag of suck or *what?*" Then she noticed Diana's suit. She took an appreciative moment. "Sexy."

"I'm dropping in Marcus's chair," Diana said.

Liz raised an eyebrow, looked at Greg crumpling his dive suit in two hands.

He shrugged. "I'm not diving. Unacceptable risk. Don't blame me."

Diana sighed. Here it was.

"Let's see what Liz thinks of me going," she told him.

"I don't frankly care what Liz thinks," Greg snapped, "I'm not doing it. It's ridiculous! Tell her, Liz. She's claustrophobic for god sake!"

"Never in the Spears," Diana couldn't help protesting. "Liz?"

"Well, I say Diana does whatever the hell Diana wants," Liz said slowly, eyes on Diana.

"Wow," Greg snorted disbelief, balling his suit and turning away. "I guess I'm the adult. I'm not going. Dive's off."

"Fuck *adult*," Liz announced, her fiery gaze almost consuming Diana. "*I'll* drop with you Di. We can go together. We've always wanted to."

Diana saw Greg freeze. She might have reasoned for hours and never changed his mind, because sometimes reason is just the wrong tool to negotiate with. She regretted the relationship damage this would probably do. But Namaka needed Greg in the sub. There are the important things, she knew, and the things you can fix later.

"You're a *crap* pilot," he was protesting to Liz.

"Says you," she laughed, "I *built* those subs."

"Well who cons the mission if you dive?" he demanded.

"A monkey, Greg, that's idiot work. Give me your suit. *Here.*"

Her hand was out, but she watched Diana. Greg looked between them, cold but spectacular in deck slacks and a pullover.

"Fine," he finally said, tossing up his hands, "fine I'll go. Liz can... but this is just a *very bad idea* so if anything, and I mean *anything* goes sideways, we call it and surface. Can we agree to that?"

Diana nodded. Liz shrugged. Greg gave Diana a final glance. He shook his head.

"Just don't pretend you wish this wasn't happening," he said. "I know you." Then he stalked off into the wind. Liz and Diana watched him go.

"I think I just got used a little bit," Liz said, "which feels dirty in a good way."

"Let's get the countdown rolling," Diana sighed. "We're losing light."

"My god you're ruthless. But that Greg. So competitive, am I right?"

"Greg's doing this because it's the best thing for the project."

"No. He's doing it because he's afraid to leave us alone together even seven miles down in separate subs. He knows I could have you back in a hot second. As if I even wanted you." Liz's voice was soft, a murmur as she stepped closer with her furnace eyes. "But who needs you? That's what I want to know. Your type's a dime a dozen—brilliant-sexy-as-shit CEOs who won't *ever* commit, though you dedicate your entire career to their idiot dreams? Please. There's dating apps full of you people."

"We both know... it's more functional this way," Diana said, and endured the disbelief in Liz's face. "This way we're doing impossible things, we're going to—"

The deck pitched, and before she could gather her balance Liz grabbed her. Fingers dark with lizard tails wrapped Diana's pale wrist, where the one tattoo anywhere on Diana's body lay open; a butterfly with stars on its wings.

"Butterflies," Liz sniffed, "you'll regret this cutesy bullshit. He'll regret his too."

Diana shook her head, freed her hand, and turned toward the Spears.

"He'll never win this rivalry," Liz told her, "and it's sad he doesn't realize."

Diana spun back. "You two are not rivals."

Liz sighed. "Not me." She jerked her chin at the shock-red submersibles rocking like temple guardians at the rail. "There's no way any of us compete with your ghosts. And by the way Greg's right. This is a shit idea. I really hope you know what you're doing."

Two HOURS and forty minutes later the hoists were grappled, the subs locked at the starboard rail, and it was time to board. Diana gave her Spear a last examination and couldn't repress a tiny shudder. Just the cold wind. Not the dropping seven miles in a PressureGlass aqua rocket.

She saw reporters on the bridge and saw Greg climb into Spear Two. Usually there were comments on the public comm as pilots prepped. Little jokes. Today there was silence. She put that disappointment aside as she climbed the ladder and dropped into her capsule.

The crew sealed the hatch above her and the world grew still. She heard only the soft waft of fans. She fit in this place the way she fit her favorite pajamas. She'd simulated hundreds of hours in this capsule over the last five years. By this time, it was the most peaceful place in her entire world. Nothing could touch her. The air was a perfect 76 degrees. A magic bubble of control.

She flipped dive computers live and settled in her harness, then gimbaled the seat 360, the control surfaces spinning with her. She knew she should be nervous, but all she felt was a rising urge to go. Just *go*.

"Namaka team, this is Stalwart dive control," came Liz on the comm. "Status?"

"Spear One, all systems nominal," Diana said back.

"Spear Two, green on the board," Greg said, voice measured, professional. For all his protests about the safety of the dive, Diana knew how eager he was to go. This dive was the first step in his own dream, studying extremophiles in the crushed oxygen-free zone beneath them, the closest an Earthly astrobiologist like him would ever come to life on other planets. Homemade aliens.

The sudden jolt of the hoists jerked her. Gears spun, thunked as the starboard deck slipped away, then she hung over rolling water. Her stomach twisted. The sims couldn't ever do this part justice. On the stern she saw Spear Two suspended, Greg visible in his harness.

"Spear One, we're dive ready," Liz's voice cracked. "On your mark."

"Let's get wet, dive control," Diana said.

The Spears dropped. Eager swells gripped her impeller housing and her sub bucked, still tied to the ship and vulnerable to swells. She fired thrusters and eased the stick to stay vertical. Just like the sims. And slowly, engines yearning downward, Spear One pulled itself into the sea on a cable.

Water coursed and rose around the capsule and suddenly there was light above and dark below. And she was under, an inch of dome in the air, her spear still latched to the cable like an infant with an umbilical cord.

"Spear One, ready to slip," she said.

"Spear Two ready," Greg echoed.

"On your mark Spear One," Liz said.

Diana took a breath. "Go drop."

The latch snapped, her sub jerked and all sensation of movement ceased. The view above went glassy blue, then riotous bubbling green as ballast spilled. The whine of thrusters momentarily rose. She peered across at Spear Two, the dark fuselage already indistinct in fading light but the capsule lit, with Greg clear as a thought bubble sinking beside her, down into immense dark everything.

"Spear One, Spear Two, prepare for glide," said Liz.

"Roger, Stalwart," Diana said.

"Spear Two ready," came Greg's voice. They were so close she could see his mouth move. He gimbaled his harness around from pseudo-screen to pseudo-screen, powering up the samplers. Greg carried the laboratory and prospecting sensors in Spear Two. Diana had the comm links in Spear One and the beacons to for satellite uplink.

"Glide in three, two, one, go," said Liz, and mission control cut power to thrusters in both subs. From this point they would let gravity do the work, while Stalwart monitored their position and did course correction. Why they'd wanted a fighter pilot like Marcus for this was beyond Diana. There was nothing for her to do until they went ambulatory. Greg would have his hands full for the hour dropping, overseeing a sample stream, but for Diana it was sixty minutes of waiting.

"Everything's green, Spears," Liz told them. "Remote guidance operative. We'll wire you down. Have a snack. Let us know if you see mermaids."

"Roger that, Stalwart," Diana said.

The environment around them would change now—pressure growing, gravity squeezing, until seven miles of saltwater ocean lay atop them. Machines stopped working at these depths, she knew. But her machines had passed every test. Mistakes people made could be fatal down there. But her teams didn't make mistakes. Well, there was Marcus and his broken hand. But she'd started thinking of that as a net positive.

In the distance were groups of jellied Medusozoans, like phosphor stars in the ether, and a moment later a cloud of iridescent fish schooled by, almost within reach. But the black grew with every passing yard. It billowed out until it was just her and Greg, falling through a dream, a dream that had started long before she'd taken over Roark Pharmaceuticals, before she met Liz and Greg, back before her sister had died, when Atticus Roark was saving the world with Immpenta.

SEVEN-YEAR-OLD DIANA FOLLOWS *her sister through their enormous house, copying the way Phoebe sits and eats, reads and types and talks. It's a game Diana loves. Phoebe is fifteen today, and they've just been told she will be leaving soon for MIT on a biotech scholarship. Phoebe the genius. Phoebe the future of Roark Labs, as their father tells them all. Phoebe will answer impossible questions. She will do the undoable. Diana imagines that future. It seems wonderful and close.*

They drive to the airport the day Phoebe flies off to school. Diana is sad on the trip home, watching her father, filled with pride, listing the diseases Phoebe will cure with him, once they finish with Ebola 3. Diana wishes she could make her father say nice things about her, but Diana is not a genius, not like that. When the car passes a lemonade stand, leaning and forlorn, Diana sees a girl she knows, a classmate, miserable behind un-poured pitchers. The girl's father watches, mute. Diana sees how unhappy that father is. Perhaps every father has one daughter who makes him unhappy?

Right then Diana asks her father to lend her $500 for a lemonade stand. She promises she'll double the money and return it in thirty days. He scoffs at the idea. $1000 from lemonade in thirty days? He agrees only when Diana's mother intervenes, with an encouraging smile at Diana. Neither parent believes in Diana the way they believe in Phoebe. But Diana has a plan.

Before her plan can run its course, however, the future of the Roark family is shattered. One night the phone rings. Diana hears her parents, her mother crying; Phoebe, in the dark on the MIT campus, has been kidnapped. Tense hours pass, a day—waiting. Police shepherd Diana everywhere. And then suddenly, though the family pays the ransom, begs for her return, Phoebe is dead at the hands of her captors. A month passes. The heart of family Roark is torn to pieces, the house laid hollow. Diana is almost forgotten, except for the servant, Charles, who minds her like his own child. But she doesn't mind.

Thirty days after their ride from the airport, hoping to help her father in his despair and knowing no other way, Diana enters his darkened office and sets an envelope on his desk. Inside, $1000, made not by selling drinks from a lemonade stand—an obvious impossibility— but by building and selling an improved lemonade stand to her classmate and her wealthy father. Diana wants to tell her own father this *story. Ask him questions about value, markets, negotiation—the many ways money can be made, the thing she is good at, as Phoebe was good at science.*

But Diana freezes when she sees his face. Atticus eyes his remaining daughter. He lifts the envelope as though she has put a soft, dead animal on his important papers.

"Nothing will bring her back."

Diana knows. But she wants to help the family. She can be something, not what her sister was, but something to make her father proud, if he will...

"Money?" Atticus's despair sweeps down on them both. Pulled thin by sorrow, he stands from his chair, leans heavily on his desk, and points at his young daughter "Money? Money won't help us. Money's not the solution to impossible problems. You borrow five hundred dollars and give back a thousand—that's arithmetic! We're not BANKERS! A Roark expands frontiers, A Roark shoots... for stars... why did she go? WHY DID THEY TAKE MY BABY?!"

Diana shakes. She lacks the experience to separate her father's heartbreak from the reasonable and true, and she can only stare. Her father is bent. His pain and hopelessness are hot around them. He tosses the envelope at Diana, sickened.

"The debt this world owes me can never be repaid. That is yours. Invest it, give it away, it makes no difference to me."

Diana takes the envelope, turns, and stumbles from the office. She is trembling, but even then, she's thinking of the future. She seals the envelope and finds a place to store it, and there she leaves it, unopened, while the stars spin her forward through years.

Liz's voice over the comm brought Diana out of her reverie. She realized with a start that it had been many minutes since anything had come over the radio from the Stalwart.

Something didn't feel right.

"Spear One," came Liz's voice. Diana groaned. She could tell there was another problem. Broken retrieval carriage? Changing weather? There were plans for these contingencies.

"We have, ah," Liz stammered, fumbling, "we don't know... we have a situation... oh my... god..."

Liz, at a loss for words? Not a hoist, Diana realized. Something badly wrong. She focused on her instruments. The Spears were just passing the five-mile mark. Without needing to think, she snapped forward and ran her indicators. Emergency protocols. She threw on exterior floods and whipped her harness in a circle, scanning the water. It was all instinct. Nothing in the data was saying anything dangerous.

"Stalwart," she said. "I'm green here, all indicators. Greg?"

"All systems clear in Spear Two."

"You need to see this," Liz's voice came back, after a moment.

"See what?" Diana asked. Silence. "Stalwart, what is your situation?"

She listened to Liz breathing for two full seconds. Was the ship sinking?

"I don't know our situation. Go to visual, Diana. Greg. Visual *now*."

Diana flipped a pseudoscreen up over her dash. She saw Greg in Spear Two, forty feet off, scanning a duplicate screen. She expanded it, and a view of the deck of the Stalwart resolved, the crew, the technicians, the sailors, all pressed against the aft railing, looking up.

"Stalwart, I can't tell what you're seeing..." Diana started, then someone zoomed the camera into the sky. There were shapes there. She couldn't parse it. Birds? Airplanes?

"What am I looking at?" she asked. "What's in the sky?"

"We... those are... ships Diana. Those are, they're massive. They just entered the atmosphere. And all long-range communication is cut. Massive electromagnetic surges. We can't reach the mainland."

Liz stopped talking, left the mic hot, and Diana heard shouts and footsteps on the deck, saw crew pointing at the sky. Above Earth.

Diana saw, were dozens of shapes in a circle; the scale was hard to judge, but they had to be truly massive.

She'd stopped breathing. Which was wrong. You always keep breathing.

Her body felt small, gluey, and hard to use; something must be wrong with the topside camera. Whatever those things were, she had to get topside and get control of the camera. A fear-cavity opened inside her. Trapped five miles from the surface in a tiny fishbowl.

Capsule, heat, her breath fast and the chair like a tomb, squeezing tighter and tighter. She could feel herself gasping for air, her mind scrambling for an explanation. Fans failing? Water pressing, dark fears, missing people, grief and debt... Wiping sweat and tears, Diana scrambled out of her harness on instinct, her mind racing... air, get to the hatch... wait, not the hatch, not underwater...breathe, breathe, breathe, breathe...

"Stalwart, what's telemetry from NASA Deep say?" Greg's voice, smooth as air traffic control. Their private pilot channel snapped open while Greg waited for Stalwart's reply. Diana trembled and stared into the dark. Frozen.

"I forgot my Xanax," Greg said, calm, hands on the Spear's instruments, methodical and precise, "can I have one of yours? Hey you know, Diana, I'm thinking maybe put these harness straps on the other side of the impact racks? Because that gives us three extra inches, and we can slide the whole assembly back so we relax. What do you think? Can you see me over here? Look at me butterfly. Deep breath. Look. Over here."

She shifted her head. Saw him. Wanting air. She hung watching his face, air... and in a rush she found her breath. She scrambled back to her harness, trembling. This had never happened in a Spear before. So, maybe Greg was right, there was a first time for everything. But she was right too—he belonged down here. This was his element.

"Negative," came Liz's voice, at last, "we can't raise NASA. All communication cut."

"Ok, look," Greg replied, "there's a comsat you can try at period 92.7. I'm sending config data now."

"Roger that," Liz said. "Hold."

Greg was back on the private channel. Diana felt her arms shaking and listened for Liz's reply, trying to relax.

"Diana, I have something very important to ask you," she heard Greg say.

"What? Ask what?" Oh god, what now...?

"How do you make an octopus laugh?"

"What... ?"

"With ten tickles"

"What?"

"Funny right? Do you know why the lobster blushed? Because the sea weed!"

She saw him smiling, really enjoying himself, only fifteen feet from her own capsule. He just wasn't funny. No one could convince him. Why she ever laughed she didn't know, you couldn't encourage him...

"Hey Diana what's a dolphin say when he's confused? He says *I'm sorry, can you please be more Pacific than that?* Hey, guess what's the strongest animal in the ocean—it's *mussels.* Did you hear they put the ocean in jail? Yeah, it keeps showing divers its bottom. Hey..."

—she gasped, snorted, *please not a snort laugh*—

"...what do you call a lazy shellfish, do you know? *A slobster* get it?"

She snorted—*no*— "Stupid shut up..."

"Stupid oh really? *Whale* hello there Diana! I think you're *fintastic* Diana! Hey Diana I think we might be lost at sea but I'm not *shore*! My god those people up there on that boat are missing this, they don't appreciate me."

It was a character flaw she had. His idiocy sometimes shook her body and left her in stitches and she had no control. She bent forward, trying to make it stop, panting tears.

"Don't say *anything*," she warned, as control returned. "*Stop.*"

"You're the only one who laughs at my shit. Why is that?"

Then Liz was back. "No satellites to ping. Everything's down, we're blind."

Diana watched Greg through the floodlit murk. They were still falling. Detritus floated up between their subs.

"So, what's the plan, control?" he asked. "We calling this?"

"I'm pulling you," Liz agreed.

Diana tried picturing what was happening on the Stalwart. Liz was mission control, but Captain Anderson might have his own ideas about what to do with his ship. Suddenly, a warning chimed. Diana saw termination indicators on her board.

"Strap to abort," Liz commanded.

"Stalwart, no!" Diana cried. This was moving too fast. "Don't go off half-cocked. Let's see what the data…"

"Oh, I'm fully cocked, love. Strap *now*, I'm blowing ballast in five, four…"

Diana's hand flew to the override and palmed it before Liz could finish. The red indicators flipped to green and Spear One and Spear Two shifted to local control. By default the thrusters spun up and their descent stopped. They hung. She checked, saw Greg's surprised face hanging even with her own.

"Diana!" Liz sounded scared now. "What are you doing? The situation's changed. There are—Diana there are *alien ships* in orbit over the Earth—you get your asses out of the ocean *NOW!*"

Diana didn't answer. The ship to ship channel opened, though Greg didn't speak. Seconds passed, miles beneath the surface, the subs literally treading water, while Diana spun contingencies through her mind.

"What are we doing, Diana?" Greg asked finally. "I thought we agreed. If anything happens, we call the dive."

"I know. I have to go though." She saw him get ready to argue and cut him off. "Because who knows what'll happen after this? It might all—who knows what this means? Anything might happen after god damn alien ships! I can't just give up—I just... there are beacons to drop. The mission's not finished."

"The satellites are down!"

"They'll come back."

Liz, increasingly desperate on the public comm, was demanding they respond. Diana muted her.

"You go up," she pointed for Greg.

"We both go," he argued, "you *agreed*, Diana."

"You can't miss first contact! I'll just drop the beacons and turn around."

"What are you saying? It's totally crazy staying down here!"

"I know—so go back! You have local control, go!"

"But you're the one—you shouldn't even *be* here, you want *me* to go up? You're not a biologist, you're not a pilot, Roark Pharma's minting *billions,* there's no need for this risk but nothing's ever enough for you, is it? Atticus is *dead,* Diana, an here I am—you're missing the life that's right in front of you! And just no. I'm not going without you. The only reason I'm here at all is you—you *negotiated* me into it!"

The pseudoscreen over her control console swung to a new view. Liz had dug up a handheld camera and was holding it close to her face, furious, still muted. Diana could lip read her own name within a string of obscenities. She pushed the public comm live and Liz's voice flooded the capsule.

"... and I can read your biometrics so I know you're not *dead,* so god damnit *ANSWER ME!"*

"Stalwart?" Diana commed. "This is Spear One. Do you copy?"

"Yes! What the hell's going on?"

"Stalwart, Spear One is proceeding to the trench. I'm going to drop these beacons. I'll be up as soon as they're set."

"Are you insane? Listen, these ships are doing something new. We have no theories. Look!"

Liz cut in another camera and Diana saw huge, distant space wings, smudged like noon white moons, a dozen of them parked in a ring. They pulsed color across the spectrum, each ship a hue. In the center of the ring, a dark cloud was forming.

Liz spoke off camera.

"We don't know. Are they attacking? Communicating? And those aren't the only ships either, we see three more groupings, horizon north, east and south. Seems like... 27 ships in every group. Is it fucking weird for this to be happening up here miles away from you, while you're all the way down there out of touch? Yes, it is fucking weird! Come up here! Greg," Liz pleaded, "get her out. Do something."

"My hand's played, Stalwart." Greg stared at Diana from his sub, head shaking in disgust. "Open to suggestions. Tried logic, psychology — we know she doesn't respond to human kindness — I'm out of ideas. You're mission control. You be the boss of her."

"Additionally, Stalwart," Diana said, "please prep to retrieve Spear Two, which begins turnaround *immediately*."

"That's a negative, Stalwart," Greg snapped. "Spear Two goes where Spear One goes."

"Jesus Christ," Liz snarled, "it's like I gave my submarines to a couple of second graders. Let's get this drop over and get you *out*."

⁂

THE DESCENT CONTINUED. A loud pop from the mantel over Spear One's batteries shook Diana as they passed six and a half miles. It was virgin depth now, a record for both subs. The pressure was titanic, a deep-sea car crusher straining in at every seam. Some deformation of the materials was expected under these conditions. It's hard to worry about aliens when your submarine is pressure popping, Diana found.

"Stalwart," she heard Greg on the comm, "we're point five klicks from terminal depth. I'm hearing material deformation on the exterior, joints around the battery flexing. Note for topside review."

Him and his unflappable focus, Diana thought. You loved it and you hated it.

"Any updates?" Greg continued. "On our alien situation?" Fifteen minutes earlier their pseudoscreens had gone dark when the antenna on Spear One failed. It had been a last-minute addition, with some thought of live streaming the landing. Now they'd be audio-only until they were topside.

"That dark cloud in the middle of the circle of ships is almost black now and sparking— could be lightening," Liz reported, voice muted, "nothing threatening but I can't say it looks friendly."

"Come on people, focus," Diana said. "Five minutes to contact. Prepping inversion."

"Roger," Greg replied. "Inversion sequencing."

They were falling fast, a few thousand meters from the ocean floor, though the only evidence was the picture sonar was painting. If they landed in their current orientation, thrusters down, they'd be blowing silt for five hundred yards, wiping out any chance for fine observation or gathering clean bio samples. So the Spears had been designed to flip capsule down, while gimbal and harness reoriented heads up, whatever the vector of the sub.

She keyed the inversion. Slowly the Spear tumbled end for end and stabilized. Greg did the same in Spear Two. Now she sat in her harness with thrusters above and nothing but the blackest sea beneath her—free falling in a pickle jar.

"Inversion in process," she said, "going ambulatory."

The second stage of the landing sequence was just as specific to their mission. From slots in the housing—now behind and above her— six multi-jointed actuators thrust, telescoping past her curving control capsule to hang, eleven feet in length, below the bottom of the dome. She flared them and suddenly they were legs. She was hanging in the thorax of a plunging water spider.

"Spear One ambulatory," she said.

"Spear Two ambulatory," she heard Greg say.

"Systems clear for contact," Liz confirmed.

Diana spun up thrusters, now pulling from above, and threw the landing lights on. In less than thirty seconds she had a visual below.

What had been a dream for years, a dream even Atticus Roark could be proud of, was now real: the Challenger Deep.

The brilliant floodlights cast razor shadows against canyon cliffs that rose on either side of Spear One. This was a moonscape of blunted edges and gray forms, an ancient aquarium of micro sand. The Challenger Deep was the subduction trench where tectonic plates, the Pacific and the Philippine, met, where heat and pressure sucked the Pacific under like a pancake into the molten mouth of the earth.

Spear Two was intended to touch down a hundred meters up canyon from Spear One. Diana shot Greg's capsule a glance just as it slid behind an outcrop of basalt. The original mission called for exploration from opposite directions, then meeting in the middle, marking a perimeter for the permanent structures, but now they would skip that. She would land, deploy the beacons; Greg would take a sample if he had time and then ascend. To aliens.

The cliffs were towering now, flashing past the windows. All thought of the surface vanished. Now she focused on bringing her Spear down without breaking it. She'd done it a thousand times in the sim, but she found herself falling too hard, sixty feet away the sea floor glowed up in her lights , she dug in thrusters, forty feet, flex and prep the legs, twenty feet, ten—and contact, ambulatory systems taking strain, pneumatics flaring... her capsule bobbed, once, gently, and hung.

Around her spread a blue-grey waterscape. She hung four feet from the deepest solid surface on planet Earth. The most foreign place imaginable.

"Stalwart, Spear One down," she said.

"Spear Two, landing confirmed," Greg said from up the canyon. "One small step for man, one giant leap for spidery machines."

"Roger that," Liz said. "Do what you need to do, people, and get the hell out of there."

Diana gentled the stick, tilting the sub toward a rise that suited her payload. The spider legs swept out around her, guided by sensors and feedback—a ballet akimbo. Like swimming in a dream.

"Arming beacons," she said when she topped the rise. She flipped through nav subsystem. She was sorry, suddenly, that it would be over so fast. That she'd never come back here. It was the end of a long...

Her hands flew to her ears as the radio let out a deafening shriek. It rose and rose, a thousand skidding tires screaming, then chopped off, speakers spitting and snapping a burst of static then falling silent. She shook her head to clear it, and flipped her com.

"Stalwart, my radio... did you catch that?" She waited a moment. No response. She tried again.

"Stalwart, Spear One, do you copy? Stalwart, respond. Stalwart, if you can hear me, something's..."

"Diana!" Greg's voice cracked on the ship to ship channel. "Are you okay?"

"I'm fine. What was that?"

"I don't know but... look, can you lock on my position?"

She checked, saw Spear Two several hundred yards up canyon.

"I see you," she said.

"Get here. Get here now, Diana."

System failure? Was he stuck?

"Is the Spear okay?" she asked. The first thing that occurred to her.

"Just come fast." His voice was thin.

"On my way," she said, reversing thrusters and lifting the sub. Silt rose in a cloud; she put it behind her with a hard twist and pointed up canyon.

"I'm two hundred yards north," his voice, almost to himself, "I was here deploying a collector, then this ... whatever... feedback? Not sure..."

"Greg, are you all right? I'm closing on your ping, are you..."

"I don't know what I'm looking at."

One more canyon turned and she knew where she'd find him:

behind the slanting, serrated wall hiding Spear Two there pulsed a blooming ball of light. It cast disorienting silhouettes on the chasm walls— monsters, grotesques. The radiance seemed more than illumination, it seemed solid in some way. Not a light sourced from a point but a growing viscous cloud, as utterly and completely out of place in the Challenger Deep as sunlight.

On the sea floor she saw Spear Two's shadow stretching and twisting as Greg worked his stick.

"What's that light?" she called. "I'm almost..."

Then, as if from a thrown switch, the light snapped out. All she saw was what onboard floodlighting showed: the face of the slope a few yards to her right.

For one instant she felt, rather than heard, a resonant throb before a brutal shockwave slapped her sub back. Rocks exploded off the ridge and cycloned down; as the Spear surged her harness straps pinched her windpipe. The sub tumbled, gimbals twisting to keep her upright, while she clawed the stick, then her restraints snapped, she shot from her seat, her arm splintering into the capsule window. She saw bone and blood, and just before losing consciousness exploding gas from a spare tank.

Greg, she thought.

Then blackness.

TWENTY HOURS LATER, on an ocean surface torn by wind and tempest sleet, the Stalwart, following Spear One's transponder, found her floating inoperative but for life support, just below the surface. The crew, hollow-eyed, dragged the battered sub onto the deck and removed Diana, bloody, arm and leg shattered, to the sick bay. A pair of Roark choppers rendezvoused and raced her to a hospital, where round the clock interventions saved her life, though at the cost of the arm and leg.

WHEN, months later she emerged from the hospital half a cyborg to greet the swirl of human civilization on tentative new limbs, all she found above her was empty sky. The rings of 27 alien ships were gone. They had orbited the planet just three hours that day, and vanished. But they'd left behind The Augmentation. And that had already changed everything. Staring upward at the vault of blue atmosphere, Diana felt optimism amid her sorrow. Humanity had at least lived through its first brush with extraterrestrial life. Or, as the aliens were already coming to be called, The 27.

2

All debt flows from the Sentient One. Debt is the second highest form of enlightenment. Seek, then, to acquire it in all you do. Secure bold loans and write them to the Metaspatial Blockchain. The greater the debt you accrue, the closer reality comes, as nearer and nearer to the Sentient One you stand. There can be no learning without pain, no happiness without sacrifice, and there is no enlightenment without debt. Only through debt may a stakeholder reach the highest form of sentence: ownership.

—From *The Book of* Ω64, of the Swandeen Pracis

San Francisco wavered through the windshield; a phantom painted in rain. Diana was surprised to recognize so little of it. It had been too long since she'd left her compound. The popular press called her a hermit she knew, and she felt like Rip Van Winkle, wandering down off her mountain after thirty years. She felt a little shocked, actually, though she'd seen it all in reports.

Her limo wove autonomously through the once familiar hills. Now these hills were thick with PopuPods. So many people, all of them needing homes, or anyway that had been the thinking in the beginning. Diana had funded the PopuPods and now prefabs tumbled everywhere; white and haphazard up the slopes, like cliff dwellings. She glimpsed doughty, broken Victorians deep in the shadows, pining for daylight.

"It's so cold," she said, her voice muffled within her deep red parka. Why hadn't she tinted those PopuPods something more organic? Anything else, why this sterile white?

"I'm sorry, Ms. Roark," Charles said, sitting across from her. "There's another blanket in the trunk."

"I don't mean I'm cold. I mean the way the city looks. Besides, a little chill won't kill me at this point." She regretted it the moment she said it because his brow wrinkled, a little tapestry of youthful concern. They both knew what would kill her.

"I'm perfectly comfortable, Charles," she said. The limo was a frosty forty-five degrees inside, no different from outside, but she was fully mummified in her antique down jacket, hood snugged around her face, comforters swaddling her legs. Nothing but a pair of glassy eyes in a polar explorer's outfit.

Charles, on the other hand, wore a translucent, short sleeve suit jacket and delicate, cream-colored half pants, cut mid-thigh. Dress shoes. No socks— conservative business attire in the modern style. She thought it looked ridiculous and so did he, but everyone would be wearing something similar at the meeting, and his professionalism required event-appropriate attire. But it made him look like a lingerie schoolboy.

A schoolboy. It was so utterly ridiculous.

"You're how old now?" she asked. With the original physical signs wiped away, it was hard to remember anyone's age. No more neck-wattles or thinning hair. He looked a healthy twenty-three.

"I will be one hundred and twenty-eight this February third."

"And you remember when cars had heaters—they did, right? I'm not imagining it?"

"No, Ms. Roark," he laughed softly. "I remember when they had heaters. I'm fifty years older than you. I remember driving your father back when cars had *drivers*. I can even remember when cars had ashtrays."

Ashtrays in cars. For an economist, you couldn't ask for a better example of market forces. Ashtrays had disappeared from cars when consumers had stopped smoking, just like heaters had vanished from cars when consumers had stopped feeling cold. Or feeling hot or any other temperature. Every human but Diana.

She tucked her icy left foot beneath her blanket. The only truly comfortable things on her body were her right leg and her left arm— her prosthetics. And they were casualties of market forces too—the market for human prosthetics had vanished and had left her limbs to fend for themselves after the Great Augmentation. After that single day thirty years ago when The 27 had appeared and then vanished, prosthetics had become obsolete and their manufacturers had gone belly up. Hers had been the pinnacle of cybernetic tech when the doctors had installed them. But now, three decades on, they were wearing out, and no one made parts to fix them. She was thinking this while watching her left hand power through some kind of factory diagnostic, fingers lifting and dropping on the seat at lightning speed, spasming, starting over. No one had asked her hand to do that. Charles pretended not to notice.

Dear Charles. He had been with the family since the beginning. Now he would outlive them all.

The car piloted them into the city center where Diana's offices, the Roark Foundation Towers, soared like twin knife blades and the road dipped into the rain shadow of buildings in the commercial district. The windshield cleared. The squall still prowled the streets though, driving wind into the PopuPods. They were tilting everywhere, even on this, the most expensive real estate in the bay area. The pods were ever-expandable housing for a surging human population that looked like it might continue to grow until the sun burned out. Twenty-nine billion humans and counting. The irony was, after all the expense, the pods were rarely used. The Needless didn't like them. The Needless preferred the streets.

Traffic was heavy downtown, but though she could easily bid to the head of the routing queue and arrive at her Towers in minutes, now that she'd arrived and was actually seeing it, she couldn't tear her eyes from the view out the windows.

The sidewalks were thick with the Needless; men and women and children, all of them naked. Completely nude, despite the weather. None of them noticed the cold, any more than a fish would notice water. The bitter gusts of the storm whipped remnants against their exposed backs and chests and legs, but protected by their Augmentation they thrived, here, as everywhere else on the planet. Utterly comfortable.

Charles's body had been Augmented, just like the rest, and he could easily have gone naked, but Charles was a PreAug, born before the Augmentation, and remained a child of his times. He liked wearing underpants. The Needless, on the other hand, had all been born in the world The 27 had made. The Needless took what The 27 provided, all their basic needs perfectly delivered and wanted nothing else.

She heard a chime. Charles reached to his pocket and pulled up Diana's phone.

"Text," he said, holding it to her.

"Who?" Charles was the gatekeeper now that she often didn't have the energy to lift her hand, let alone answer her phone. She'd given him the device permanently. They had no secrets, not at this point. She was an open book. Well, she thought, though there was the one secret. But she planned to keep that. It was hers.

"It's Ms. Mustang," he read. "She encourages you, again, to come to the opening at the Roark Oceanic Institute. The Museum of Nautical History. Will you be going?"

"No, Charles. I will not. I will be on vacation."

"Your mysterious vacation."

"My mysterious vacation."

"And you won't let me help you plan it? Make reservations?"

"Thank you Charles, no. I've taken care of it."

"Then shall I tender your apologies to Ms. Mustang? Again?"

"Tender away." He started to type. Thumbs to screen. So familiar. Cell phones, one of the things The 27 hadn't changed. Part of humanity's frozen technology, the same as when she was a girl. She eyed the unclothed throngs on the sidewalk. The planet was such a hallucinatory mix of the familiar and the unseemly. Nothing like she'd imagined 2077 would be.

"Wait Charles," she said suddenly. "Say this. Tell her, say, *Liz, I'm sorry I haven't been...* how many years has it been? Charles? Since I saw her?"

He considered. Nearly perfect memory, one of the bestowals of Augmentation she would never enjoy. Her own memory was a bit of a grab bag these days.

"Let's see. The 27 arrived almost exactly thirty years ago... you last saw Ms. Mustang on April 9th, 2039. Nearly 28 years ago."

"That can't be right."

"I'm afraid it is. You... when you discovered that you had not been affected by the Augmentation, you sent her away."

"I know, Charles. I remember that part." She sighed. Charles had never forgiven her for trying to save Liz the pain of watching her slide into what she now was. He had liked Liz almost as much as she had, and Diana still thought of her almost every day. Her tattoos and her flashing smile. She thought of Liz and she thought of Greg.

"It's really been that long?" she asked. "Ok. What about, *Hey Liz sorry I haven't seen you in 28 years I've been busy?*"

Charles offered an uncertain frown.

"Fine. Just say goodbye. How about that?"

"A bit final sounding?"

"Do it."

Traffic stopped near a park and she turned to look back outside. The Needless lay on the grass, relaxed in the freezing mist like it was a big beach party. High on the PopuPods she saw a group of children playing. They ran out over the birdcage balconies. They balanced on the railings, skidded, laughed. It took her a moment, but then she realized just how dangerous that game was. They were sixty feet up. Rain slick surfaces. Leaping and racing in bare feet.

"Look," she said to Charles. "What are they doing? That drop would terrify me."

He shrugged. "These are the Needless."

"It's not safe. Where are their parents?"

"These people were born after the Augmentation," he observed. An explanation she struggled to fit to the situation. Her mind was foggy these days. What was he saying?

"They'll fall," she insisted. "Isn't anyone afraid they'll fall?"

"I'm told fear is only a learned response, Ms. Roark. Hot stoves and such. The Needless never learned, I suppose."

She had just decided that the children must really be tethered somehow, that there had to be a rope or a net she couldn't see, when one of the boys leaned too far. His arms windmilled, and he teetered for strung-out seconds. Then his feet flipped up.

He grabbed for the rail as he fell but it only spun him and he went over backward and slammed the handrail on the Pod below. That folded him like a wallet. He spasmed. Diana gasped. He slipped and continued down, like a toy doll without bones, hammering terrace by terrace like Pachinko ball, rail to beam to rain-slick gable until he got to the sidewalk and stopped falling in a pile. She couldn't possibly have heard it, not from the car. But her mind offered a sound— speeding train intercepts dumpling.

Without a thought she opened the door. She was out, on the sidewalk, running into the park, stumbling on wet grass, heading for the tiny body. Charles followed.

"Charles, call an ambulance!"

"Ms. Roark, come back!"

She was the only person who'd seen anything. Not another soul was stirring. She pulled her hood open as she ran. Her breath was instantly ragged. She heard Charles sprinting behind her, calling out, *come back to the car*, but she ran until she stood, panting, looking down at the tiny, unclothed mess in its pool of red.

His body was a pulp. One arm snapped open like a pea pod with bones arching out. A rib pierced his side. A leg bent back at a nauseating angle. His thin chest, skin so young, ribboned with cuts and torn like shredded paper. She shrugged off her jacket and knelt on the grey concrete. She knew enough not to move him. He was still breathing. She could keep him warm until help arrived. Where was help? Why was no one rushing to the scene? No one in this park was even moving!

Then the boy laughed.

And from high above came shouts and jeers, boys and girls who hadn't suffered the terrible inconvenience of plummeting sixty feet to crush themselves on the cold sidewalk. They were happily mocking him and he began to yell back, defending himself from their taunts, yelling past teeth stained red, with childish, embarrassed bravado. Feeling no pain at all.

"Ms. Roark, please," Charles whispered. He knelt beside her and looked grave. He wasn't concerned for the boy. He was watching her.

"Did you call an ambulance?" she asked, her mind shock blank.

"No. Please. Come back now, come to the car." He looked behind him and tried to pry the jacket from her hands to put it on her. "Please, your coat."

People in the park had finally stirred. A curious crowd was drawing close. Diana let Charles help her up; the Needless were ringing them in, a circle of homogeneously young, perfectly nude spectators, white, brown, yellow, and black, un-groomed, carelessly feral, beautiful. They didn't spare a glance at the crushed boy. They were fixated on Diana.

"What's wrong with you?" asked a woman. She carried a sandwich. Whole wheat bread perfectly sliced, mustard dripping to the ground. Ham and lettuce. She bit it as she talked.

"Ms. Roark, we..."

"It's all right, Charles."

She understood. Of course. The boy was Augmented. As Diana was not. Suddenly she imagined how she must look to these people, without her jacket. She was sixty but appeared older. She was almost a different animal. Something they had never seen. Her hair had once shone red but now hung in gray patches. Her face was sunken, her cheeks were shadowed pockets. A puppet of joints and bones, a skeleton—all except for her right arm and left leg. Her plump and muscled prosthetics, pink and strong, archival copies of the woman she'd been thirty years before.

"You look pretty funny," chewed the woman. "You're all shrunken."

"I'm..." Diana paused, looking for the word. "Old. I suppose." She wanted to ask about the boy's parents. But the stares of the crowd held her.

"How old?" the woman asked.

"Sixty."

"My dad's sixty," said a man to her left. Flat belly. Bright eyes. Teeth like polished mirrors. He was dubious. "He looks normal."

Normal like them. Diana raised her jacket and pressed it close to her chest.

"Well. I'm sick," she said, then thought, why tell? Because. It was liberating to confess to strangers. Only Charles had known, and the few anonymous doctors she'd consulted. Former doctors, she reminded herself. No patients, so now non-practicing.

"What's *sick*?" asked another woman, her breasts heavy. Her smooth brown belly swelled with her coming child. She was sipping a blended strawberry margarita, salt rimming the edge of a simple gray cup.

The ring of people pushed close now, reaching for Diana. Curious. She backed away and felt herself step onto the broken child behind her. She gasped and looked down.

He was broken no longer. The wounds on his torso had vanished. His arm was re-knitting as she watched. Only the injury to his leg remained. He scooted away, laughing.

Charles caught her arm before she could fall.

"Ms. Roark, please, come away. Come." He pulled, and she went. He held her waist and pushed toward the car, clearing a path through the crowd. As they passed, the Needless reached out. She shrank but they stroked her hair, her shoulders. They felt her legs and hands and stomach. Charles shoved, yelled, but they did not disperse until he got her into the car.

He climbed in the other side. Instantly he covered her legs with the blankets and tried to dry her face and arms with the edge of his transparent suit jacket.

"Put on your jacket, Ms. Roark. Please. You can't afford a cold."

She unclenched the parka and let him work her one stiff arm and her one balky prosthetic back into the sleeves. He drew up the zipper. He pulled the hood tight and wrapped her in covers until she was once more nothing but a glint of eyes above a red nose, observing the world from a cave. She looked back at the park as the car pulled away.

The Needless had forgotten her. She saw them on the grass. The boy who fell now ran back up to join his friends. The pregnant woman with the margarita settled at the base of a four-sided Obelisk, forty feet high, and reached out— the air wrinkled, and another margarita appeared at its base. The park fell behind them and Diana looked up the sides of the Obelisk. Its slate faces shed rain in friction-less gouts. It resisted water the way it resisted every human tool, the same as any of the hundreds of millions of monoliths that had grown over the Earth after the Augmentation. She looked all the way to the top. In huge black strokes, visible for a block as the car sped toward her towers, she saw the omnipresent, stamped sigil: 27.

Charles held the door open as Diana limped into the noisy conference room, confronting a pageant of roiling clouds outside the 52nd-story windows. One of the many reasons she'd stopped going to meetings of the steering committee was she'd come to find these floor-to-ceiling PressureGlass bays disquieting. She had been talked into something breathtaking by an architect who would not, in the end, ever have to sit in the room and conduct business. Because the tiles on the floor were a reflective blue and the windows so seamless, the effect was of a long conference table suspended in the sky, ringed with the members of the board of directors of the Roark Philanthropic Foundation. All ten of them, laughing and chatting, their busy assistants hurrying about the room.

She took a moment to overcome the sensation of an endless plummet. Here, at least, she was warm, though not yet ready to take off her parka and hood— warm for the first time since leaving her compound this morning. She sniffed. A hint of combustion and old dust hung in the forced air. When she had begun to plan this farewell appearance several months before, she had given the order that the furnaces in the East Tower, unused for decades, be brought to working order. It was a monumental waste of resources, this heating a sixty-story building for the comfort of one human being. But, as she was about to be told ad nauseum, there was little else for the foundation to spend its money on these days.

She looked from the windows to Sanjana, deep in debate with one of the board. Sanjana was the acting Director of the Foundation, empowered in Diana's absence to make whatever decisions needed making. It had to have been a thankless, frustrating job since Diana had stepped away twenty years before. A losing battle, the charity game. They often exchanged emails but had little other interaction. Sanjana noticed her. Diana saw the look: attempting to interpret Diana's iconoclastic apparel. Parka formal. Polar business?

Diana turned away. Sanjana would understand soon enough. Let her puzzle over it for a while. Diana felt so tired of managing everyone's expectations. Doing for everyone else. *What an idiotic, childish complaint,* she thought. *I must be getting hungry.*

In the corner of the room stood a small Obelisk. Atop, as always, the boldly stamped 27.

"Charles," she said quietly, "will you get me a melted cheese?"

"With pleasure, Ms. Roark. Would you like Darjeeling?"

"That'd be nice."

Assistants connected to the other directors were doing the same thing, withdrawing refreshments in little crumples of distorted space, then delivering these to their employers. Steamy soup was popular today. Just a psychological thing, since no one could be affected by the chill. She saw one assistant carrying what appeared to be a whole thanksgiving turkey into a corner, presumably to slice it into manageable pieces. It would not be strange for Charles to do the same for her. No one need know that this was the *only* way Diana could interact with the Obies.

Sanjana approached deferentially as Diana watched Charles. She did Diana the service of not staring, but instead faced the conference room and watched the directors getting settled.

"It's a pleasure to have you back, Diana," she said. "We missed you."

Sanjana looked 23. Human standard, circa 2077. She had the olive skin of Punjabi royalty, black hair bound in concentric braids, and wore a variation of the diaphanous business attire that everyone in the room—Diana excepted—had on.

"It's been a few years," Diana admitted. "I... ah, I've been pretty busy." She kept both hands in her jacket pockets, not ready to reveal the unhealthy pallor of her flesh hand, and also hiding her prosthetic hand which had begun a slow *grip*-pull, *grip*-pull, as though milking an imaginary cow. She nodded across the room at the Obie to distract them both. *That* had not been here last time.

"You made someone sleep in here just to get an Obelisk?" she asked. "I hope you gave them a cot."

"One of the interns volunteered, about fifteen years ago. You don't mind, I hope?"

"I suppose it's convenient."

"We got tired of running down to the lounge every few minutes during meetings. A few of the directors have grown..." Diana looked where Sanjana was pointing and saw the man whose assistant had withdrawn the turkey. He had moved to the corner and was holding the entire carcass to his face, taking slow, sensuous bites, his eyes closed. Diana was startled, but no one else in the room noticed. After a few bites, he cast the entire, mostly uneaten bird into a disposal crate, wiped his face with the napkin his assistant provided and sent her back to the Obie with new instructions.

"Maybe we should have put some of the foundation's money into eating disorders," Diana said.

"It is interesting, isn't it? The Needless are not afflicted this way. It's only us PreAugs. The ones that grew up before the Obelisks. Those who developed, ah, maladaptive strategies around food, before eating was so easy."

Diana watched the man begin devouring a cake. If you could eat anything you wanted, and as much as you wanted, and never deviate from ideal homeostasis, Diana thought many people she had known might do just that. Since drugs didn't work anymore, and alcohol had no effect, what was left? People still had their demons to feed. Not the Needless, though. Only PreAugs. Interesting. She'd sheltered herself so completely, working away in her offices generating money, maybe she'd missed more important and subtle behavioral changes than she'd imagined. *The world has really and truly passed me by*, she thought.

Charles returned and handed her a gray plate on which an open-faced, sesame-crusted cheddar sandwich melted, steaming and perfectly delicious. Beside it was a pickle. Her childhood favorite. Charles used to grill these for her as a girl on the Roark estate and had snacked on more than a few himself. That meant this taste had been imprinted in his mind. That allowed him to withdraw it exactly as she herself remembered. The Obies only dispensed what you knew to require from them. You required a meal and the extraordinary nano fabricators of The 27 did the rest, throwing in a plate for good measure.

She took a bite and watched the Obie do its work. They were impossible to reverse-engineer. Impossible to break. Impossible even to move, once established in a location. The Obelisks of The 27 had obsoleted agriculture, fertilizer, the meat and dairy industries. Wiped out a third of all transportation on the planet, not to mention the makers of flatware. Now, in order to receive, all anyone had to do was ask.

Anyone but me, that is, Diana thought. *Poor me. Oh god, shut up.*

"Sanjana, excuse me," Diana said, handing the food back to Charles. "I see someone I need to talk to."

Dr. Rance Fishman had been one of the first people Diana had seated on her board, just before the Augmentation. She had leaned on him heavily, in the early days. His knowledge had guided much of the Foundation's medical work. She'd been trying to reach him for months, but after his vocation had been eliminated in the Augmentation, his behavior had tended more and more Luddite. Not so Luddite that he refused food from the Obies, of course—in reality they were so magical they hardly seemed like technology. But Luddite enough not to have a phone or to answer his email. But, as she had hoped, here he was.

"Dr. Fishman?" He was seated by a window, broad-shouldered, black hair draped around heavy obsidian eyes, holding something to the skin of his leg where it was exposed below his dress shorts. She still pictured him as he had been when she met him: careful white hair, mannered, polite to a fault. An old-school practitioner. She had never gotten used to the youthful, post Augmentation Dr. Fishman.

"Yes?" he answered, without looking up from his leg.

"It's me. Diana Roark."

It took him a moment, fixated as he was, and when Diana saw what he was doing she froze. The implement he held to his leg was a scalpel, and he was carefully, surgically, drawing it up the long flesh of his thigh, opening deep, pink cuts— cuts which sealed instantly as the blade passed. Efficient as a zipper. Like a magic trick. A small sound escaped her, muffled by her hood.

"Ah, here she is," he said, looking up, smiling. In that smile she could see the warmth she remembered, the familiar cordiality. But it was doing battle with something dark and wild. Back and forth the two impulses strained. It looked like he would really, really like to go insane, but somehow couldn't. He stopped his cutting and lifted his blade, examining the edge carefully. He flicked it like a professional knife sharpener. "Come to grace us at last, is that right? In your fine parka?"

She tried to process it, unsure how to answer. He continued as if she had greeted him enthusiastically. Old friends.

"It's good to see you. The Seer of Sonoma! Come down from your castle by the sea, is that right? She pulls the strings! She makes the financial markets dance to her song!"

She watched him return the scalpel to his skin, brooding again, black hair a watery cascade. He stared at the knife. Considering where next to cut? The room spun for a moment, and she steadied herself on his chair. Everything had changed, more than she could have imagined. She scanned the room. No one was watching Dr. Fishman. No one seemed to care.

Ok, she thought after a moment. I can do this. It's not like he's doing permanent damage. His Nano Sphere is fixing him right up. Maybe he's doing an experiment? I'll just ignore this man, this Byronic youth making sushi of his leg, and picture the person he used to be. The 84-year-old oncologist, cultured and brilliant.

"Dr. Fishman, I wonder if I could ask you a question," she said slowly, wondering how much he was actually hearing. "A medical question."

"Well, *that* would be an odd thing to do, wouldn't it?"

"Do you mind?" She reached down and stopped his hand. There was only so much she could take.

"For you?" he said, meeting her eyes again. "Anything! I'm on your board of directors, for heaven's sake. My sworn duty, to guide you and provide my wisdom."

"Thank you." She marshaled her thoughts. "In your experience with cancer patients..."

"Oh! Cancer! None of that left now, we're all free of that."

"I know. But still, when you worked with people with osteosarcoma. Bone cancer? Do you ever remember having any patients with symptoms of... visual spots?"

He frowned. "Spots?"

"Yes. Black shadows that whirl around in the room? Like they're alive? They block your view, they stick to the walls even when you look away? I've gone through all the research, and I can't find any reference to anything like that."

"You've been looking through the old cancer research, is that right?" He peered at her. "Looking for people who saw spots?"

"Yes. Spots. Moving shadows." She was quickly deciding that Dr. Fishman was not going to be the help she had hoped. She wished she'd been able to reach him months ago. Three *years* ago, when it had all started. If she had known he was... like this, she might not even have come to the meeting.

"Does it sound familiar?" she urged him. "Is this visual anomaly a known cancer symptom?"

He closed his eyes. When he spoke, he seemed to be drawing up words from a long-lost story. A wonderful fantasy.

"Osteosarcoma, the most common type of bone cancer, begins in cells that form bones. In rare instances it can occur in soft tissue outside the bone. The prognosis and treatment decisions depend on where the osteosarcoma begins, tumor size, the type and grade of osteosarcoma, and whether the cancer has spread. Osteosarcoma softens the bones where it develops. In advanced cases bones collapse under the body's own weight. Osteosarcoma is typically treated with a combination of surgery and high-dose methotrexate, doxorubicin, and cisplatin, sometimes including ifosfamide. After completion of treatment, patients will need lifelong monitoring for potential late effects of intense chemotherapy and surgical intervention."

He looked back up at her. His eyes were lidded, shelves barely affixed to their wall. "No spots. No one had spots."

Then he returned to his leg. Diana backed slowly away.

"Another text from Ms. Mustang," Charles said behind her.

"What now?" Diana asked, jumping. "Didn't you tell her what I said?"

"I did. She writes: *You should come. Greg would want you here. It's the thirty-year anniversary of his death.* What shall I tell her?"

"Tell her screw yourself, I'm not coming."

"I will not."

Sanjana clapped her hands and the faces around the room pointed her way. She moved to the chair at the head of the table and pulled it out, gestured for Diana to sit, but Diana shook her head.

"I'm just one of the board today," she said. And as soon as I can manage, not even that.

She took the seat directly in front of her and the rest of the board came to attention. She had decided not to take off her parka. She needed the buffer and from more than just the temperature. Unlike the Needless, the board members were still attached enough to ancient decorum that they hesitated to stare. But they wanted to. Her parka was a collector's item.

Sanjana gaveled the meeting to order.

"Alright, we have a lot to cover today, but since it's been some time since we've had the pleasure of Ms. Roark's company in person, I wanted to begin the meeting by thanking her for coming. The Seer of Sonoma!"

"I hate that," she muttered to Charles, seated beside her.

And around the table the youthful assemblage applauded. The fresh faces gave the proceedings the feel of a student council meeting rather than a gathering of the most accomplished financial and operational minds on the planet. Given this permission to face her, they happily stared. Diana slouched and made certain there was little to see. Then Sanjana pointed their attention to several large pseudo displays that shimmered up over the table. The lights dimmed. A generally dour seriousness settled over the room.

And then the board proceeded to conduct an examination, almost a post-mortem, of the strategies and procedures by which the Roark Philanthropic Foundation had failed at every single thing they had ever tried.

If only the shadow spots will stay away, Diana thought. It was so hard to concentrate when they started dancing around the room.

It began with a summation of the day of the Augmentation. As if anyone could ever forget, Diana thought, or find anything new to say about it. She watched the alien ships spin in the sky on these screens, just as she had watched those other screens, miles beneath the sea. 27 ships in a ring, a total of 27 rings all around the globe. She watched the footage of the dark clouds forming within each ring—the Swarms—and saw these Swarms dropping from orbit, dispersing in clouds of nano particles; the Nano Spheres which had bonded to them, all the humans on Earth. After the Swarms dropped, the alien ships vanished, and then the Obies began to appear, wherever a human slept for a few days in a row. The Needless tended to share huge, communal Obelisks. Families had smaller examples in their living rooms. Experiments had shown that humans interacted with the Obelisks through their Nano Spheres. *Except for me*, she mused, *my Nano Sphere is broken. Doesn't keep me young. Won't let me connect to the Obelisks.*

It was all the same old information.

Then archival footage was replaced by recorded experts providing the expert consensus; the ships had come from a consortium of 27 individual species, together forming an interstellar civilization, spreading this technology throughout the universe to prevent intelligent species from destroying themselves. Enormous resources had been devoted to the search for star systems where these civilizations resided. Occasional successes—traces of signal, bright flashes in the dark heavens—kept mankind focused on the hunt, though data was scarce. The 27 were out there, the experts agreed. They were simply not interested in being found.

Diana was bored. She found herself watching the directors as much as the presentation. Some of them were riveted, though many, like her, found it tedious. They were an oddly twitchy group, she decided.

But as she watched them, she saw that more than mere twitchiness was at work. Across from her a man bit his fingers, over and over, placidly peeling thick strips of skin from the tips. It grew back instantly. Sanjana herself plucked her eyebrows endlessly as she gazed at the pseudoscreens, never feeling a moment of pain, a limitless supply of re-growing brow hair at her disposal. The gorging man stepped over to the disposal, softly threw up, then returned to the Obie for a leg of lamb; she noticed other people doing the same, board members and assistants in a soft buffet parade. Dr. Fishman sat quietly, slice, slice, slicing away in his chair. All apparently feeding their demons, in the dark, with no price to pay.

"Are you seeing this, Charles?" she asked softly. "It's like an OCD ward in here."

"Yes, Ms. Roark."

"Does it seem unusual to you?"

"It is not so unusual. Not now. Not among the PreAugs."

"I would have noticed this."

"You seldom leave your compound. I manage your staff very carefully so you are not interrupted in your work."

"What about you? I'm around you all the time. You're not like this."

He shrugged and, she thought, pretended to watch the screens.

"We each have our obsessions, Ms. Roark."

When the Augmentation had been effectively rehashed, the real presentation began—a dissection of the Roark Philanthropic Foundation, which, they all knew, had foundered. The problem was singular and simple: no one, not the board, or anyone else in the organization, could think of a way to spend the Foundation's money and provide human beings with anything they needed.

She examined the slides and graphs. This, at least, was real data, and she pulled her attention away from her aberrant board to parse it. After the Augmentation and the Obelisks, when people had discovered that their most basic requirements could be had for free, there had begun dramatic, global upheaval. The first thing many had done in that vast, corporatized economy was quit their jobs. Why work, they had reasoned, at meaningless careers, when food and water were free, health care unnecessary, and when the natural elements had been conquered? In the beginning only a few walked out, five percent of the global work force. But that was enough, because it happened so suddenly. Industries collapsed. Everything followed from that, financial dominoes toppling with relentless, unavoidable effect.

Unemployed workers paid no taxes. Governments began to fold. Roads went unpaved. Laws went unenforced. Even warfare ceased —anyone you shot just got up and started shooting back again, a costly undertaking with zero results. People the world over hunkered down as the changes set in, eating and drinking better than they ever had before, watching civilization fall to pieces. If the World Bank hadn't stepped in at that point, providing loans, loans of truly epic proportions, to governments large and small, it would certainly have been the end. To this day the World Bank remained everywhere, a stable, guiding hand. There were rumors that it had a more nefarious side, but nothing was ever proven. People just hated banks, she supposed.

Diana had created the Foundation just before the Augmentation, and she poured vast resources into it after she sold Roark Pharmaceuticals. She had wanted to make a difference in the topsy-turvy new world. The Foundation had originally been chartered to handle health and hunger, the two scourges of what had been, at the time, the modern world. But after most governments stabilized, and hunger and disease were no longer issues, the Foundation had found itself without a viable mission. And so began their search for a purpose.

They had tried pouring money into the environmental tragedies of pollution and global warming, but those were only human tragedies as long as they affected human health or caused human suffering. Once humans could live in perfect comfort in cities dense with smog, or bathe in rivers thick with industrial pollutants, environmental tragedies became just... the environment.

Animals were still dying, of course, and the Foundation tried throwing money into extinction mitigation. People were living longer, so the Foundation tried spending on overpopulation. They did manage to fund the PopuPods, but it turned out that no one used them. They tried funding poverty relief and disaster relief and education. But increasingly it became clear that Roark Philanthropic was locked in a spending arms race with every charity or foundation on earth, all of whose missions had begun to evaporate. Everywhere Roark looked they found too much charitable money fighting to relieve ever-diminishing pools of human misery.

And so, the Foundation's funds had accumulated, mostly unspent, for almost thirty years. They pivoted one direction and another, searching for a way to make the world a better place, before finally concluding, just recently, that the world had gotten to be just about as good a place as money could possibly make it. At least as far as the homo sapiens of the planet were concerned.

The question was, finally—what could they do with all the cash?

The presentation ended there. The lights faded back on. And every eye in the room turned slowly to Diana, Sanjana's included. They were flummoxed. And Diana was the world's financial genius. The Seer of Sonoma. They expected a solution.

She stood, forcing her aching spine straight. She had a prepared speech. Charles opened it on a tablet and laid it on the table in front of her. She cleared her throat and unfastened the strap over her mouth so she could speak clearly from within her hood.

"Thank you, all of you. That was very informative. Excellent job. I'll just tell you up front, I don't have any idea how to put the Foundation's money to use. The fact is, I hate to tell you, I'm about to make your problem a whole lot worse."

She lowered her eyes to her notes. She just wanted to get this over with now. She had come hoping for answers and found nothing but a room full of neurotics. She'd never enjoyed public speaking, though she'd often been called on to do it. And she'd never mastered the trick of being particularly relatable. What was she really supposed to say to these people? Greg had been like a pig in slop in front of a crowd. She remembered once asking him for advice, and he'd said, *Just speak from the heart, Butterfly. Try pretending everyone in the audience is naked.*

Now she knew how ridiculous that advice was, since only three hours earlier she'd stood before a completely naked audience and it had been far more unnerving than this. Abruptly, she decided that she was not going to give the speech. She would just go on her vacation and get the slate cleared up.

She reached to the tablet to close the file, but realized that her swiping hand, her prosthetic, had gone on a little vacation of its own. Despite her instructions to reach down, it was nowhere near the device. It was rising out to the side of her body.

Her audience saw it before she did. They were puzzled, but polite. The arm rose higher, like a train crossing arm, then began an inscrutable flapping. Up, pause, down, pause. Like one wing of a large, lazy bird. Really, she thought, this is just too much. So many things a person simply can't plan for. What's the point of even having a plan?

The board was entranced, however. Why, she could see them wondering, is Diana waving that arm like an ostrich wing? Is she pointing at that wall there? Will there be another presentation? Several heads turned that direction, hopeful.

She reached across her chest to yank the prosthetic back in place, but it was determined and *strong*—many times stronger than any limb made of flesh and bone. They had told her she could smash through a door with that arm. She hoped *that* little performance was not on the agenda. With all her yanking and pulling she only managed to unbalance herself, so Charles had to jump and catch her. He was left gently holding the recalcitrant wrist as it meandered up and down. All the activity was starting to make her hot.

The board was absolutely enraptured. This was *far* better than the presentation about how bad they were at their jobs. The finger-eating man had stopped chewing on himself, his index finger forgotten in his gaping mouth. They were watching Charles work her arm like a human water pump.

"Just two things to add," she said, wondering whether she could ignore her arm into invisibility. "Just give me another moment and I'll be out of your way. First, I am resigning! I hereby resign from the board of the Roark Philanthropic Foundation and from any operational control of its resources, effective immediately."

That got them to look at her hooded face. But they seemed confused, wondering if they'd missed something important earlier in her presentation.

"And secondly," she said, now that she had their attention, "I am donating the entirety of my remaining personal estate, all cash and all property, to the Foundation. This bequest, in the sum of approximately 18 trillion dollars, will be managed to the best of the board's ability in the pursuit of the Foundation's chartered mission. Such as it is. I understand the irony of this grant coming at a time when the Foundation is having a hard time finding ways to spend its *existing* endowment. I guess... I don't know. You'll deal with it somehow."

A moment passed, during which dazed board members looked back and forth in confusion. This was more new and unsettling information than they'd heard at a board meeting in many years. And then the room erupted.

Charles was at her side, still gripping her delinquent limb and drawing her backward toward either a chair or the door, she wasn't sure which. Sanjana was demanding order, but no one could hear her. The board members were gesticulating, shouting to be heard above other board members also shouting to be heard.

"Charles," she said in the tumult, "get this jacket off! I'm going to boil!"

To her immense relief her arm chose that moment to come in for a landing and Charles was able to unzip her. She shrugged the hood off and slipped out of the parka. Blessed cool air hit her body.

And the board finally got a look at her. The pandemonium in the room slowly ebbed into a wide, puzzled silence. *Go ahead,* she thought. *Go ahead, look. I weigh seventy pounds. I have eye sockets like cups of chocolate pudding. At least I'm not eating my own flesh.* After a moment, Rance stepped forward, a fevered gleam in his eye. He swept his hair from his face.

"It was you," he said. "*You* are the cancer... patient. Can this even be possible?" He raised his hand toward her face. "May I?" he asked.

She wanted to cry. She felt like running. But she'd never outrun this crowd. She'd never outrun any crowd, ever again. Why try? She'd come for Rance's professional opinion anyway. She nodded. Tentatively he lifted her eyelid. He peered into her mouth. He drew her arm up and felt her lymph nodes, swollen, she knew, like eggs. He asked her several times if he was hurting her, forgetting, it seemed, how out of the mainstream that simple human question had become. How impossible. He queried her about her symptoms. And then at last he turned to the assembled board of directors, who stood, utterly absorbed, absolutely silent, watching this medical examination of their former Chairman of the Board.

"This woman has cancer," he said, with astonished solemnity. "Bone cancer, I think. Osteosarcoma." He turned back to Diana. "Does it hurt?" She heard a frail, yearning note in his question.

"Yes," she said. "In waves. It comes on fast. The pain is..." She found she didn't feel like describing the pain. The bone pain. There weren't any good words to describe it anyway. "I don't think I have much time left. A few weeks."

He was hardly breathing as he asked, "Are there others like you?"

"None that I could find," she sighed. "Believe me, I looked."

"Of course there aren't," Sanjana said into the silence. "No one has cancer. It doesn't exist anymore."

"I wish that was true," Diana told her. She felt useless. "I re-engineered the tests. Took me a year or so. Crude but accurate. There's no question."

"How is it possible?" Rance asked. All Diana could do was shrug.

It was the question she'd spent the last three years trying to answer, without success. Her father had died of the same cancer. That was the only explanation.

"Ok people," Sanjana announced. "Out. Give me the room. I need to talk to the Director."

"Not the Director," Diana said. "You're the Director."

"Out!" Sanjana yelled. "You too, Rance. Everyone. Now."

Rance was last, after everyone else was gone, staring back like he was losing a cherished treasure. And then the big, soundproof doors of the conference room closed, and they were alone.

Exhaustion took her legs from beneath her, as if the rubber band squeezing everything that was *her* together had finally snapped. Charles caught her, no great feat of strength for his strapping, twenty-three year old body. As he settled her into a chair she saw her plate on the table, the sandwich uneaten, the pickle wet and firm. It would remain that way for twenty-four hours and then the plate and the food would disincorporate, like everything produced from an Obelisk. If only it could be that easy for her.

"Don't do this," Sanjana said, very quietly.

"It's done," Diana said. "Everything's been transferred. I'm officially a pauper." She shrugged. "As far as resigning from the board? Who cares. I've been an absentee landlord, sitting in my office making all the money I just gave you. You won't miss me. This is your time now."

There was a reason Diana had chosen Sanjana to replace her. The woman was smart and hard to stop. She processed her disbelief and jumped swiftly past any confusion. She began generating solutions.

"Look, we can fix this. We can set up a lab for Dr. Fishman."

"There's nothing he can do, Sanjana. What will he prescribe? The drug industry is gone. Market forces. No consumers."

Sanjana nodded. "We'll bring it back. The Foundation will do it. It's in the charter. Health services."

"Sonja, please. There's no time. I'd have done it myself if I thought there was a chance. This thing is fast and it's almost done with me."

Sanjana shook her head.

"Don't give up."

"There is actually a time where that's the right move."

"No. I'm older than you, Diana. I was on the Board of Roark Pharma. I knew your father. He wouldn't want you to give up."

"My father?" Diana could sense it breaking over her then. She was a ship, a vessel caught against a reef to be broken by waves of sadness. "The truth is my father never cared what I did. Honestly, he wouldn't care whether I gave up or not. I'm not the person he wanted, not to run his company, not to be his legacy. I'm not the daughter he wanted. He..." her voice caught.

"That's not true, of course that's not true." Sanjana was aghast.

"Oh, it's true. I live with it. It's all right. My father spent his life on science. He was an incandescent mind. Creating impossible things. Saving people and... and all I've ever done was make money. That's all I can do. Money and more money. Never anything good from it. I never did what he wanted Phoebe to do. I'm not that person. In the end, that's what killed him."

"STOP," Charles yelled. He was shaking. He pointed at Diana, and *his* was the face covered by tears. Not hers. His.

He stood. "You will not speak of yourself that way!"

"Charles. You were there. You know it's true."

"No!" He knelt by her. "Listen to me now. There are things about your father you don't know. He wasn't the person you think he was. I swore to myself I would take this to the grave. It's not my place. But I *cannot* listen to you say these *things* about yourself!"

Diana's mouth slipped open, but words failed her. Charles had just yelled at her. This was not any version of Charles she had ever seen. Not in all the years they had been together since her father's death, not when he had taken care of her as a child in her father's house. He was crying now. He struck himself in the stomach with his fists, over and over. It was reminiscent of the PreAug behavior she'd seen from the board. The first time she'd ever seen anything like it from Charles.

"I was there," he moaned. "I saw it all. Your father... Atticus was *not a good man*. The things he did, Diana. The world never knew. *Ebola* 3, oh, lord... I stayed, for you, Ms. Roark, for your sister. My god. For your mother. While he did horrible... I should never..."

And suddenly the doors to the conference room were thrown open with a thundering smash and through blank, amazed eyes Diana saw an unfamiliar man step into the room. He wore a charcoal suit, a suit like people used to wear, when she had first built these towers. He had pants with long, pleated legs. Shiny black shoes. He had cotton candy blue eyes, and a small mustache as tidy as a recurve bow.

"I hope I'm not interrupting, Ms. Roark," the man said. "The door was open. My name is Jianguo Tsou. I am with the World Bank."

3

Like a fish to its school, like a bird to its flock, so are sentient Stakeholders to the Known Economy. If we want to change the Known Economy, we must first change the assumptions we have about the reality that created it. Conversely, even the smallest alteration to the Known Economy will soon change our assumptions about reality. The two are conjoined. Separation from the Known Economy takes a different name in every sentient tongue, but each one translates to a single concept: death.

—From *The Book of* Ω64, of the Swandeen Pracis

"You *are* interrupting," Sanjana said after a moment. "How did you get onto this floor?"

"I walked," Jianguo Tsou told her. He regarded them with a calm, friendly expression. "I've come for Ms. Roark."

Diana looked behind him at the lobby. Was that a body on the floor? And blood? It was. Dr. Fishman. She saw another pair of motionless feet just beyond him which dangled from the cushion of a fallen couch. But Jianguo Tsou—from the World Bank?—stood before them composed and banker-friendly, so she wondered for a moment if it was only a coincidence that there were bodies scattered behind him in the lobby.

"Who are you?" Sanjana said, walking right up in front of him. She hadn't seen the bodies, Diana thought, or she would be asking different questions. She might not be standing so close.

Charles had seen the bodies; he was facing the man, and Diana watched as his eyes narrowed, calculating angles.

"Don't move, Mr. DeLarusso," Jianguo said, and Charles stopped. Mr. DeLarusso. No one called Charles that.

"I don't understand," Diana said. "You're looking for me?"

"Yes."

"Why?"

"I think we both know the answer to that question."

Sanjana looked back. Diana shook her head. *No idea.*

"You say you're with the World Bank?" she asked, trying to squeeze sense into the scene.

Sanjana pulled out her phone. Jianguo shook his head, sadly, and raised his arm so fast it was difficult to see him move, and when he swung the long knife that appeared in his hand Diana thought, *there's a knife in his hand?* She watched in stunned disbelief as it formed a dull gray arc that splashed in one side of Sanjana's neck and out the other, the way you could almost completely cut off the top of a carrot but leave just a flap behind.

Blood splattered over Jianguo's face as Sanjana collapsed across the board's long table. Diana tried to scream but could only watch. Papers scattered as Sanjana's body slid off the tabletop and onto the floor, her head twisting loose.

Jianguo wiped blood from his cheek with an economical flick. His friendly expression changed a little, as if he didn't like it when people got their blood on his face.

"Ms. Roark, please come with me," he said, holding out his hand.

Charles began to circle again.

Diana was weak with shock, but still her brain churned known data. There was a small possibility that Sanjana had managed to text security—she couldn't take her eyes off the body—but that didn't seem likely. That meant she needed to call them herself. No. Charles had her phone.

"I hope the situation is clear to you, Ms. Roark," Jianguo said and gestured to the spot under the table where Sanjana lay. "To kill an Augmented human, the most certain way is to cut off their heads. But I have sliced the throats of your confederates. They are not dead. Still, their Nano Spheres cannot keep them conscious while those complex tissues and nerves are re-connecting and so they will remain comatose for a day. I tell you this so you will understand how hopeless your situation is, and not attempt anything dangerous."

It was almost sickening how polite he remained, as though he were only there to serve her. It reminded her of other bankers she had met—obsequious while they lured you into debt. He gave her a good-mannered smile, then took a gray disk the circumference of a cereal bowl from within his suit. He spun it in his hands as if to find a particular edge, and at that moment Charles struck from Jianguo's blind spot.

Charles was fast, panther-like, Diana thought with surprise and approval, and his silence seemed a deadly advantage; but it appeared that Jianguo didn't have a blind spot after all. Quick as a factory automaton Jianguo swung his arm and again he did the magic trick to make a knife appear. From one frame to the next, like a badly edited movie, the blade pared Charles' throat in two. Jianguo managed to skip to the side this time and avoid the blood. Charles continued forward a step, Jianguo watching him fall.

Then Diana saw another kind of movement from the corner of her eye. A dot. A shadowy pirouette. *Not now,* she thought. But that's what she always thought, and always the same result: the specks twisted into the room like living creatures, like a swarm of bats. Her mystery cancer symptom, usually nothing but a bothersome intrusion that made rooms a challenge to navigate. They never brought addi-tional pain. In fact, no physical sensation at all accompanied these visitations, just inconvenience and quiet dread. Charles would usually help her to her room where she would stay, half-blind, and wait for the spell to pass.

"Ms. Roark," Jianguo said as he closed the conference room door and came back toward her. "I'm going to have to ask you to take your clothes off."

Her mind wobbled. The room spun with dark embers, a whirl of anti-sparks. She backed away, keeping the table between herself and Jianguo. She blinked, staggered, and trained her focus on the blood-smeared banker who stalked toward her. This was the most damnably tiresome part of dying of cancer, these god damn vulture circling spots!

Jianguo reached her quickly but walked right past, straight over to the huge PressureGlass windows, while Diana leaned against the side of the table and tried to keep her balance. Tried to keep her hands out of Sanjana's blood. Through her cloud she could just make out Jianguo as he squatted and laid his gray disk on the floor. He appeared to depress illuminated buttons on its surface.

"We are almost ready," he said, "now, please, remove your clothing."

Her clothing? None of it was tracking. Jianguo finished with his disk, stood, and backed up several feet. Diana squinted from the corner of her eye and saw him counting down under his breath. When he reached zero a pressure wave washed over her and there came a tiny thump, like a bomb going off fifty miles away, and then an Obelisk appeared in the room where none had stood before. She had to shake her head and look from several angles, as swirling shadows clogged her sight lines. It was really there.

To Diana's knowledge no one had ever managed to move an Obelisk, to nudge an Obelisk, to tilt one, to make the tiniest mark on one. You didn't do anything with Obelisks except get breakfast from them. If you wanted an Obie to appear somewhere you slept in that spot a few nights, and that was the extent of any control they were subject to. You definitely did not make them spring into existence using gray cereal bowls. Early on there had been feverish research involving just that question: was it possible, in any way, to affect a Dispensing Obelisk? But those programs had shut down as the money fell away. Many of the labs had been taken over by the World Bank.

A puzzle piece settled in her mind like a bit of vapor. Jianguo was with World Bank. An Obelisk had appeared in the conference room. The World Bank—developing Obelisk technologies?

Jianguo slung his suit jacket to the floor.

"I have to insist that you take off your clothes *now*."

"I'm an old woman," she protested, gripped to the edge of the table. She was unbalanced and half blind and disinclined to get nude on general principles. "I'm cold."

His shirt followed his jacket to the floor. And then he was undoing his fly and dropping his pants. Jianguo didn't wear underpants. This was all moving so fast. It must be easier and faster to throw your clothes off in conference rooms if you came in without underpants, she thought. If that was your thing. She squeezed her eyes open and shut. It was surreal. Men entering rooms, slitting throats, stripping.

"You say you're a *banker?*" she asked. He was naked now. As far as she could recall, his was the only banker penis she had ever been shown, certainly this soon after being introduced. She waved at her shadows. *Go away!* Jianguo removed his watch and laid it on the table where he could see its face.

"We are on a tightening schedule," he insisted. "You *will* take off your clothes."

"Are you kidding me?"

"If you do not take off your clothes, I will cut your throat and take them off myself."

She saw how serious he was. And then she felt the tables turn, just a few degrees. A measure of control was possible here. There was a deal to be made.

"If you're trying to seduce me," she offered, her voice becoming calm, despite fear and her orbiting maelstrom, "you should have brought chocolate."

"I am very serious." He showed her his knife. She almost told him that he'd get nothing by cutting her throat and taking off her clothes except a naked corpse. Broken Nano Sphere, no Augmentation. Easily killed. But the explanation would take too long. If only these damn spots would…

And then they swept away. The shadows seemed to fly upwards and disappear through the ceiling, like a mourning veil drawn up off her face. The room dropped back into sharp relief.

Clear thinking became possible. Just clear enough.

The skill Diana had grown rich using, her superpower, was her acute sense of value. Her ability to perceive it, her ability to negotiate around it and her willingness to take risks and make them pay. These had made her a legend. Negotiating, she was fearless. And right here, she smelled value. A chance to get some answers. Her fatigue faded further, replaced by something familiar: the sizzle of the hunt.

"Ok," she said. She began to undo the buttons on her shirt, wondering whether security would ever come, would find the bodies in the lobby in time to break down that door and save her from what-ever was about to happen. But in the meantime, she would do deals.

Why not?

"Let's play a game," she said as she worked on her blouse. "I'll take off a piece of clothing and you answer a question. Clothing, question. Before you know it you'll have a naked old lady. Deal?"

She watched him struggle, then relent. As she had somehow known he would. He spun his hands in a circle. *Go faster*. She went very slowly. But after a moment she had dropped her blouse to the floor and she faced him in her bra. It had been many years since she'd disrobed in view of any male genitalia. She felt it ought to be a shock. But it turned out to be just another peculiar turn in a very odd day.

"Ok, my question," she said. A warm-up. A feint. "Are you a ninja?"

"No, I'm an Economist."

"Come on. You're really good with that knife."

"That's not a question. If you say anything else which is not a question I will cut your throat and take your clothes off—we are *running out of time.*"

Pressured, she thought. *Why? Hard to say yet. But a good sign.* She took off her shoes, thinking about her next question. Jianguo had just made an Obelisk appear. *What was the World Bank doing with the Obies?* Fan him for answers. Make him give something away. He'd already done it once: he was an *economist?*

"Do you know who invented the Obelisks?" she asked.

"The 27, I presume. *Faster.*"

Was that the truth, she wondered?

She slipped out of her pants. At one time her legs had been so shapely and toned that Greg had composed a sonnet to them, put it to music and serenaded her in the material sciences lab. But now, not so shapely. Well, she thought critically, one of her legs was still pretty nice. She examined Jianguo. He had begun to bounce impatiently.

"Ok, next question. Why don't the Obelisks work for me?"

"What do you mean, the Obelisks don't work for you?"

Okay. Addition by subtraction. Unaware of her defective Nano Sphere? She reached behind to undo her bra. For the first time she saw Jianguo stare, apparently just catching on to the fact that she was old. All over. Bent. Wrinkled. Which was important information; whoever she was dealing with here had the massive resources needed to get into this building and assault this room, but her physical condition had not been known to them. She dropped her bra to the floor. *Second to last question. Make it count.*

"Why did you make that Obelisk appear just now?"

"That's not an Obelisk it's a Field Relay."

It looked like an Obelisk to her—though now, without dancing shadows matadoring her eyes, she realized that there was no 27 imprinted on its top.

"We need the Relay to actuate the Landerson Field," he said.

Three answers in one. He really wasn't very good at this. One: he *had* been responsible for making the Obelisk, she'd been right. Two: it wasn't an Obelisk; it was a Field Relay. *So, wrong there.* Three: *Landerson* Field? Why did that sound familiar? *Terrance* Landerson? Terrance Landerson was Director of the World Bank.

She pulled off her underwear. And there she stood. Naked. Aged. Dying. She pulled herself up as straight as her soft bones would permit and studied the naked economist ninja from the World Bank facing her. Her fatigue had been seeping back and now, all at once she wondered what good any of it was going to do. She'd negotiated so many deals in her life: contracts with prime ministers and church fathers, Nobel winners and thieves and she'd always come out on top. She didn't really know why, but that's the way it worked; the prize was always hers. But the time had come to stop. It was late. No more use for prizes.

Jianguo was pointing his strange, gray knife at her. Her last question, she realized.

She sighed. Just no sense in any of it.

"Do you think I'm pretty?" she asked him.

"No," he told her.

So at least his other answers had been honest. Any man who could hear that question from a naked, vulnerable, cancer-ridden old woman and not at least offer up something about her beautiful eyes, or say that real beauty was on the inside, was a man obsessed with truth to a laudable degree. She should know. People had often told her in years past how beautiful she had been on the outside. She had never been beautiful on the inside, but no one ever seemed to notice.

He pulled her to the windows and made her stand with him on a gray mat extending from beneath the Obelisk—no, the Field Relay. She had lost all interest in the game they were playing. Through the windows she watched dense clouds tumble upward, like San Francisco far below was just a boiling pot expelling steam. This was what the Needless felt, she thought. No clothes, no money, no goals. Nothing to strive for. No fear. It was emptiness.

Under the conference table she saw Charles, his body extended in an exotic pose, a human made of putty. She knew he wasn't dead. She knew he would be fine. But she couldn't help the sadness. The poor man: to the very end he had protected her. Those things he'd said about her father—outlandish gibberish pulled from thin air, anything he could think of so she would feel safe. *Immpenta. She'd grown so tired of hearing about Immpenta.* She almost wished she'd told him the details of her vacation, suddenly thinking it would be nice to have company.

Though it appeared she wouldn't be going on vacation now.

"I've had enough," she said abruptly.

"Shut up," Jianguo told her, his body tense.

"I'm putting my clothes back on."

He gripped her arm so tightly she could feel a swell of blood build behind his grip.

"No. Your clothes aren't part of your Nano Sphere. If you're wearing, or even touching, anything outside your Nano Sphere when the Field forms, you'll get disincorporated or you'll blow up." He looked at her, threatening. "Do you want to get disincorporated or blow up?"

"Kind of."

"Hold your breath," he squeaked as he inhaled deeply.

The doors of the board room bashed open. A long-delayed security detail rushed in. They carried immobilizing rifles and advanced quickly.

"Over here!" she called, "he has a knife..."

But that's as much as she got out. The Field Relay keened and something took away her breath, as if she'd been pushed out an airlock into space. A queasy lack of pressure velveted her ears and she was encased in absolute silence. Some of the security staff continued to rush toward her, but most of them stopped. She fell to her knees. Her hands gripped the edge of the gray mat. Her mouth opened. Her chest spasmed.

A jumble of impressions bombarded her: the Landerson Field—she presumed it was that—now enclosed them. And it had eaten—

was eating?—an empty half circle from the side of her building, forming a globe with the Field Relay floating inside. The wall and windows were just *absent* and she hung, clouds above, clouds below, clouds behind, half in her building and half out, on a mat, in a translucent bubble stuck in the side of the fifty-third floor.

Her breath rushed in at the moment the whole bubble shifted backward. She was on a train departing a station. Detritus from damaged panels fell past them as they eased out into space and then they floated several feet from the gaping hole, leaving behind a throng of people with rifles, crouching and pointing. The bubble continued backward and in a moment the tower was only just visible through massed cloud, perhaps fifty feet away. Then it rose. It reached the top of the building and kept going. Up, up where there was nothing but cloud. And then it burst into the sunshine, high above everything, and stopped and hung, with San Francisco seen through patches of white far below, the bay and the ocean beyond it reflecting the sun.

She looked slowly up to Jianguo. He was arguing into the air in a language she didn't understand, his expression vexed. Someone was telling him something he didn't like. Diana felt sick to her stomach, had horrible vertigo and it hurt her neck to look up, but looking down —several thousand feet down—gave her guts a sickening yank, while looking inland or out to sea was just as bad. Her gaze finally alighted on Jianguo's penis, comfortably situated at eye level. It seemed to settle her stomach. Small favors. Well, that wasn't fair to Jianguo. Average sized favors.

He was uncircumcised, because there wasn't a circumcised penis left on the entire planet. She wondered, as she floated a half a mile above the surface, trying not to vomit, what it must have been like during the Augmentation when all the humans had had their limbs regrown, their tattoos erased, their scars healed and eyesight corrected. What had it been like when all the missing foreskins had Augmented back? Plenty of men must have tried to have it done over, in the beginning. Were they still trying, even now, thirty years on?

After watching Rance Fishman flaying his leg in the dark, she thought she knew the answer to that question.

Then the Landerson Field began to move. There was no sensation of acceleration but she could see the clouds below her stream past. Soon they left the storm front behind and were out over populated hills, covered with PopuPods, thick with humanity. No wind ruffled her hair. There was no sound. Very carefully she turned so she was no longer traveling backward.

"What are you... doing with me?" she squeezed out.

"Taking you to Lab One," Jianguo said. "Director Landerson will speak to you there."

"Lab One?" She groaned as her leg gave her a warning throb. She hoped this didn't portend a full-blown episode. The bone pain was unbearable. To distract herself, and until she could form a better plan, she chatted up Jianguo. "What's Lab One? A dance club?"

"The Director will ask the questions."

"This technology... what is this?" Around them pulsed a faint, oily field. No moving parts, no heat, no engines. Just motion. "Who *are* you, really?" Throb. *Keep talking. Make the pain go away.* They now seemed to be flying south down the coast, their crazy speed apparent even here, high above the ground. What she wouldn't give to have a week to tear this technology apart. The money she could make with this. Worldwide markets would open. How could she never have heard of it?

"This is a Landerson Field," Jianguo said, with a quiet pride that she noted as possible leverage. "A nano enclosure created and maintained remotely by our corps of Economists."

Where to start with that one.

"A *corps* of them?" she asked. "What does that make you?"

"An Economist, of course. MBA. Top of my class."

"You're no economist."

"Oh, I am," he said softly, as though he could visualize a thing, just out of his reach, that he wanted very badly. "And soon, you will see, the standing of Economists in the world will change. There will be a revolution."

"A revolution." She wanted to make sure she understood. "Of economists?"

He nodded. His arms were stained with blood from his work with the knife. His shoulders were broad and powerful. He was fast and dangerous and very well trained. She had to admit that *something* different was happening in the field of economics.

"So, where'd you go to school?" Keep your mind off the leg, she thought. It will pass. *Please, let it pass.*

"Chicago School of Business, class of 2074. I was going to study Quantitative Economics, but I was talked into a specialization in Monetary Policy." *Chatty, this one.*

"Ok. You must have known... Marty Sinclair?" She wasn't sure she recalled the professor or the school. Stab in the dark.

"Applied Econometrics. 3rd year."

It was true, then. Something she could work with.

"That makes you a little free market nut job. An anti-Keynesian pretty boy?" she asked. She groaned. It was hard to tell if the leg was getting worse. And hard to ignore it too. "So, you're just some crazy, Monetarist ... asshole?"

She'd never been great with insults. Still, maybe she could get him riled up. Maybe he'd make a mistake—land the sphere, try to beat her. Maybe she could escape. It wasn't much of a plan, but economists were notorious for unreasonable passions and commitment to untestable theories. MIT had hosted a forum once where one professor had heaved another off the stage over a disagreement about the rate of inflation. She knew there were buttons to push if she could find them.

But he just lifted his head and smiled. He had his hands on his hips and as he looked off into the middle distance she thought he resembled a young, mustachioed George Washington crossing the Delaware without any pants.

"I'm neither Monetarian, Keynesian, Austrian, or anything from the past," he said. "I am the future. I am a New Capitalist. A Landersonian."

What in the world was Terrance Landerson doing? Was this a cult? An economist cult? What did Landerson want with her? As far as she could remember she had never met him. She had never taken any debt from the World Bank, of course.

"Hey, class of 2074. You were born post Augmentation," she realized. He shrugged as if to say *what of it?* "You're one of the nudists, the Needless. But you were wearing pants! What's up with..."

She watched revulsion curl his face.

"The Needless are a *scourge!*" he spat. "Pathetic, cowardly, slaves! I'm not one of the Needless—I'm an Economist, regardless of my birth year. And you; you're a *traitor*, regardless of yours."

"Traitor's a pretty strong word," she observed. "Who am I supposed to be betraying?"

"As if you didn't know."

Something else had just occurred to her. She threw it out there. *Keep talking. Keep hoping.*

"At least I'm not a liar," she tried.

"I haven't lied to you once."

"You said I had to take my clothes off because they'd make me explode."

"Yes. Anything not impregnated with the particulate cloud of a human Nano Sphere disincorporates within a Landerson Field. Anything inanimate. Anything other than your flesh. And if you're touching it when it disincorporates, the covalent bonds of your body are reversed, and you explode."

She shook her head.

"Bullshit. I have an artificial leg." She pointed to it. "I'm touching it right now. It's *attached* to me. It's not flesh. It didn't disincorporate. Nobody exploded. So, *you* are a *liar*."

She watched him for a response. He gazed down at her, calm eyes a brilliant, fluorescent blue. How would he explain it? Give me a thread to pull, she urged him. This might lead back to some real data.

"What's an *artificial leg?*" he scoffed after a moment.

"This one," she pinked the artificial flesh. "This is an android leg."

Jianguo's attention was pulled away abruptly. He looked ahead of them and spoke into the air. Then he looked below them.

"We're almost there," he pointed down. Down at the Mission San José.

ALIENS FIRST INVADED California in 1789, when the Spanish priests of the Franciscan order built a score of Catholic Missions up and down the Pacific coast, magically provisioning the indigenous humans with food and medicine in order to convert, educate, and transform them into Spanish colonial citizens. The church bell towers, though tall, had been nowhere as benevolent as the Obelisks and the food, medicine and conversion had mostly destroyed the native people who accepted the alien largess.

Then those Spanish aliens had lost a war and gone home and the Missions lay empty for a hundred years. After that, for another hundred years, they had been tourist attractions for the State of California. And then finally, in 2049, as part of a collateral settlement with the California state government, the World Bank had taken possession of the whole California Mission system and closed them to the public. No one had purchased a Friar Junipero Serra keychain at any Mission gift shop in almost thirty years.

The Mission San José, which Diana and Jianguo had begun diving toward at what Diana felt was a dangerously high speed, had been the largest of all the missions. Diana saw the city of San Jose expanding below them like a hoary ocean, waves of white ceramic PopuPods rising wherever they could be stacked, in broad avenues slicing up the flat land around the Mission but ending abruptly before reaching it.

The Mission sat isolated behind an invisible dike holding back the cresting city, within broad fields of golden grass and coastal oak. The main building, a long red shingled rectangle with a three-story tower at one end, stood enclosed in a plaza courtyard of paths and dark foliage. She could see all this very clearly as they plunged lower. Beyond the courtyard, the empty fields stretched all the way to a PopuPod tidal wave cresting against an imperceptible levee. A shocking no-man's-land of unused space in this day of population growth. A defensive perimeter?

Their Landerson Field careened down toward the precise center of the courtyard. Diana's shoulders were tensed all the way to her toes. There was nothing to hang on to. She wasn't a fan of conventional air travel and this descent was worse than anything she had ever bad-dreamed. It wasn't an airplane slipping from the sky out of control; this was someone bombing themselves straight at the ground, open throttle crazy.

"We're coming in a little fast," Jianguo muttered. "The landing will be rough. It's not my fault."

"I don't care whose fault it is!" she screamed.

"They may be training a new recruit on this approach."

"Make it stop!" She wanted her eyes to close, but they wouldn't.

And then it did stop.

No sense of deceleration, no bump, no bounce. Just them, one minute traveling blindingly fast, the next not traveling at all. Hovering. In a courtyard.

Diana exhaled. The plaza where they had fallen—or landed—was a cemetery. Fitting, she thought, trying to unclench her body. Almost fitting. Could still be fitting, sometime in the next week or so. What's a better way to die, cancer or impact? When she thought about it, she thought she'd prefer impact. *Too late now.*

She and Jianguo floated one foot from the ground on their mat, the Field Relay beside them, still inside the sphere of the Landerson Field, a huge bubble floating in a graveyard— like the Good Witch of the West visiting her buried sister.

"Brace yourself," Jianguo said.

"Why? Aren't we here?"

"No." He squatted down toward his gray cereal bowl, on the corner of the mat. "The pilot was unable to balance the inverse spatial forces. There is accumulated acceleration still in the Field. When I disincorporate it... I'll buffer as much as I can."

He placed his full palm on his disk. The Relay beside them stopped humming, which was a bit of a shock because she had stopped noticing that it was humming in the first place.

And then *gravity times ten* reached across the final twelve inches between her and the ground and crushed her down. Ah, she thought, as the back of her head hit a flagstone and pink and green light flashed over the scene—there it is, the accumulated acceleration.

4

The emerging economic sentience, seeking to postpone the final crises, makes two false assumptions. These are: *I am the possessor of things*, and, *I am a vessel for debt*. The developed sentience knows the truth: *I am the maker of choices*. Only by writing choices to the Metaspatial Blockchain can the Known Economy be expanded and the final crises postponed. But only postponed. The final crises will ultimately consume us, regardless of all false assumption or truth.

—From *The Book of* Ω64, of the Swandeen Pracis

"I am Terrance Landerson," Terrance Landerson said to her. "This is my office." His first words. The first words anyone had said to her since landing thirty minutes earlier. She already didn't like his voice.

They'd hustled her out of the cemetery, through the darkened, stained glass blur that was her single impression of the interior of the Mission San José, past an ancient door and down into an underground facility, where all the white corridors and white garbed people and white light made her eyes hurt.

Now she sat in Terrance Landerson's office feeling woozy from the knock her head had taken. Terrance sat behind his desk. He watched her with mottled eyes, like frost on wet, dead wood.

"Water," she said. Her voice was weak.

Landerson rose and dispensed a cup from a small Obelisk beside his desk. He wore the same clothes they had dressed her in, white fabric that billowed when it moved. He handed her the cup and settled his weight back into the solid desk chair. It creaked like old bamboo. *Apparent age of 23. Corpulent but abnormally light on his feet. Most of humanity was slender but Terrance was fleshy.*

"You'll never get away with this," she said. It felt good to say that. She got a feeling of controlling her own fate when she said it. The pain in her leg had receded. Things were looking up.

She recognized him now that she got a look at him. He'd been in the news for a while, then he'd faded away. Director of the World Bank. Apparently, also inventor of magical flying spheres and kidnapper.

"You are wrong," he said. "Lab One is secure."

She eased her eyes around the space: curved swords hanging behind his desk, Japanese art framed on the walls. Books. It didn't look like a lab. When she tried to look behind her a pain shot through her head. She winced and felt for the bump on her scalp.

"Your head was cut," he observed in his motionless way. "While landing. You hit the ground." Terrance recalled the incidents for her as if she hadn't just lived through them. She wondered if he were as strange as he seemed, or if she just needed to recover from bouncing.

"It continues to bleed," he pointed out. "Even now. Without healing. Forty minutes of bleeding." He stared at her head, his gray eyes unblinking. His entire body was statue still, except when he limber-danced over to give her water. And then suddenly he smiled. It just appeared— *display teeth!*

"Explain your blood to me," he suggested.

Explain her blood. Explain why the Augmentation had worked its magic on everyone in the world but her? She'd always presumed she had been too deep, too far from the alien ships when the Swarm descended. If Greg had lived, he would probably have been aging right along with her. But it strained reason to think she'd been the only human unaffected. And even if she did have theories about why she bled from wounds when no one else on earth did, she felt no particular impulse to discuss those theories with Landerson. Why should she be the one to explain anything? He was the kidnapper.

Terrance grunted like he'd been struck in the stomach. As he rose from his desk, Diana wondered if they were going to begin the interrogatory beating so soon, but he turned his back on her. His arms lifted straight out from his sides, his spine arched and he pinched his breath out in chopped-up pieces like a breath choo-choo train, *ak...ak...ak...* His arms began to tremble, his palms turned up and his head tilted back until it appeared he might be trying to see behind him to view her upside down. It looked like an epileptic episode. But of course, no one had those anymore. Something else was wrong with him. *PreAug,* she realized. Maybe that accounted for the robotic conversational style too.

And then he relaxed. He turned back around and looked at her.

"Yes?" he said.

"Yes?"

"Explain your blood."

Right back to that? Did he even know about the trembling fit she'd just seen? Or did he know and not care?

"I bleed when I'm smashed," she shrugged carefully. "My whole family's like that. Why am I here?"

"To speak to me. About Immpenta. Let us start with Immpenta."

Immpenta *again?* She'd spent so many years doing so many other things. To go beyond Immpenta and father's *brilliant legacy.* To do something even better. But it always seemed to come back around, this reminder of her inadequacy. She had stopped giving interviews because of it. She actually grew queasy when she had to talk about it. She always had.

"I knew your family," Terrance told her. "Atticus Roark. *Very* poor businessman. A brilliant scientist." He was watching her bloody fingers as he spoke. He rose and limber-danced over to her again and offered a white handkerchief.

"You knew my father?"

"Seventy years ago," he recalled. "I was Bank chairman. Through Immpenta and Ebola 3. Yes?"

Immpenta. *Please, stop* she thought, feeling small and strange. *Why Immpenta all the time?* She didn't know the first thing about it. She'd been at MIT, and her father had created Immpenta out of nowhere. Suddenly there had been a cure for Ebola 3, a disease which had itself sprung and spread like a human prairie fire. *Can we all move on?*

"I don't feel like talking about it," she said.

"But we must. Roark Pharma. The World Bank. Ebola 3 and Immpenta. Our shared legacy. It made your company."

He was so motionless his speech so distant, like he was being phoned in from orbit. Like there was a part of him missing, off somewhere, doing other things, leaving behind a moving mouth and these disturbing eyes and his trembling fits. He reminded her of Dr. Fishman; something hidden was wrong with all the PreAugs. *Neurosis bubbling up but without a natural limiter?* There was no price to pay for any of the darkness inside them. People could chop themselves up and go on and on, no worries. She wished he would stop saying *Immpenta*. It made her guts twist.

"Immpenta made your company," he offered again. "It made Atticus."

"Hey. Why are we talking about Immpenta?"

It made her stomach lurchy, down where the secrets lived.

"Because I know," he said. "Your father. His debts. We helped each other."

He barked a quick laugh, like a dog. The smile came and went. He nodded to her, and all the while her throat was closing. She felt vomity. She could see he wasn't going to stop saying *Immpenta Immpenta*. She wished he would stop. *Stop.*

"Immpenta. The money they spent!" he cried. "Such a small investment. A thousand fold return."

"What investment?" she demanded. But why ask? *Don't encourage him*, she begged herself.

"The worldwide plague," he said. "A world desperate to pay. Whatever the cost. Your father built a machine. A machine to make money."

"Ok. I'm done." She was suddenly dead tired. Maybe it was the blood-letting, maybe everything else, but her body sagged like it needed to stop listening. Yes. She needed to stop him from talking. *But do it smooth.*

"You might not know it," she said, "because you're crazy, but you're not making any sense. So thanks for the compliments to my family. Are you done kidnapping me now?" *So sassy! What was that about?* She wasn't usually sassy.

"We are the same."

"Please stop."

"I can be your friend. I was your father's friend. I ate with him. With your mother. A business partnership."

She wanted *out of this now*. The insides of her stomach clawed to become the outsides of her stomach and she couldn't move. What was happening? Every time he said *Immpenta...*

"Yes?" he asked. "Can't we meet halfway?"

"What do you want?"

"To make you see. We are the same. I know the secrets. So indelicate to say it. But I will. Friends sharing secrets."

Terrance rose from his chair like a helium whale and blimped to his Obie. He got her more water. She watched it all from inside what she assumed now was her concussion. He leaned on his desk and creaked it like a dying bridge. She wanted to look away.

"Well, here," he shrugged, "the secret: Atticus created Ebola 3. Repaying his debt to us. Ebola 3 and then Immpenta. The cure. And endlessly profited. Now. We are on the same page?"

"Yeah, a page from the book of *crazy*," she said. Had she heard someone say that somewhere? It wasn't the kind of thing she usually came up with. She didn't feel like herself at all. She felt sideways. Something was coming up in her guts.

"Yes! Wit. Your father lacked that. We are aligned. Roark Pharma and the Bank."

No. But something was tickling the back of her mind— a memory of... Phoebe? And Charles had started saying something about her father, right before Jianguo...

"Why?" she asked, and it sounded like she was begging, "why would he do that? That is insane."

"To fail because of debt? *That* is insane. We freed him." Terrance pulled up a pseudo display showing accounts, from years ago, which only her father could have accessed, and saw money flowing between Roark and the World Bank.

"That didn't. Happen." Somewhere deep in her, where her insides were rising to the sky, someone was nodding. Very emphatically *nodding.* Someone was *punching the air.*

Someone said *knew it! KNEW IT!*

And she threw up. It came up and out and she had no chance to hold on and no desire. The very little she had eaten and drank in the last twenty-four hours pitched forward, striking the front of Terrance's desk. She kept heaving and a minute or two passed before she had finally heaved up an empty stomach and a blank mind.

"You're saying...?" she whispered, at last, into the silence, and wiped her face.

"And you've simply carried on. Perfectly free. Your empire."

"And I somehow knew it all along. That's what you're saying."

"Your secrets are safe. In fact, immaterial. Except now. Because on our shared history. I have hope. We see a resolution. To our mutual benefit."

She was being led somewhere.

This sounded like a business proposition.

"Fine," he nodded. "We understand each other. So, we move forward. Speak of your alliance. With The 27."

Her mouth was sticky sweet with bile, and her thoughts that something inside her had always been dead and she hadn't known it. But she knew it now and something inside came newly alive. This new, living part stepped up and took a shot at the conversation.

"What alliance?"

"With The 27. As I said."

Such endless little circles, she groaned. Going round and round from clarity to confusion.

"The 27?" she asked. "The aliens?"

He nodded. She looked at the display with her father's accounts, the huge sums from private accounts.

"Our shared advantage served," he said, glancing at his watch. "The negotiator's art. All parties benefit. Though some see it differently. The steering committee don't agree. They mistrust your alliance with The 27. And now, come. It is time."

Terrance and two company white attendants escorted her from the office and through the underground complex. White walls slipped past. Windowless doors. An ancient oak portal with a round, metal handle she remembered coming through on the way to Landerson's office. And then there was an elevator, and a blur of white.

An alliance with The 27, her old, dead brain thought. *But the 27 are gone.*

I've always craved approval from my father, her newer brain thought. *But my father was a monster.*

The astonishing thing—well, there were so many astonishing things—but one of the astonishing things was how *fast* she absorbed this new idea about her father. She just hooked it in and sucked it down and planted it in ground that felt like it had been prepared long ago. How else did certainty grow so fast? Her new brain saw it, and things that had meant something... now meant the opposite.

She got a hold of herself, she took new stock; it was all so clear—everything had been a lie. Her father's legendary brilliance. His company's legacy. Nothing but lies, made crystal clear by new data.

Amazing how crystal clear and brilliant this new world is, where everything meant the opposite.

SHE HAD ONLY BEEN twenty-two when she had seen him last; he had been sixty-one, unconscious in a hospital bed. His cancer had hollowed him out a spoonful at a time. A scoop from his cheeks. A dollop from the temple. And then he had caved in all over, and she had thought to herself *this wrecked ship cannot be my father*. He had always shaved.

She was there to sign papers to end his life. She had struggled, come to this with an open heart. But in the end the best she could find was a washed-out place inside where deciding became an act of utility—cost, common sense, the needs of others for the bed he occupied. Because she couldn't bear an open heart. She couldn't bear the feeling she had. So, she never did. And that's why she was never able to wonder *why*? Why had she felt such *relief* when she signed the papers collecting her father's life?

She understood now. Ending her father's life had meant the opposite.

When she'd walked from the hospital that night, into the cool air, through the halogen brilliance and into her waiting car and begun to gird, even then, for the fight to control her company, she had seen meaning in her father's life: hope, discovery, truth. Noble goals she could strive toward to earn his approval, even after his death.

But.

Unable to love.

Self-deceiver.

World wrecker.

Madman.

Her measuring stick had been broken. His life had *not* meant hope, discovery, truth; it had meant the opposite.

WITH GREAT EFFORT she pulled herself back into the elevator. She had a new best friend named Crystal Clear; it was helping her move around in this white-walled labyrinth and not bump into things, so another part of her mind could focus on examining her captors and discovering where she was, why she had been brought here and devising a plan to escape. And after that, what?

Why, your vacation, her friend Crystal Clear reminded her.

So, when the elevator stopped, gently, and the doors slid apart, she tried to start noticing things again. The first thing she noticed was furnace heat, which blew into the elevator box. It was like a hammer blow. She followed Terrance into the corridor and was covered with sweat by the time she took her first breath. Her guides didn't notice; augmented bodies didn't sweat. Presentable and relaxed as patrons at an opera, they led her on.

The floors and walls here felt alive, as though an engine rumbled somewhere in the basement transmitting piston strokes into her feet. When she trailed her hand on the wall she felt it in her fingers. Terrance led their troop to a lonely door at the very end of a long hallway, then opened it and gestured to her.

Inside was a large, hot room, hotter than the hallway had been, where vaulted beams held up a ceiling inlaid with carving. Woven carpets spread across the floor in patterns matched to the rich, paneled walls. The lights were dim except where a single bright pool that fell on a table. Several chairs stood around it. In one corner of the room stood a small Obelisk and Terrance pointed at it.

"Refresh yourself."

She glanced at the Obie, then limped to the table and pulled out a chair.

"I can't use that. But I could use a scotch. If you want to be my friend."

She sat. Just a tiny throb in her leg; Crystal Clear couldn't do anything to help with that. Terrance went to the Obie and drew down a tumbler. He brought it to the table.

She sucked in a mouthful of kidnapper's Scotch and it expanded over her tongue, expensive and very aged. She kept herself from draining it, but promised she wouldn't leave the room without finishing, because whoever had bartended for Terrance 30 years ago had set a very fine model of Scotch in his mind.

So, let's get this going, she thought. *I've got vacation plans.*

With no preamble from Landerson, four large pseudo displays spun up along the wall, casting their own light into the room and revealing more of the carved wood. Terrance strolled to a corner where he could see everything at the same time. Each display held a face. She recognized none of them.

"First," Terrance announced, "introductions." He gestured to the faces on the displays. "The Steering Committee of The World Bank. Meet Diana Roark."

"Is this really necessary?" asked the woman on the leftmost pseudo with an accent Diana recognized, probably Liberian. She wore a formal shawl in bright colors. Terrance pointed to her.

"Akeelah Bartuah. World Bank Director, West African Union," he said.

"I am that and busy. I am *busy*, Terrance. Why the charade?"

"Here," Terrance said, indicating the next three pseudos, "the Directors, variously: Estonia, United Korea and the Brazilian Confederation. Maksim Linna, Felicia Pak, and Paulo Silva. Ladies, gentlemen. Thank you for attending."

There was a moment while the committee observed Diana and she them. With the exception of Akeelah, they were each wearing formal, gauzy suits. Without looking away, she raised her glass and sipped. Damned if she was going to be the first to talk.

"What the *hell* is wrong with her, Terrance?" asked Akeelah. "She looks four hundred years old."

Diana's shadows appeared then, swirling like volcanic ash. Well, when it rains it pours, she thought and my life is just a living thunderstorm. This time they didn't come *from* anywhere, they were just there, hanging in the air. But only a few of them. It was a tasteful visitation, a cozy clutch of motes, arrayed over the table. When she turned to Terrance, they swung out of view; when she looked back, they were still there. It was possible, barely, to resist swiping at the air. It could be worse, she supposed. Onward.

"What is wrong with her. Indeed. Diana can address that," Terrance said. "Put it to her." He gazed with raised, interested eyebrows and his smile flashed on and off like a vacancy sign.

"Just for clarity," she said, then stopped and let her eyes range over the faces that hung before her, searching out the dynamics. Who was in charge? Who needed something, and from whom and how hard could any of them be pushed? Could they be pushed at all?

"Just for clarity," she repeated, "you are all aware that I have been kidnapped and am being held against my will."

"Yes," Akeelah said, "we know. And *just for clarity*, the arrangements you made to prevent us from tracking you left us little choice. So: petard, meet hoist. You have no one to blame but yourself in this."

"On the contrary," Diana observed, "I can think of six people to blame, starting with the people I have just been introduced to, and I plan to blame them in public to the authorities unless I am released within thirty seconds." She sipped. Really good Scotch, pointless opening salvos.

It was a mildly interesting problem. She had no idea—yet—what any of them wanted. But she was under no illusion that she'd ever be given the thing she desired herself: vacation time. They would never release her now, not after she'd seen them all. So, the stakes were low. It was more an existential exercise than a full-on negotiation. What could they do to her that the cells turning her own bones to chalk would not do anyway and soon?

The stakes were so low she almost began to enjoy herself. *Immpenta*, she said to herself. *Immpenta. No gut lurching. First time ever. Nice.* Crystal Clear was still pumping through her veins, keeping her mind sharp. Keeping the world new. If only it wasn't so god dammed hot in this room! Sweat slipped into her eye. She squinted. She pushed hair from her forehead, her hand coming away traced with blood. If she wanted to intimidate these people with her negotiating prowess she'd need to stop bleeding so much.

"Start on the right foot," Terrance advised. "I've confessed our shared complicity. Immpenta. Our alignment with Roark Pharma. Let us help one another now. Hold that goal."

"Akeelah raises a relevant point, though," said the Brazilian. Paulo. His face drew nearer his pseudo, no doubt zooming for a closeup on her. "She absolutely appears aged. And... is she bleeding?"

"Yes. Cut when landing. On her head." Terrance nodded and made a quick slicing gesture to indicate the problem. He was remarkable, Diana thought, in his oddness. Was the steering committee anything like her own board of directors? *Let's see.*

Yes. Paulo was a lip licker. Oh, was he ever. But never a chapped flap of skin. He could lick forever and never ever need a Chapstick. Akeelah seemed pretty normal. But hiding something, if the day's experience was any guide. How about the rest?

"Intriguing, no?" Terrance asked. "Her cuts are open. She bleeds. All over my settee."

"Explain all this to me, Roark," Akeelah demanded. Ah, thought Diana. My invitation. She wants an explanation; how much is that worth?

"Maybe she doesn't have a Nano Sphere?" said Pak, the United Korea director. Pak, Diana thought. *Are you crazy too? Hmm.* Was Pak... masturbating? Off camera. He was, almost certainly.

"Maybe that's why she's bleeding," Pak continued. He seemed very capable of doing two things at once. "Could The 27 have removed her Nano Sphere for her, for some reason?"

"Her nano-sphere exists. She survived the Landerson Field. It would have disincorporated her," Terrance said. "I assume The 27 did this. Yes. Somehow they caused this. But why? We are here for that. To understand. How does Diana command The 27?"

"You people are crazy," Diana said. She felt quite certain of it.

Maksim Linna, the Estonian, rumbled, his English like a cascade of broken rocks, "Is possible disincorporation would have been best thing," he said. This made Akeelah roll her eyes, while Pak and Paulo carried on with a certain irritated dismissal.

These people are so sloppy, Diana thought. They leak information like five-year-olds playing telephone. Was it arrogance from too many years spent in charge of the world? Terrance had been the head of the World Bank since before The Augmentation. Had this same ruling coterie been in place since The 27 left the planet?

She wished she had a perfect, Augmented memory. She'd probably be able to remember who the steering committee members had been for the last hundred and fifty years. But her regular brain wasn't totally useless, and Crystal Clear put an extra giddy-up in her step. *Let's see... founded after World War II by the western powers. Primary charter? Promote capitalism by financing loans to developing governments.* But instead of creating economic stability, the Bank had quickly become just another burn the barn financier, stalking the borders of the most vulnerable nations and binding them in debt. It faded quite a bit as the 21st century rolled in.

But the day The 27 vanished and left behind the Dispensing Obelisks and the Augmentation, the World Bank had roared back. It mainlined money into the financial veins of the world, pumped the faltering heart of the global economy back up, raised nations, transformed industries and kept the lights on. The sums thrown around had been vast, and frankly surprising, backstopped by gold. And now thirty years on, the Bank was like a creeping fog. It went everywhere, unfettered by any charter. It operated on its own, crossing borders, more powerful than any sovereign government. No one minded.

The World Bank in a nutshell—*thanks, flesh brain*, Diana sang softly to herself. Oh, was she getting drunk? Was that a good idea? Well, what else could people expect her to do. Her father was a child slaughterer. Her shadows seemed to observe her drinking, just a little bit censorious. But she didn't care. Crystal Clear was steering her straight down the middle, and it felt pretty damn good.

Linna, his pugilist's nose compressed in a growl, spoke again, rumbling Diana's seat. "Solution here is simple. This one interfered, plan is too far along, we must dispose her. Quick."

Terrance tsked and did not even bother to address this suggestion. Instead, he turned to Diana directly.

"So much for introductions," he said, flashing a smile between his cheeks and then putting it away like an accordion of lunacy. "The time has come. Offer your explanations. You are allied with The 27. We need to understand. What is the scope of your arrangement? Its terms and conditions? We will meet and exceed them. And Maksim is correct. We are constrained by time. And patience."

He nodded and crossed his arms over his big fat chest and waited. Diana was used to negotiations that developed fast, but this was *fast*. She took another sip and a drop of red sweat rolled off her brow and fell in her tumbler. It was so hard to concentrate in this sauna! Very non-optimum for deal-making, at least on her side of the table. More shadows filtered into the room. She took another sip.

There is a time for gathering information. There is a time for playing games. But sometimes you get what you want by telling the truth.

"You've got me all wrong," she said. "I have absolutely nothing to do with The 27. I don't know anyone who does. The 27 are…" she made a twinkly motion with her real fingers. Off in the universe.

"We know that's false," Terrance said. He looked at the faces on the pseudo displays. They nodded, all impatient and angry. "Our information is compelling. So please. Drop this pretense. Seek a mutually beneficial exchange."

"Nobody likes a mutually beneficial exchange better'n me," Diana insisted. "Ask anyone. But I'm telling you, I'm not hooked to The 27. I'm not a joiner. Never ever. Not even a softball league. Hate to poop your party."

He walked close to the table, bent and looked at her from inches away. "The Seer of Sonoma. Such astounding insight into the *markets*. Everything you touch turns to *gold*. How do you explain it? Your extraordinary wealth?"

Diana couldn't figure out where he was going with this. But she was willing, and they were going to spill the beans soon enough. She was convinced they had beans, it was just a matter of time. They weren't the kind of gang that kept things to themselves for long.

"My family has always been wealthy," she shrugged. "That's how I explain it."

Terrance was losing patience. That was good. She liked it when the rest of the room got jumpy. More mistakes.

"No! The 27 fed you information. Your succession of financial bets? After the Augmentation? *All* of them paid off. And you carry *no debt!* The 27 helped you. We can help you. But first, tell us. How did The 27 assist? And *why?*"

Now they were insulting her, just to add some spice on top of the kidnapping, she supposed. As if the things she had done were just the result of *alien intervention?* Did they think she had grown to be the richest person on Earth because The 27 had fed her information?

That pissed her off.

"Terry—can I call you Terry, Terrance? Terry, you're completely full of shit, and your friends are all assholes. What do you think of that?" Her anger made her head swim more, the heat and the head wound compounding the problem. But it felt good and her father was a homicidal child slaughtering madman. Everything meant the opposite. What did she care?

"Why we play games?" Linna demanded. "Tell her everything, make things move faster!"

Terrance spun toward the display and flashed Linna a smile, but this was bad smiling. It hung on his face for seconds, a dead smile-threat. It was, Diana had to admit, chilling, the way he stared. She updated her opinion of Terrance Landerson. He was probably pretty dangerous.

Linna seemed to feel the same way because he stopped talking. Terrance watched until Linna began to squirm.

"Remember how close Estonia is, Maksim." Terrance snapped his fingers, the sound sending sharp echoes around the silent room. "That close. Yes?"

The big man nodded. Terrance turned back to Diana and took a breath.

"Maybe step by step. That might help. Walk us through an early investment. The first big splash. How did you do it?"

"Do what?"

"Three weeks post Augmentation. You sold Roark Pharmaceuticals. Just a month later, it went bankrupt. No one saw it coming. Other than you."

Those first weeks. Life after losing Greg. The pain of learning prosthetics, of lacerations and broken bones, the emptiness where Greg would have stood if he hadn't loved her so much he sacrificed himself at the bottom of the sea. Those early days. Yes. When almost instantly, within the first days after the Augmentation, running her company from the hospital, she'd seen anomalies in the data. No one but her had understood how that data meant doom. The data said people had stopped using prescription drugs; she didn't understand it, but she believed it.

She'd tried to make the board see and take steps, but they wouldn't. How could they? They couldn't imagine that the world could take such a devastating, head spinning turn, become so different so fast. But for Diana, devastation was easy to imagine. She had come to this new world pre-devastated; Greg was dead because of her.

One night soon after her first surgery, ready to end it all, she sold every single piece of Roark stock she owned. And then the company imploded, while she escaped free and liquid. And so began the streak that turned her into the Seer of Sonoma.

It didn't take a rocket scientist to connect the dots. People weren't going to get sick, so they wouldn't buy insurance. So, she shorted the insurance industry. Those bets would pay off if insurance faltered, but she bet the industry would evaporate, so the bets would *really* pay. The size of her wagers made heads turn and if she'd figured wrong she'd have lost every cent. But risks didn't stop her. This wasn't the world she knew, and it wasn't the world she wanted. What did she care about risks? She put every cent she had—the money from the sale of Roark and any liquid assets she could find, billions of dollars—against insurance.

And then the insurance industry collapsed. Her wealth grew billions.

On she rolled. The Dispensing Obelisks started dispensing food and water everywhere, so she shorted corporate agriculture, petro-chemical fertilizers and grocery chains. She bet it all, every cent, and won, every time. Energy, more than a third of it worldwide, was used producing, transporting and storing food. She optioned energy at rock bottom prices with every. last. cent.

Fearless, young, amazing, she became the darling of finance. Like magic, they said, the highest high-risk poker game ever played and won. But the truth was, she wanted it to stop. She didn't deserve anything she had, she knew it and it wasn't worth anything to her anyway. She wanted to leave it behind but something drove her; she couldn't help it. She kept thinking of her father, what he would have wanted and what she couldn't do that he had been able to do—save the world and do impossible things. Pushed to financial extremis, begging for failure, she bought half the world and sold it again, hoping the edifice would bury her. But every time she made a move, she made money.

She hated the The Seer of Sonoma. She was The Seer of Sonoma.

When she realized her body was different, that the Augmenta-tion had skipped her, she retreated from the public eye to her Sonoma Coast compound. She sent Liz away, buying her off with the director-ship of her oceanic research institute. Charles just kept coming back, again and again, until she gave up. And then she got cancer. And now here she was.

And at no point, not at any time, had a little green man whispered her an executive summary. It had been her. It had all been her.

The mistakes were hers.

"Diana? Are you with us?"

Terrance looked at her, a few feet away, and she realized she'd drifted. The memories were powerful but seemed tied to a life other than this one. The whole mental exercise made her feel rubbery and dislocated. Plus, she was now officially drunk as shit.

The heat! Sweat drenched her. Her palms slipped where they held up her chin, and her clothes were soaked. The shadows were really coming on now; apparently they'd only sent a small advance guard to see how many would fit into the room and it turned out the answer was *a lot*. It was easier to look at Terrance if she closed one eye.

"I'm here," she said. "Or I'm not. You pick."

"Why did The 27 help you?"

"Oh. They didn't."

"Your trades. Regression analysis proves it. What you did was impossible. You had assistance. The 27 guided you. Why?"

"I'm telling you they didn't!"

"Yes! They did! No one bets their *entire fortune*. But you did. Over and over. On sheerest speculation! No one does that!"

"You're getting testy," she said with a smile. It was coming, she could tell: the beans were on their way. "I suppose you're right about my fortune, though. I guess it's a question of value. You know I have an econama... economics degree? Economics—the science of human value. The science of *what matters to people*. The only thing I valued was gone by the time I started my streak. I didn't have a fortune. I didn't have anything. So that's what I bet. Over and over."

Now she was the one at the end of his cold stare. She matched it, daring him to strike her. He thought he knew what she valued. He thought he knew what she wanted—he thought she wanted to live. But she had the leverage here. She had it all.

"We have captured your operative," he told her softly. "He is here. In this facility. We have Robert."

There was a long silence. She heard Linna's rock fall, "Finally we tell her."

"What's that supposed to mand? Supposedly mean?" she scoffed. "My operative?"

"Robert. He is here. Asking for you. I destroyed your ship."

"My sheep... shiper? I don't have a ship."

"Not anymore," he agreed. "I destroyed it. With my Field Projector. You must have been given this ship by The 27. It was quite remarkable."

"The 27 never give me anything, damn you!"

"Do us this favor. End your dumb show. My thoughts? Your ship failed to rendezvous. You had a scheduled meeting. But it's cloaking failed. I saw it. Enclosed it. The range of the Field Projector grows daily. Sadly, the ship was lost. But Robert survived."

"Who?"

"Your operative! Stop this, Diana! You make it harder on yourself. Your man is Robert. He is in a Containment Field. Below us in Lab One. He insists he must speak to you. Only to you."

Landerson waved up a pseudoscreen and on it a face rotated. Diana tried to study it. She really did. But her shadows went absolutely crazy at that moment and swirled around her head like black flies on dead meat. She saw a little... a man, vaguely Asian, thin black hair, sallow skin the color of a pine countertop. 23 years old, like everyone on the planet. It was no one she had ever seen before in her life.

"I must speak with Diana Roark," said the man they called Robert. "I can only speak to Diana Roark," he insisted while Diana batted at substanceless flies and didn't remember.

"That's a stranger one to me," she pronounced. Bat, bat, drink.

"Stop! Did Robert drop from the sky, in a spaceship, asking for you, without knowing you? Unlikely. He is your operative. Is there another explanation?"

She tried to imagine how she could explain it. She couldn't think of an explanation. Or keep her head up very well. Or anything.

"Your *plans*, Diana, your... *congress* with The 27. It is time to tell us everything."

Well, here were the beans at last. They came out in a nice stream. But instead of piling in her hands in a neat little stack they fell through her fingers and scattered on the floor. Terrance had captured an operative, in a ship, and he thought it was her operative; they thought she was in league with The 27. But it wasn't her operative. Someone named Robert? In an alien ship? She couldn't bring it all together. Crystal Clear was long gone, maybe stealing her vacation. She needed to regroup, she needed a distraction... *she needed to stop drinking.*

"I have cancer," she announced.

As conversation stoppers go, it packed a pretty good punch. It seemed to work here, given that it took Terrance several moments to respond.

"What?" he said.

"I have cancer. Bonity cancer. Of which I'm dying. Of." She hiccuped. *Cliché. A hiccuping drunk woman announcing she's got cancer.*

It was fun to see Terrance confused. *Good old Terrance*, she thought.

"Think, Terrytotter," she told him. "Akeelah said it, I look like a crap on a napkin." Terrance turned to look at Akeelah. "That's because my body don't Augment. I'm bleeding, see? I'm old, bloody bleedy Diana, I have the cancer. You want to keep it aliving, a little longer? Gotta get me outta this heater. I'm right... the edge of mine. That's advice. Take it, leave it, who knows."

"She's bluffing," Akeelah said without conviction. It wasn't obvious what sort of bluff it might be.

Diana noticed her face tip toward the tabletop and saw her sweat, fruit punch red, pooled there. Her eyes began to close. She couldn't resist it and she didn't want to. She hadn't expected to do it, but just before her forehead met the table she thought it might have been the most effective negotiating tactic she had ever tried: passing out.

5

As falling water clouds the surface of a reflecting pond, so the great mysteries bring uncertainty and inflationary pressure to the Known Economy: who made the Obelisks? From whence the Nano Spheres? What preceded the first link of the Metaspatial Blockchain? These questions seem eternal and unknowable and thus only the purview of the Sentient One. We can never know the answers. Yet, failing to search for them, we advance the moment of our doom.

—From *The Book of* Ω64, of the Swandeen Pracis

She awoke in a small white bed in a small white cell in the grip of Terrance Landerson's large pink hands. He was shaking her as if she were a broken promise. He shook and shook until she opened her eyes. He had pressing business today. Was she ready to cooperate? She mumbled something affirmative. Diana's friend Crystal Clear had fled and she had a new roommate named Vicious Hangover. But Crystal had left something behind on the bedside table. An idea.

"The Director says you're going to cooperate," Jianguo said as he led her down a long white hallway toward the elevator doors.

Crystal. So smart.

"Fully," Diana nodded. "I plan to tell you everything." The idea: maybe it only seemed like an idea, instead of a slide down the path of least resistance, because her skull still pounded with sparkling poison. But the idea was to lie about everything and keep moving; it was the best she could do. It's not hard to survive surrounded by lies, she knew. Sometimes they made you throw up, but otherwise you could go on for years that way and even get fabulously rich.

"The Director wants me to bring you to the Lab," Jianguo said. "We'll join him when he's done. He's recycling failed operators."

"Let's go." She limped after him into the elevator.

Down they trekked through Landerson's Habitrail hideaway with its population of white robed rats. Diana felt like her mind had shut itself into a room deep inside her brain, still a bit shocked and wondering what would happen next. She tried to keep track of their route for potential escapes. When they arrived at another elevator, sized for freight, waiting minions stood aside and Jianguo and Diana entered alone.

"Why's it so hot everywhere?" she fanned her hand. He looked at her. "How long was I out?" she asked, pulling her shirt off her chest. He shrugged. "What day is this?"

"March eleven."

Only one day since the board meeting then. She had three days left. Greg had died on March 14th, the day of the Great Augmentation—easy to keep track of. She heard herself complain softly about sweating like a sponge and she clamped her mouth shut. The idea called for complete cooperation and no complaining. It was a very simple idea and she wished she'd thought of it the second she'd gotten here, because now she had a lot of ground to make up.

"Do you know about Immpenta too?" her mouth decided to say out loud. *Not part of the idea.*

"That was something from before the Augmentation? Some technology to keep bodies from breaking?"

"It was a drug."

He shrugged again, *what does that have to do with me?*

"The Director hasn't mentioned it?"

Jianguo shook his head and ended the conversation by pulling out his phone. Apparently her secret was safe. Only the most powerful maniac on the planet and his steering committee had heard the news: her father the mass murderer, with his billions in debt, repaid through suffering and death, and Diana grown rich on his lies. So many lies. At least he'd never told her that he loved her. Apparently even Atticus's lies had limits.

When the elevator doors opened she saw a crowd milling, though they stepped away when they saw Jianguo. Diana disembarked into a cavern hewn straight from the Pacific coast bedrock. Someone had peeled titanic, precise ice cream scoops out of the solid metamorphic stone. The chamber was so long that the far end blurred in her sweat-stung eyes. The ceiling was seventy feet above her head. Repeated deployments of a huge Landerson Field could have performed such an excavation, she thought. Even disincorporation had practical applications. *Leashed nothingness.*

The floor was concrete and level and the chamber bright as a surgical theater. Workers, white dressed like ghosts, hurried everywhere with tablets. They ministered to row after row of man-high, glass-sealed, cable-injected pods, rank after rank across the huge catacomb, like statuary in a Chinese tomb. Jianguo looked out at it all like a proud father, twirling his little prance of a mustache.

"Lab One," he said.

The pods all had curved glass doors and inside each there was room for a person to stand. What looked like boots were form-sealed to the floors, spread apart from each other and a thick, silver circlet hung wired to each pod ceiling like a mini chandelier.

Some pods were lightless and empty, but many were lit and each of those held a person. The people were posed like Da Vinci classics, arms out and legs wide. Their hands were bound in restraints on the walls, their feet locked in the boots on the floor and their foreheads encircled by the hanging headpiece.

They strained against their harnesses and appeared to be screaming, though no sound escaped the pods. She was sure they were screaming though— their backs were arched, faces pitched up in blanched agony, gums flaring teeth. Outside each pod a technician stood, with electrodes trailing from temples to a pod-mounted control board. *Some sort of brain wave interface? Monitoring the people within the pods?*

These pods were the source of the heat that wrung her and the deep, subsonic thrumming she felt in the floors and walls. The entire cavern vibrated like an idling bus. This pod farm was drawing untold joules of energy, the waste heat only incidentally vented somewhere above.

"The Director has asked me to be very frank with you," Jianguo said as he surveyed the chamber. "To answer any questions you might have. Do you have any questions?"

"What did these people do to deserve this?" she asked, mouth dry. She wanted to sound off-handed because her idea called for lies and guile. Lie about everything. But it was hard to lie around horror.

"No," he said, "no, these are Pilots. Economists. The best of the best."

"Pilots? And you're torturing them?" she asked.

"They're working. They don't feel pain," he assured her, as he looked at the man squirming in the nearest pod with a slight, puzzled frown. "It's an honor to be chosen."

"You're a Pilot? You've been inside?"

"At least twice a week for the last four years."

They watched the nearest pod. Once Jianguo looked, he couldn't look away, and there was something unsatisfied in the cock of his head. He delivered a lecture as he watched, a speech he had clearly given many times before. Maybe even to the man who screamed only ten feet away.

"After the Augmentation," he began to recite, "World Bank Director Terrance Landerson began to acquire any science laboratory pursuing Obelisk research. He knew even then that only he would be able to save humanity. One of his labs was the first to model the individual nano fragments of the Swarm. His scientists created a theory to explain the interactions between human Nano Spheres and the Obelisks—how humans required things and the Obelisks provided them.

"But if the Obelisk nano fabricators could create atomically perfect food, the Director thought, why not computers? Space ships? Ball-point pens? Well, no one could say why not, but that never worked. You can't get Obelisks to fabricate anything they are not programmed to provide. But his scientists soon found ways to control the particles of the Swarm, those minute nano bits making up human Nano Spheres.

"The earth's atmosphere is saturated with them. With enough energy—a very, very large amount—the nano particles could be manipulated by a human subject. This eventually became the Field Projector technology we see here today.

"There were problems controlling these particles in the early days. The research, conducted at Cornell, cycled Cornell students through the first machines in cadres—groups of athletes, groups of physics students, groups of engineers, creative writing students— because research showed that certain groups were slightly better at manipulating particles and others had no ability at all.

"When they tried a group from the Economics department, they saw two things: several of those students went mad, despite their Augmentation, and *all* of them managed massive interactions with the planetary nano cloud. The mad ones suffered mysterious misalignments of their Nano Spheres. The ones who didn't go mad refused to enter the machines again.

"But the Director was not afraid. He was, and is, the foremost economic theorist of his or any generation. He wondered if his economic expertise would allow him to reproduce the student's results. It was an amazing success! Within days he was able to form what we now call Landerson Fields out of nothing but a shell of particles! And he learned to make other simple things. Building materials, the strongest in the world. Knives and tools. And so, he created these labs, and he taught us."

Jianguo looked behind him at Diana to check—make sense?

"So you can't make a Landerson Field unless you're an economist," she summarized. "Why economists?"

"Our training analyzing costs and benefits simply makes us superior."

"Okay. So you don't know why economists. Just say that."

"It doesn't matter why economists. This is all in preparation for battle with The 27. That's the only important thing."

Jianguo had moved closer and closer to the pod and then he stopped talking and stared, like a man at an aquarium, as his economist co-worker tried to thrash and rip himself to pieces. If he hadn't been bound by the hands and feet he would have succeeded. She suddenly thought he bore a remarkable resemblance to Terrance when he'd performed those epileptic back bends in his office. From beneath the crown on the Pilot's forehead a steady rivulet of blood ran and she thought, *how could that be?* Augmented bodies heal immediately, unless they are smashed, like falling boys, or neck-snicked, like members of a board. *Don't they? What's going on under that crown?*

The thrashing came to an abrupt end and the pod door rose with a rush of air. The attendant dropped her electrodes from her temples and checked her tablet, quick, business-like—a bus driver pulling up at the designated stop. She slipped past Jianguo into the pod. Her Pilot was slumped, hanging. She removed his crown. It sucked free with a pop and a jerk and the Pilot inhaled a deep breath. Diana felt herself sicken. Inside the crown was a gray, three-inch spike, now dripping bloody ichor, which had been punched through the Pilot's forehead. There was a hole through his skull into his brain, and the attendant shone a light into the hole like a dentist. Diana could see swirling pink tissue. The attendant ticked a field on her tablet, as the hole sealed itself quickly shut.

The attendant wiped blood from the pilot's face and in a few seconds he was able to straighten. She tapped a few more fields on her device and the boots and wrist clasps opened. Then out he stepped, blinking like a newborn.

It looked as though he had nowhere to go. He seemed absolutely without affect, like a newly minted cyborg. Diana expected the attendant to take him by the hand and lead him away, but she hung her tablet on the back of the pod and left and the Pilot soon walked off in the other direction. Jianguo took her tablet and flicked through the data, then turned back to Diana, his lips tight.

"That was sloppy," he said. "They were off by fifty feet."

Pilots. A piece suddenly fit together with another piece for Diana.

"When we crashed in the cemetery," she said, "you said someone was landing us, someone was piloting the Field. These Pilots?"

Jianguo was distracted. "Yes. Although this team will have to be recycled."

"It kind of looked like there was a spike in his brain," she offered, still slightly shaken.

"Nano Interface. It can be off-putting the first time you see it."

"Sure. Just the first time. So, some of you economists are Pilots. And some others like you get ferried around breaking into buildings and kidnapping people?"

"I'm a Pilot," he said sharply. "One of the best. And no, we seldom perform extractions, only when the Director sees a special need. We usually track a subject's Nano Sphere in the mesh and tag them remotely. But since your Nano Sphere doesn't appear in the mesh, I had to locate you physically and emplace a Relay. The director sent me because of the sensitivity of the mission."

"What's this mesh? Why don't I appear in it?"

Jianguo pulled out his phone. He looked after the Pilot, and seemed to change his mind. Sighing to himself, he muttered, "It'll have to wait." Then to her he said, "Come, I'll show you."

***

"THIS IS A MAP," Jianguo told her, "of the mesh."

He had taken her off the main floor of the Lab, through a locked portal and into a squared-off, polished-stone meeting room of bookcases, tables, seats. No Obie, she noted. He was pointing to a ten-foot pseudo display holding an isometric map of the world, continents colored red, shading to pink at the poles.

"Population heat map?" she guessed.

"Only incidentally. Population heat coincides with the mesh."

He spread his arms, and the map zoomed into North America, solid red, with lighter shades of pink on mountain tops and inside deserts. *People everywhere these days.* He did it again and brought them to Central California, solid red everywhere. A couple more zooms and the red separated into tiny, discrete dots, moving infinitesimally, over a street map.

One more zoom expanded the view and brought them to Mission San Jose. The dots were spread some inches apart, and many moved. She recognized the plaza graveyard where she'd fallen. Dots strolled the paths. They paused and started and turned and passed each other. And then Jianguo zoomed once more and she saw a schematic of the meeting room where the two of them stood. The table, the bookcases. The dot representing Jianguo, positioned precisely where he stood.

But there was no dot representing Diana.

"You can track anyone on earth?" she asked, stunned. "Through their Nano Sphere? Where's my dot?"

"You're not in the mesh," he said with a shrug. "We thought you'd cloaked yourself by working with The 27. But now the Director understands: you've been abandoned by The 27. That's why you have cancer; your Nano Sphere has been disabled. That's why he's sure you're cooperating now in good faith. Because they are your enemies also, and we can help you." He looked back and forth from her to the screen as if to confirm it all. "They broke you. But there is hope. Watch."

He swept his hands back in to expand the view to its farthest vantage. Could it even be possible? Could she be looking at a real-time tracking system for every human being alive on earth? Every human being except for her...

A new color scheme was superimposed on the world. On this scheme most everything remained red except for four small sections carved out in navy blue: Eastern Europe, United Korea, the western United States and the Brazilian Confederation. The rest of the globe had been cut into a dozen roughly equal shapes.

"The world here is divided into its New Capitol Zones. The four blue spaces are the Bank's inholdings, where the steering committee and the Director will remain. This is the Director's master plan for defeating The 27. He will win us our freedom back."

"I don't get it."

"Humanity will once again earn. And pay. And work."

"As a master plan, it's pretty vague."

"The 27 are space-going philanthropists! They enslave by making everything free!"

"Oh, got it," she lied, but not very well. Jianguo was insistent.

"You're an Economist," he said. "You must understand. Capitalism? The economic theory pitting the strong against the weak to allocate scarce resources?"

"Capitalism, yeah I guess, but it's not a strong versus weak dichotomy..."

"Scarcity drives innovation, but scarcity has been eliminated by your philanthropic aliens!"

"I don't have any aliens."

"Think—we're still using mobile phones and it's 2077! We still have internal combustion engines! It's a wonder we're not using horses and carriages. We were on our way to fusion engines and induced telepathic congress and now it's 2077 and we live like we did in the 2020s! It's because there's no fear of death. Everything you need to succeed is within your grasp. You see? No fear of death, no drive to innovate. No drive *at all*. And we're sliding quickly toward a world where the Needless so vastly outnumber PreAugs that any new markets we create *will fail*. And still the Needless lay torpid, sucking the giant alien teat!"

He paused, so incensed that he couldn't go on for a moment. She took a moment to appreciate his imagery.

"Think of the power, Roark! The raw power it takes to maintain their system of Dispensing Obelisks. An unimaginable quanta of energy, *given away for free!* Where does it come from? We don't know, we don't pay for it. But the Director will defeat them. He will let us all pay again!"

Diana recognized the tag showing on her brand-new, upside-down world, where everything meant the opposite, where getting less free merchandise was someone's fervent, longed-for dream. People needed to struggle again, he was saying. Was that it?

"So you're planning to defeat The 27?" she started. "Don't they have access to, like you said, um, incredible power? They came here in giant spaceships and covered the planet with alien technology and vanished."

"We defeat them by defeating their philanthropy," he said. He pointed to the map. "We eliminate the Obelisks in the New Capital Zones. Like this."

He put his palm against the wall on a gray plate. A small Obelisk seemed to vaporize up from the floor in the corner of the room, as if it had been laying on the ground in a thousand million pieces. 27, it proclaimed on its crown. He pressed again, and it sloughed down like a melting candle, and was gone.

It took her a few seconds to process. First she had to unpack the idea that Landerson could somehow break the unbreakable Obelisks. But when her mind shifted to the implications of that power...

"Your New Capital Zones cover most of the planet, Jianguo. If you get rid of the Dispensing Obelisks, there won't be food. There's no way people will be able to feed themselves."

"The human race will struggle. But they will buy and sell again. Capitalism will save us!"

"No clean water?"

"Humanity will have to innovate! Grow food! Invent!"

"Most of humanity will *die*."

"Possibly. Certainly *the Needless*. Strive and achieve, or fail and die. It'll be the haves and the have-nots, tied in a capitalist utopia, like the days of old!"

She checked the map. She couldn't stop herself.

She cast Crystal Clear's idea out the window. *We were so close, Crystal.* She whirled on Jianguo and pointed at the map.

"Human civilization is *totally dependent* on the Obelisks, Jianguo! If Terrance takes away the Obelisks, we'll drop back to the Stone Age! That's the *plan*? So people can relearn capitalism and ultimately come back and invent—what, better lasers? More comfortable couches? Instead of living in comfort and enjoying themselves like they are now? While in the *meantime* Landerson and the rest of you bankers wait it out—for how many generations? Happy as clams with the Obelisks you don't destroy, in these," she pointed, "blue zones? Behind very tall walls, I'm guessing?"

Did she see a flicker on his face? Just a flicker of doubt? A tiny kernel? She pushed.

"All of that seems like a *good idea* to you, Jianguo? Because it doesn't to me."

His eyes narrowed. He gave her a set, cold stare, doubt clearly gone.

"Only capitalism will set us on the path to our ultimate goal. For that, we need scarcity. We will dominate these aliens. The Director will lead humanity back to sustained GDP growth and we will triumph. It is unfortunate that you don't share the vision. Come with me now."

Jianguo turned and left through the portal and a moment later

Diana limped after. They crossed the main floor of Lab One—were there other Labs? In the other Missions? Labs Two through Twenty? —until Jianguo reached another sealed portal and he motioned her to enter. She turned to look back at the highly organized, highly homogenous New Capitol economists laboring in the heat and noise.

For the briefest moment she considered her doubts—could the problem be her? It was true that human civilization hadn't progressed technologically. Markets all over the planet transacted an ever-diminishing pool of discretionary purchases. She had seen this in her own data. Could there be something realistic and necessary in this project, this *New Capital* plan, that she was missing? Landerson had convinced all the people in this room, these highly educated economists and they weren't drugged, they weren't gibbering idiots. How could they all be so committed to this vision of violent capitalist devastation if it was as insane as it seemed to her?

She was turning back to Jianguo when a Pilot and her technician walked past and then both of them, locked in step, slowed down, then stopped. All around her the white-robed Economists seemed to be powering down. Their mouths dropped open, their arms hung limp at their sides, and their eyes rolled back into their heads. Their bodies began to twitch as though minute jolts of electricity ran through them. Everyone in the enormous cavern stood the same way. Not a word, not a footstep—quiescent as a field of dream-bound anemones. She turned to Jianguo and saw that he also stood with rolled back eyes, his body shuddering quietly. She stepped close and passed her hand in front of his face. Nothing.

Before she could really get her mind moving in the direction of *running for her life,* the assembled Landersonian Economists spun up back into motion.

"The Director is waiting," Jianguo told her, gesturing again.

She stared. "What was that?"

"What was what?"

"You... your whole..."

His gaze was frank and unfriendly. She was an adversary now, she saw; she wouldn't be getting any more answers from him.

She followed him through the door.

It was quiet in the new chamber. One of the dark walls was covered with pseudo displays that rippled characters and graphs. Secondary displays near a main console showed a video feed of another room. On these displays she saw Robert, her purported operative. Shown crouched, from various cameras in a brightly lit, completely empty concrete cell, with a single door and no windows, he floated a few feet off the ground inside the oily outlines of a Landerson Field.

It was apparently a live feed. Operatives in the room observed Robert carefully. He squatted with his feet on the same kind of gray mat Jianguo had unrolled to transport her. He had his arms wrapped around his knees while he stared at the wall and wore a simple outfit: khaki pants and a neatly tucked, plaid short-sleeve shirt. He had a pen protector in his shirt pocket. No pens. Robert appeared calm.

Behind her Jianguo closed the portal and from the corner of her eye she saw Landerson, now wearing one of the swords which had hung in his office. The sword belt was black and the scabbard was black and the pommel was black, and in his white raiment he looked somehow holy and swashbuckling at once, like a self-help samurai.

"Now she believes," Terrance said to Jianguo. "You showed her?"

"I did, Director. She's seen everything. I answered every question."

"She is convinced?"

Jianguo gave Diana a narrow look. He shook his head.

"I did everything you asked."

"But?"

"I don't think she's on the side of mankind. I think she's with The 27. Or the Needless."

Diana pushed both her hands out at chest level in a quick gesture to say *now hold on just a minute!* But it failed to say that because her prosthetic arm didn't lift. It dangled, useless as a piece of rope, so instead of two hands raised saying *now hold on just a minute!* she was raising one hand saying *may I please ask a question?*

"Yes?" Terrance said. "Question?"

"No. Yes. Listen, Jianguo's wrong," she said. Now her prosthetic began jerking spastically. She worked hard to corral it. *I probably look crazy.*

"I have..." *Arm come back! Sit. Stay.* "Look, I don't know anything about The 27. But I think there's something important we should talk about. I think your New Capitol plan needs... adjusting."

"I am disappointed." Terrance might have felt disappointed but that didn't stop him from flipping his lips wide in one of his smiles. His teeth glittered in the cold light from the pseudos.

"Can we talk about the New Capital Zones?" she asked.

"No," he said. "I need information. We lack time. One of you will confess."

"One will?" she asked. "I don't understand."

"You or Robert."

Terrance nodded toward a wall between two of the console stations and she saw a door, well concealed. One of the Landersonians pushed it open and stood at attention there. On the pseudos displaying the inside of Robert's room, the cell door opened. Adjoining rooms, Diana realized. Robert stood up. His expression didn't change, but his mouth moved and from the speaker she heard his voice, firm and clear.

"I must speak to Diana Roark."

"Why is he wearing clothes?" she suddenly asked, looking at Terrance. "What about the Nano Spheres? Shouldn't he have exploded?"

"You tell us," Terrance suggested. "He is yours. What are his powers?"

She turned back to the feed, surprised. She hadn't thought Terrance and the steering committee had been lying, but she'd assumed that they were at least misinterpreting. But here was the man, *Robert,* asking for her by name. She studied him on the display.

He still didn't appear concerned. In fact, he seemed very calm for a person trapped in a magic bubble six feet off the floor. She was certain she'd never met him.

Jianguo lined up behind Minion One at the open door and Minion Two pushed her forward to get her in line also. Terrance stood behind them all, like a train engine ready to nudge his cars into the station tunnel.

"I am Robert. I must speak with Diana Roark," Robert said again. "I can only speak to Diana Roark." Robert's voice over the speakers was insistent. Minion One stepped through the open door. On the pseudo displays she saw Minion One enter and stand to the side, which seemed to be the single trick he was trained to do with doors: stand at attention beside them. Next in line, Jianguo disappeared from the control room and on the display she saw him stop and look back, waiting for her. Another push came from Minion Two, behind her.

She went through the door.

But only part way. She stopped and Minion Two bumped into her and grunted. He gave her another push and she stumbled forward. She looked at the walls, the high ceiling; the room seemed to be the one she'd seen on the displays. It held Jianguo and Minion One at attention and had walls and a Landerson Field.

But there was no Robert. Instead, there was a very tall, plum-colored broccoli in the Landerson Field where Robert should have been.

Minion Two pushed her again, but she didn't move. She stared. *Some kind of sculpture?* It was floral, purple—half again as tall as a man — and not at all the hunched-over biped in khaki pants she had seen on the pseudoscreen. She wanted to step back into the control room and get another look, but the Minions were having none of that. The sculpture was disturbingly alien, *emphasis on disturbing with additional emphasis on alien*, and her mind grabbed for similes. The best it could do, the image she kept returning to, was broccoli—lavender broccoli as high as a standard ceiling, hunched beside the Relay inside the Landerson Field. The broccoli had its base pushed into a four-foot square cube of translucent jello and that's what held it up. A big square block of jello.

Terrance watched her stare, his expression a little sneery. Sort of out of synch, she thought, for the circumstances.

"Yes," he said. "We have him. You doubted it? We quarantined him. Nothing penetrates the Field. No toxins. No viruses. No sound."

She ignored Landerson, stepping closer to study the thing in the Field. Through the open door to the control room, she heard the voice of *khaki pants Robert* say, "Thank you for bringing Diana Roark. Now release me so I can confer with Diana Roark."

Terrance faced the broccoli in the Field. "No. Confer with *me*."

The broccoli didn't move. Hadn't moved to speak. Didn't have a mouth. From the speaker in the other room came Robert's voice, "I can only confer with Diana Roark."

"She is my captive," Terrance said, his voice low. "So are you. Either *she* confers with me or *you* do. One or the other."

From the other room came Robert's response, "Well, I won't confer with you. I can only confer with Diana Roark."

Landerson, she observed in confusion, was having a conversation with a broccoli sculpture. Although now that she was closer to it, peering through the slight distortion of the Field, she saw that it was not a sculpture, because it was moving. It swayed this way, and sometimes that way and the jello cube shimmied a little bit, which made the broccoli it supported flutter, though no sound escaped.

"What is it?" she asked the room, wonder in her voice.

"A Landerson Field. I thought you knew," Terrance said.

"No, what is... that thing?"

Terrance shook his head, like he wanted more information.

"Why?" she asked, "Why does it look different in here than on the pseudo displays?" She waved vaguely back toward the video feeds in the control room. Landerson shook his head again, his irritation clearly growing. He was not getting what he wanted from her. Had he expected her to scream and cower?

She stared around the room for any kind of clue she could possibly find, checking the faces of the Minions and Jianguo and Terrance. And then she saw that her shadows were back. They'd come in sneakily and they had done a thing they had never done before: they were lined up against the walls. Evenly spaced. Motionless. *They were never motionless.* But now they were, like soldiers in a parade, or musicians in a marching band. Marching in a square around a room. But not marching. Just hanging around.

"What's going on?" she demanded. "Is this a show?"

"It is no show," Terrance insisted.

"But what is it? Where did it come from? It is alive?"

She saw Terrance look at Jianguo and saw Jianguo shrug. Then Terrance looked at his minions and they made *we have nooooo idea* faces. Then he looked back at her and he spoke very slowly.

"My patience expires." He pointed at the Landerson Field while looking at her. "You deny knowing Robert?"

"I don't know the big purple jello broccoli," she confirmed.

Two things happened at the same moment then. From the other room she heard the voice of Robert say, "I must confer with Diana Roark." And in front of her, within the Field, the square of jello that supported the stalk of the lavender broccoli stuck out a tube—a shiny, pencil-thin, five-foot pseudopod with a sucker at the end, which affixed itself to the curve of the Field entrapping it, level with her head.

And a voice came through the Landerson Field, out of the sucker. It said, "Diana Roark *shut the fuck up!* We're in enough trouble already!"

She jumped, stumbled, and fell backwards toward the door; one of the Minions caught her, because he thought she was trying to make a run for it, but she wasn't. Not in a million years. She wasn't about to leave this room until someone explained what was going on.

"What ... that jello ... what?" She gathered her thoughts. "The jello talks?"

Terrance and Jianguo and the minions exchanged more confused looks.

"Jello?" Jianguo asked. Diana pointed.

"The jello, the jello in the..."

"*Fucking. SHUT! UP! ALREADY!*" bellowed the sucker, still attached to the inside of the Field, with far more volume than she had imagined a sucker could produce. She was shocked silent. She looked at the others so they could all be shocked together.

The others weren't shocked; she would have described them as a little bit confused. They watched her warily, some of them frowning. But no shock. And then, finally, she understood; they didn't see it. They didn't hear it either. They saw Robert, in his khaki pants, trapped in the Landerson Field, and not... whatever *she* saw in there.

It dawned on her that biped Robert didn't really exist at all. He was some kind of simulation or illusion, appearing for the cameras and in the eyes of other people. But she saw... whatever this was. It was a crazy theory that called for testing.

"Quick question," she asked the room. She grimaced and rubbed her eyes, just a dying old lady with a headache. "My vision's getting blurry. Ah... what color are... ah, Robert's... pants? Right in there?" She pointed to the broccoli.

Terrance took a deep breath, then considered the Robert/Broccoli as if he was wondering what sort of trick he was about to fall for. Jianguo crossed his arms. The minions watched in frank fascination.

"Khaki," Terrance said after a moment.

"Right," she said. She stared at the Landerson Field. "You see a Robert in there wearing some pants and a shirt." She was about to describe the thing *she* saw, but decided she'd wait until she had a better idea of what was going on. The jello sucker had cursed at her both times she mentioned it directly. The better idea would be not to say anything for a moment.

"Enough!" Terrance proclaimed. He pulled out his sword and

held it out to Jianguo. Jianguo took the sword in his hands by its handle and cocked it like a baseball bat, gently, with an expression Diana couldn't read.

"One of you dies," Terrance said in a quiet voice. "To convince you I am serious. You waited too long. You were warned."

Diana wanted to protest—no, she had *not* been warned. Not in any way. But Landerson wasn't finished.

"But which one?" He seemed genuinely undecided. "Diana knows The 27. A longer relationship. Robert just came from space. Not yet debriefed. More recent data. And Diana *is* dying. Soon she will be dead."

He nodded to himself, working it all out in a moment like an algebra problem. She found it easier and easier to imagine him commanding the massacre of billions of helpless human beings. He would just weigh the pros and cons.

Terrance pointed to Diana. "She is the one. Kill her."

Jianguo did not hesitate. He held the sword straight in front of him, his elbows bent, his shoulders loose, his face calm. He looked at her.

"On your knees," he said.

Diana's flesh leg seemed absolutely willing to follow directions—eager, in fact, to collapse—but her robot leg was feeling less cooperative. It stood straight up. This was actually what her brain wanted, to remain standing and she observed her prosthetic with a certain fond appreciation. *In the end, it is our tools, our externalizations of ourselves, that keep to the course. Our flesh just buckles.*

One of the minions struck her from behind and then she did fall. She brought her hands up and her flesh arm was not fast enough, but her robot arm was there. It stopped her, keeping the concrete from meeting her face, spinning her onto her side.

The minion lifted her and set her on her knees.

"Watch closely Robert," Terrance said. "See what happens. Observe the consequences."

Diana's shadows had been frozen around the walls like sepulchral guardians, but now they began to move. They gathered into a single mass near the open door, right in front of her, and then flowed back to the walls. They did this again. And again. And she noticed that the broccoli on the mat in the Landerson Field was shifting its position, compressing and sliding its gelatinous base, so that it faced the main bulk of the shadows as they moved.

The broccoli moved with the shadows. It became clear then, in her odd new world where everything meant the opposite, that she had misunderstood the nature of her shadows. The shadows weren't a symptom of her cancer. They weren't related to cancer at all. Her shadows actually existed, present in the real world. Others could see them too. *Some* others. Purple others.

Jianguo approached her softly. He seemed made of grace, pure impulse. Not a step was wasted as he padded in, his feet and arms and the core of him flowing like a mountain stream. The sword he seemed to have been born with, his grip so certain and expert. And then he was only two feet from her.

The pace of the dancing shadows increased, the broccoli in the Field in synch with them. Somehow, the broccoli was a creature too. She understood that. *So many things to understand in the very short time she had left.*

Jianguo brought the sword slowly to her throat, his face soft and calm. She felt the edge against her skin.

Then he flashed the sword back. It stopped, for the merest second suspended behind his shoulder and she saw the eyes of the minions across the room, wide and amazed. *What is this going to look like?* their brains seemed to be asking. But all *she* could ask was *why?* Why this? Why not anything different? Why had she made the choices she'd made? Why had all the things she valued come to nothing? Why had she valued any of the things she had at all?

Why was that long, stiff pseudopod with the sucker stretching down *out of the Landerson Field* toward her?

The sword glinted and came for her.

The pseudopod came faster.

6

Jianguo's blade shattered icicle bright when the sucker on the pseudopod tapped it. Outside in the control room there was an explosion and the cell lights failed and returned and then faded to half. The Landerson Field vanished and the broccoli hit the floor like a jelly sumo wrestler, the mat and the Relay beneath it.

The Minions sealed Landerson between them instantly, arms spread, bodyguarding despite complete confusion, wide eyed and bewildered. From the control room came loud questions and yelling. Jianguo stared at the stub of sword in his hand and then whipped his gaze around the cell the way the Minions had. No one seemed to spare a single glance for Diana or the fallen creature.

"What happened?" Jianguo shouted, peering through the dim light. "Director! What's happening?"

Landerson ignored him and stepped away from the bodyguards. He turned a slow circle. He was the only one not panicked. His eyes were suspicious slits. They paint-peeled the room. He drew his gaze over Diana where she knelt on the floor, but he did not pause for even a flicker of a second. She looked straight into his eyes and got back not a twitch of connection. He turned and scoped the room like the second hand on a clock, micron by micron.

Her breath caught. Did he not *see* her?

On the floor at her knees, the pseudopod sucker stretched taut from the fallen creature. The jello cube had not deformed at all when it hit the floor. Instead, it had bounced an inch and stuck, though the thick purple stalk leaned low to the ground, like a stop sign someone had plowed into.

"The less noise you make, the less this will cost," she heard the sucker beside her knee whisper. "Get out of the middle of the fucking room!"

She watched the gelatinous mass stiffen its purple stalk upright and saw the whole gluey mess slide back against the wall, fast as a striking snake. And then Landerson began to walk directly at her, his eyes skittering this way and that, looking but not seeing.

The fury on his face forced her backward. She watched it build, watched him not-look at her, like a child playing *let's pretend I can't see.* He came closer, and then stopped and stared at the spot she'd vacated only seconds before. He looked up slowly and met her eyes. She knew, *knew,* that he was staring at her. A million years of animal evolution said it was true. That's how eyes worked. The other three people in the room watched but didn't shift or speak.

"No," Terrance muttered. He turned toward the door to the control room. The smell of smoke was now wafting into the cell.

"No, no, no," he said. His head shook. His hands clenched at his sides while his arms rose and stuck out from his shoulders as rigid as oars and he began to bend backward. His spine was a python rising from a basket. It was much more unnerving than it had been in his office.

Jianguo and the Minions went slump-shouldered, their eyes rolling back in their heads. Their arms slid limp to their sides and their bodies twitched as if tiny jolts of electricity ran through them. She looked from Landerson to the others. *Was Landerson doing this, in their minds somehow?*

"To me, *to me,* all agents of change!" Landerson screamed at the ceiling, but none of his agents of change could move to him even if they wanted to, because they were all being electrocuted motionless.

Landerson's fit passed. Jianguo and the others rolled urgently to attention and had not a clue that anything had changed, as far as Diana could see and she *would* have seen because she couldn't look anywhere else. She wondered if Landerson himself had any idea what was happening. It all seemed sickeningly unconscious, the ultimate co-dependent relationship.

"My pod," Terrance said and then swept from the room and drew the others after. For just a moment the room was silent.

"What a total *fucking* disaster," she heard. It was her cellmate, the broccoli with the speaking antennae strung across the floor. Tiny lips on its tip were hissing angry words. "Get closer to me. The closer you are, the less this erasure costs."

When she declined to move, because she declined to understand that she was hearing anything meant for her, the sucker snorted out a disbelieving rasp and then the whole mass of jello broccoli smooched along the wall in her direction. It made sounds as it came like wet cookie dough being mixed. One part of her—the little girl part, the part who had feared monsters in her closet—wanted to scream. It was a nightmare made real, a vision from beyond the edge of reality.

But another part of her felt suddenly giddy. This creature wasn't simply alien looking—*it was an alien.* A life form not from earth. Here. Doing what? One of The 27? How did it move? How had it learned English? Why was there never an astrobiologist around when you needed one?

This was Greg's dream. She was living his wildest, most impossible fantasy. What would he have done? He would have stayed rational, collected and analyzed the data, and asked questions. Would he have greeted it? *Should I greet it? What should I say?*

Hello, and welcome to earth. No, too late for welcomes, considering they'd already captured and imprisoned him. Maybe, *do you come in peace?* Hm. Same problem. It might have *come* in peace, but what it had in mind now was probably different.

"You saved me, didn't you?" she croaked softly. Somewhere during the last few minutes, she must have done some screaming because her throat felt raw and hot.

"You're welcome," the sucker said. It was just a short stump now, as the jello square slid in beside her. Then the sucker retreated into the sheer, translucent side of the cube and became just a small hole with lips.

A smell came off the alien: astringent, with a touch of peaches. It wasn't unpleasant. The lip hole in the glutinous cube was only a foot from her own mouth and she had a disjointed feeling wondering where she should look as she talked to it. Did it have eyes? Should she look at the lips? Up at the purple fronds, garnishing it?

Who cares where you look, she thought. This is the first alien ever to visit the earth. Maybe the thing to do was negotiate some basic interactive conventions, so they didn't accidentally insult each other and create an intergalactic war. She was so far out of her element it wasn't even funny. Greg, she thought, so many reasons I miss you. Oh my god, I hate myself for killing you.

"You speak English," she finally observed. Not great. In her mind, Greg grimaced but tried to look positive.

"No shit, Sherlock," the lips said, its voice derisive. "Albert fucking Einstein. *You speak English.* Jesus christ, is that the best you can fucking do?"

Despite the singularly extraordinary nature of the situation, she felt a flash of annoyance run through her. Ok, she was out of her element. Maybe a bit confused. But was that tone really necessary? Maybe the idea of setting ground rules hadn't been half bad. From outside the cell came more smoke and more screaming. But the world had narrowed, for the moment, to herself this alien, and his tone.

"Just so you know," she said carefully, "the particular English phrases you're using have pejorative overtones, and may tend to present you in an unfavorable light." Greg nodded. Nice and clear. That's the way.

"Oh, *so sorry*," the alien replied, "I didn't realize I was talking to the Queen of fucking England." The tone was very clear. "Just so *you* know, I don't give a shit what light my phrases present me in, Diana Roark. I've got real problems."

At that moment one of the control techs rushed into the cell. Diana froze, eyes wide, and pressed against the wall like a mouse viewing a fox. Why hadn't she found someplace to hide? The tech knelt beside the Relay laying on the floor; she looked as terrified as Diana felt. Her fingers shook as she lifted the small gray cereal bowl from atop the mat. Gaze skimming the cell, she looked right through Diana without so much as a quick blink and then ran from the room.

"Why don't they react to me?" Diana asked after a moment.

"Because I'm erasing us in the mesh."

"How does that work?" she asked, amazed. She looked down at her own hand, fully visible.

"I don't fucking know. I'm not a scientist. I'm *paying* for it though, I know that."

"In theory," she asked. "How does it work in theory?"

"In theory? In theory there are nano particles sitting on nerve pathways inside their brains. This erasure app lives in the planetary nanomesh, interrupting optic nerve impulses. A tweak here, a tweak there, boom, you're erased. Or tweak this, tweak that, now I look like a human being to you. All I know is, it's fucking expensive and the longer we hang around down here the more it's going to cost. We need to leave, like, *right fucking now!*"

You know, she thought, if you let yourself relax into this profanity it had a kind of bracing, almost rejuvenating effect. And now Greg wanted more, her mind filling with questions.

"You just broke yourself out of that Landerson Field," she said. "So why did you wait until now to do it? Why did you let them keep you a prisoner?"

"Because I couldn't get out before! I'm not budgeted for fucking prison breaks!" Robert's topknot of bushy purple vegetation thrust up and down in the jello and she could almost picture alien arms thrown up in frustration. "There's no fucking line item for breaking out of weird, primitive, nanomesh cages. I don't even know how he was making that cage. I've never seen anything like it."

"But you *did* break out. You saved me. How...?"

"When your head was about to get chopped off, *then* emergency funding got released. It's fucking ridiculous. I used that to break his cage. It's a weird fucking time to be having this conversation."

Too many questions. *None of this makes sense Greg!*

"What's special about *my* head that you get... emergency funding?"

"You're signatory on the account. If you die, I'm fucked, so I spent the funds even though I have to justify *every fucking expenditure* and believe me it's not going to be easy. Listen to me Diana Roark, we *have* to *leave*, like, *as soon as possible*."

His insistence on evacuation finally penetrated. She wasn't satisfied with any of these answers, but he was right. It was a weird time to have this conversation.

"Ok," she said. "Let's leave."

"Yes!"

She waited for Robert to move.

"What do we do?" she asked.

"I don't know. It's your fucking planet."

Yes, all right. It was her planet.

"Then let's go up," she plotted. "I think we should go up. I saw a door I recognized, it might take us out through the old Mission, if I can find it again. I think I can...we can escape across the..."

"Blah blah blah blah *escape*. That. *Go!*"

She stood and was happy to find that all her limbs worked together in reasonable harmony. Her flesh knee felt bruised but usable and her prosthetics were remembering their jobs. She wondered how long it would last.

She tiptoed across the darkened cell, careful and quiet and slow all the way to the open door and peered through. The control room was dark. Empty. Beyond the closed outer portal to the Lab One cavern, she heard voices and running—out where she needed to go for any further escaping. Was she really invisible? Was she really *erased from the mesh?*

From the control room doorway, she saw the pseudo displays, still carrying a live feed of the cell and she saw Robert waiting to follow her through. He was a conservatively dressed homo erectus from toe to tip, tapping his foot impatiently. She turned to face the hallucinatory fruit salad that actually trailed her; she turned back and forth.

"Why do you look human on the pseudo displays?" she asked.

"Shit. Forgot to turn that off," Robert muttered. Human Robert flicked suddenly into broccoli Robert on the screens. "Cheaper to hack a display than a roomful of brains. We're just *bleeding* money. Are we still escaping, or what the fuck is going on?"

She did her version of darting by crossing through the dark control room at a slow limp. Robert followed, and he was much, much faster than a nine-foot gummy cube had any right to be. He moved by shooting thin pseudopods ahead of him and drawing his bulk forward along the floor. He must weigh two thousand pounds, she thought, but he's swift as a cat. The gluey feelers were so thin; she could imagine a dozen products built around that concept, just off the top of her head. Later, she reminded herself. Well... no. Never.

"The people out there might not see us," she said, her hand on the knob, "but they're going to see this portal opening."

"They better not or I'm getting a refund, I'm paying to *hide* us."

She pushed, the portal swinging open. The Lab chamber had also darkened and what were obviously emergency lights glowed along the walls. The chamber hung with smoke. Something Robert had done—*Robert*, she kept calling the alien *Robert* in her mind *its name can't possibly be Robert*—something the alien had done had burned through primary circuits, overloaded breakers. Short-circuiting that Landerson Field the way it had might have shut down more than one Capsule and Pilot. *Had the effect cascaded through Landerson's system?*

Pilots and techs hurried by, but panic had been replaced with straightforward urgency. Diana stepped into the flow of people as though easing into a swift river, mistrusting Robert's erasure. She took a few steps in the current of people, then slowed, then stopped. They stepped around her without comment. *It's amazing,* she thought. She tried to visualize what was happening in their brains, where a million billion nano particles circulated and where, on nerve pathways between eyes and frontal cortex, sub microscopic engines were somehow sorting the impulses that created her image and lifting that picture away and replacing it with — what? Nothing? A blend of background elements? Something entirely new? This wasn't actual invisibility. It was more like being photoshopped out of reality in real-time.

She turned toward the elevators and then tripped on a fallen cable and fell straight into the chest of a rushing technician. He staggered to the side and caught himself and stared at her.

"Hey," he called over his shoulder, "we've got a loose primary panel over here, off the back of 107. Sending a flag." He pulled a tablet off the back of a Capsule and flicked data in, then continued away.

"What just happened?" she breathed to Robert.

"Who knows? Mesh apps are smart. It did some on-the-fly shit, built a reasonable explanation. Same thing when we opened that door. These apps are adaptodynamic. And every time it has to cover up some mistake, I get charged up the ass. So fucking walk a straight line, will you?"

She set off very carefully, tired of getting cursed at. When they got near the elevator, she discovered a problem; a small crowd waited before the closed doors.

"I don't know what to do here," she said.

"I thought you had a plan."

"I did have one. I *do* have one. In order to do my plan, we have to go up this elevator, but there are thirty other people who want to do the same thing. Can we just barge in and have your *mesh app* built reasonable explanations for an elevator full of people squeezed up against a cube of sloppy, disgusting goo?"

It was a moment before Robert answered. "Probably. But it'd be expensive."

"Look, why don't you contribute something proactive?" she demanded. "Do you have any ideas? You're escaping too, you know."

"Hmph," said the tiny mouth in the cube of undulating, disgusting goo. She felt a twinge of guilt describing Robert that way, since he actually looked well sealed and dry, but what did he expect of her? The tiny mouth vanished. A moment passed while Diana wracked her brain for solutions.

Then the elevator doors opened, and a knot of techs exited. The waiting group started to file in.

"Well?" Diana asked, looking at the alien. "Bright ideas?"

She heard an outraged cry and when she looked back she saw the group of technicians tumble out of the elevator like action figures emptied from a toy chest.

"Come on!" Robert called and shot ahead. He was faster than she was, she realized. How quickly could he move on that slippery cube?

The doors were closing as she slipped through and she heard one tech complain to another in disgust, waving a hand in front of his face, "What did you eat?"

"It wasn't me," said the other "Daryle did it."

"No way!" someone else, presumably Daryle, protested. "I'm a vegan. We don't pass gas."

"Vegan! That's pretentious bullshit. We're all vegans. No one's eaten an animal in thirty..."

The doors slid shut with a snap and the voices were lost. The elevator pressed them down gently as it rose. She thought she saw the alien quiver, its jello jiggling. As she watched, its sprouts quaked, leaving no question it was quivering. The pattern repeated a few times, then stopped, then began again. Was it laughing?

"Was that you?" Diana asked.

"This mesh app works on any nerve pathway." It paused for a moment while it shook, then continued. "I made them smell a fucking fat, cheesy fart. It wasn't even expensive!"

She wrinkled her nose. "What are you, an alien frat boy?"

"Don't complain to me because you don't have a sense of humor. That was fucking brilliant!"

Her sense of humor was a discussion for another time. Or maybe not; what did this alien blob know about humor? Suddenly Greg was back, asking questions.

"So, your people have humor?" she asked.

"Yeah, my people—we so stupid, we so sad and backward, but we have big laughy time, roll in mud, eat own feces." Robert drew up in what could easily be indignant hauteur. "Diana Roark, *my people* have a technological culture that's *five hundred thousand* years old, we're a Tier 3 Accountancy and we've had fucking calculus longer than you've had *any words at all*. So yeah. Me have humor."

"Fart jokes, though?"

"Farts are funny throughout the reaches of the Known Economy. Farts are fucking hilarious. Lighten up."

They had to table the conversation then, because the doors opened and a waiting crowd of Pilots and techs stood poised for the elevator to empty of the people they apparently saw and Diana and Robert skittered out. She headed off as fast as her exhausted legs would carry her. Behind her, as the elevator doors closed, she heard an outcry and someone shouted, "Oh my god, who laid that...?"

She had started through the hallway at a good clip, but quickly she slowed. Her clothes hung on her like rags straight from the wash, heavy with sweat. The air here was cooler, and for the first time in many hours she breathed without feeling like someone had stuffed hot socks down her lungs. But her heart was beating too fast. Now, allowing herself to imagine a real chance of escape, hope was about to give her a heart attack. She stopped, panting, and leaned against the wall. The hallway was full of scurrying techs. She squeezed to the side but still felt absolutely exposed.

Robert slurped to a stop beside her.

"Is this it?" the lip hole piped. "Escape into a hallway?"

"No... give me a minute," she gasped. "I need to drink. I'm going to pass out."

"Fine. Ok. Where does drinking happen?"

"Obelisks. I can't work them, though. I can't make..." she tried to swallow. Her throat was so dry she could hardly speak. "I need water."

"Water? Like, straight up, one oxygen, two hydrogen, covalently bonded?"

She nodded. If she didn't get something to drink very quickly she was going to overheat and collapse. Running and stress and high temperature and possible freedom had simply overwhelmed her.

Beside her came a sloppy *pop*, and from the alien's jello base a pseudopod extended. At the end of the tentacle was a firm, translucent bowl filled with clear liquid.

"What's that?" she asked.

"Water."

"Where did it come from?" she asked carefully.

"From me, where the fuck do you think?"

"You just... you have water in there?" She pointed dubiously at the semi-transparent cube. "You carry water around?"

"In my *bladder*, yeah."

She'd been reaching. Now she stopped.

"Here!" Robert insisted. "Drink the water already."

She shook her head. And he snorted, suddenly angry.

"Oh, I see. Yeah—you know what? —you're all the same! You animals are all the same!" The alien foliage started wildly waving, like a tree in a windstorm. Robert's voice got shrill. The jello cube began to whip out pseudopods at random locations and the little bowl of water the first pseudopod carried sluiced back and forth and almost spilled.

"I mean, I'm not a speciest or anything," Robert said, and now he was shouting, "but it's actually *true—you ARE all the same!* You'll eat us, chop us down to make fucking houses. But you won't drink my piss. Is that it? Dying of thirst, but you're too good to drink my piss?"

"You're a plant," she started, some of it sort of making distant sense. How she wished for Greg...

"Oh, look at the *Rhodes scholar!*" Robert snarled sarcastically "What gave it away? The fucking foliage?"

"You metabolize... water? Into... a bladder?"

"Let me tell you something, you fucking arrogant little biped, ninety-nine percent of all sentient life in the universe is photosynthetic. Yeah I metabolize water into a bladder!"

Robert began to slide back and forth in the hallway, circling tight in violent ovals while the passing technicians danced this way and that for who knew what *mesh app* created reasons, and it became clear that Robert was hardly even talking to her. The alien was venting out a tirade of grievances accumulated from long before she'd ever met it.

"A universe of worlds that don't even *have* animals," the voice from the little lip hole raged, "in all the Scattered Pieces there are barely any, and there's a reason for *that*, believe me, fucking self-destructive...the animals that do survive are totally dependent on plants! But they don't admit it, oh no! Even this backward shit hole planet where plants take light and water and carbon dioxide and eat glucose and then *shit oxygen!* You animals have been breathing *plant shit* for millions of years but now, to save your life, you won't drink a little pure water from my bladder? Well, fucking *fine* then!"

Robert halted and without another word turned the bowl over and emptied it onto the floor. They both stared.

A moment passed.

"Oh, great," Robert said. "Now you made me piss on the floor."

"I'm sorry," she croaked.

Another moment.

"No," Robert said. He groaned and sighed "I'm sorry. That was totally uncalled for. You didn't make me piss on the floor. I did that. I'm a fucking idiot."

"Look," Diana said, "could we back up? I feel like we really got off to a bad start. I don't know why. It's probably me..."

"No, no, it's totally me. I haven't been myself; I don't want to totally unload on you but I *do* have a lot on my mind, and..."

"Let's reset. Do you want to?" Diana asked. "I'd be very happy to drink... to drink your urine. I'd be honored. I'm so thirsty..." She held out her hand for a peace-making handshake before she even thought it through.

Robert, misunderstanding the gesture, extended another pseudopod toward her with a brimming bowl of water. Taking a breath, she cupped her own hands under the vessel and found it—and the tentacle connected to it—stiff and motionless, tensile as a steel rod. She bent her head down and Robert tilted the bowl toward her mouth. She drank. When it was gone, she looked up at the foliage.

"Thank you."

"My pleasure. That's a first. Kind of fetishy."

"Can I have more? Do you have more?"

"Three? Well, the chox in my family have shy bladders. But..." he retracted his tentacle and after a moment a new bowl emerged. She drank it off.

"God that's great," he breathed. "I've been holding it for days. So. Are we good?"

She nodded, surprisingly good. Her heartbeat had dropped back to a reasonable gallop and her body had begun to cool. She pushed off down the hall and hugged the walls to avoid bumping people. It was hard to abandon herself to being continuously photoshopped into non-existence, but after a while she gave up and just went for speed, straight down the middle of the passage, speechless as the app cleared her a path. Finally, turning another corner, she saw what she had been looking for: the only door in the entire Lab that wasn't white. It was deep brown, oaken and scored by priests and the passage of time, with a round metal ring to pull it open.

As soon as she reached it she was pulling but found it too heavy. Robert grabbed the handle and whipped it back. She watched the alien drop the black iron ring from its gelatinous appendage. *Strong like an elephant.* When she saw the staircase behind the doorway she wondered if they would have to find another route, but Robert was unfazed. The alien slid up ahead of her with balletic grace.

They reached the top of the steps without hitting anyone coming down. Robert waited for her behind another closed wooden door and she labored up beside him and caught her breath, then failed to push it open until Robert extended a thin tentacle to help. She saw a white stucco hallway with a terracotta floor. Only a few people passed, none glancing at the open doorway. Across the hall she saw windows and to the left, an arched opening that led into sunlight. The cemetery. Freedom.

Robert spoke behind her.

"We've got to find someplace to hide. I have to return this erasure app, it's bleeding us dry. There, go there!"

He extended a pointer toward a vine-strangled, tile-roofed structure which she realized after a moment was a standalone restroom, from when the Mission had been a tourist attraction. It had been built out of stucco and rough-hewn wood to look like the rest of the historical structures. It seemed as good a next destination as any. That was the way she was doing things these days, all her plans just one visible destination to the next.

She stumbled out under the arch and into the sunlight, feeling like it had been months since she'd seen the sun. It was even harder to believe in her invisibility outside in the bright light, with so many variables and so much to hide, her cast shadows, her reflections in the windows, the bounce of white light off her shirt and pants. And what about her footprints in the soft dirt of the path? How much processing power did this app have, to perform all these calculations in real-time, not just in one person's brain but in the brains of everyone who turned an eye their direction?

They made it across the cemetery. The doorless entrance to what she saw was the Men's room was blocked by shrubs and a pile of ancient gardening equipment but it only took a moment to slip through the barricade. Inside it was cool and dark.

She slumped to the floor. The ceiling vaulting over them with its exposed oak beams was probably larger than the nave of the original church the Fathers had built to convert all those suffering native souls.

Robert stopped on the dusty tiles beside her, fronds bent and wilted. There was a long moment where neither of them said a word.

"Talk really quiet," Robert finally told her. "We're not being erased."

"Fine," she said. *Almost free.* She kept repeating it to herself. *Almost free.*

"What is this place?" the alien whispered.

"Bathroom," she whispered back. "For getting rid of, you know, animal waste products, though now our waste product just disincorporates, we put it in a little can; it doesn't even smell, and it's gone, and just, ecologically you wonder, what would be the impact if humans started creating metabolic waste suddenly and..."

Rambling. She just needed a minute to marshal her thoughts.

She levered her body around so she could watch Robert but watching didn't help. She collected no clues from its appearance. No readable body language. She *did* notice that its cube smelled different, less peaches now, more pine needles, but just as much rubbing alcohol. Was that indicative of anything? A thought occurred to her.

"You must have a mesh app translating your speech. Scrubbing and replacing impulses on my auditory nerves?"

"It works different with you than anybody else. But yeah, something like that."

"There's a lot more to human communication than speech. Humans need visual cues for real understanding."

"No duh. Same here. My translator is making you look like me. I picked up all the subtle details of your amazing, thought-provoking lecture about human shit just now."

"Could your app translate you for me? It would make things clearer."

The alien grumbled. "That's very expensive. Like I said it doesn't work the same with you. You're not on the same network as anyone else on the planet, so I don't have access to your network. I can't manipulate your Nano Sphere. For you, translation has to happen externally. Photons have to be captured and shaped *before* they get to your eyes, so your optic nerves are actually hit with an edited image. You get it? I can't affect the nano-particles in your sphere directly. I'd have to buy an adjustment using the fabricators *just outside your eyes*. Fucking expensive."

"Please do it."

"I kind of freak you out, don't I? Admit it."

She nodded. It was true. It would take a long time to get used to the visuals.

Finally, Robert sighed. "In for a penny, in for a pound, I guess."

And then Robert shifted, blurred, and reformed. It was like looking into a heat mirage where the background and the illusion blended back and forth for a minute and then the alien jello broccoli was gone and in its place was a sallow-skinned, thin-haired human man. The transformation was total and utterly convincing. She waved her hands before her face. The fabricators in front of her eyes didn't seem fazed. She reached out and touched his shirt. Total immersion. All her senses were addressed; there was absolutely no difference in the apparent reality of the previous alien Robert and this new, human version.

"You're really one of them, aren't you?" she whispered. "The 27?"

Outside she heard people talking and in the distance someone yelled.

"One of... what, now?" he asked. He frowned. She was astounded. So much information, translated from plant body language to human facial expression. And, she realized, she was appearing for him as though she was a huge, purple broccoli. Breathtaking. The 27 had finally returned, and they were more surprising and astonishing than anything she could ever have imagined.

"Where are the rest of you?" she asked

"Who are you fucking talking about?"

"The 27."

"The who?"

"The 27. You know, on the top of the Obelisks. The 27. The aliens—I mean, you're not aliens to yourselves..." She sputtered to a stop. They were missing something in this conversation.

"Oh, right," he said, nodding. "Yeah. Look, The 27 isn't what you think it is."

"Oh." She waited for him to continue. "What is it?" she asked.

"I can't tell you."

"Why not?"

"First you have to sign the account agreement.

"What account agreement?"

"I can't tell you."

His voice was irritated. He seemed to understand the absurd inconsistencies in what he was saying and not to like them very much. He appeared to be struggling to keep his voice down. She wondered what that translated into in broccoli. High-pitched pheromones? Weird light shows?

"This whole assignment is totally fucked up," he spat. "Everything! I got held in orbit—a bureaucratic fuck up and I'm held in space for thirty years! Then when I do get inserted this crazy fuckwad *caught my ship.* Which is absolutely not supposed to happen. I don't think it's even supposed to be possible. So, on behalf of my own fucking idiotic government and bureaucracy, sorry for the inconvenience. But as soon as your agreement is signed, I can tell you everything."

"Let me see the agreement," Diana said. She wanted him to tell her everything. She wanted *someone* to tell her *something.*

"Well, see, when dick nard in there caught my ship, I had to disincorporate it to avoid the impound fees and the document pericarp separated. I'm pretty sure it got to the destination, but I was pulled into this dank fucking lair. We'll have to get back to where the pericarp landed."

"Where is that?"

"I was supposed to land at your Sonoma Coast compound. It has to be around there somewhere. It's just waiting for us."

Not her compound. Her *former* compound. She'd donated it to her foundation along with everything else. Before it was her compound though, it was the Sonoma Coast State Park, which she had purchased when the state of California was selling off its assets. Its proximity to Bodega Bay, where she and Greg had first come together, had moved her. She'd built a grand estate on its bluffs, overlooking the Pacific Ocean and had lived in two rooms and an office of that mansion for the last 20 years.

"I'm not going back there," she told Robert.

"Why not?"

"Because," she said. *Because it belongs to another life, because I'm running out of time, because it's cold. Too complicated.*

"Listen, Diana Roark," he whispered. "I just saved your life. I watered you. You fucking owe me."

"I don't owe you anything."

"What are you talking about? Your head was getting chopped off! Are you saying you didn't want me to stop that?"

Robert's question held a touch of desperation. Whatever technology was doing the translating, it was fantastic with nuance and it made the alien's voice sound vulnerable and fearful and indignant all at once and his plain face appear earnest and pleading.

"Okay look," he said, "I know I've been kind of an asshole. No, I'll say it, I've been a complete asshole. I'm really sorry, you know. You have to believe me. I'm not usually like this. Well. I mean I *am* usually like this, if I'm being honest with you. But usually people deserve it. You, though, you seem like a nice lady animal. Can you just help me out? I don't even know why I got assigned here. They usually give me type M dwarf suns where nobody's even paying attention and there's, like, some sentient algae or some shit in a methane sea and I'm in and out. But this assignment is a much bigger deal. It could make my career." Robert paused. Then quietly, as if he could hardly believe the words, he said, "I could pass my pod shrouds."

The words held such a degree of honestly trembling reverence that Diana had to ask.

"What's a pod shroud?"

"One third of a Neoooxcolu zygote. The way we reproduce. My species. The Neoooxcolu. Oh shit, I forgot the...I haven't done the legal..."

Robert surged upwards then, transitioning back into a massive purple vegetable, and rising toward the roof of the bathroom. When its cube was firmed and its fronds thrust fully erect the alien's height easily exceeded 11 feet. It became very still and its voice took on a formal evenness as if reciting prepared information.

"Greetings   Diana   Roark,   my   name   is 2x2x2x5x5x17x37x43x43x43x

71x89x89x89x227x863x907x2477x2503 of the Neoooxcolu, but for convenience you may call me Robert. I am your Account Representative, assigned pursuant to Section 18.2 b of the F.I.L.A. I am to assist you in the legally required exegesis of the Terms and

Conditions of your account. Diana Roark, on behalf of the Interstellar Trade Commission, welcome to the Known Economy."

And then, formalities observed, Robert reformed into a smallish, harried, vaguely Asian human in rumpled khaki pants.

At last, Diana thought. Something she understood: governments and agencies.

"What's the F.I.L.A.?" she asked. Outside she heard more yelling. Some panic was finally developing and it had spread to the upper levels of the Mission complex.

"I can't tell you that," Robert replied. "We haven't executed our agreement."

"Ok, can you tell me what Section 18.2 b stipulates?" she asked.

"Not really."

"Let me hear the Terms and Conditions?"

"I'd like to. But I can't do it."

"What *can* you tell me?"

"I told you everything I can tell you. Please, Diana Roark. Help me finish this job. Help me pass a pod shroud. Help me breed. I'll ... I'll be your best friend."

"I don't need a best friend."

"Bullshit. Everybody needs a best friend."

"My best friends always die."

"That's totally a left turn, but I'm really sorry, that's..."

"I killed one of them myself."

"Jesus fuck, fine, I take it back, it's just a saying, you know, *I'll be your best friend.*"

As far as she could see, sitting there in the dust of this empty, forgotten restroom, she had one of three choices, each problematic in its own way. She could go to her estate and search with Robert for his pericarp, hear his Terms and Conditions and satisfy her curiosity. She could attempt, somehow, to stop Landerson from creating his New Capitol Zones and wiping out humanity, which sounded like probably the right choice. Or she could go on her vacation. To Bodega Bay.

For just a moment she felt the burden of obligation crush down, a deep black ache. No way to do it all and not even her responsibility to. Something must be forfeited. She felt it as a gravitational pressure, the damage she'd done, the carnage wrought simply by living her short and privileged life. She was conscious of it, heavy in her tissue, in her deepest flesh: Sullen and hot.

She gasped. The pain was no illusion, this is the way it came. Distantly, up soft and lazy trails like a dream billowing in. And then, in an instant, it fell on her, and it raged.

The bone pain.

She groaned, twisted and gripped her thigh. Her hands left streaks of grime on her white pants. There was no way to stop this. Now the excruciating episode would come, protracted and intense, It made the choice before her, on the floor of this abandoned restroom, much easier. She glanced at her wrist, at the single, fading tattoo, the butterfly with the stars. The only tattoo left on earth.

"I'm going on vacation," she hissed, as the pain started. "Come with me if you want. But stay out of my way."

7

It is important to understand that the Known Economy refers to more than an economic system; it reflects the state of a consciousness of opposites. A sentience who understands this has achieved the condition of commercial Mind. This Stakeholder has learned tolerance in the face of duality; happiness and sadness, giving and receiving, life and death. Just as a planet remains unchanged through cycles of day and night, so the commercial Mind is untroubled by cycles of profit and loss.

—From *The Book of* Ω64, of the Swandeen Pracis

I n the end, she'd never have made it without Robert's help.

For hours she writhed, unable to walk. She kept herself from screaming, somehow, and no one ever searched the restroom. Only after night had hidden the plaza and the cicadas had finally come out could she sit up on her own. Robert helped her stand.

She remembered limping off the grounds as the stars appeared, down a stone staircase gritty and bowled from centuries of traffic and through a pale gate in a low stucco wall. Then the two of them had followed a road, straight as a ruled line, toward the PopuPod border in the distance, at every step being erased from the mesh.

She leaned on him the whole way, until they passed into the PopuPod maze, dizzy and only half aware. She heard him say they were far enough from the Mission that erasing them now had a poor cost-benefit ratio; he stopped, so they were fully visible, though he still appeared to her as a human. She asked for directions to a train station from a Needless girl who stared at Diana, one leg bowed, skin loose, neck so very weak, and then stroked her arm. Diana wondered how she would get on the train. Surely they were tracing her accounts. Old-style cryptocurrency would have come in handy here, but of course that dream had died in the Augmentation. They would find her and she felt like a moth trembling at a pin, a pin that would descend and fix her to a map.

They stood on the station platform, she hunched, Robert stiff as a khaki-clad tourist. She waited for the prick between her shoulder blades, but it didn't come. Instead, the train arrived, and Robert erased them both so they could board.

As the train swept into motion, she slept. And had her dream.

GREG MOUTHS words to her from within his capsule.

In the trench, ocean dust cascades in slow watery sheets like ash from a burning paper mill. It settles everywhere. On the Spears. Everywhere. Greg is in his Spear, Diana in hers. Their capsules are so close. She can't hear him, but she knows what Greg wants.

Tell me, he is saying.

The dust pours, redoubled and the light is going out. The dust piles atop the pilot capsules and rises around them from the ground. She puts her hand up to the PressureGlass and watches.

Tell me, he says.

He is there, just inches from her. He reaches his own hand up. Dark ocean compresses everything. Nothing is alight now. Only the capsules, lit in the deep.

Tell me, he says.

The dust has risen up the flanks of the capsules. It slides down the dome roof. It seals a thick shroud everywhere. He's disappearing. He's almost gone, his mouth, his eyes, his beard. Then his capsule is buried. Her own is sheeted opaque. They are two mounds, deep in the sea, eternally separated by inches.

Tell me, he says in his Spear. But she can't.

THE SUN HIT her closed eyes, so she raised her hand for shade and squinted. Her forehead leaned against glass. *Was that right?* A window. Outside, sunlight spun kaleidoscopic. It flashed through trees and her seat rocked as she came awake: the train. The first thought she had was *food.* How long had it been since she'd eaten? She was thirsty. Her pain was gone. For now.

Robert was beside her and watched her wake up.

"Howmp," came out when she opened her mouth.

He held his finger to his lips. "We're not being erased," he said.

"Can I have some water?" she groaned, "I'm dying... of thirst."

He held a bowl to her mouth, a bowl he raised from nowhere. It was, in reality, a pseudopod appendage holding metabolic waste but it looked like a bowl. The water was delicious. She bent and drank and wondered if it was selfish to wish that his species sometimes peed coffee.

Her seat was comfortable and part of her wanted to slip back to sleep, rocked senseless by the gentle motion. But her dream lurked down there. She decided to stay awake and find something to eat instead.

A passenger across the aisle stood and walked toward the restroom, leaving a plate with a breakfast burrito on his tray. She stood, legs wobbly, and grabbed it. Presto. Manual disincorporation. She brought it to her seat and felt a prick of guilt, which she knew was ridiculous; he'd be surprised that his free mind-food breakfast was gone, then he'd get another. Bacon. Fried eggs? Potatoes. She ate it all.

She watched the pseudo display at the front of the car draw a schematic of their trip, including location, weather and attractions along the way. Here and there among the seated riders, she saw the gorging, the picking, the half-conscious flagellation that evidently plagued PreAugs across the planet. They went at it quietly, with methodical, low-key craziness.

The rail line they all rode wove up the coast, past seaside villages and PopuPod shanty towns. Three hours away was her Sonoma Coast estate; an hour closer sat Bodega Bay. Robert watched the display beside her.

"So. Bodega Bay," he nodded to himself. "Bodegabay."

"You know it?"

"No, I don't fucking know it."

She raised an eyebrow and shrugged while chewing her stolen burrito.

"So," he said after a moment. "Good old *Bodega Bay*." He nodded up at the ceiling, pretending to recall it really well.

"Do you have a problem?" she asked, mouth full.

"I don't have a fucking problem."

"You're free to get off the train. Any time."

"Yeah, *not. Not* free to do that. So I'll just fucking sit here and *ride the train* to fucking boh-day-gah-*bay*."

She wasn't going to be able to sit and listen to him for two more hours.

"If you have something to say, say it!" she challenged.

"Why are we going to Bodega Bay and not to your estate where the pericarp is?"

"I told you why." She swung her face away. *Translator, translate: I'm done talking.*

"Your vacation. Right. You know, *I've* had vacations, some really outstanding fucking vacations during which if a fucking *alien* ever crashed from fucking outer space to get me to sign really important documents *I'd* put my *vacation* on hold for an hour and do it! I'm sure Bodega Bay is fucking beautiful and everything. I'm just saying."

When she didn't respond, he added, "And I'm the alien crashing down in that reverse scenario, in case it wasn't clear." When she still didn't respond, he threw up his hands. "Fucking animals and their vacations."

Several of her shadows chose that moment to swoop down the car between the seats. One flew between her and Robert and they both ducked. Diana stopped chewing. Robert frowned.

"What are they?" she breathed. "You can see them. My shadows."

"Shadows?"

She pointed as another one flitted past and at another hanging in the air near the pseudo display.

"Those," she said. "You can see them. I know you can. *What are they?*"

"Tiisii," he muttered with distaste. "But you shouldn't be able to see them."

"What's Tiisii?" she asked. *The shadows. My cancer shadows. They have a name?*

"A race. A species. Like fucking flies, but dumber."

"I've been thinking I was losing my mind." She felt a shiver of sudden relief, at least on one front. She wasn't going crazy. "You can see them. How come you and I can see them, but no one else can?"

"It sounds like you *don't* see them. You see shadows?" She nodded. "They're not shadows, they're tiny, shitty little Brussels sprout leaf balls. They have wings and they're the cheapest fucking Appraisers in the Known Economy. Your planet is *infested* with them, by the way. It's disgusting."

"I see transparent blotches, not little winged plants."

"Oh. I get it," he snorted, throwing an eye roll, "I see what's going on. It's got to be. ITC regulations require contractors like the Tiisii to purchase client masking." He gestured around the train at the other passengers. "Standard mesh erasure removes the Tiisii for all these yokels, and the Tiisii can afford that. Barely. But you're not on the network, so they have the same problem I have. For *you* the Tiisii have to do what I'm doing: pay to manually redirect photons and scrub themselves out of your vision. Only the fucking Tiisii are too cheap to do it right! They're Tier 1000 Appraisers—who even hired these fucking pests? There're too many of them, that's the problem, so many they can't afford a decent external scrub, that'd cost trillions of Neu. So they're just smearing themselves into a blur for you. Amateurs. The ITC is going to yank their license. Let's just ignore them."

He set about doing just that, looking conspicuously everyplace they weren't.

"Hold on," she said. Her brain was so fogged with exhaustion, the by-product of fighting pain. "You're saying there are *lots* of these Tiisii on Earth?"

"Yeah, I mean, they're everywhere. You should spray or something. Now, *there*," he pointed out the window as they passed a series of PopuPod tenements tumbled up against the track's protective fencing, "*there* is a true professional."

Diana looked. All she saw were a few people wandering a series of narrow, haphazard alleys. One of them had a dog.

"The dog?" she asked.

"What? Fuck no. There's a Swandeen Pracis by the fence."

"I didn't see a... Swandeen Pracis?"

"Yeah, no shit. Those guys are. Bad. *Ass. They* could afford manual erasure, let me tell you. You know shit's serious when you see Swandeen Pracis on a job site and I already saw *two* this morning!"

Diana was getting a strange feeling in her stomach as she looked out the window and failed to see any of the aliens Robert saw. It was one thing, getting erased from other people's fields of view. But aliens that were getting erased from *her* perception... well. That was unsettling.

"So there's a another kind of alien on Earth, besides the Tiisii?"

"Oh yeah. Swandeen Pracis, Tier 1 Forensic Accountants. Best in the business. They're like priests." The strange feeling in her stomach right-turned into a sneaking suspicion.

"Are there any *other* aliens I can't see? Around here?"

"Oh, *hell* yes."

"How many?" she asked, numb.

"Fucking impossible to say. Hundreds of thousands? Something's bat shit crazy down here on this planet."

"Is it The 27?" she breathed.

"I fucking told you The 27's not what you think." Before she could form the question, he held his hand up. "And no. I can't say anything about The 27. Not until everything's signed. Do this by the book, keep our heads down, nobody gets written up."

"What's the Swandeen Pracis *doing* here?"

He shrugged and raised his hands. "Can't tell you that."

"Fine," she said. "Can you tell me what one looks like?"

"Inverted beet. Walks on its fronds."

Out the window she saw trees and dappled sun and stacks of wasted housing. And that was all. Another Tiisii sped through the car. As she glanced after it, her eyes fell on the man whose burrito she was, at that moment, having a difficult time swallowing. Was he what he seemed? The train sounds, clickity clack, rolled through her brain. She wanted to stop thinking and let the world go. Was *everything* upside down?

"Ok," she tried. "Are there any aliens on the train right now? Other than you?"

He looked down the car. "There's an Unzyfwymn in the car behind us. Tier 5 Employee Resources. Best description of him... sideways pine tree with a big soap bubble on the end. That's his tongue."

"All plants. Beets, Brussels sprouts, pine trees."

"You better hope so. The animals... you don't want to meet the animals of the Known Economy. No, you do not."

The burrito was not going down well at all.

"Is that why you're all here?" she asked. "The Known Economy? Are you trying to study us and figure out how humanity created advanced economic systems?"

Robert almost choked. Then he started laughing and he took a long time about it. He slapped his leg a few times and carefully wiped his eyes. She thought he *might* be stretching it all out for her benefit.

"Oh! That's fucking rich! Your advanced economic systems? The entire universe is a fucking *feeding frenzy* of production and distribution and consumption, you animals didn't *invent* fucking *cock turds!*"

"You know Robert, you're a very rude plant. Did you ever take a god damn executive communication class? You leave a lot to be desired as an Account Representative."

He seemed to shudder and freeze. Taking a deep breath, he looked down at his hands and nodded.

"I'm sorry. I suck. I know. I'm fucking terrible at this. It's not what I should be doing *at all*. No excuses, I mean, it's all my own fault. I'm only here because..." he shrugged. "I don't even know why. Look, you have questions? Diana Roark, I'll tell you whatever I can."

He seemed sincere and she almost felt sorry for him. But how sorry could you really feel for a twelve-foot broccoli?

"Fine. So, you, the aliens... you're all out there conducting business? Outer space is like..."

"Like a really big, practically infinite mall. The Known Economy."

"Does the Known Economy have money?"

Robert bit his lip, frowned, and looked around furtively, figuring something to himself. Then he made up his mind and the moment he did, his eyes fired up.

"The money, the coinage of the Known Economy, is Universal Currency," he told her, his voice low. Wow, she thought. Now this is a change. The animation. The focus. Like it's his favorite topic in the world. "Every sentient species has access to Universal Currency. Spend it, save it, loan it, invest it. Do whatever."

And now she was interested too. The fogginess in her mind seemed to drop away. A *universal* monetary system?

"Do humans have access to Universal Currency?" she asked.

He looked disappointed. "Can't say."

"Who prints this money? A central bank?"

"It's not printed. It's mined. A unit of Universal Currency is called a Neu. As soon as it's mined, it's registered on the Metachain."

"Metachain?"

"The Metaspatial Blockchain."

It took a moment to understand what he was saying. Metaspatial Blockchain? *Metaspatial?* "A blockchain. You're talking about an interstellar *cryptocurrency?*"

"Yes, that!" he chirped with surprise and growing excitement.

"Verified by consensus mechanics?"

"Yes! Right, a side effect of quantum linking, with temporal..."

"It's *temporal?* Not the GHZ state? We tried...how did you get that to work?"

"The Metachain's just there, some say the Sentient One made it, anyway, it's immutable because the photons it contains—"

She interrupted him, she couldn't help herself.

"—don't exist at the current time but they're still extant in the most recent block! It's so extensible you could record everything in the universe on it—you could recreate and record the actual, physical universe! Endless universes!"

Their eyes were locked. It was like being back at MIT, conversations in the cafeteria with strangers, tumbling down into a theoretical wonderland when all you'd been going for was lunch. In that moment their thoughts seemed perfectly synchronized. He felt it too. He looked like he was trying to peer behind her corneas, into her brain. Maybe that was possible, who could tell anymore?

"Diana Roark, how do you know any of this?"

"My doctoral was Temporal Blockchain Theory. I was going to start a new cryptocurrency, I was going to... how do *you* know it?"

He shrugged. "I'm a Tier 3 Appraiser. Blockchain's the foundation of what we do. Value Commission 101."

It all felt like ancient history, her life's work.

"We were *this close* to quantum blockchain," she said, softly, "I could have solved so many problems."

He leaned away, still watching, with a new and calculating look.

"Diana Roark, you're a very surprising animal. You're more like a plant than any animal I've met in five thousand years."

"Thanks. And I think I really mean that. You're a pretty different plant, too."

As they'd talked, a whirling swarm of shadows—Tiisii, she reminded herself—had begun spinning above them. Robert seemed to notice them for the first time, eyeing them uneasily.

"So your coin, this Neu," Diana asked, enthusiasm bubbling, "how's it mined? Algorithmically? A system that expansive, how do you possibly calculate a hash?"

"I can't tell you how a Neu is mined," he said, beginning to look a little rattled. He flinched away from the circling Tiisii and cast his gaze up and down the car. His current body language was translating as, *oh fucking shit.* He scrunched himself lower like he wanted to hide from the Tiisii. "I really shouldn't be talking about this."

"Who's going to know?"

"Are you fucking kidding me? I'm a government employee. I work for the Interstellar Trade Commission. Everything I do, *everything,* is written to the Metaspatial Blockchain. The whole history of the fucking universe from the beginning of time is written there. Believe me, they'll know. The document you and I have to execute, it registers our relationship on the Metachain, but we haven't signed it yet. Stop asking me questions. *Fuck.*"

She decided to do exactly that. She would stop asking him about his alien cryptocurrency, and in turn, she wouldn't tell him she had no intention of executing his document. Fair is fair, she thought.

Bodega Bay is a stubby, rounded oval, like the tab on a puzzle piece where the Pacific Ocean snaps onto the edge of North America. Fish enjoy this bay. People built homes there because they enjoyed the fish. And after people finished building, nothing much changed ever again. Diana descended from the train platform and remembered it, a town of single-story houses, exposed wood worn gray by 200 years of coastal wind. Beautiful and soft. But today it was different.

Brassy mariachi beer bands battled ColdTone dodecaphonic street music as she and Robert hit the main boulevard along the beach. A wash of color and costume swept around them, and it all looked nothing like she remembered the town looking. She ducked her head and pushed through crowds of laughing, masked tourists as she led Robert toward the hotel. She'd made the reservations two months earlier, but no one had mentioned anything about crowds.

Robert seemed disinterested in the crowds. Instead, he watched her.

"This is a waste of time," he complained. "If we'd stayed on the train it would have gotten us within a mile of the pericarp. Are you fucking crazy? Are we really going on vacation? You know, you have three days to get your account registered with the IFC. Three days! I can't help you until you sign it and good fucking luck if you don't have my help. Are you listening to a fucking word I'm saying? Diana Roark?"

She wasn't. By the time she got to the hotel she had wrapped her mind around the situation. Bodega Bay was hosting a Food and Costume Festival and the party was just getting started. It would last a week, a celebration of the Augmentation Anniversary.

She edged between two laughing men and entered her hotel lobby. What she wanted to do would be meaningless anywhere but Bodega Bay, so she'd just have to live with the inconvenience of a festival.

"Welcome to the Star Hotel!" cried an enthusiastic 23-year-old woman behind the counter with a swinging ponytail. "Are you here for the Festival?"

"I have a reservation," Diana said. "Prepaid. Gay Clovis."

"Gay Clovis," hummed the clerk. She was so profoundly dedicated to hospitality as a calling that she almost convinced Diana that her swollen, sagging black eyes, her partly missing gray hair and her stumbled lean against the counter were not even worth a second look. "Here you are! Thanks! You're in the Butterfly Room! Key! Come back down later. We have a tour! Sample the food!"

An artist's rendition of the Milky Way spanned the stairs. Diana took her key and limped beneath it, then started climbing. She passed a high-resolution image of Andromeda after a few steps. Higher up, a dramatic color photo of a solar flare hung a little crooked and she stopped to straighten it. In her memory these had been brighter images, but maybe the wind had done its work in here just as it had outside the houses, blasting gray into this celestial gallery. She stopped on the top landing to get her breath. Thirty years since his memorial service and not a single change except for a general graying. It was almost boring. Not at all like the rest of the universe.

Robert followed and seemed to sense she wanted quiet. They came to the door of the Butterfly room and she keyed it open.

The room had not changed in thirty years. She watched through the open doorway at diaphanous drapes straining yellow crepe sunlight. She stepped inside. The simple bed. The chest and mirror. She turned to the wall. The flaring wings of cloud and vacuum, in purple and green and gold, yearning upward across a background of velvet black space that stopped her breath—the star factory, lithographed across the entire wall beyond the bed.

The Butterfly Nebula.

She stopped, transfixed by the ten-foot smear of stars, small and large, born and dying, within the great gossamer wings of gas. Robert came to stand beside her.

"I've been there," he said. "The exchange rate's terrible."

"You've been to the Butterfly Nebula?"

"Sightseeing, yeah. Honestly? The museums were ok but public transport is a mess and they could all stand a bath."

"The whole *nebula*?"

"Probably. I don't know. We mostly stayed in the hotel."

She checked the bathroom and found it unchanged and the closet, which had held the ugliest penguin print shirt she'd ever seen. The chest of drawers was the same, where they'd put a single pair of sandals, just to feel as if they'd moved in. She sat on the bed and bounced. She was so much lighter now and the mattress barely moved. Her hands rubbed the beaded quilt, where their bodies had rolled, naked. Her eyes closed.

"Diana Roark. I'm going out on a limb. You've been here before, am I right?"

She nodded and Robert came and sat beside her and together, quietly, they watched the giant image of space hold utterly still, just as it would in real life if seen from Earth. The mariachi band stopped and the sounds of surf came through the sliding doors. It was warm and a little sticky. Perfect. The afternoon aged them a moment that way. When she spoke, her voice was thin.

"Robert. Does your species marry?" She refused—refused—to look at her tattoo as she said it. "Would you ever commit your life to another... person or plant? Forever?"

"Yes. I would. But Diana Roark, we're not right for each other. You're much too little."

"What..." She looked sideways at Robert—was he serious? For a second he kept a straight face, then he giggled. He slapped her arm and she pushed him, then *she* was laughing too despite herself, and it came out in a snort and surprised them. Robert found it hilarious and pointed and made a snort to mock her, but it was like a foghorn and scared them and the floodgates opened: in that room on that sticky, boardwalk afternoon, gales rang while the day waited.

"I'm warning you," Robert shook his head, "my species, don't make us laugh we can't help it we..." and he let out a massive, flatulent harmonic chord and she couldn't believe how it smelled, *really*, and she slipped off the bed, which brought five more chords in a row like melodious choir farts.

They gasped on the floor, rolling. While above them the wide, dark wings of the Butterfly Nebula, frozen open, reached for the corners of the room and the sun sank a little lower and the stars, the real stars, invisible behind Earth's domed blue sky, moved where no one could see them, along merciless paths.

Finally, they had laughed themselves to exhaustion. Or they just stopped, for whatever other reason it is that laughing eventually forsakes a room. They lay side by side with the crowns of their heads against the wall of interstellar space and Diana took a sharp breath.

"My leg is starting to really hurt," she said quietly. "I'm going to die soon."

Robert took a moment to respond.

"I understand, Diana Roark."

"I have something complicated to tell you."

"You don't have to say anything. It's obvious why we're here."

"It's obvious?"

"I'm not a fucking Tiisii. I understand. You came here to die."

"Robert," she said in a rush, "I want to tell you how grateful I am. I would never have made it here without you. You're a credit to your people and your profession. Tier 3 is not nearly high enough for you."

He shook his head. "That's bullshit. You don't know what the fuck you're talking about."

"I know something valuable when I see it."

"Yeah, ok." He shrugged. "All in a day's work for the worst Account Representative in the Known Economy."

She still felt like she ought to explain, at least a little.

"I wanted to wait until the actual anniversary," she said. "That's in three days. That was my plan, you know. Three more days. Isn't that stupid? But the pain... it's unpredictable. I saw it happen to my father. One day he was up, giving orders and the next he couldn't hold a pen. And that was when we still had pain medication. He couldn't stay conscious." How many years had it been since the universe had paid the tiniest lip service to her plans? "So, I have to do it now. While I'm still... you know. Capable. I'm going downhill fast."

"No one else can execute your document," he reminded her, without really trying to persuade her of anything. "That deadline's coming. I'm sort of bound by law to remind you, that's all."

"I'm truly sorry. I hope you understand."

Robert stood up, then helped her up too. Then his human disguise flickered and was gone. As he rose toward the ceiling, expanding the tight purple foliage at his top into its full, solemn expanse, his translucent base seemed alight with motes of phosphorescence. Diana gave a start, holding her breath; she had already forgotten how utterly alien he was. How amazingly, completely alien. No eyes. No arms or legs. But a talking, thinking being. His fronds began bending slowly toward her and at last, froze in a bow. His voice issued deep, in a way she hadn't heard before.

"Diana Roark, among the Neoooxcolu, the path you are choosing is a sacred path that *each* of us must choose at the end. To do it in sunlight, to be conscious when we go. We spend years in consideration and are surrounded by family and shroud mates and friends when we decide. It's a very plant thing to do, what you're doing... it's surprising. For an animal. This is a sacred... these aren't the right words. Fucking shit."

The alien bent even lower and its purple foliage was actually within her reach. She raised her hand to stroke it. So soft. Soft like a cat's fur.

"Diana Roark, I will bear witness in the name of the Known Economy to your passage back to soil. Even though what you are doing is going to totally fuck everything for me. May your pod shrouds flower in sunlight forever, Diana Roark."

Then, because it seemed polite and felt perfectly correct, she returned his bow, as much as her cancerous spine would bend. She hoped it translated somehow to encompass everything she felt. And then she crossed the room and took the stairs to the lobby. There was nothing else to say.

DIANA APPROACHED THE RECEPTIONIST, who gazed at her cheerily. "Will you be heading out on the food tour?" she asked. Diana shook her head.

"We're still unpacking," she croaked. "But I have a blouse I need to cut the tag from—do you have some scissors, or a knife? I can bring it right back."

Her original plan had included a suitcase—packed herself, so Charles never knew—with a selection of options. A bag to tie over her head, a knife, a pouch of Nightshade berries...just so she had some choices when the hour arrived. But those choices were gone now. She watched the receptionist pull open several drawers and then smile. *An X-Acto knife! Perfect.* Diana took the instrument, wrapped it in a thick paper brochure, and ducked outside.

The sun was low and the wildly costumed crowd in the street was just getting warmed up. She could limp through them, just one more masked celebrant done up like a zombie, she supposed. They were all PreAugs like her. The Needless would never celebrate the Augmentation, not any more than they already did every day. The Needless were no past, all present. But PreAugs retained a craving to memorialize.

Diana passed stall after stall where people lined up to taste from the minds of Flavor Artists, artisans and travelers who ate their way around the world sampling food from Obelisks in the Andes and the Gobi, from France and Appalachia, bringing back the tastes those people had grown up knowing. Once a Flavor Artist had fed one person in a community, that taste would propagate, perfectly formed, like a contagion. Tastes spread and faded in fads. There were stories of hidden flavors carefully sheltered by secret societies, dishes that only the most privileged would ever access.

She wasn't hungry though, and soon she'd come to the trail. It led over the top of the dunes and down to the beach. As she climbed, her shadows dropped down, like bats in the gathering dusk, circling and flitting. They looked the same as they always had, just dark smears through her field of vision, but now she could visualize them as tiny round plants. Flighted plants. She wondered how many other creatures were standing, crawling, flying around, maybe just yards away, hidden from view. It was a strange world, filled with amazing new things to discover. Someone would make those discoveries someday, she hoped.

She navigated her way down the dune on the sea side without tumbling and at last she found herself on a tide-hardened beach. The air was cool and the the clouds were purple. The sky was ten minutes from the first stars. It smelled like seaweed and distant lands. Thirty years since his memorial service here, on the beach where they should have been married. *Ten years I knew him, and what did I do with the time? Spent it on the ideals of a dead man, a man who never saw me, or said a single honest word to me.*

She fell to her knees near the waves and laid the brochure open beside her, taking up the knife. It looked like the one in the pictures on the internet. The funny thing was how old the information had been. Actually, it was funny how old the internet was, how nothing had changed in so long. Landerson had been right about that, at least. The pages she'd found on suicide had been archived thirty years ago and not added to since. The most useless possible information.

She hadn't been able to drink a lot of water and swell her veins, as the posts had suggested. Wrist cutting had not been her preferred mode of suicide anyway, but it was all she had left now. There weren't any cliffs to jump off. And she really, really wanted it to happen on this beach, before the suffering was unbearable. So.

It was up to her prosthetic left arm, which was probably a good thing. Less than 20% of those that attempt suicide by cutting themselves succeed, she'd read. It takes a lot of strength to cut deep enough. Strength she had, if nothing else.

She held the blade against her arm near her elbow and felt the pressure of the tip, just before the skin folded open beneath it. There was pain, but it was nothing compared to the pain she was avoiding. And this was *her* pain, in her control. So, different. She shifted her grip, prepared to pull the shiny triangle deep down her forearm to her wrist, to cut open the package Diana. She heard a gull call, as if encouraging her. A gull behind her.

Wait. Not a gull. A voice.

Despite herself, she turned. A figure was tumbling head over heels down the long sandy slope she'd descended herself a few minutes before. She was surprised at how much darker it had become. Time was like a train: whether you woke or slept, it kept moving. The voice called again, most of the words lost in the wind.

The fallen figure stood and rushed toward her over the sand. Broad shoulders. Shock black hair. Unfailing dedication.

"Ms. Roark!" Charles yelled. *He is so fast*, she thought. "Ms. Roark, stop, stop!"

Her prosthetic twitched and the knife dropped. He came closer. She was running out of time. She reached for the blade but missed. Her prosthetic was aiming four inches to the left, doing its own thing. God damnit. She reached slowly, targeting her fingers like she was watching in a mirror. A little up. A little to the side. Got it!

"I found you, Ms. Roark." Charles stopped, barely winded despite his mad scramble. "There was no trace. Nothing. The police were watching for credit cards. But I thought, perhaps, you would be able to escape. And if you did, I knew you would come here."

"Oh Charles, you shouldn't have come."

"No, Ms. Roark. *You* shouldn't have. Not this way. Not without me."

"You don't know what's going on. Just, go back."

"Ms. Roark, I know. How do you think I found you?"

"You know my plan?"

"Your *vacation*? I guessed. You did a fine job hiding it. But," he spread his hands and smiled sadly, "I've been with you too long."

He seemed conflicted to have found her, almost sad for figuring out how to interrupt. She was thinking this, but her eyes kept returning to the other figure. *The other figure.* The one who had followed Charles down the dune and out onto the beach. The naked figure stalking toward them.

"Who did you bring?" she asked, her voice low.

"I brought no one," he said. "Why?"

Diana shook her head and pointed over Charles' shoulder.

"Please do not move," Jianguo called, raising his voice to be heard over an incoming wave. He still managed to sound polite, using the same tone he'd use to call to his best friend, or inquire if a person wanted a glass of water before he cut off their head.

"Do not run," he commanded. "Do not make this unfortunate situation any less convenient than it already is."

Charles saw and rose, fast. He took the razor knife in Diana's hand and spun toward Jianguo. Jianguo didn't break his long stride, coming on like a tide across what beach was left between them, oblivious to obstructions. Charles charged, reached him and slashed with the razor. Jianguo stepped past the swing and took Charles by the arm and heaved him up, throwing him over his shoulder, not even breaking his stride toward Diana. Charles spun eight feet through the air like he'd been hit by a car. He landed on the hard sand, and Diana heard bones crack.

Jianguo underhanded an object into the sand without even looking where it landed and a Relay sprang up. He was loose and dangerous, performing practiced tasks with utter confidence. No rage. No hesitation. Did her eyes play tricks, she wondered, or was he glowing? Gray against the darkening bluffs?

She had fallen backward and watched him from the ground, propped on her elbow. Jianguo held his arm out, as if waiting for his invisible girlfriend to take him by the hand; over the sound of the waves, she heard a buzz from the Relay, like a transformer spinning up.

And then the same way there had just *been* a knife in his hand when he'd cut his way through her boardroom, there just *was* a sword. It grew from his palm, in the tiny space between one second and the next: gray, obsidian sharp, glowing for a moment just like Jianguo, before its luminance ebbed.

Jianguo didn't ebb, though—he overflowed. His eyes were high blue and dead. He rushed her and raised the gray sword and it fell as he came. *Knives for throat slashing,* Diana screamed inside her mind, *swords for head chopping.* No words came and no negotiation, just vicious forward action. She leaned backward but couldn't get up, so she rolled forward and hoped to stand and run.

And then he was there. He swung for her ear, to split her neck from her shoulders. She could simply have frozen and let him do the job she had come to do herself. Instead, she threw her arm high instinctively, despite knowing his swing wasn't something she could stop.

But neither Jianguo, right-handed, nor Diana, with her left, had factored in the decades of lost technology—lessons gleaned from battlefield losses, money spent putting soldiers back together to re-risk death—that had informed the long-ago creation of Diana's left arm. Jianguo moved faster than any human could move. But Diana was not human, at least not in that limb.

She caught him just below his wrist, she and her ceramic reinforced prosthetic hand. It had only happened because he didn't know about her prosthetic and because Diana had moved on purest instinct. He wrenched, but she wrenched back, piezo hydraulics *strained and spun* and she heard something sizzle in her shoulder and pop. She twisted, levered him with a final jerk and pivot and felt herself snap the bone in his forearm. His sword dropped and vanished.

Before the Augmentation a man would have screamed—an oath of rage, wail of pain or fear. But all Jianguo did was stop. He shook his head like a bear doused with frozen water and did a quick recalibration, glancing just once at his arm. Something in his carriage, in the set of his shoulders and the dissolute thrust of his neck, made her think: *Landerson.*

He still simmered gray light, or gas, naked, Greek statue perfect. He pulled another long blade from the air with his working hand and stepped close, ignoring his broken arm, swinging his new sword at her heaving throat.

But Charles had risen off the sand. He lunged from behind, razor in hand, and plunged it deep into Jianguo's shoulder; instead of slicing Diana Jianguo over-spun, his broken arm unbalancing him. His nicely timed stroke did not separate Diana's head from her body. But it did sever Charles. Severed him in two pieces, just below his lungs. Bone and blood spilled for a beat, then somehow sealed. His arms and chest and head fell to the sand. His legs stood for a moment on their own and then, slow as a tower, collapsed the other direction and stopped moving.

Diana found herself on her back. Jianguo stepped away from Charles, still getting his balance, and ended astride Diana's legs facing her feet. It did not occur to him that he was in any way vulnerable. Or he saw it too late, a fractional second after she did. But a fraction is long enough for a war-tuned prosthetic leg.

It rose from the sand between his knees and connected. There was a snap, a wet crack like an egg roll caught in a mousetrap as his testicles burst. And perhaps on instinct, or perhaps in actual, simple discomfort, he finally dropped his sword and doubled over, one hand going to his groin. Diana scrambled to her feet. He turned toward her, bent over.

He was exposed. She saw it. She had a chance. And she'd come this far, and she was dying one way or another. She might as well play it out.

She needed to see his face.

"You... will not... escape this beach," he growled, head down, already recovering. "You're without allies, weak, weaponless." He hardly felt a thing, she saw. His broken arm hung and brought no pain at all. But flattened testicles—that was simple male instinct. Even the Needless, apparently, had a protective instinct. But no pain.

He was numb to pain. It was his one vulnerability.

"Sorry I hurt your arm," she rasped. She herself felt like she might have broken a rib. Her soft bones were not cut out for this kind of thing. She reached out and laid her prosthetic gently on his shoulder where he hunched near her belly. The arm was balky. *Please arm*, she thought, *I need you this one last time.* And then, *come on, Jianguo. Look up here. Up.*

His hand flexed open for a new blade.

"Sorry about your balls too," she said. She patted his shoulder to get his attention. *Look, Jianguo. Look.*

"You've betrayed your planet," he snarled, "you, your philanthropy. You fear pain and suffering. But from human suffering comes greatness. You are weak. We are not."

A sword stretched from his palm, a tracer of gray that flickered then froze into something real, and he looked up at her. *Finally.* His mouth was stretched in a terrier grin, freezing her heart. Landerson's grin. He lifted his chin.

Now.

Her prosthetic fingers shifted two inches to the razor knife Charles had buried in his shoulder. She plucked it. Swung. One last cybernetic burst of speed and strength down her arm sideways, and she sliced his throat. Her machine arm made it feel like cutting through a pillow, though immediately afterwards, it went completely numb. Jianguo froze.

"Human pain does have a purpose," she said, in the silence. "Not to make anyone rich. Or spread capitalism. It's supposed to warn you," she panted, showing him the bloody blade, "when you have a knife stuck in your back."

The blood coursed from his neck and down his chest. He brought his hand to his throat, and held it as he slipped to his knees. She stepped away and watched, just to make sure the wound was deep enough. She didn't want to watch, but she knew she had to.

It took only a moment for his Nano Sphere to move his body offline. He fell to the sand and lay still. She stepped toward him. She knew she needed to kill him, that it was the only wise course. But the bloody razor fell from her hand. She couldn't.

She stumbled to Charles. Something was fatally wrong with her prosthetic arm. It was locked in position, bent across her waist. There was only a ghostly absence where she used to have fingers; something had splintered and broken and was now gone. Forever.

Charles. His body was tossed in two pieces. She went to the piece with his torso and arms and head, near the waves. The tide would push over him. She used the last of her one armed strength to pull him up on the beach, falling beside him.

He was awake. The severed bottom of his stomach was not bleeding. It was just flesh and chopped bone and viscera open for inspection, like a medical diagram of the inside of a torso. She lifted his head into her lap.

"Ms. Roark," he whispered. She shook her head. But he said, "I'm sorry."

"Charles, shh."

"I came too late."

"Too late? You saved me."

"Too late for everything."

His voice faded. He was being taken offline too, she supposed. How would this work, a whole lower half to regrow? His breath came slower.

"You've always been on time for me," she said. "Always."

"The things I said... about your father? I'm sorry, I had... no right."

"I know about it, Charles. Immpenta. So, no worrying."

"It was so dark in that house. He was so dark. But I stayed for you girls. I wanted children, you see. My own. But..."

"Charles, hush."

"I'm cold now."

"You're outside."

"I'm glad I'll go first. At least..."

And his eyes closed. And the blood inside him, held back for a few moments against gravity and sense, poured from him. He deflated like the most precious balloon, folding in on himself like a flower, fading in her lap until he was empty and very light. No Nano Sphere was proof against this injury. Not even The 27 could hold him together.

Now, she thought, maybe we're the same. Empty.

She drew a deep breath.

Without warning Robert shimmered into view, wearing his human semblance.

"Why are you here?" she asked, simple and low.

"I thought you were going to kill yourself," he said softly and if she wasn't mistaken, a bit reproachfully.

"That didn't work. Did you see it all?"

"I said I'd witness. I came in the name of the Known Economy. I didn't want to intrude." He looked at Charles, in pieces on the sand. "Was he one of your best friends?"

"No... what? Why do you say that?"

"You told me your best friends always die."

She had no idea what to say.

"He was an employee," she decided.

He gestured at the bodies. "Diana Roark, you are either *really bad* at killing yourself, though surprisingly good at killing other people, or you changed your mind at some point. Which is it?"

She knew she'd come to the beach to end her life. So why had she fought Jianguo so hard? Why do that?

"Robert, does your species ever hate your children?" she asked.

"Oh no. We really like babies. We love them."

"You'd never lie to them? So they wasted their whole life on...illusions?"

"Is this a trick question?"

What was it she really wanted? She looked at Robert. He wanted to have babies. She held up the hand she could move, which blood and sand covered like a glove.

"Okay," she sighed as he lifted her with broccoli strength. *So confusing.* "I guess I'm not killing myself. I'll die the horrible way."

"Awesome!" he said. "Let's get to the train. Clock's ticking."

She stood staring at what was left of Charles for a moment, aching and cold and one armed. "We have to get this done as fast as possible," she muttered. "I'm wearing out."

8

Does the water wheel turn more powerfully for a just cause or a good intention? No. In the same way, a stakeholder fearful of the fruits of their actions and clinging to doubt is no different than one free of attachment and devoted to good works: none of that matters. A sentient stakeholder simply turns, like the water wheel, creating choice through motion, and adding Currency to the Known Economy. In the end all sentient behavior is economic behavior.

—From *The Book of* Ω64, of the Swandeen Pracis

Along the western coastline of North America, where the Pacific Ocean pounds the continental plate, are a patchwork of micro climates. Bodega Bay sits in one protected pocket, a fairy land of temperance. But ten miles farther north, thick forests cascade down coastal foothills to the high, rocky edge of the continent, before backpedaling from cliff tops at the very last minute. And the weather becomes colder. And wetter. Everything Diana had hoped to leave behind.

She sat with Robert aboard the Surf Liner, the last big engineering project the state of California ever completed before it ran completely out of money. Her ribs hurt. How many of them were broken, she wondered? She hadn't heard a peep out of her artificial arm since Bodega Bay. She was broken and empty and dirty and tired, but at least she wasn't hungry. Beside her was a pile of sandwiches she'd collected from the festival on their way out of town. These would last twenty-four hours and disincorporate. Robert kept insisting that they had less than forty-eight hours left. So, she was only off by a day's worth of food from the end of the world. Or something.

The fact that the anniversary of Greg's death and the anniversary of the Great Augmentation and the deadline on Robert's timeline all coincided was a coincidence she'd asked about several times. But it was one of the things Robert couldn't talk about.

"Ok," she said. "Here's a question."

Robert sighed. He'd been distracted since the beach, not his usual happy, profane self, though he still seemed determined to try answering whatever questions he could.

"On the beach you said something you never said before," she began. "You asked if I was ready to *save my planet*. Didn't you?"

"Diana Roark," he said. "I say a lot of shit. What difference does it make?"

"You never said that before. Do The 27 have something planned for the planet where it needs to be saved?"

He shrugged, looking even more uncomfortable. Then he said, "The 27's not..."

"Yeah, I know," she interrupted. "Fine. But how come you never acted like there was any danger before? All you ever said was that I had to go sign some documents. Did something change?" She watched him. He squirmed, not meeting her eyes. "What changed?"

"Nothing!" he said. Several passengers looked their way. Apparently the passengers were allowed to hear everything Robert was saying, but they couldn't *see* him. Or not the real him, him that might make a fine coleslaw. When she had asked him about it he just complained about his budget.

"It's not *nothing*," she whispered. "Obviously. It's my planet,

Robert. If it's in peril, don't I have a right to know? You're the one who said it."

Robert appeared ready to argue, but saw something over her shoulder, something outside the window that she couldn't see. More extraterrestrial vegetables, she presumed. She shuddered.

And then he didn't argue but bent toward her to whisper. She couldn't even hear him at first. She doubted if whispering kept things from being written to the Metaspatial Blockchain, and it was hurting her ribs to lean, but she couldn't help listening.

"When you were on the beach not killing yourself," he said, choosing his words carefully, "you attracted quite an audience."

"Yeah. I was there. It was crowded. What's your point?"

"Not your stalker. And not your employee."

"I'm sorry I said he was an employee. He was more than that. He was..."

"Ok, whatever, fucking listen. I'm talking about *everyone else*. You couldn't see them, but the beach was full of..." he was obviously struggling to figure out how to say this. "There were... you were being watched. Your whole fucking planet is crawling with professionals, I've never seen anything like it. Ok. Let's do this another way. There are things I can't tell you yet. But maybe you can answer some of *my* questions. Ok?"

Diana nodded. It was the game she'd played with Jianguo, only in reverse. She hoped she would get to keep her clothes on this time; she was just now starting to warm up.

"Diana Roark, what is so special about the Earth?" Robert asked with the most intense stare.

She waited a minute for the rest of the question, the part that would give it some sense. But Robert was done.

"Special how?" she asked.

"There are hundreds of thousands of sentient species in the Known Economy. All of them have been introduced at some point into the economic sphere. There's a protocol. So, what makes humanity so different that the protocol would be... bent this way?"

"Bent how?"

"Can't say."

"Ok, how are we different? What do you mean? Different from what?"

"Other species. You're not being treated... per protocol. Why not?"

"You're asking *me*?"

"Just guess. Take a fucking guess. What makes you so different?"

She threw up her hands, or rather her one hand, and frowned.

"I give up, what makes us different from the aliens?"

"This isn't a fucking riddle! And *you're* the aliens, just to be fucking clear. So what is it that's so special about you?"

"I don't know. Is it our... ability to love?" She had read a few science fiction books on that theme. Robert snorted. "Ok, how about war? No other species has war?" He shook his head impatiently.

"Cruelty? Fear of death? Hope?" No and no and no. She dredged up every trope she had ever come across. She knew it wasn't humor; apparently fart jokes were a universal staple. "How about our fashion sense?"

He leaned back, confusion in his eyes. He looked worried, she thought. Then he bent near again and he looked deep into her eyes.

"Diana Roark, are humans just fucking with us?"

She waited. She had him.

"You mean, fucking with The 27?"

"No...the god damn shit fuck 27 is not what you..."

"Okay, okay." She didn't have him. "I have no idea what you're talking about. Honestly. Look at me. Fuck with *you* aliens? I can't comb my hair."

He sighed and looked defeated. "Well, there's a huge, fuck old economy up there." He gestured up. "And there are very strict laws governing it. Laws written to the Metachain, to prevent financial meltdowns, monopolies, whatever. And there are always Stakeholders trying to get around the laws. Looking for loopholes. I work for the Interstellar Trade Commission, Diana Roark. The ITC's charter is consumer protection. But I can't protect you if you're going to keep secrets from me."

Hey, she thought. Actual information.

"Consumer protection? So, I'm a consumer?" she asked. "A consumer of what?"

"I can't fucking tell you," he said.

"Robert, I swear, I'm not keeping secrets." Now it was her turn to sit back, full of bitter disappointment. "There's no vast human conspiracy. Humanity isn't special. We're insane. You know what insanity is? Making the same choices, over and over, but expecting a different result. That's humanity. We never learn."

Robert looked thoughtful. "Now *that's* interesting. The same choices. Most sentient species make a choice once. Once in the entire existence of the species."

She shook her head. The translator must be frizzing, she thought. "What choice do you make?"

"No I mean, most sentient species *literally* make any single, given choice, as a species, only once. Remember, with a few exceptions, it's a universe of slow movers, photo synthesizers. And the exceptions are the scary ones." He stared at her and now he looked more than worried; he looked frazzled and outright scared. "Only the animal species sometimes make a given choice more than once. Not all of them. Thank god there aren't many. But a few do and even then, only in on very narrow choice tree: predation." He shuddered.

Of all the things she had heard him say, this was far and away the most alien. She ran the last few minutes of the conversation back in her mind. He was talking about a common concept but it wasn't tracking. How could a choice be made only once per species, then never again, and still be available to guide individual behavior? Either choose to act or fail to act. Right?

"I don't understand," she admitted. "Choices are how sentient creatures navigate the world. It makes us who we are. I make choices constantly. Every second."

Robert's snorted, and his voice took on a didactic cadence; from the tone, she was the child and this was a pre-school lesson.

"Choices are the way a species evolves," Robert sing-songed. "Most sentient species are plants. We make choices so slowly we can't afford to repeat mistakes. Thankfully, every choice gets encrypted in our genetic code. If the choice was productive, that's what individuals of the species do, forever after. If it was a bad choice, that's what they don't do. And so a choice tree evolves."

They had to be using the same words for different concepts. "Choices don't evolve for humans," she told him.

"That's a really dangerous concept, Diana Roark."

"So wait, are you doing what you're doing right now," she asked, "based on choices made by other Neoooxcolu in the past?"

"Life presents an individual a never-ending stream of options," he said, in the same formal, teacher-pupil tone. "Which course is best is a choice that only needs to be made once, if it is preserved and its outcome recorded. This is natures safest, most economical path."

"What about you?" she protested. "When you pause, aren't you trying to choose how you want to insult me? Or figure out whether you're allowed to answer one of my questions? Isn't that a choice you're having to make?"

Robert paused to think. He didn't seem to notice the irony.

"No. In those cases, I'm just going farther back on my Choice Tree. In the genetic record. Common choices at the top, easy to access. The most exotic, unusual choices could be carried thousands of branches deeper, and take a while to get to. The Neoooxcolu are a Tier 3 Accountancy, which means I carry most of the Neoooxcolu Choice Tree with me individually. The fucking Tiisii are Tier 1000 because each one of them has only a tiny shard of their Tree, and they can't make the simplest choice unless enough of them are gathered together at one time."

"What if you can't find a choice on your Tree that applies to your situation?"

"That never happens. Remember, the Neoooxcolu civilization is five hundred thousand years old. That's just the civilization. We've been around as a species for millions of years. The choices have been made and recorded. But if it did ever happen, a circumstance without a recorded choice, I would have the high, inestimable honor of making a new choice for my species."

"But that's ridiculous! Even choosing which choice to choose from your Choice Tree is a choice! It's endlessly recursive. Do you store all the choices to tell you which choices to make from the Choice Tree *on the Choice Tree?* And then store the choices about the choices about the choices?"

"No. Choosing from the Choice Tree is the meta choice. A special case. It's called Right Action. And just because it works in a way you don't understand, Diana Roark, you fucking arrogant animal, doesn't make it ridiculous." He didn't seem mad. In fact he seemed amused. And condescending. She was out of her depth here, by a wide margin. "It's like you're complaining that gravity is ridiculous. Not a good look for you."

She was having a hard time picturing a functional planetary culture, let alone a hugely distributed interstellar civilization, working this way. Clearly her experience of the world was fundamentally different from Robert's—and from ninety-nine percent of all sentient species. *You wouldn't know it from talking to him,* she thought. *Or listening to him, fuck this, fucking fuck that, because he seems to be making choices all over the place.*

It was, apparently, a very big, extremely alien universe.

"That's not the way we work," she said at last. "Not at all."

Robert nodded. "Yeah, I'm catching on there. I've got to tell you, your species is doing shit I've never seen before. Anywhere. Fucking crazy shit." He was shaking his head and seemed almost to be talking to himself. "Crazy, wasteful shit. Like those swords your stalker was using." He looked at her. "They should really, *really* not be doing that. It is so wasteful, it's... insane." He stopped himself. Stared at her harder. "It's insane," he repeated.

After that he was quiet, either not wanting to talk to her, or mulling over the insanity of human choices. The train climbed through streamers of low cloud as it crossed the final pass that led to the Sonoma Coast station, at least a mile from her compound. The prospect of wandering the hills and clifftops of her estate with no jacket, no raincoat and no place to go when night set in made her cold all over again, but Robert had assured her he was budgeted for this phase of the trip. He would take care of everything.

His budget. As the train eased down the long grade toward the cove where Sonoma Coast Kayaking and Adventuring stood rustic watch over the Russian river, Diana kept thinking about Robert and his budget. The budget of Universal Currency that he dispensed, accomplishing his various astonishing technological feats the way she might have bought coffee with a credit card. Where did all this money go? Where did it come from? It sounded like someone, somewhere, was building up a lot of debt.

"This is as close as we can get to my estate," she said as they pulled into the station. "We walk from here." He nodded and rose, but she stopped him.

"If Landerson's people followed Charles to Bodega Bay, there's a pretty good chance they'll have agents here, too," she said. "It might be a good idea to, you know," she made a twirling gesture in the air above her head, "magic spell me."

"Already did it," he said and walked off the train.

She followed.

The first thing she noticed as she stepped onto the platform was the wet fog, the wind stretching it in banners from the heights of the surrounding foothills. The second thing she noticed was that, though she could feel the fog and the wet and the wind, she remained perfectly warm.

It was a revelation and she felt an incredulous smile break across her face. She followed Robert as he led them off the station platform. They walked along the shoulder of the narrow road, away from the collection of quaint stores and she marveled. The wind blew. Her hair and clothes flew. The fog left a wet shine on her skin. But she was impervious. Cocooned.

About twenty minutes into their walk, the highway left the flat coastal bluffs and turned inland, winding through the ancient redwoods. The giants gathered deep, ancient gloom around their feet on either side of the road, where feathery swards of emerald fern dripped and coiled in spiderish nests. A woodpecker tatted echo holes in some hidden trunk, a hollow valley of sound. Faintly, far overhead, she heard the wind pulling the tops of the trees. And through it all, she strode invulnerably. *This is what being a god feels like,* she thought, and then, *what a crock of shit.*

Robert peered from one side of the road to the other. He looked worried again. Distracted. Why? Were they drawing another crowd? She didn't want to know.

"We're almost there," he said. Twenty more yards and he stopped, pointing into the trees. "The pericarp came down back there."

She nodded and waited for him to cross and enter the sward. Instead, he surveyed the road they'd come down and the forest behind them and the sky, where Tiisii crowded. They kept a respectable distance, but Robert looked very troubled.

"This is your last chance," he said when he turned to her. "If you have something to tell me, if there's some secret you want to share, now's the time."

"Robert, stop it. I'm not hiding anything."

"I'm on your side, you know," he said. She tilted her head, to show she appreciated the sentiment. "I mean, yeah. It's my fucking *job.* But you're a very unusual animal. I really like you."

"Ok, Robert. And you're the most hospitable alien I've ever met."

She just wanted to get on with it. There were shadows coursing through the trees, spinning among the bowels of the redwood titans. Hundreds of them. Thousands. Flying plants, rated as Tier 1000 Accountancy. Despite the warmth, she felt a chill.

Robert sighed and crossed the highway and they stepped beneath the high, seamless curtain of evergreen. So little sun reached the forest floor that everything here, the sorrel, ferns, fungi and duff, phantomed open as if she had entered a nursery of ghost greens. She wondered if the foliage was really so indulgent or if the sensation was a product of whatever Robert was doing to her.

Ahead was a shaft of light that struck down through the canopy. Robert was leading them toward it. As they drew near she saw where massive redwoods had been snapped in half. The broken trunks lay shattered on the forest floor, white shards like broken teeth in the shadows. She stepped over long, shredded strips of wood and bark. Something had hit, come down from above. She ducked under one huge, leaning trunk, and found Robert. He had stopped and was pointing.

In a lit pool of forest floor was an impact crater, twenty feet across and within it lay a shape. Gray. Obelisk gray. The pericarp. It was oblong, twice the size of a football, laying like an Easter egg in a basket. *Would they crack it open? Would there be candy?*

There would just be documents, she thought. And possibly planetary destruction? Because really, it was just now occurring to her— what did she know about this alien broccoli? About his intentions? Was she about to hand the keys to the planet over to him? Where had her usual suspicions gone? Sixty years of business had bred a methodical caution in her. How had she come this far without a single question concerning his motives? Mind control? Her lack of misgiving made her feel she should have a lot of misgiving.

Robert stepped through the ferns and down into the crater and stood at one end of the pericarp. He motioned her, pointing to the position opposite him across the gray oblong. She waited to move, wanting to make certain that she had the choice. *Refuse if you want,* she told herself. It made her feel conspicuous and strange and Robert got fidgety as the seconds passed, so she stepped over strips of fractured redwood and into the soft earth of the dug-up crater and stood on the spot he had indicated.

He transformed, then, unfolding upwards and assuming his

branching, gelatinous form, and she noticed how at home he looked. Much less alien, here in this kingdom dominated by his distant brothers and sisters.

"Diana Roark," said a voice from the jello cube, "now we both touch the pericarp. Keep touching it until I say to stop."

Robert extended a pseudopod to the smooth surface. Tiisii whirled around them, a vortex of shadow. How many other alien beings were watching, invisible, beneath the trees? She squatted down in the moist earth so she was even with one rounded corner of the pericarp. The forest was very quiet. Not a drip of fern green water could be heard. The world held its breath and waited for her to do something; she reached out and put her palm down.

"About fucking time!" Robert said instantly. He withdrew his tentacle and reformed into his human disguise. Diana was left with her hand on the gray, wet egg. Several seconds passed while she waited.

"What now?" she asked.

"That's it. Contract signed, registered to the Metaspatial Blockchain. I'm now officially your Account Representative."

"That's it?"

"Yeah. Now I can get you up to speed on your account. There're a couple of ways we can do this. There's the standard introduction, something the ITC put together to help new account holders get oriented. Then there's the non-standard introduction, which I hacked together myself out of the ITC standard one and mine more or less tells the actual fucking truth about what's going on. Which do you want?"

Diana didn't hesitate. "I want the actual fucking truth."

He nodded, and the forest vanished. Words and images swept over her in a tide:

Welcome to the Known Economy! The Known Economy is over ten million years old, possibly as old as a hundred billion. [*This first part is a bunch of corporate bullshit, but just get through it.*] It is composed of hundreds of thousands of sentient species coordinated in a vast, interdependent web of production, trade and consumption. The glue which holds all the Scattered Pieces together is Universal Currency, and access to Universal Currency is made possible by the Obelisks, a gift the Sentient One bestowed upon all the peoples of the universe before disappearing forever. [*Or possibly before never having been there to begin with; nobody really knows shit about the Sentient One. It probably existed. Something sure made the fucking Obelisks.*]

Every sentient species ever to emerge from the mud or the seas or the skies of their home world must develop an indigenous economy before being welcomed into the Known Economy. Economic urges are a natural outgrowth of sentience. They take an astonishing variety of forms! If a species has not developed a monetary system of its own and does not have a banking system serving a supermajority of the population — a stage of development known as Full Economic Expression — strict regulations prohibit the races of the Known Economy from contacting them. [*Yeah. Strict regulations prohibit premature contact, so it fucking NEVER happens, right? Riiiight.*]

The reasons for these regulations are twofold. One, the fear of contamination. The races of the Known Economy regard a species' indigenous economy, the system by which it exchanges goods and services, and assigns and transfers value, as the highest, most sacrosanct assertion of its identity. To contact a species before the flower of its economy can mature and blossom, to make that species a soulless caricature of the contacting race and enfeeble them with alien money and goods, is to kill the very lifeblood of the Known Economy: vibrant economic diversity. [*Bullshit. The very lifeblood of the Known Economy is, Get Whatever You Can Without Getting Caught.*]

The second reason regulators delay First Contact until after Full Economic Expression is more practical; a sentient species does not begin accumulating Universal Currency until it develops an economic mentality. Premature contact can stunt, or completely end, the growth of a budding economy and prevent essential infusions of new Universal Currency into the Known Economy. [*More bullshit. Everybody knows Universal Currency accumulates long before there's any fucking banking system. What they really mean is that it's a LOT MORE WORK to protect really young economies. They can't say that. This is a cover-your-ass regulation. The truth is you're a target for a loan as soon as you're half-sentient. It's just a matter of whether anybody finds you.*]

Universal Currency is a natural byproduct of operating sentience. [*It gets technical in here. Stay focused.*] In mechanistic terms, UC is the fifth quantum force: Electromagnetism, Gravity, Weak Interaction, Strong Interaction, Universal Currency. It is closely related to electromagnetism and accumulates in the magnetic mantle of a species' home planet, a glorious, [*Hah! Fucking hacks, these guys. Glorious. Riiiight.*] ever-expanding manifestation of the thoughts—and more specifically, the choices—arising from the cognitive activity of a sentient species. As a species makes choices, it subdivides the fabric of reality [*Really? The FABRIC OF REALITY? Hilarious.*] and formally separates one quantum option from another, reducing the local incidence of entropy. [*If this is making your head explode, I'm sorry. Personally, I find it fascinating. Class is almost over.*]

This anti-entropic field accumulates in the *quantum* realm the way matter accumulates at the level of *General Relativity* and has all the hallmarks of money: it is measurable, exchangeable and is a store of value. In other words, it *is* money! But it is also a fuel, a commodity like a petrochemical. It can be tapped using the technology of the Obelisks to power nano machines and fabricate all the wonderful material goods which spread joy and happiness throughout the Known Economy. [*Goodbye science. Hello happy land.*] Scientists have given many names to the charge of Universal Currency which surrounds and infuses the home worlds of sentient beings, but it is colloquially known as the Golden Field. [*More like the Golden Goose.*]

The second great gift given to the peoples of the universe by the Sentient One was the Metaspatial Blockchain. A blockchain is simply a record which cannot EVER be altered and which is readable by EVERYONE. [*It's more complicated than that, but that's true.*] The Metaspatial Blockchain is a *quantum* record, spanning all of space and time. As soon as Obelisks have been emplaced upon a species' home world, they can spend Universal Currency from their own Golden Field within the Known Economy and these purchases, loans, investments and debts are recorded on the Metaspatial Blockchain. The unquestioned integrity and limitless reach of the Metaspatial Blockchain is what makes interstellar commerce possible.

Your world has already experienced First Contact. An Account Manager [*Me.*] has been dispatched. If Obelisks and a mesh network have already been emplaced on your planet, [*They have.*] your Account Manager will assist in the process of registering your Universal Currency to the Metaspatial Blockchain. However, if Obelisks have not been emplaced, you have several options:

Option One — The Interstellar Trade Commission can emplace, at no cost, a fully functional mesh network and seed Obelisks onto your planetary surface. [*If only! Unfortunately, humanity picked Option Two. Not that you probably had a fucking clue what was happening when you did.*]

Option Two — Various third-party providers are available who can emplace a fully functional mesh network and seed Obelisks onto your planetary surface. These third-party providers often furnish additional services which you may choose to engage. You should consult your Account Representative for guidance. [*I got frozen in orbit for 30 years and now it's too late for fucking guidance. Wow, do you think that was a coincidence?*] The ITC makes no warranty nor does it underwrite or certify any individual third-party provider and to the extent that—

[*Blah blah blah I just chopped out the rest. You asked for the actual fucking truth, so that part starts here.*]

The vast, cold reaches of interstellar space are patrolled by soulless pirates. They're officially sanctioned by the regulators of the Known Economy to spread despair and endless pain. [I'm sorry. I'll try to keep the cynicism to a minimum. But here's the truth: your planet's fucked six ways from Sunday.] *These pirates are known by many names: bankers, revolving credit purveyors, black-hearted fucking sharks. But we'll lump them all together and call them Predatory Lenders. They traverse the dark, uncharted byways between the stars in search of victims—I mean, borrowers. Unsophisticated borrowers, to be exact.*

The Interstellar Trade Commission was created some time ago [Look it up if you want the exact date. It was millions of fucking years ago.] *after one of the greater Great Economic Meltdowns, to protect those unsophisticated borrowers who had, once again, been lured into unsupportable financial arrangements and had, once again, brought the Known Economy to its knees because there had been, once again, a total fucking disregard for the norms and practices of the financial industry. So, the ITC was established and real, clear rules put into place to prevent future disasters and if anyone had paid any attention to those rules, the universe would be a wonderful place.*

But Predatory Lenders don't give a fucking shit about anything but getting rich. These fuckers are always looking for loopholes, for ways to slip between the rules. And the Trade Commissioners mostly look the other way, because the Predatory Lenders fund their pet projects and recycle hydrogen on their pet worlds and generally weasel their way into the heart of the VERY INSTITUTIONS that were set up to control them, like the ITC. Foxes ruling chicken farms.

So, the Predatory Lenders head out into space to offer credit to unqualified, unsophisticated borrower species and rob them blind. These Lenders are leveraged to their eyeballs, by the way. They take out HUGE loans themselves, because they're not about to put their own money at risk on this credit scam. They loan out money other assholes higher up the chain loan to THEM. It's a clusterfuck of greed.

They find a new world with a field of Universal Currency: a Golden Field. [This part is actually difficult and they're providing a useful service by expanding the borders of the Known Economy and discovering new sources of UC. That's the argument they always use, too.] *They offer to seed Obelisks onto planets and emplace the mesh on the new world. The sentient species has no idea what any of it means; they've never heard of the Known Economy. And the Predatory Lenders* [The group that came to Earth were called The Fund.] *never explain the terms. They make it seem like free money. What could go wrong?*

They seed the Obelisks. But here's the insidious part: instead of powering the Obelisks and the mesh with the client's own Golden Field, they give the sentient client a line of revolving credit, like a credit card, from their own leveraged funds. So, every time the client uses the Obelisks to eat, or drink, or power their health, they are running up a charge on a credit card. The client falls into huge, unsuspected debt instantly and never finds their way out. They don't even tell the client the billing cycle, which can be no shorter than 30 years. [Your billing cycle is 30 years. Are you starting to see what's happening here? How long ago was your Augmentation?]

These are lines of revolving credit and the interest accrues in Universal Currency. But they are not unsecured loans. There is collateral. Can you guess what the collateral is? Can you guess what the funders are able to repossess, legally, in the event that the client fails to make a payment, or is late on a payment, or looks at them sideways?

EVERYTHING! The whole fucking shebang. Every last erg of Universal Currency the client possesses. [This seems unfair to you? Complain to your Account Representative. Oh, your Account Representative got held in orbit for 30 years? I guess that's just too fucking bad.] *They take the WHOLE PLANET and everything on it.*

But.

There are two rules they can never fully sidestep. These are the heart of the ITCs charter, and no amount of inside weaseling can ever get them eliminated:

1. The client must always have the resources to repay the loan. Somehow. So, there is a SINGLE OBELISK on your planet that can be linked to your own Golden Field and a SINGLE PERSON who can connect to that Obelisk. [You are that person. You need to find the Obelisk. Your billing cycle ends in approximately 48 hours and after that you lose your planet. Good luck.]

2. *The interest rate of the loan has to be prominently displayed in the language of the client species, at all times.* [They slip and slide around this one. They plant stories in the client culture, try to make the displayed rate appear to mean something else. But it's always there, somewhere.]

So, congratulations! And, in the name of the Sentient One and the Known Economy and all the sentient species ever fucked up the ass inside it, welcome! [That's all. It's a pretty shitty situation. But don't give up hope, okay?]

THE BUBBLE of sensation and information that had enclosed Diana faded and she seeped back into her body like water into a dry lake bed, slowly, inch by inch. She was lying on her back, propped up on one side of the impact crater, her head resting on soft pieces of redwood bark. She thought maybe Robert had arranged her like this, because she didn't remember doing it herself. She wondered how long the presentation had taken. She blinked at the canopy of branches, noticed the deep gloom. It had been streaming light the last time she looked. Had hours passed?

Robert squatted on the rim of the little crater, looking down at her with eyes that seemed, if his translation app was still doing its job, deeply unhappy. She might even say sad.

"You ok?" he asked.

"I don't know."

"Your question is answered, at least."

"Which one?"

"It's your interest rate. In the client species' own language. That's the rule. Consumer Protection, you know?"

She didn't see what he was getting at. There were too many

pieces to hold in her mind at once. The pericarp lay where she had seen it last, a dull gray in the dampening gloom. The same gray. Always the same gray. Obelisk gray.

And then she saw it. Her question *had* been answered. It was there at the top of every Obelisk. Every Obelisk on Earth had the imprint. Over and over, she'd asked him about it. And now she understood.

The interest rate of the credit card that was about to destroy the Earth: 27%

9

Seated on your cushion, wise student of the Sentient One, you meditate on this question: which came first, the act of *purchase*, or the act of *sale?* For within this dichotomy lies the frisson that gives Universal Currency its expansive power. But take care. For while you are lost in thought considering the nature of *purchase* and *sale*, other sentient Stakeholders are traveling the Known Economy, engaging in purchase and sale, so you may one day find that you no longer own your cushion.

—From *The Book of Ω64*, of the Swandeen Pracis

Diana stood. The shadowy trees around her leaned inwards, crowding her, stealing the air she needed to breathe. *A bit of claustrophobia?* she thought. *Something closing in on me.* Robert hadn't moved. He crouched on his haunches and watched her.

"Diana Roark. Sorry for all the shitty news. You must have other questions."

"The 27," she said.

"I told you," he shrugged, "it wasn't what you thought."

"But everybody thinks it's... why did we think...?"

"That's The Fund. They're experts. They've done this to a thousand other worlds. Whisper campaigns, urban legends. The Obelisks are always the same; the number is always there, just the story changes a bit. *'The 27 is an alien Board of Directors,'* or, *'There are 27 steps to enlightenment.'"*

He laughed, a lonely sound within the murk and the chill of the trees and the ferns. "Your planet was a sitting duck. The Fund did it with Facebook. Twitter. Fake accounts—*scientists,* don't you know, respected *world leaders*—a few hundred posts here, a few hundred reposts there and before long you're convinced you *know* what The 27 is. *A consortium of federated species.* Just total fucking bullshit. But you bought it. They always do."

"I'm thirsty," she said. Without a word, Robert held out a bowl and she went and sat next to him on the wet ground and drank. It was cool and clear—the clearest thing about the entire situation.

After a minute she tried again.

"There's something I don't understand," she said.

"Just the one thing?" he asked, with a rueful smile.

"How can they do all this without...? I mean, doesn't someone on earth have to agree we want to start an account? Sign a pericarp or something?"

He nodded. "Absolutely. The law's super fucking clear."

"I never signed anything. I thought you said I was the signatory on the account."

"You are, but you're not the account originator. They like to split things up, keep any one stakeholder from really understanding what's going on." He shrugged. "It's totally fucking screwed, I know. You're the signatory, so you have ultimate responsibility for the account. But the Account Originator can be anyone, as long as they pass a pretty high bar for financial know-how. That's another ITC regulation. The Account Originator has to be a Qualified Investor. Hilarious."

"So, who's our Account Originator?"

"It's almost guaranteed to be a banker. Familiar with finances, plus The Fund *likes* to work with bankers. They can usually buy them off. Know any bankers..."

They both realized it at the same moment.

"Landerson," she breathed. "But he's not an idiot. Why would he agree to this? A line of credit tied to our actual planet, that we have hardly any chance of paying back?"

"Money, most likely. Like I said, The Fund doesn't mind paying." Robert shrugged. "Think about it. All The Fund cares about is stealing your Universal Currency. They can create as much gold as they want with the mesh. Did Landerson suddenly get richer at some point?"

Diana thought about all the loans the World Bank had made immediately after the Great Augmentation, and how no one could figure out where it was all coming from. But now the source of those funds was obvious. Landerson had spent thousands of trillions and he'd done it to save the civilizations of the world from collapse. He'd saved lives. He'd taken the largest treasure chest ever buried on any beach and instead of keeping the money, he'd spent it to save mankind. But he was also the one who had imperiled them in the first place, agreeing to the loan. Had he changed his mind? And when had he become a monomaniacal lunatic?

"Another question," she said, as the pieces continued to click. "Why does The Fund go to all this trouble? Why not just drop an Obelisk and start sucking us dry? Who would ever even..." but she saw the answer as soon as she asked. Robert nodded.

"Because everything they do is written to the Metachain. The regulators are watching. There are certain rules they can't break. They can bend them, bend them the fuck over backward. But outright theft? They're cowards. They'd never risk it."

"Right. Got it. Explain something else."

"Shoot."

"Why am I the signatory? Why me?"

Robert shrugged again, shaking his head. "Just pure chance. Look, here's what happens. They're required to provide a single Obelisk connected to a client's Golden Field and link a minimum of one person to that Obelisk so repayment can be made. But they want to make repayment as hard as fucking possible. Maybe the person is late on repayment and The Fund can take possession of the whole Golden Field, right? So, they'll scan a planet, locate an individual in the most isolated, inhospitable spot possible, designate her the signatory and drop her Native Obelisk beside her. After she figures out what's going on, she has to get back there somehow to activate it. I'm telling you, it's all a scam. They work the system. There is a reason they're called Predatory Lenders; they want you to fail. So, you're the signatory. Any idea where your Obelisk is?"

She knew. Of course, she knew. The Obelisk was in the coldest water, at the loneliest profundity, in the farthest canyon. A place she never wanted to see again. A place she saw every night in her dreams.

The trees continued to lean in, holding back the air of the forest. She wasn't breathing; black water was choking her, pressing in around her, but Robert seemed not to notice. He was flexing and shaking his hands like a boxer preparing for a bout.

"Here's the thing," he said. "All these fuck all aliens on your planet, they're here because The Fund hired them. It is completely fucking insane. There's so much money being spent on Appraisers, The Swandeen Pracis, about a million Tiisii—*hundreds* of Appraisal species. The Fund is trying to figure out what your Golden Field is worth because they can't access it directly, not without ringing the biggest bell you ever heard on the Metaspatial Blockchain. They probably need to raise money; I bet they're leveraged to their eyeballs. So, they're hiring Appraisers to wander your planet and create what's called an *estimate of value*. But I'm your Account Representative; you can give me permission to look directly at your Field. You don't have to, it's your account. But these fuckers are playing you, Diana Roark and you can't play them back without fucking information."

It was good to have something other than deep, blood-thick ocean depths to think about. Something to do other than settle, covered with dust, while a billion pounds of—

"Ok," she almost shouted. "What do we do?"

"Like an account book, you're tied to the account. You can't spend anything until you activate the Obelisk, which you still have to figure out how to do. But all you have to do is give me permission and I can piggyback your access and look at your account and we can at least see what the fuck everyone else is trying to see. Is it ok?"

She nodded.

"You have to say it," he told her. "This is getting written to the Blockchain."

"Yes," Diana said, looking up into the night dark branches looming above them. "I give you permission to examine my... mankind's Universal Currency."

Robert nodded and reached out toward her forehead with his palms.

He closed his eyes just before he made contact. He was frowning in concentration. *His translation app is really working up a storm,* she thought.

Then his palms hit the skin above her eyes.

He froze and gasped, transforming back into a towering Neoooxcolu.

And then the whole purple broccoli, which reared so high its top was lost in the redwood branches, tilted like it had been logged. It collapsed on the pericarp with a sodden crash, like a wet tree falling in the forest.

The alien jello cube slumped, softened and then ran out over the dark forest floor like clear, hot pudding. And seeped away into the ground.

Some of Robert was left. She saw it on her wrist; an ectoplasmic bit had landed right beside the butterfly. She watched it as the final light faded around her. Until the blackness in the forest was complete and night was there and in the pitch black silence the soft static of the deep woods rolled in. She heard an owl, its call a prelude to bloodshed, then all the small sounds of the antediluvian wood loosed. The trees groaned and settled. A fox bark echoed among invisible trunks, was taken up by others. Insects purred and bats pursued. And like an animal, but softer and more relentless, came the cold.

Robert was gone and the shroud of warmth upon her shoulders was gone with him. Chill rolled through the primordial rainforest and she was defenseless. But it was fine. She had nothing left to defend.

"I don't know what you want from me now," she said. She could feel them all around her. An invisible conclave. "You killed him. Was that your plan? So I'd be stuck here?"

She peered into the blackness where the woods were and saw the blackness of the sea instead. She could feel herself seated before the console of Spear One. Falling. The surface was long gone, far above.

"It's always been you, right?" she asked of her observers in the darkness. "You've always been here? Is that why I've been this way?"

From the beginning?

"Are you the reason I'm broken?"

No one had told her when her sister was dead; she had reasoned it out too late to cry. And then her mother had died, but by then the habit was set. And her father, who she hadn't mourned at all, had left her eyes perfectly dry. *But Greg. Not for Greg?*

"I should have felt that. You should have let me."

Charles. On the beach with half his body in her lap, she had known it was wrong not to cry. That something was wrong with her. Charles who had tried so hard all his life to give her what she hadn't even known to ask for, or want, split in half because he never gave up trying, not even long after it was too late. She'd had nothing for him. She'd left him for the tide to rise and soak away.

"I should have felt that. What you did to *Charles* wasn't *fair*."

And Robert, he was different, too different. Why do I care about him the most, out of everyone I've lost? And now he's sunk into the ground and gone, so why did I even care, now or ever, for that matter? Attempting to pull herself together, she pictured what her father would say to her: *Stop wondering how you're going to go on without Robert. Who even cares about Robert?*

She gently heaved forward, falling softly, like one of the ferns.

It was so dark. No one would see, only them and they didn't matter, and they certainly didn't care. It was easier to be alone with the aliens, where no one could see that she didn't know how to do it. She could do it even though it would be so bad and it still wouldn't be enough.

Tears rolled down her cheeks and dripped from her chin, held back for so many years but flowing now, unchecked. She didn't know how to cry; but Phoebe had known. She'd watched Phoebe, sometimes, when they were little and she could still copy her big sister. She knew that you cried when you lost a doll, or when boys were mean, or when the day was too short. *Come in for dinner*, Mother might have hollered and Phoebe crying back, *No I want to play!*

I want to play. Why can't I play?

Time passed in the forest, a forest as dark as the sea where she had lost Greg and she cried. Her only timepiece was the drip of water, drop on drop. As she stared into the dark, she began to hallucinate colors, stars in the ether, forms that moved in front of her, expanding and contracting, then becoming a glow. Another tear dripped from her chin, she glanced down to where it had landed, and she saw the dirt on her trembling leg in the light of her hallucination. *In the light...the light that isn't a hallucination.* The earth around her became luminescent.

The radiance grew, forming pools that began to move, collecting around the base of Robert's supine stalk. Slowly, the bits of phosphorescence rose. Then quickly, like reverse footage of an ice cube unmelting, the cube reformed around the recumbent stalk, which straightened and trembled, reverse timber-falling, until it rose back into the air and swayed.

Diana was flooded with warmth. Her sleeve of comfort returned, though her shivers continued; her body was too far gone with cold. It was prepared to shiver despite anything warm for the rest of her life. Her teeth chattered and the only way to keep them from breaking was to clamp her jaw. She watched the glow around Robert's base fade, though some bits remained, stuck to wood and leaves and gave off the softest illumination. Sometime after that, without a word, he transformed back to his human disguise. But still, he didn't move.

She held out her arm, offering him a tiny mote of florescence stuck there. He reached a finger and took it.

And then he said, "Sorry."

Her entire body shook, but not from sadness, or whatever had possessed her in the dark for a time, but from cold. She must have been close to hypothermia. She drew her thoughts in from where they'd gone shivering away.

"W-w-what... ha-happened to you?" she asked.

He took a breath, a look of wonder on his face.

"I made a choice. I made *a fucking choice*, Diana Roark. And it almost killed me."

They stared at each other. Diana still suspected they were using the same word to describe very different things, but she wasn't in the mood to be called a *fucking arrogant animal* again because she asked questions. She nodded.

"W-what... ch-ch-choice?" she asked.

He sat down beside her, slowly, still looking amazed. They gazed into the depthless black of the forest.

"I choose not to write what I saw in your account to the Metaspatial Blockchain."

"W-will you... get in trouble?"

"I'll have to write it eventually. But in certain cases, an ITC employee, in order to protect a consumer, can delay registering information to the Blockchain. You'd never need to do that, though. No Neoooxcolu ever has. But it was the only choice I could make."

"Are you ok now?"

"I am. I'm *better*. I can't describe it... a genetic rewiring. I'm rewritten."

"Ho, that sounds like what I need." She managed to chuckle because it was So. Damn. True.

"Diana Roark, I just added to the Neoooxcolu Choice Tree."

His voice was as soft as a little boy's, whispering under his covers at night, murmuring all the wonderful things that were going to happen to him when he grew up.

"Why h-hide what you saw?" she asked. It was getting easier to talk.

"Oh jesus fuck. Diana Roark." He turned away from the dark forest to look at her face. His wonder had not diminished. If anything, he looked more amazed. "Your Golden Field is..." he made some movements with his arms that communicated nothing to her and she wondered what his jello cube was doing to translate this way. *Something I would actually like to see*, she thought.

"What?" she asked.

"It's god damn fucking *huge*. And all these motherfuckers," he gestured around her, around him, shouting at the woods, "they know it, but they can't see it. So, they can't put it in a report. They're wandering around your planet trying to create an *estimate of value* but they'll never even come *close*. It's the biggest I've... by a factor of... it's a fucking supernova of Currency...it's..."

"What?" she asked. *Please Robert. You're back now. Be useful.*

"Here's an analogy they teach us. Think of Universal Currency as fire. Plants, once every ten thousand years, we light one match. Right? We make a choice. That choice is a contribution to our Golden Field—slow, sustainable growth, the way of plants. We never make the same choice twice. That's *plants*—but animals are different. Animals are like a campfire, constantly burning because they make choices so often and because sometimes they make the same choice *more than once*. You see? Now, most animal races flame out fast—it's crazy unsustainable, they just blow themselves up or some shit; there's no balance. But a few animal races find a balance. And that's terrifying. They're not smart, they're just fucking fast and aggressive and dangerously predatory... anyway. Even the craziest Tier One animals are only campfires."

He frowned, working something out in his mind. He couldn't seem to look away from her.

"But humanity... you're no campfire. You're an exploding sun. An ongoing, massive, nuclear eruption of choice. It looks to me like *every* choice you make is new. Tens of trillions of choices every fraction of a second. The same choices over and over and over, new choices... it's... fucking insane. Nothing like your Golden Field has ever existed."

Diana tried to picture it, grasping just a tiny glimmer of understanding. They were rich?

"Ok," she said. "Humanity has a huge Field. Why hide it from the Metaspatial Blockchain?"

"Something's going on, Diana Roark. The numbers don't add up. Someone suspects. Someone wants it all. And I think..." she could see him having a thought that was terrifying to him, "I think the Interstellar Trade Commission's involved. I get delayed in orbit for thirty years? No fucking way that happens without ITC knowledge. There are irregularities all over this fucking planet. Why doesn't the ITC shut this account down? Your data is privileged information, but high-clearance eyes will see it the second I commit what I just saw to the Metachain. Someone at ITC will see it. And if it's the wrong someone and I'm right... all fucking hell breaks loose."

"Well, what do we do?"

"We get to your Obelisk. You connect to your account."

"I thought I was? Connected?"

"No, you're not fucking listening."

"I am. What about the pericarp?"

"That was just for us to sign the Customer Relationship Contract. You need to get to your Obelisk, get up close to it and activate your account. Then you make the payment that's almost due and after that you'll have time—thirty years until the next payment. You can figure something out." He waited for her to say something.

"So where's your Obelisk?" he finally asked.

"Underwater."

"Let's go."

"Seven miles underwater. I can't get there."

"How'd you get down there to begin with?"

"I had a project, I had a team, I had a sub..."

She stopped. The team. The team had vanished, faded into the hills, Augmented away into insignificance. They were thirty years gone. All but one; one had actually tried to stick around until Diana had finally driven her off. But she was still...

"We need to catch a train down the coast," she said, standing. Her legs were shaky but they worked. "To Monterey. The Roark Oceanic Institute."

Where, unless something had changed, the director of the Institute was still Lizbeth Mustang. And the Institute's Museum of Nautical History was still about to open. Maybe the history would save them.

IN THE HOUR AND A HALF, it took to get back to the train station, dawn had arrived. Robert erased her long enough to get her up the boarding stairs and then the two of them fell into a pair of seats and they set off.

To Liz.

Diana had purchased the Monetary Bay National Marine Center from the federal government when it had gone up for auction. She had given it the Roark Foundation name and offered Lizbeth the job of Director. Charles had complained and Liz had pitched a fit. But Diana had discovered by then that she would never have any Augmentation to enjoy and she wanted to do her work and have her life and not drag anyone into the hole she saw closing, so slowly, around her.

Had it been the right choice? Charles said she'd broken Liz's heart. Liz kept trying to visit, but Diana stayed too busy. *So busy.* She sent money for any research Liz wanted and never saw her again.

Robert sat beside her and watched out the window as the train turned the coast of northern California and headed back toward the coast of central California. She watched too. They left the redwoods behind, and the soft chaparral and rolling hills of the cloudy Bay Area rushed to meet them. Robert spent the trip from Sonoma watching like that. He was keeping an eye on something, that much was clear, but he wouldn't tell her what he saw.

Around her danced dozens of shadow-smeared Tiisii. They were like flies, she had to agree. They never left her now. They'd started gathering when they'd boarded the train and more and more of them buzzed as the miles sped past. Robert swished them away when they got close to his face, but otherwise tried to ignore them. But they brought Diana's mind back to the 27, now lowercase. The interest rate on their loan.

She was struck by a thought.

"My Nano Sphere isn't broken at all, is it?" she asked. Robert looked at her. There was something out the window he was not happy about, but he tried to pull himself back to her questions. She elaborated for him.

"Everyone on Earth except me is walking around drawing borrowed cash from Obelisks hooked to an alien credit line. But my Nano Sphere is tuned to Earth's Obelisk. I always thought it was broken. But it just hasn't been turned on."

"You're a debit card," he agreed. "You activate the first time you're used."

He glanced out the window, then back at her. He batted at Tiisii and continued.

"Those fucking swords your stalker was making? Unbelievably wasteful." He looked a little incensed. She thought it was kind of cute —he was overwhelmed with anger at Jianguo because trying to cut off Diana's head on the beach had been very wasteful.

"I don't know how they're doing it, but Landerson is manipulating nano particles, building things out of the actual particles themselves. Swords and flying globes and shit. But the particles are just the transfer medium. It's like someone needed an expensive table, so they applied for a bunch of credit cards, but instead of using the cards to *buy* a table, they built a table *out of the credit cards*. It's not supposed to work that way. The Nano Sphere connects to the Obelisk, the Obelisk pays the mesh particles to fabricate things. Honestly, what they're doing shouldn't be possible. You people are fucking crazy."

He was in a very bad mood, which she put down to worry. He went back to scouting the passing countryside. And anyway, she agreed with him. Humanity had a long and storied history of insanity.

"That's why he needs economists," she said, almost to herself. "They're manipulating money. They're building things—swords, whatever—out of dollar bills. The only people who can make those machines connect are people who've studied the way currency flows."

"Still shouldn't be possible."

"Why does The Fund let it go on?" she asked. "Couldn't they stop it?"

"Because it's running up your debt! Every fucking sword you make! It's taking massive amounts of UC to pull that off. The Fund must think they hit the fucking jackpot, they..."

Suddenly, still facing the window, Robert froze. He reached out and grabbed her leg, her real one. It hurt. His body had gone as taut as a nail and Diana saw that something was officially wrong.

"Oh fuck," he whispered under his breath, eyes glued to the window. "You've got to be shitting me."

"What?" Diana asked, looking outside but seeing nothing, while gently trying to pry her leg loose. His fingers were actually disguised gooey pseudopods of extraordinary strength; it didn't work.

Robert spun to look around the car, his eyes huge and his face white. *Terror translates really well from Neoooxcolu,* she thought, the terror spreading to her. He looked down the aisle, jerked his eyes to the doors between the cars and then shot a look back out the window.

He cried out and stood, shoving her backwards from her seat.

"We have to get off the train!" he yelled, pushing her down the aisle. Only a few other people were in the car and no one had yet noticed Robert and Diana stumbling and shouting. Or else Robert was erasing them again.

"What's happening outside?" she asked.

"Come on!" he said, and took them toward the forward door, checking out the windows to his left as he ran.

"Robert, what is going on?" she asked again, trying to keep up. "What do you see?"

"An animal," he panted. "I can't believe it. I can't believe they brought that here."

"*What?*" she demanded.

"Wuln Vuln Drongplo. Tier 1 Private Equity. It's coming. It's the fucking...it'll rip this train..." Before he could finish, Diana felt the carriage shudder.

"What was that?" she cried. She saw other passengers stand and look out the windows. Then they all staggered as the car spasmed and rocked violently to the side.

The train was rounding a bend. Diana could see the cars ahead out the left side windows, a long curve turning like the inside of a sickle around the edge of a broad, empty field. She pulled Robert to a stop, her mind blank with amazement, as, four cars ahead, the entire carriage was yanked into the air by *nothing,* while the cars yoked in front and back clung but were wrenched up on their back wheels, throwing sparks. The middle car just floated for several seconds, and then their own car heaved savagely, throwing passengers to the walls and floor, Diana among them. Only Robert remained upright.

As she fell she saw the floating car, fifty feet off the ground, shaken one way and then another and then sent sailing—as if thrown —six hundred yards through the air, across a field, trailing people and other cars. Her own carriage spun off the tracks, pulled up to the sound of wheels grinding a maniacal shriek.

The floor tilted and the shrieking stopped and all she heard was whistling and clanking and the screams of passengers. They were airborne. Out the windows she saw land and sky spin, round and round, like she was in a giant rolling tire and she knew, with perfect certainty, that they were going to die.

"I'm sorry for this!" Robert yelled. She thought he was apologizing for getting her crushed and even in her panic she thought it was ridiculous.

He dissolved his human disguise. His cube was glued to the carriage floor and stayed that way even when they spun upside down and he hung in the air. She saw gluey tentacles form and extend toward her, felt them wrap around her waist and pull her up off the floor where she rolled. She found herself right up beside his cube, while the world rocked and swirled and he fought to keep her safe and the car spiraled through the air.

Her whole body was pressed tight against Robert's jello-cube side. She remained that way for part of a second and then, before she could stop it, she was sucked in through a tense surface membrane— pulled from the air into the jello, like a lollipop disappearing into a mouth.

It felt like missing a step on a stairway. A moment of free fall. And then she was gone.

Stuck inside the jello cube that was Robert, her body wanted to thrash and strike in panic but was held utterly motionless and bound in a stiff suit of solid wet. Sound vanished. So did air, her face sealed in a gel mask, with nothing to breathe. She felt the mask spread around her mouth and a tunnel formed from her lips toward the air outside the jello. When the tunnel reached the air, she gasped it in as if through a snorkel. She could see the world only as whirling, colored forms, blurry, as if observed through layers of semi-liquid plastic or wax.

Her stomach spun and flipped. The car pinwheeled through the air. She was cocooned motionless. Impressions came in snatches. An interval of weightless gliding. Like a bus falling off a cliff. A thud of impact. Squeals muffled by gelatin. Shapes— people, seats, pieces of luggage— flew past and then suddenly there was daylight and she realized the carriage had split open and was grinding over the field and breaking into pieces. There was a crushing impact as some obstacle struck them and then absolute stillness.

Robert wasted no time. She felt him—them—drop from the ceiling to the ground and emerge into sunlight. Inside the cube she felt squirming movement, as what passed for muscles within his tissue contracted then extended, swinging them rapidly away from the crash.

Patches of light and dark flew by. They were moving very quickly, but she had no sense of direction. And then, without warning, within a region of green and darkness where spots of light swayed—the shade under trees? —they stopped. Diana waited a moment for the rush and movement to start again, then tried to speak. It was awkward, but not impossible.

"Let me out!" she begged. Claustrophobia was settling into her chest now.

"I can't," she heard through tiny vibrations next to her ears. "The fucking thing is tracking your nano signature. If we're lucky, it thinks you're dead. My tissue is masking you. Oh fuck, Diana Roark. The fucking animals are here. Wuln Vuln Drongplo. They sent in *Private Equity!*"

She took a deep breath through her breathing tube and worked to still her panic. It was easier when she closed her eyes. It wasn't comfortable—she was pulled in strange directions, she had a cramp in her side, some of the goo was abrasive. But it was better than being dead.

Robert kept referring to Private Equity. *Tier 1 Private Equity.* Another species designation, she thought, like Appraiser, or Accountancy. In the world of earthly finance, private equity funds were the worst of the worst, investors in name only: the cruelest, most parasitic and rapacious of capitalists. They scoured the world for companies to target and acquire and then spent huge sums in hostile takeovers. They borrowed money, abusing the acquired companies and running them into the ground, until finally the dying business was broken into pieces and sold; the real estate beneath the stores, the merchandise on the shelves—whatever remained of value was shaken off the husk and sold, bit by bit, until it was gone. Careers lost. Lives shattered. While private equity grew fat with profit.

So, if there was some alien creature named after those equity funds—an animal, Robert kept saying—she did not want to meet it. She pictured the train car hanging in the air, turning one way and then another as if under examination, then cast across a field. This thing must be absolutely enormous.

"Why is it doing this?"

"Because everything I was fucking afraid of must be true! I told you none of this added up! They want to kill you before you activate your account! When you touched the pericarp and signed our agreement, I wrote that to the Blockchain. They'll know I told you everything. *They* know that *you* know about your debt and they don't want you to make your payment. They turned an animal loose and they don't care that everyone can see it—I can see it on the Blockchain right now! The whole fucking Known Economy knows they did this! It's fucking *much worse than I thought*."

Diana's mind whirled with alarm and not so much because she was being hunted by a huge, invisible monster. She was finding it very hard to contain the rising tide of claustrophobia trapped like this, unable to see or move, dependent on a tiny tube just to breathe.

"Robert," she protested, panic rising fast, "I can't stay in here!"

"You're going to have to," she heard. "I'll get us to Monterey. But we have to move fast, and you have to stay hidden. The only way to do it is to carry you."

And then they were moving again. Robert had said they needed to move fast and she knew that was true, but she hadn't known what that meant to a Neoooxcolu. Though the outside world was only a nebulous, multi-hued blur, she could see enough to judge their speed: faster than the train had ever traveled. She would never have guessed that Robert's morphology could move like this with nothing but pseudopods. She wondered what else he was capable of that she, the arrogant animal, had failed to suspect.

Her claustrophobia came in waves. She wanted to scream, to talk about the attack, to make a plan, to take control. But there was nothing she could do. Her discomfort increased, but there was no escape. Her brain began to drift, driven from her body to escape the terror of gel pressing in, immobilized limbs and nothing but a half-inch tube standing between her and asphyxiation. She grew torpid as gyrations strobed, a repetitive, hypnotic throb. Her eyes closed and she slipped into a state of half-dream, half-catatonia, stumbling back and forth through semi-lucid, semi-unhinged thoughts. She began to suspect that she was not alone. Something, someone, proceeded her here. There was something with her in this strange cockpit of foreign flesh.

Sliding into a dream, possibly *the* dream, she thought she heard a voice. Her eyes opened, gummy. With difficulty she turned her head, the gel resisting her movements. The tube respirating her moved even slower than her head, trailing an inch behind her mouth, but she got repositioned. And saw nothing.

But she heard something. Someone spoke. Was she hallucinating? Dreaming? The words came again. By this time her mind was so decoupled from her physical body she couldn't be certain what was real, whether it was a real sound or merely a thought—a wish for company, a fantasy.

[*She's moving again! 1*]

She jerked, certain this time. Not certain whether it was a voice or a thought or a fantasy, but certain it was words that had meaning. Something observed her.

who's there?

[*Giggles.*]

who's there? please? robert! robert!

[*She thinks we're Robert. 1*]

[*We are Robert. 2*]

[*Not like that. She thinks we're Big Robert. 1*]

[*Giggles.*]

hello? who is... is someone here? is someone near? i can't see you!
i can't see anything!

[*She's afraid.* 3]

[*Poor weird thing.* 4]

[*I think she's sweet.* 3]

[*Laughter.*]

A hot-soft-deep comfort suddenly spread over Diana, along every inch of her skin, from her toes to her stomach, from her fingertips to the small of her back. All the rough, continual, abrasive kneading was insulated away and in her mind she felt wrapped, enshrouded in the thickest, downiest fleece cloth the world had ever known.

And now there were almost-shapes sliding and twirling through the translucence around her. They were nothing more than thicknesses, fleeting and swift. A twist of the light. She couldn't turn her head to follow them. Something about the way they dove, then rose and twisted, made her think of seals playing and romping—twirling for the sheer joy of movement.

[*Look! Ahh. She's happy now.* 3]

who are you?

[*We're Robert's pod shrouds.* 1]

[*Who are you?* 2]

i'm diana. diana roark.

More swimming. More frolicking. Whoever they were, they'd forgotten her for a moment, but she did not mind. Her mood was changed. For the first time in many days — weeks? years? — she felt herself relax. So many questions occurred to her. She couldn't contain herself. She felt effusive. Buoyant.

you're a pod shroud? what's a pod shroud?

[*She doesn't know what a pod shroud is!* 2]

[*She's very stupid.* 1]

[*I love her.* 3]

[*I love her too.* 4]

[*Of course I love her too. But she's very stupid.* 1]

[*Yes, she is very stupid. But I do love her.* 2]

There were four of them. It was such a pleasure to be near them! She watched from the sides of her vision as they engaged in another round of swooping and she smiled. *Smiled.* Time passed, prismatic forms racing by outside the cube as Robert sped them down the coast. But the world outside now seemed like a very distant place. A foreign land that she fit into, better than anywhere ever. This was her world. This was where they loved her. She remembered her questions.

really, though. what's a pod shroud?

[*Giggles. More giggles.*]

[*She's stupid! I love her. Should we teach her? 3*]

[*Let's teach her! 4*]

[*I want to teach her. 2*]

[*I love her! Let's teach her. 1*]

The light from outside Robert's body dimmed completely, the way a movie theatre would and there was a similar sense of anticipation. She wasn't sure whether her eyes were open or closed. She wasn't sure of anything, and it didn't matter, all she knew was that her friends were happy. She had things to learn.

Robert was five thousand years old. They wanted her to know that five thousand was pretty old for a Neoooxcolu chox to still have all four pod shrouds. It took all three sexes, chox, tackeral and benzerth, to get together and make happiness. The pod shrouds from the chox could be wrapped around the pods from the tackeral and then the benzerth could pollenate. And then seedlings!

Robert had been born on the Neoooxcolu home world and had started as a very promising Accountant. He had specialized later in Forensic Accountancy and his fellow-field had been very proud. And when the ITC had selected him to come and support the Known Economy all the fellow-field had been sad but happy at the same time. Everyone thought Robert would soon find a tackeral and benzerth and make happiness.

But first he needed to do things to be a good mate, so everyone would see he was worth happiness. Robert was so dedicated. He tried to start right away. But the funny thing Robert discovered about the

ITC was that it didn't run very well. He did a few things to make it better. No one liked that. Then they assigned him his first job but it was a bad job and even though he finished without failing, he got a bad mark.

In the beginning Robert had been a very smiling Neoooxcolu. In all his fellow-field he had been most turned to the sun, always bright and facing up. But years went by at the ITC, and Robert stayed dedicated, but the ITC seemed not to like him. Poor Robert. He thought, if he just did his job better, suggested more good changes for the ITC to implement, found inefficiencies and told them, that everything would turn up toward the sun! He couldn't help himself and he knew it was the right thing to do. He was a Forensic Accountant. His job was to find numbers that didn't add up and figure out who was responsible.

They sent him farther and farther on assignments. They didn't let him do Accountancy anymore and demoted him to Account Representative. But still he tried to do the best job he could. After a while he realized that it had been hundreds of years since he had seen his fellow-field. And he got sadder and more unhappy and no tackerals or any benzerths would talk to him at all because they said he was angry and not at all upward facing. The ITC said he was a troublemaker. Who wouldn't be angry? He didn't want to be angry, but sometimes...sometimes he felt like he was the only one who cared about things being right, about numbers adding up. The only one in the whole Known Economy. It made him feel so lonely. He would never find mates.

But his pod shrouds never lost hope. Why would you lose hope? The sun always came up the next day. As long as the sun was there, there was a chance of happiness.

And then! Robert made a Choice! He made a change to the Neoooxcolu Choice Tree, and that made everything different. Now he would be famous and he could make happiness.

And then! Even better! Diana Roark came to live with them! They had never met anyone else before. Nothing had ever been as good as living with Diana Roark. Nothing! Life had never been so full of light. Diana Roark was so stupid! That was true. But she was the one they loved!

[*Why do you feel sad now, Diana Roark? 1*]

why would you love me?

[*Who wouldn't love you? 3*]

no one loves me.

[*How do you know? 1*]

[*Did you ask everyone? 2*]

i didn't earn it.

[*Silly! No one earns love. 1*]

[*It's not money. 2*]

[*You just get it. 3*]

[*Get it and get it and get it and get it like sun and water. 4*]

[*Silly, stupid, wonderful Diana Roark! 3*]

And then, before she could answer, before she could protest that she could never take something she hadn't earned, the trip was over.

It was sudden. Shocking. Horrible. Diana opened her eyes, or the lights came up in the theatre and she felt something rough yanking on her foot, pulling her away from her best friends. She felt rough ectoplasm, dragging against the skin of her cheeks and getting in her nose. She was choking. She was going away!

[*Goodbye Diana Roark! Tell Big Robert we are proud of him! 1*]

[*Face the sun Diana Roark! Face up! 4*]

[*You're silly and stupid. You're the best thing the world ever made! 2*]

[*We'll be your fellow-field. Remember we love you the most. 3*]

[*Don't forget! Tell Big Robert we're proud! 4*]

And then she fell out of acceptance, and warmth, out onto the cold, hard ground with a wet thud.

10

A hammer may be used to pound, but never upon itself. A knife to cut, but never its own blade. But the Known Economy creates a consciousness of completeness called the commercial Mind, and this is the most powerful tool of all. Not only can the commercial Mind be used to aim the hammer, and draw the knife, it is the only tool in existence which can be used upon itself. The commercial Mind can be used to remake the commercial Mind. In this lies the secret to all Profit.

—From *The Book of* Ω64, of the Swandeen Pracis

Diana lay on her back with her eyes closed and vacuumed in a breath, the first full breath in a long time. She shivered. She was damp. Lost. There was dirt beneath her hand, there were rocks in it, and they hurt. Not at all like... like what? Her jello home? It wasn't her home. It had been someplace... friends lived. It had been a gift.

She opened her eyes, Robert materializing above her. Sunlight struck her face, and she blinked and turned her head. She felt awful, like something a dog coughed up on a beach, like dead fish. Her legs were weak—her prosthetic foot hardly worked at all. She levered herself onto her functioning arm and stared.

They were on a low hill, within a stand of eucalyptus and below them ran a thin strip of highway. Beyond it stood the Roark Oceanic Institute astride a long spit of sand and coastal chaparral. The sand ran out into the water, pointing west into the Pacific sea. The complex looked very different than it had twenty-five years ago.

Where there had been a low collection of nondescript, government-issue laboratories and administrative buildings hunkered against the wind, there now was a glittering, PressureGlass bubble, rising in the afternoon sun. And in the ocean adjacent, what looked like a deep-water harbor, dredged and fortified. The harbor was empty but for a single long, slender craft, with huge polymer sails. They looked like butterfly wings, flexed up off the deck. Lizbeth had been very busy.

As her mind cleared she sat all the way up. Robert was once again a slightly unkempt biped.

"Is this it?" he asked.

She nodded and struggled to her feet and found her prosthetic leg at about fifty percent strength. She had the feeling it could fail completely at any moment; maybe it was trying to keep her dead arm company. She could have a collection of useless, paralyzed limbs all her own.

"I met them," she said softly.

"Who?" he asked.

"They're beautiful."

"What is?"

"Your pod shrouds. Your children to be." She watched his face to make sure she was not overstepping any boundaries. Cross-species communication—a minefield. She remembered how mad he'd been the first time she'd hesitated to drink his urine.

His eyes filled with sudden tears.

"You did?" he asked. He waited, pleading quietly for confirmation. "Are they... do they think about me? No, no. Never mind. I don't have any right to ask. I'm just... I failed them. I failed, is all."

"No." Diana smiled. "They're beautiful, Robert and all they

talk about is you. They're proud of you. Now that you changed your Choice Tree you can finally find your mates. And have seedlings."

He dropped heavily on the dry leaves and gazed at the sun and the waves and shook his head.

"It's too late for that," he said quietly. "I realized it on the way down. I never fit in at work. Or anywhere. I'm too fucking... I don't know. And now I'm expendable. That's why I'm here; I'm never getting off this planet alive." His expression was distant, soft as the waves washing up the distant beach. "I've always tried to do the right thing. I've always tried to face the sun. Make the numbers add up. But... the universe is fucked up, Diana Roark."

"What are you saying? Why won't you get off the Earth?"

"None of us will! The fucking Wuln Vuln Drongplo are loose! The Fund is going to repossess this planet, sell it to Private Equity and they're going to rip it to fucking pieces and suck every piece dry and there's nothing we can do about it. You can't fight them, Diana. They're animals."

She squatted down slowly until she could look into his face. She grabbed his shirt with her one hand, forgetting for a moment that it was only an illusion of a shirt.

"You know who else is an animal?" she breathed, pulling him close. "Me. I'm an animal. And I still own this planet."

He squinted. "You're an old lady. With cancer. And one arm. You don't stand a chance against Private Equity."

But Diana was deadly serious, in a way she hadn't been in a very long time.

"I got richer than anyone else on this planet feeling like I had nothing to lose. What a pointless waste. But now I *do* have something to lose. And listen to me, Robert the Alien; I choose *not* to lose it. You understand? I *choose* to keep it. And I choose you to help me. Because that's your job. I need Consumer Protection."

He snorted, but she held his eyes. He shook his head, but she wouldn't look away. And finally, he threw his hands up. "Fucking fine. Okay fine." He stood up. "Let's go look at your fucking Institute. I bet we'll totally be able to save the world with fish tanks."

She smiled at him from her position at his feet.

"Thank you." She cleared her throat. "Now help me up, my leg just completely stopped working." He rolled his eyes and held out his hand.

THE SIGHT they presented as they approached the paved entry to the Institute and the attached Museum of Nautical History was an odd one. Diana knew it; she could feel eyes upon her from within the building. A limping partly paralyzed elderly woman was an unusual sight in a world where no one else had so much as a pimple. They turned toward the Museum doors where the walkway split; their slow, conspicuous advance made Diana imagine a different set of eyes observing their progress—other animals seeking her. Hunting.

"I'm vulnerable to the Wuln Vuln Drongplo now, aren't I?" She gestured to his jello. "You're not masking me anymore."

"I'm spending emergency funds to hide you in the mesh at this moment. Your life is in danger. There's a line item for that. I could have done it when they attacked the train, but I saved us a lot of money doing what I did the way I did it." He sounded proud of himself. Diana could only hope there was enough money left in that particular account to hide her for another thirty hours.

They arrived at the wide entrance. The door handles were shaped like harpoons, but when Robert pulled them, he found the Museum locked. When they turned back, an Institute employee was hurrying up the path and when he got close, he froze, unable to hide his shock.

"Um, the museum is closed after 3," he said.

"I need to talk to Director Mustang," Diana croaked. "Tell Lizbeth her boss is here to conduct her three-decade performance review. That's Diana Roark." When she said her name, the boy—the man? For all she knew he could be a hundred years old— looked closer. His expression changed. He pulled out his phone.

"Stop!" she said.

"I'm calling the Director."

"No phones! Nothing on the network. No one can know I'm here."

He nodded, absorbing it quickly. Someone had trained this person very well. "My name is Chang. It's an honor to meet you, Ms. Roark. This way please."

He led them to the main facility and held the front doors open. The vaulted, glass-domed lobby was mostly empty, but within a few seconds it began to fill with people. Chang passed word that no one was to use devices. It felt as though every employee, scientist and research assistant in the entire Institute had gathered to watch her walk across the tiled foyer and wait for the elevator. It was like standing before a crowd of the Needless, until they began applauding.

The sound faded when Chang escorted them into the elevator and the doors closed, but it didn't disappear. She could hear it outside as they passed the second floor, heading to the third.

"What the fuck?" asked Robert.

"Just impressed to see an old lady hobble into a building, I guess," Diana said.

"No, Ms. Roark," Chang said. "They—we all—are... it's an extraordinary honor to meet you at last." He seemed unable to say more.

"They know who I am?"

"Of course. We all do. It's an extraordinary..."

She stopped him. "Ah, ok. That's good. Make sure no one gets on Facebook about this, right?"

"I'm hiding you in the mesh," said Robert. "I don't think..."

"I'm not worried about The Fund. Does the mesh include Facebook? Are you hiding me on social media? Because I guarantee you, Landerson has a worldwide digital dragnet in place, right now and I don't think I could handle another visit from Jianguo." Robert looked thoughtful. She guessed that the mesh did *not* include social media.

The elevator doors opened. Chang leapt out and called, "Code blue! No phones! Network silence, people! Everybody—code blue!"

Diana was impressed. There was a code? Only one mind that she could think of would have thought so far ahead as to put a network lockout into the standard operating procedures of a marine research facility. A mission control kind of mind.

A crowd was present on this floor. In the midst of the crowd stood a figure in high black boots, beads and bracelets on her arms and around her neck, with black hair wild as a feral horse: untamed, unrestrained.

Liz came slowly toward her, a shocked expression on her face and tears pouring down her cheeks.

"Jesus, Diana," she said softly. And she flew forward and they were embracing. Well, Liz was. Diana needed to hang onto Robert with her one arm to keep from falling.

"Diana," said her husky voice, the voice Diana remembered so well, even thirty years later.

"Liz," Diana said.

Liz looked down at her, a few inches taller. At one point they had been the same height. Diana wanted to look away.

"Charles kept telling me." Liz mastered her tears, but her throat kept gripping tight. "I tried to come."

"I'm here now."

"You came for the opening. Oh, Diana, look at you, I'm so..."

"Just stop. Please, Liz. I can't do this now."

Liz stepped back. She even smiled. She nodded and swept her hands wide.

"Okay. Well. Welcome to your Institute."

They stared at each other, the faces in the crowd watching them. Diana still thought of Liz sheathed in an almanac of tattoos. But here she was. Unmarked. Unmarkable.

"Come to the office," Lizbeth said. Diana shook her head.

"Liz, we don't have time. Can we go to the museum?"

"Now?"

"I'll explain. Let's walk." Without further question Lizbeth assented and they stepped into the lift. She motioned two people to join her, but Diana shook her head.

"Alone," she insisted. "And please remind everyone, my presence has to remain secret."

"They've been told," Lizbeth growled. "My people don't talk. They're mostly post-augmentation babies, you know. But our program finds them young. It turns out, if you catch them early and teach 'em, the Needless are almost normal."

Diana couldn't help it. She stared at Liz. *Normal.* Was Liz normal? She wasn't stabbing herself in the eye or chomping on a whole deer. She stood, relaxed, steady and smooth as a coiled snake. Did she not have ticks?

As the elevator doors closed and they dropped to the bottom floor, Lizbeth was frank in appraising Diana. She measured her with the dusk soft eyes Diana remembered so well, the eyes she'd first seen behind a pair of protective goggles in the material science lab at MIT.

"This is Robert, by the way," Diana said. Liz acknowledged and dismissed Robert in a glance. She only had eyes for Diana.

"How long do you have?" Lizbeth finally asked.

"I don't know," Diana said. "A few days... doesn't matter. Long enough."

Together the three of them limped Diana out of the Institute. She tried to think of where to begin the explanation she needed to give to Liz. She didn't even know if she would find what she was looking for here. Didn't know if she wanted to find it. But her silence didn't seem to bother Lizbeth in the least. She walked a few steps ahead while Diana leaned on Robert for support, and reached the doors with the harpoon handles. "Open," she murmured, then pushed them aside. Voice-activated locks. *Old tech or new?* Diana and Robert followed her in.

"Just a warning," Lizbeth said before she threw on the lights.

"The design evolved a bit over the years, until we came to this. Just happened naturally."

And then the lights came on and Diana saw a huge portrait of herself, suspended from the ceiling. In it, she was dressed in a bright yellow jumpsuit. Her hair, a glorious red, was blowing across her cheek and clouds towered behind her. Her green eyes were fixed on something very far away, something beyond the horizon. She hung from a ladder on the deck of a ship, and below her the crew, frozen and staring upwards, waited to be told what she had seen. And under the portrait were the words, *Diana Roark: The Debt We Owe.*

Diana looked at Lizbeth in confusion and Lizbeth raised her brows in what was, she saw, a challenge.

"You told me I could do whatever I wanted," she said. She dared Diana to deny it.

Diana could only shrug and frown.

Lizbeth held her arms forward, pinned together, the way a prisoner might, begging to be unshackled. The trinkets on her arms clicked and swung, the only sound in the building.

"When my mom died," Lizbeth said, staring down at the bare skin of her forearms, "I was only ten. A street kid. I started the ink for her; I had her name, Dragisia, on this arm, in black and red. And I just... kept going. All the things I wanted to remember, I wore 'em. I wanted something permanent. It kept me sane. But then those ass-fingered aliens came and took it all away."

She met Diana's eyes.

"They took my memories, Di. Stole 'em, the bastards. Right off my skin. They left us here on this whore shit planet, not a memory to be found. Whitewashed. But the world needs a fucking past! We owe it to the dead. And I can't get a god damn tattoo to save my life. So, I made this." Lizbeth threw a thumb over her shoulder at the hung placard and beyond that, to the tastefully lit interior of the vast space.

"Some people cut themselves, Diana. Eat, pull, pick themselves apart. But I do this. No one's going to remember my mom. They sure as shit won't remember me. But they'll remember you, Di. I'm going to make sure of that."

Could it be true, Diana wondered? Was Liz's tick... Diana herself?

The interior of the museum was divided in two. One side was devoted to the trappings she might have expected in a navel museum, ships and sea history. There were roman galleys cut in half, depictions of cultural diasporas that had expanded and contracted across the seas, naval warfare, exploration.

The other side seemed to be all Diana Roark, as far as the eye could see. She limped through the gallery, approaching each fresh installation with trepidation, like the next of kin called to identify not one, but a hundred different bodies, the remains of some devastating tsunami. Here was the natural disaster of her life, cataloged, labeled, and organized. But all of it had been slanted, somehow, to appear laudatory and selfless and successful.

Images of her mother. Her heart rose. Publicity pictures, but also photos that Lizbeth's archivists had found elsewhere — mother holding her tiny hand as they walked a mountain path. Feeding her with a happy spoon. Pictures of Phoebe. The two of them, explanatory placards detailing their upbringing, and a corner devoted to the kidnapping that had wrecked her family. She almost couldn't go on. The tears had come back now. It was no easier to cry; in fact, it felt harder. But now there was a furrow worn inside her where they bubbled forth.

She kept walking and was told about her remarkable early achievements in blockchain theory, the papers published, the patents. There were lists of every hospital she ever endowed, every program underwrote, every illness ever researched. A single section examined the death of her father and her own struggle to retain control of her company. She could only stare and wonder who it had been behind those eyes. Who had that woman been who had wrought such things on the world?

Then the Swarm. The Augmentation. And the Roark Philanthropic Foundation with her humanitarian achievements and her awards, how she had been considered the foremost humanitarian of the twenty-first century. It was too much. Her years making her fortune. The Seer of Sonoma. *Always that.* Claustrophobia began to close around her.

But Diana understood that the gallery was guiding her inward to some curated, penultimate exhibit. She couldn't even limp now, her leg a stiff board. Robert practically carried her. She kept onward, inward, because what else was there at this point? Until she came around a final turn where the secret heart of the museum waited.

Namaka.

At the very center of the vast interior, lit blue and green and golden in watery bands down the walls and floor: Spear One.

Diana stopped. Lizbeth had actually done it. She'd dropped secret clues in her text, Urging Diana to come to the inauguration to see a *special display.* In her heart she'd known. It had to be this.

After they had lifted her from the water, nearly dead and red with blood, they had sealed up Spear One. And saved it. Diana limped around its base, ignoring the images and the displays. She gazed at her submersible. It looked to be in perfect condition, the PressureGlass capsule unscarred, of course, and the fiberglass housing complete, though much cracked. The batteries were missing and the ballast. But everything else was present.

Lizbeth watched her, arms folded.

"Will she still dive?" Diana asked.

Lizbeth uncrossed her arms. She cocked her head and narrowed her eyes. Not the question she'd been expecting, it appeared. Diana turned to Robert.

"This is the only chance we have," she explained to him. "It's what I took down the first time."

He nodded and examined the capsule carefully. Diana turned back to Lizbeth.

"Listen to me, now, Lizbeth. We have less than a day and a half to get this sub in the sea. Can you do it?"

It took five long seconds before Lizbeth decided what she thought about *that* question. There was no rushing this conversation, though every single second was likely to count.

"In the sea for what?" Lizbeth asked, carefully neutral.

"I need to..." Diana could not believe that she was going to say it. "I have to go back. Into the Trench."

"In Spear One," Lizbeth said.

"It's the only way."

"The only way for what?"

"To stop, oh god, what's going to happen."

"You want to die underwater? One last sendoff?"

"No. It's a real mission."

"What kind of mission?"

"It's so complicated. I'll tell you. But first—can she dive?"

"You can barely walk, Diana."

"Yeah, well. The ride is one hundred percent sitting. So."

"Tell me you're not serious ... are you?"

"I can't do this without your help."

"It's a thirty-year-old rig, Di. So, no. She can't dive. And if she could, it's a one-way death trap."

"One way's fine. All I have to do is get there. Getting back's not important. Wouldn't even matter."

Diana was leaning against the boarding ladder, her back against the sub, using it to keep herself upright. She hadn't figured out how to start the explanation yet. Lizbeth stepped closer but stopped a foot away and stared at Diana.

"The answer is no. No batteries. No dive weights. The hydraulics are dry. The nav boards—who knows if they were working after you blew up at the bottom of the ocean the first time and crapped out under my boat!"

"The capsule will hold, Liz. PressureGlass could be a thousand years old and I'd trust it. Throw a respirator in there. Hang some ballast on a net and tie it up. All I have to do is hit the floor."

"Honestly, Diana. You look like shit on a bone grill. I'm sorry to be blunt, but I guess I'm the grown up here." Diana remembered someone else saying that, once long ago. Lizbeth turned to Robert suddenly. "Is this quiet little dog fucker making you do this?"

"He's my associate," Diana said. "He's helping with this... project."

Lizbeth stepped closer to Robert, her eyes flashing menace. "Is this your idea, you slimy pig fuck? What is it, blackmail? Are you drugging her? I know she's not Augmented. Drugs? Psychotropics?" She glared back at Diana, giving that idea serious consideration, then whipped back to Robert. "You know, the second I saw you, I wanted to shove a hot poker up your ass. I don't like your eyes."

Robert raised his brows and looked at Diana but said nothing. Diana could understand exactly how Lizbeth must feel. There was only one way to skip all the arguing and move the discussion to the next stage.

"He's an alien," Diana said.

"I don't care."

"An outer space alien... you know. God damnit." She sighed. "Robert, show her."

It was a few seconds before Robert moved. Diana imagined that he might have to go a long way back on his Choice Tree to get this one right, but after a moment he nodded.

As they watched, his khaki wearing, schlumpy-looking number cruncher façade began shimmering and distorting, one image overlaid over the other for the briefest of seconds, until suddenly an ominously huge, alien shrubbery on a translucent jiggling cube was in front of them. Even Diana gave a little gasp, still not used to his real form.

To Lizbeth's credit, she didn't run. She met the apparition with the same attitude she used on hundred-foot waves, PressureGlass formulas and recalcitrant submarine pilots: you can't fix a problem unless you understand it. She didn't move and she didn't speak. *Perfect.* So, while she was quiet, Diana filled her in on the details, a huge data dump, up to and including Landerson's crazy plans, while Liz stood without taking her eyes off of Robert.

Finally, she was done. Lizbeth still didn't move. Diana asked Robert to transform back, and only then did Lizbeth turned her eyes toward Diana, unwilling to face away from Robert.

"We trust him?" she asked, her voice steady.

"Yes," Diana said. And just like that, Lizbeth accepted Robert. She turned to the sub and took a long, slow walk around it, deep in analysis, reappearing on the other side.

"I can get her ready."

Diana almost collapsed with relief. She turned to Robert.

"How long will it take to move the sub over the drop site?" she asked him.

"What drop site?" he asked back.

"The...you know, the drop site." He didn't understand. "Above the Obelisk? Under the ocean? To put this submersible into the water?" He was shaking his head. "So I can go and make the payment... what?"

"The fuck, Diana Roark? What do I look like, a fucking container ship? I can't move this anywhere. *Especially* not out into the ocean; it's a big poisonous bowl of piss."

"But how are we going to move it?"

"I thought you had a plan."

"I did. You were it."

Diana felt cold dissolve over her chest like she'd been hit by a nitrous pendulum. She had presumed too much. In all her planning, with so little time left, she had simply assumed that Robert would be able to transport the sub. The Marianas Islands were over five thousand miles away. Ship-based transport would take weeks.

Realization broke that they would never make it. Whether or not Spear One worked was immaterial. They had no way to get it to the site.

"That's it, then," she murmured. "We're finished."

The three of them gazed at each other in silence.

"I have something to show you," Lizbeth said, stirring as if from a dream. "Come with me."

She left the Namaka gallery. Robert helped Diana follow. Diana found that most of her remaining strength had deserted her. She was leaning more and more on Robert, as the path forward faded.

They found Lizbeth standing at the end of the Timeline of Nautical History, past nuclear subs, beyond carbon fiber trimarans. She waited for them below a model of a strange, lean, corkscrew shaped craft, part submersible, part catamaran. The display was titled, simply, *The Black Marlin*. Above the ship rose two odd, delicate butterfly sails. They were the sails she'd seen in the harbor adjacent to the Institute. How the wings could possibly be used as sails escaped Diana, however, since they were fastened fore and aft to the craft's hull and could never be turned into the wind.

"My baby," Lizbeth purred.

"What is it?"

"A prototype. The ship of the future. For one thing, it's fully autonomous. She drives herself, if you need her to."

"Liz ... why are you showing me this?"

"This placard's long-winded," Lizbeth admitted, pointing to the explanatory material. "But here's the short version; the Black Marlin's the fastest ship ever built. She travels just below the surface. Aqua dynamics modeled on the real Black Marlin, world's fastest fish. This," she tapped an infographic, "says she goes about 100 knots per hour. But she's a hell of a lot faster than that. Just didn't see any reason to get more specific."

"How fast?" Diana asked.

"She and her sister, Green Marlin, could get from here to the Marianas in six hours."

It was several moments before Diana trusted herself to speak, hope trickling back in.

"Well. You *have* been busy," she said, gazing at the Black Marlin's sleek form.

"That's what you pay me for," Lizbeth agreed, slowly smiling.

LIZBETH HAD CREATED and trained the most efficient, intelligent corps of sailor scientists the world had ever seen, Diana decided. It quickly became obvious that they were even better than the Namaka crew. Lizbeth pulled a handful into a private briefing. They were introduced to Robert's real appearance, then given broad instructions: within twelve hours, move Spear One aboard the Black Marlin, wired with pressure-resistant batteries in quick-chop banks, stock her with emergency respirators and test all systems. If done on schedule, they'd arrive at the drop site with a three and a half hour window to do a ninety-minute dive. Cutting it close, but it was doable.

Diana kept herself out of the way. She was exhausted, and there was nothing she could do to speed the work. She watched the interior launch bay from an upper office as Black Marlin and Green Marlin were readied for sea—the decision had been made to crew both ships, just in case. And then, six hours into the twelve hour watch, she felt a deadly familiar knot build in her leg.

Over the course of an hour it spread, pushing through her every fiber, worse than ever before. Every time was worse than the last; eventually, it would become so unbearable that her brain would stagger and quit beneath the load.

Lizbeth found her stiff in her cot when she came to deliver an update. She sat down and pulled Diana onto her lap. She stroked Diana's cheek and caressed her arm until she came to the butterfly.

"I told you once you'd regret this. I hope you never did. Regret it I mean."

"Not a day."

Liz nodded. She kissed Diana's burning forehead.

"I think I like your new friend," she whispered, smiling.

"Who's that?" Dry mouth.

"Robert. He told me *all* about your trip."

"Oh."

"Diana. Sweet light. For the love of god," even through her own pain Diana saw the pain in Liz's eyes...so much pain, "were you really going to go? On that beach? And never say goodbye?"

"It's been a long time, Liz. I figured ... I don't know. What's the point of goodbye?"

"God. Diana."

"Ok, goodbye. Happy?"

"And Charles. I was so sorry to hear about Charles."

"I couldn't say goodbye to him." She would regret it for the rest of life. It would have to live in the queue behind all the other regrets. "I didn't know he was dying."

"Robert thinks you're some kind of special." She stroked Diana's hair. "I think he thinks you're badass."

"He doesn't know what he's talking about."

Liz watched her, tears streaming. "I love you, Diana. Do you know? I never stopped. I'm actually obsessed with you."

Diana thought about the Diana Roark gallery, the massive photos, the intimate placards.

"No one would ever be able to tell," she wheezed.

Liz choked a laugh. Diana gave her voice a serious edge.

"Look, Liz, I have an idea for the ballast release."

"What idea?"

"Skip the release. Save time and complexity. *Look at me.*"

"No, Diana. Very no. We're prepping release. You're coming back up."

"One way is all that matters. Time..."

"Why won't you heal, though? When you connect to the Obelisk?"

It was so hard to talk. She shook her head.

"Different networks," she breathed. "The Fund gave humanity access to the mesh through their own Obelisks and specialized nano machines in our atmosphere. Trillions of programmable quantum fabricators give you anything you can pay for. But Earth only has one native Obelisk. It connects to our Currency, but not to the Mesh. So. One way's really fine."

"So basically, we get a pile of money, but we can't buy anything?"

"We can buy our freedom."

A tech came to the door and motioned for Liz before hurrying away. Liz rose but stopped at the door.

"Those days at MIT, when the three of us were together? Those were the best years of my entire fucking life. I think about him, you know. Greg. I loved how fast his mind was. Like lightening." Lizbeth paused, thinking. Or pretending to think. She knew perfectly well what she was going to say. "What about you? Why did you love him?"

Diana didn't have to think about it. She knew that answer. *Easy.*

"He made me laugh."

Liz nodded.

"Yeah. He wasn't at all funny, you know."

"I know."

Liz was being pulled out of the room, but she couldn't leave. She had to ask.

"And what about me?"

"My god, Lizbeth, don't you all have perfect memories? Why do you make me do this?"

"Just tell me."

Diana cast her mind back down all the long years, the hours together and the connection. There had been such a connection.

"Because you made me horny."

Liz stared at her for a long second. Then flashed a wide, white smile.

"Just wanted to hear you say it," and she was gone.

Diana rolled in and out of delirium after that for another two hours. It was easier to let her mind go. Escape. Just like old Atticus. The human body has a built-in escape mechanism for this kind of experience; she had seen it in operation. Atticus had succumbed, loss of consciousness. She drifted closer and closer herself.

Then she felt hands lift and carry her to the loading area.

Time to ship.

The loading bay was a warehouse built out over the quays. The massive doors stood open and starlight from the western sky cast a cold luminance on the slips where Black Marlin and Green Marlin lay, high in the water. The floor of the bay was ordered chaos, a giant game of pick-up sticks; girders and beams, ropes and cable, boxes, crates, netting, and forklifts scurrying everywhere, stowing provisions within the sleek ships.

They set Diana on a cot. Lizbeth, Robert and another woman approached. Diana tried to sit up. Lizbeth didn't tell her to stop, though Diana could see she wanted to.

"Diana," Lizbeth said, "this is Captain Cybil Donaldson. She's taking Green Marlin with a support crew. You and Robert'll come with me in Black Marlin. We're crewed to deploy the Spear, she's aboard and ready."

"Nice to meet you, Captain," Diana rasped, extending her hand. Cybil reached to shake, but halfway there she froze and gaped over Diana's shoulder. Shock transfigured her face, pink to white. The warehouse had grown very still. Diana levered around and looked behind her.

Robert, in full purple glory, towered.

Panic flared through the bay. Only a few people had seen Robert this way and even they were jolted by his sudden appearance. Shouts rang; people dropped tools and scattered.

"Robert!" Diana yelled. Or tried too. It came out an indistinct croak.

"Get your ass covered back up!" Lizbeth shouted at Robert, then turned to the bay yelling orders. Captain Donaldson had been in the earlier meetings and had seen Robert, but still she stood poised a hair from flight.

"Robert," Diana tried again, "for god sake, mask it!"

"Diana Roark," issued his voice. "I fucking *can't*. Someone just zeroed my account." Diana's mind was stuck. Robert explained. "ITC just figured it out. They're in on it, them and The Fund together. They cut me off. We're fucked, Diana Roark."

"Ok. It's inconvenient. But..."

"Don't you fucking see? I have no funding! None! You're visible! They suspected I had you masked. They pulled my funding so you'd fall clear!" He paused, accessing his Choice Tree or some other set of sensors, or something. "The Wuln Vuln Drongplo is coming," he said, his voice low and trembling. "It's coming for us *right now.*"

Lizbeth returned, still bellowing instructions. She caught the fear in Robert's voice.

"What's wrong now?" she asked.

"We have to go Liz." Diana said. A sick surge powered her and she pushed herself from the cot with her one arm and tried to face the Black Marlin.

"Diana Roark," Robert said. "At sea, on land, we can't hide anymore. They found us." The translation app must still be working, Diana thought, otherwise his voice could not have sent chills through her body.

"Look, just put me back in," she pointed at his cube. "Mask me, like last time."

"They know that trick now. If your Nano Sphere pops off the mesh, there's only one fucking place you could be hiding. They'll find me and rip me to pieces. They will anyway. Oh shit. Oh, fucking shit, Diana Roark."

Lizbeth was looking at Diana for an explanation. "Other aliens," Diana said, her breath tight again. It was hard to talk, pain rushing through her like a river of jagged glass. "Tracking my Nano Sphere..." she attempted a gesture with her broken prosthetic to indicate the field of tiny particles around her. On top of all her other problems, she had this god damn useless arm to drag around and the leg which barely worked—she'd be better off without either of them!

She froze. *Wait.* She pushed through the fog clouding her mind. Something—her arm and leg. Her Nano Sphere. *Oh, think,* she groaned past the pain. *Think!*

It came to her in pieces. *Jianguo. Jianguo kidnapped me. Made me get undressed. The Landerson Field. Jianguo had me undress because... the Landerson Field disincorporated anything... what exactly had he said? Anything not impregnated with the particulate cloud of a human Nano Sphere...*

Blows up or gets disincorporated.

Her robot limbs had passed that test.

Bioelectric energy seeps into wedding rings and favorite necklaces and fillings; her Nano Sphere must have spread, through all those years of exposure, to penetrate her inanimate limbs. Her limbs must look exactly like the rest of her, infused with her Nano Sphere.

"She's exposed!" Robert was screaming at Lizbeth. "There's nothing I can do!"

Institute crew stood dumbfounded seeing the giant alien scream at their boss. Diana lay on the cot in the middle of it all, a calm place inside her. She nurtured it. *Can I remember the code?* Her mind focused back, her mind without perfect Augmented recall, striving to remember the kinesaudio password they had given her, all those years ago, during therapy after the hospital. She could almost picture the sequence. Only to be used, they'd said, in the most extreme emergency.

She ran it several times in her head, the gestures and the words, and then she swept her right hand over her dead arm and dead leg and muttered the phrases. And gasped.

Her left arm fell off. A moment after that her right leg, from the calf down, dropped to the floor. Emergency dislocation, they called it. In case of catastrophic malfunction; fire, electrocution. She hadn't imagined how unbalanced she'd feel, minus her pieces. She toppled from the cot.

The absence wasn't painful. It was cold and immensely strange and had the benefit of silencing Robert and Lizbeth. Lizbeth cried out and lifted Diana back to the cot. Distress pulled her mouth into a hard circle. *So many parts gone now,* Diana thought. *Shirt sleeve and pant leg just empty flags.*

"Robert," Diana gestured him close. She could only whisper.

"The prosthetics. They have my signature. My Nano Sphere. You have to... put me back inside. And then take the prosthetics away."

"How?"

"Green Marlin. Fastest ship on Earth," she whispered. "Fully autonomous. Send her out with my leg and arm and no one aboard."

Lizbeth shook her head. "Green Marlin doesn't have the autonomous systems yet. The Black's the prototype."

"Put my limbs in the Black."

"We *can't*, Spear One's already on the Black! It took three hours to get it stowed. We don't have time!"

Lizbeth, still kneeling, took a deep breath. She bent close to Diana.

"I'll do it. This makes sense now. I can buy you time," she said.

Diana's disorientation was growing.

"Buy what?"

"I'll be the decoy." Lizbeth turned to look up at Cybil. "You're Captain of the Black now. Get these people moving." She gathered Diana's limbs from the floor and stood, like a goddess of war bearing grisly trophies.

"What are you doing, Captain?" Cybil asked.

"I'm taking Green Marlin. I can pilot her alone." She looked at Diana. "I finished the retrospective, Di. What am I supposed to do now? Just remember me. Remember for all of us."

No one else moved.

"Private Equity will fucking destroy that ship," Robert said quietly.

"Captain, let me..." Cybil began.

"Let's *go*, monkeys!" Lizbeth bellowed. Then she was running toward the pier. "Move!"

They moved. Diana was confused. Her plan was in motion, that much was clear, but she wasn't sure she was getting what she wanted. Pseudopods reached her, lifted her. She could feel her body's bizarre new balance and counterbalance. Bit by bit, she would disappear. Chopped into smaller and smaller pieces.

Then she felt stiff-soft resistance against Robert's cube, and then the pop of transition.

Inside, where sound vanished and colors blurred, she drew weak breaths through a tube. She watched a shape she thought was Lizbeth disappear into shadow. She felt the draw and grind of Robert moving and could see she was headed to the Black Marlin. They were on the deck beside it.

Then the sky broke open, black shapes falling from the ceiling and Robert spun violently and dropped. And then nothing.

11

Which is the truer sky: the sky filled with driving rain or the sky still with fog? The peaceful sky? The sky torn by wind? None are truer. They are all sky, with many faces. Likewise, there is but a single job, wearing many masks. A stakeholder is commissioned for a task, and earns compensation, not based on time spent or labor exerted on a job, but for choices made in commission of it. The only job is the job of choosing. Every job is the same job.

—From *The Book of* Ω64, of the Swandeen Pracis

She woke up late in the day. Around her the fellow-field stretched toward the horizon, a beautiful fellow-field of Neoooxcolu, happy and warm and above them the sun, handing down sweet syrup, golden red and warm and endless. She had a feeling she couldn't remember ever having. Provided for. Providing. Pleasure ran through her. Surrender to the whole, yet still, somehow, differentiation. Not a hint of pain. There should be pain. *Shouldn't there be pain?*

Thoughts swept the fellow-field like wind as Diana and her field mates carried forward ancestral conversations. Thoughts, combinations, life, propagation. Comfort. Acceptance. Love.

The sun set and rose and years passed and she grew toward the sun, because its sweetness was a kind of gravity. A contract. It provided, as long as she stretched; so, she did.

Then high above, she saw a cloud. The more she grew, the closer she got to the cloud, until she had risen far above her fellow-field. Soon she would touch the cloud and pass through it to whatever lay beyond.

[*What is she doing?* 3]

[*She is leaving.* 4]

[*Diana Roark, stop.* 1]

[*Don't leave the happiness, Diana Roark.* 2]

But Diana couldn't stop. She needed whatever lay behind the cloud. She grew higher.

[*Stop, stupid-funny Diana Roark!* 4]

She could see it all below her, could see she was different. The fellow-field knew everything-together. But she was not a many. She was a one, a stronger-alone.

[*You mean a stronger-together.* 2]

[*Stop having your aloneliness!* 3]

She reached the cloud and grew through it and came out the other side into pain.

Diana woke for the second time, very swiftly, and the fellow-field snapped away behind her. Now she was in a world she knew. There was no fellow-field. Not for her. She was curled in a fetal ball and there was gel around her and a tube in her mouth.

[*We don't understand.* 1]

understand...

[*You left our dream.* 1]

that dream makes me weak.

[*Silly Diana Roark. You have a disease.* 2]

cancer.

[*No, aloneliness! Let us help you.* 4]

She came fully awake and remembered the loading bay. Black Marlin. Dismembering herself. Robert absorbing her. Lights moved now, outside Robert's cube. So, they had done it? They'd escaped? How long had she been sleeping? Where were they now?

[*Let us dream you back. 2*]

[*Into togetherness! 4*]

a fellow-field is just a crowd. there's no wisdom in a crowd.

[*Of course there is! Silly, stupid Diana Roark! 2*]

She could feel them, pulling her down. They wanted her to disappear and be happy.

[*Let us help you! 4*]

stop, please. that makes me weak. togetherness is weak. humans are strongest when they're alone. leave me alone!

Around her she could see the pod shrouds as they flitted, X-ray negatives on the film of Robert's tissue cube, diving, rising, so deeply concerned. Come play! Slide down! Join! Become part!

stop.

[*But why? 2*]

[*We can have happiness! 4*]

[*You don't have to be lonely. Silly Diana Roark. 3*]

loneliness is the price I pay.

[*I love her. She is a stupid love thing. I love her to sadness. 2*]

[*What does she have to pay for? 1*]

[*What are you buying, silly Diana Roark? 4*]

solutions. solutions to unsolvable problems. humans in fellow-fields are weak. they accomplish the most when they're alone.

[*That is very sad and stupid. 3*]

i have to be alone to do impossible things.

[*What? You have one leg and one arm and cancer. 1*]

[*You can't even walk around alone. You fall over onto the ground! 2*]

[*Giggles, images of Diana Roark falling over onto the ground, FUNNY!*]

[*We don't want you to be a stupider version of Diana Roark, Diana Roark. You are already too stupid. 3*]

[*Just stay here with your best friends in happiness. 4*]

The sinews in Robert's cube tightened and pulled so she knew they were moving. She had to stay awake. Alert.

Then she heard Robert's voice, that little vibration in her ear.

"Diana Roark. We're here."

She expanded her lungs slowly and pushed her words out the tube. Word drops. A thin stream. A few at a time.

"The drop ... site?"

"This Captain says the Spear's in the chamber, ready to go."

"Ok. Time to... board."

"The Fund will find you three minutes after I disgorge you."

"Then get in... with me."

"No room, Diana Roark." Though his voice was tiny and distant, she heard the desperation in it. "I don't know how the fuck to get you into that submarine. It's too small for me. But if you get in alone, you won't make it down. You're a sitting duck in there."

"Drop me. What other ... choice? Put me in. Drop me."

Diana could feel herself sliding back out of consciousness. She fought it, fought to stay lucid, to solve this one last problem. She'd solved all the others. Alone was fine. She could do this. But only if she ... only if she ...

[*We can help.* 1]

[*Diana Roark, you are our best and only friend.* 3]

And then she passed out, losing consciousness just a few minutes shy of surmounting this one last obstacle.

———

SHE WOKE AGAIN, into cold this time. Around her it was dark, though smeared points of a blue glow bobbed before her eyes. No, the lights weren't moving. It was her head—down and up, a lolling sweep, a come awake jerk.

Sticky film coated her eyes. That's what smeared the blue lights. But when she reached to clear her vision nothing happened. She remembered; *armless.* A strap crossed her chest and held her in a webbed seat. *Ah ha.*

Her pain was gone, but she was so weak. And wet. *Again.* She reached to clear her eyes with the hand that actually existed, but her fingers were coated with the same sticky slime. She swiped patiently, digits like windshield wipers, until her eyes were clear; she was strapped into the capsule of Spear One, the dim console before her, while outside the dome, bioluminescent specks, life forms too small or distant to identify, swept up and away.

They must have placed her, unconscious, into the Spear and dropped it. It was a pretty desperate move, but they'd done it. She tried to smile in appreciation but she didn't have the strength. Someone up there was admirably hard-hearted. Cybil? Lizbeth had trained her scientists well.

Lizbeth. She had no strength for that, either. But she knew what must have happened. Lizbeth and her sacrifice. One last voyage. A decoy. Diana felt herself falling just a little bit faster.

There was a tiny beep in the cold cabin, repeated at regular intervals, coming from the console. The comm. She tripped a display and saw a message. Robert's flat voice issued out.

"Diana Roark. I'm recording this as they strap you into the sub. We don't know if you're going to wake up. There's no fucking time left and all we can do is hope. It's 2:17 now. Payment due by 5:55. There's a countdown timer in your sub. Now, a couple of things..."

She heard shouts in the background and metallic clanging. It was hard to tell, but the boarding ladder slipping free was her best guess. The latch had always been finicky. Then Robert was speaking again.

"There are a couple of things you should know. Ah, first, once you're in range, the Obelisk will automatically connect with your Nano Sphere. You'll know it when it happens, believe me. So then, making the payment. I strapped the pericarp in there with you. Look down, to your right."

Diana tried, but her belt stopped her. She tried to loosen it but her hand kept slipping. What was this goop all over her? She slipped a few inches loose and looked toward her feet. Yes. The pericarp, webbed to the capsule wall, barely visible in the glow coming off the console. A timer was clipped to the webbing.

"So, once you activate your account, all you have to do is touch the pericarp. The pericarp manages the transaction, writes the payment to the Blockchain, everything. Simple. Also, um ... something else." There was a new note in his voice, something she'd never heard before. A burr. Was he crying? Almost crying? Trying not to cry?

"My... when I disgorged you, I... my pod shrouds..." he was clearly weeping. He got his voice under control and continued.

"My pod shrouds insisted on going with you. To keep you hidden. They have my Nano signature. So, ah, they're wrapped around you. They can't talk. They... they said you were... best friends. Diana Roark. I don't deserve to ask. But all I ever had was hope that... bring them back. They are children. Please. They won't last long the way they are."

There was another ringing clang and cursing and the message ended.

She checked the timer: two hours forty-seven minutes. There hadn't been enough battery to wire everything functional, so the scopes were offline; she had no idea how long she'd been falling, but knew she was falling with, at best, 32% of nominal power. They had decided to rely on the short-range scanners; when she got within five hundred meters they were supposed to pick up the bottom.

She was aware now of the sopping layer of plasm that coated her from head to toe. When she concentrated, she could feel them moving, inching over her skin like cream drifting unstirred through a cup of coffee.

Drifting. Down. She closed her eyes and fell.

DIANA IS SEVEN. *Phoebe is fifteen. Tomorrow the family will drive Phoebe to the airport and she will leave for school.*

"Why do you have to go?" Diana asks.

They are in a house made of blankets and chairs in Phoebe's room. It has been a while since Phoebe built one of these for them to play in. Phoebe has so many important things to do now. It's dark in the house and warm and they have a flashlight and a tea set.

"I'll come back, Didi. It's not forever."

Diana pretend drinks. She looks to make sure Phoebe is pretend drinking too. Her sister has red hair, just like she does. Phoebe finishes her tea. Diana pours her more.

"Ten million dollars," she says. Phoebe hands over the money and Diana records it in pencil in a little account book. Diana thinks Phoebe looks sad. Even though Phoebe is denying it, it seems like Phoebe thinks it really will be forever.

"Why are you sad then?" Diana asks.

"I'm not."

"What are you then?"

"Thinking."

"About what?"

Phoebe puts her teacup down on the table like an elegant queen. She does it right. Phoebe does everything right. Diana knows for certain Phoebe is not just thinking, because she is crying. She takes Diana's face in her hands.

"Didi, I just want you to know, I'm going to fix it."

"Fix what"

"I'm not going to let anything happen to you."

That seems right. Phoebe looks out for her. Diana looks out for Phoebe. If there are spiders, Diana will get them, because she's not afraid of spiders. But this seems like something else.

"What's going to happen to me?"

"Nothing at all. Listen. Daddy's a very good daddy. But sometimes grownups get confused."

"Is that what you're thinking about?"

"I'm going to stop him being confused. I'm going to make sure he

doesn't hurt anyone. I'm going to fix it. Ok? And you'll always be safe. We all will."

It seemed pretty straightforward to Diana. That's the way the world was supposed to work. Big sisters protected little ones. No big deal.

"I'm going to fix it once I get back from school," Phoebe says, leaning away into the dark tent. And disappearing.

DIANA WOKE UP. The world had turned again. More things that had meant one thing now meant the opposite; Phoebe had known about their father.

Outside the capsule the phosphorescence had grown, star bits in the ether, out beyond the tiny lights coming from the console. Star bits... *going down?* Something was funny. Diana reached for the console to check the altimeter, but her flesh arm wouldn't move now. She didn't need it anyway; outside the dome, lights and swathes of milky glow passed, stretching far away from her. And everything was moving down, which meant she was moving up.

Above her she could see it. A starscape. She *was* rising.

Her body felt light and the stars almost made her cry. It was so much like the bottom of the sea—so much, but opposite. The bottom of the sea was filled with nothing. But the stars were filled with everything.

Solar systems swiveled. Constellations and galaxies swaggered and flamed in the dark. Nebula. There, the Butterfly Nebula! Two roiling crucibles of super-hot gas spreading apart like wings, welcoming, terrifying, opening upon a dying star and unleashing a wash of radiation, making the gas glow neon red and white.

The capsule continued up, higher and higher and she felt how easy it would be to rise through the thin glass above her and escape out among the lights. Like she'd been born to do.

Part of her brain, still bound in her body, sent her a message. *I'm dying now.* The thought rose. She found herself rounded up against the top of the pilot capsule, longing to pass through. To join them. To join them like friends and play upon the Metaspatial Blockchain.

But her brain reminded her she still had something left to do. *They'll die too*, it said. *If I die here, my friends will die.* Up on the ceiling, she almost laughed. She didn't have any friends left. That's why it would be so easy to go up. Nothing to leave behind.

But there is now, her brain reminded her quietly.

<hr>

A WARNING SIREN brought her back. How long had it been sounding? The interior of the sub was much colder and the landing floods had activated outside the capsule—the near-field scopes had found the sea floor. Impact was less than ten minutes away. Groggily, Diana checked the scope—the sub was plunging far too fast. Lizbeth's team had done their best with the ballast, but the specs had been lost and they'd erred on the heavy side, the side of, *get-Diana-down-there-fast*. So now she had a problem.

She snapped on thrusters. Checked the batteries. Thirty-year-old training came back to her like the path home from grammar school. *Walk it in your sleep.* She was going to have to throw more of her reserves at the engines than she should if she was going to pull out of this dive. There was no way to tell how much she'd have left after she hit. She tried to do some mental math, but mental math was out of the question. There was falling. There was slowing. That's what she could handle.

"Invert sequence initiated," she said to herself. It was easier to track all this if she held to training. *Vocalize it.*

The Spear spun topside down.

The thrusters kicked in, and she was pressed into her seat. The Spear trembled—something in the engine housing was about to sheer loose. With no possible solution for that other than finger crossing, she watched the battery bleed out, watt by watt. Blades labored to brake her headlong fall, pulling full speed. All too quickly she saw the walls of the trench outside, narrowing around her in the landing floods. *Too fast,* she thought. If she hit the bottom at this speed, the capsule would explode.

She cut the thrusters entirely. Every erg counted now. Only one chance.

"Going ambulatory," she muttered.

The telescoping limbs flashed out. The engineer in her cheered that they still functioned at all, while the plummeting human pilot felt increasingly panicked. A minute from impact, proximity alarms began to ring. She swiped them off. She could see the bottom and it was coming fast.

Diana ranged the legs out to maximize the torsion the piezo constrictors could exert and pushed herself deep into her chair. It was up to the autonomous systems now. She watched past her feet as the gray, rocky floor of the Challenger Deep rushed up toward her. She hit.

The sub groaned. Thousands of pounds of kinetic energy transferred directly into physical systems—hinges, connecting interfaces—and the Spear almost gave in. One leg shattered in the first half second and the sub tilted. Ocean dust spun up everywhere. Groans rose to screams, a piece of housing flashed free and another leg snapped off. Her battery dropped charge like a shotgunned bucket. But she slowed. Slowed. The bottom of the capsule kissed the gray of the ocean floor, the remaining arms holding. She was down.

Frozen, tilted aft, at the bottom of the Challenger Deep.

So. Next. No time to waste—reserve whatever energy remains. She snapped the exteriors off, locked the legs and cut all power to the ambulatory systems. She scanned the list and took system after system offline. Navigation. Sensors. Everything she could find that wouldn't kill her, until finally she was just there, sitting in a dead sub, seven miles down. The one place she'd been certain she would never be again.

Stress had lit up her synapsis and she felt just a touch of Crystal Clear, a helpful analytical bump. Adrenaline probably, but it wouldn't last. The timer said two hours ten minutes remaining. She'd made the drop in record time. It was black inside the capsule, black outside too. She closed her eyes, then opened them. No difference.

The question now was, what next? Instructions from Robert had been to find the Obelisk to activate the account, then touch the pericarp. But where was the Obelisk? And why hadn't she asked for more details? *Unconscious,* she reminded herself. That's why. She tried to recall everything Robert had said.

There hadn't been much: *once you're in range, the Obelisk will automatically connect with your Nano Sphere. You'll know it when it happens.*

It hadn't happened yet then, which meant she wasn't in range. She thumbed positioning ops back on and checked her location. The Obelisk was at Greg's landing site, up the trench. Did she have to be within sight of it? Was *range* just one way The Fund made her job as impossible as it could? She had to get closer.

She fed juice back into the legs. Only four of them were functional now. Spear One was looking more and more like Diana herself. Missing limbs, limping to the finish line. But the autonomous guidance had been designed to solve for missing legs. In fact, she'd tested the Spear in that scenario. It might even save a bit of energy this way if she was careful. She grabbed the joystick, squeezed, gave a twist. The sub shuddered. She felt the capsule level as the legs flexed.

"Come on, girl," she murmured.

Battery stood at 11%, enough to crawl a few hundred yards up the trench and still work the ballast latches; there was no way she was getting stuck down here now. *Precious cargo. Save enough for the ballast latches.* She flipped on a single flood and babied the hobbled Spear north, noticing her hand on the stick trembling. There was a chance, small but real, that she'd see Spear Two down here. She'd spent so many years wondering what had happened. Broken open? Trapped and whole? The idea that she might find out for sure made her heart race.

Slipping and teetering on overburdened articulators, probing the ocean floor as she picked her way forward, she inched up the trench. She traversed what she thought was the midway point and silenced the *Critical Battery* siren when it rang. 9%. No need for sirens.

The instant she connected, whatever that really meant, she wanted to freeze the sub and save every erg of power. But it was possible she was connected even now; what was it supposed to feel like?

7%

5%

3%

Still no sense of *connecting*. You'll know it when you feel it, he'd said. It was all she had to go on. But she was growing more and more *disconnected*. As the cold settled deeper, fog flooded her mind.

Suddenly it was little warmer. There was something wonderful...

Head up! Crystal Clear told her. *Focus. Have a bump.* Another volley of adrenaline hit her. *Almost nodded off. Keep your eyes on the road, your hands on the wheel. Hand.*

The video-harsh floodlight suddenly revealed the canyon wall where Greg's sub had hidden, where she'd seen light bloom so violently as she'd rushed to him. She saw rockfall to her right, sloped over the canyon floor in front of her. A section of wall had crumpled, boulders still sharp and hard with only a few decades of sediment erosion softening their edges.

That light. What else could it have been? The Obelisk, it had to be there, just around this bend. Still no *connection*. She flared the lead leg, urging the Spear into the rockfall despite questionable traction. With the missing legs, autonomous drive threw warnings, *unstable terrain,* until she upped the threat tolerance—maximized it and pushed forward. The handicapped Spear slipped and picked its way up one side of the scree and down the other. She swung around the bend.

0.9%

There it was.

Ten yards away.

Sixty feet in height, it towered above the Spear, not a fleck of dust on it, frictionless above sea level or below. And at its peak, where Earth's interest rate was so prominently displayed on every other monolith across the planet: nothing. Mankind's native Obelisk.

Blackness flooded in again as she flipped off the lights. She needed that last 0.9% percent to blow the ballast and get her passengers back to the surface. She was already cutting it close. 0.9% would be enough—if the readouts were accurate.

Still no *connection*. She'd come all this way—maybe Robert had it wrong? Was she the wrong person?

The pod shrouds stirred at her waist. Robert said they wouldn't last long. She wished they hadn't come. They were the only thing hiding her from some ravenous invisible monster, but she wanted them safe. In a cradle. In a house made of chairs and blankets. Not here in the cold.

Why were they swirling around like that? The cold plasm seemed to shift itself up her chest, thickening into layers at her shoulders and then at the back of her neck. Her ears. They were suddenly sealed and she felt liquid flowing down her ear canals. The beat of her heart and the click of her jaw were magnified in hollow drumbeats.

When the plasm met her eardrum she heard a voice. A word.

[*Touch.*]

"Touch?" she asked. "Touch something?"

[*Touch it. Stupid silly. Diana Roark.*]

"Touch," she breathed. They wanted her to move the Spear up and touch the Obelisk. "I can't move the Spear!" she said. "I'll kill the batteries. I won't be able to get you home!"

[*Touch. Best friends forever.*]

"Don't say that god damnit! All my best friends..." The plasm drained away. The shrouds had nothing left.

Then she was beset by cramps, in her back, her hips, her arm, moving without an arm and leg and over balancing, muscles exhausted. But why now? What was happening? *The pod shrouds are failing*, she thought. The shrouds had been protecting her, keeping her from freezing. Keeping her hidden. But now they were running out of strength like the battery in the sub, maybe channeling everything into keeping her Nano Sphere hidden. Maybe they were simply dying, now, as she frittered away her last chance.

With a juddering finger she could barely control, she flipped the ambulatory ops live, and tipped the floods up 5% so the world was a black paper with rubbed gray shapes barely visible. Her hands shaking with cold, Diana tipped the joystick.

0.7%

Please, a few more yards.

0.4%

Almost, almost... she wasn't going to make it.

She killed the flood. *Grab the last erg.* She knew where she was going.

0.1%

The stick tightened in her hand, lost power—the Spear was about to seize up. It was too dark, she couldn't tell how far the Obelisk was, she could be three feet away but she wasn't going to make it. The stick died. There was no torque left in the piezo systems... the piezo systems. Her own limbs were piezo—a desperate thought. With just the tiniest momentum still left in the sub she dropped the stick, reached to the roof, five hundred hours of training guiding fingers, ripped the caution stop off one single toggle and jammed it.

0.0%

Outside she heard a pop, then a clank and a scrape and the foremost spider leg popped from its mount and grated down the front of the capsule, sliding invisibly to the sea floor. Emergency release, in case a leg ever got trapped in rocks or mud. So now there were only three spider legs. The Spear tipped forward, unsupported, no faster than a falling feather. And stopped.

There was a click on the PressureGlass capsule as the Spear tipped and kissed the Obelisk and died. Not a light, not a sound. The battery indicators themselves were dead. She was a hollow stone at the bottom of the sea.

Diana unbuckled the safety strap. With the pod shrouds fading, the pain they had held back now rumbled up into her leg and back, bone pain just seconds from crashing down. She forgot her missing leg and fell forward with no way to catch herself. But she extended her single arm and smacked her palm to the inner surface of the capsule, just a breath from the surface of the Obelisk.

And that, finally, was close enough.

12

On achieving commercial Mind, a Stakeholder lives alike in cold and heat, pleasure and pain, praise and blame, fitting itself to each as it chooses. To such a one a clod of dirt and a golden crown appear no different. Impartial to duality, this sentience rises to great heights, arriving finally at the Metaspatial Blockchain. Nothing is higher than the Metaspatial Blockchain. Everything in the universe is strung on that, like a thread through the jewels of a necklace.

—From *The Book of* Ω64, of the Swandeen Pracis

A pulse of heat passed from her palm through the inch of PressureGlass. A gray-blue light grew on the Obelisk, where black patterns spread in polygon ripples to vanish around the corners of the pillar. It felt to Diana as though someone had flipped on a light.

Earth's Obelisk glowed. Glowed *gray*. And multitudes of... somethings circled the Spear. There were hundreds, or maybe even thousands; propelled on wisps of lime tinted wings, they were round, variegated green and about the size of golf balls. Tiisii! She gazed wonderingly as a swarm of them wheeled past the sub. They'd been shadowed, lurking here in the deep. The perfect camouflage. But now they were revealed.

How had the Tiisii found her? Had her masking faltered? The shrouds still oozed over her, though more slowly as the moments passed. Diana peered hard outside and looked for other species, but the Tiisii were the only ones she could see.

The black, polygonal light ripples had circled the Obelisk and now jittered back from opposite ends, wavelets rebounding across a pond. She still palmed the capsule wall, her one hand the only thing preventing her from dropping to the deck of the sub. On the other side of the PressureGlass, the thin lines on the Obie collected beneath her hand, then ramped up in complex geometries, faster and denser, the world's most intricate lace doily. And then froze.

A pulse of warmth passed *back* into Diana's hand.

Account Activated.

The sensation was at once subtle and profound; it was a stampede of weightless elephants, it was showering in a Niagara Falls of confetti. It was a promise and a threat and the cold-warmth of unlimited potential. For good or for ill, she was now connected to mankind's Golden Field. All she had to do was touch the pericarp and the payment could be made.

She'd done it. The pod shrouds had forced her. *Touch it*, they'd told her. And now they were stuck as surely as she was. She let herself slip sideways off the wall and stumbled, one-legged on the tilted floor, to the console. She stretched out her arm and threw the ballast toggle, just to make sure—battery spent. The ballast bolt was locked closed, latching her here to the bottom of the sea.

"Why did I do it?" she implored the shrouds. "Why did you want me to do it? We could have fired the ballast! You could have lived! And now..."

Robert's precious... Her head dropped. More friends lost. Below the capsule were Tiisii, pirouetting wildly. Several passed inches from her face and drew tiny trails of light behind them which glowed gray, then faded. The same gray light the Obelisk gave off.

But it wasn't light. The Obelisk wasn't glowing, wasn't throwing off light; her surroundings were dark. She couldn't see the canyon walls or the ocean floor and the console and the rest of the Spear were invisible in the blackness. But she could see her own hand; the glow was something other than cast light. More Tiisii gathered beneath the capsule and like a car barreling down a dirt road, each trailed a cloud that rose like dust, flared, and evaporated.

She was seeing the nano particles themselves. So numerous and loosely bound to their host—the Tiisii—they were stripped by their passage through the water. And the Obelisk—so full of nano particles it effervesced them from its surface like champagne bubbles. The Tiisii whorls were so beautiful, she wished she could have shown them to the pod shrouds. She wished a Tiisii would fly close so she could look. *Come, little Tiisii, let me see you,* she thought, and a Tiisii changed directions and passed near. Diana started. Could she...? She urged it to come even closer.

The Tiisii ignored her, but its nano trail did not, the cloud rising toward Diana. She gasped and jerked back and it dispersed. Another Tiisii passed and she urged it closer and again the cloud shimmered up to spread against the PressureGlass and fade from view. She could *feel* the external curve of the capsule where the cloud dispersed, as if she were *connected*.

As a scientist she'd been trained to approach the physical world with intellectual discipline and skepticism. Things that shouldn't exist, but seemed to exist anyway, usually proved to be mistakes or frauds. Nano particles that came at her call? The scientist in her recoiled.

But economists were trained to look for market forces at work, to watch for signs of the invisible hand: resources moving from place to place, drawn by consumer sentiment, by scarcity, by need. And the economist in her was convinced that she herself had caused those nano particles to move. She had *paid* for it. But how? *Earth's Universal Currency. With Earth's native Obelisk mediating?* It didn't matter, because the simple truth was, you don't need to know how money works to buy a candy bar: you wanted it, you paid for it. Money functioned seamlessly *because* of its intuitive mechanics. And intuitively, she understood that she was buying the behavior of these particles. *Come closer.* That's the behavior she'd purchased.

Robert had been scandalized that Landerson had been—had even been *capable of*—buying the behavior of nano particles, of wasting enormous amounts of borrowed Universal Currency on his swords and Fields, the debt written against Earth's credit account. But she was doing this with her own Universal Currency. *Right?* Maybe a waste but incurring no debt.

A sudden hope bloomed. *No,* she thought. *Don't hope.* But if it was possible to spend Universal Currency and attract a cloud, could she spend more and get more?

She levered herself back upright on one leg, gritting teeth; the agony in her skeleton was such a distraction. She palmed the PressureGlass again, her Obelisk just a few inches away. With the dehumidifiers dead, the glass was cold, smooth and wet with condensation.

I would like to make a purchase, she thought at the gray surface. *Nothing. Of course. Purchase what? Be specific.*

She pictured it.

She pictured the long Mariana Trench, gouged like a Grand Canyon in the Pacific Ocean floor, filled with two hundred billion gallons of ancient, compacted water. She pictured the Spear, crippled and tiny at the bottom of that vast trough. And on the Spear's broken housing, she pictured its most recent addition: Lizbeth's last work, a bulging epoxy scar fixing a solenoid to the hull. The frozen ballast latch.

She visualized the water around the Spear, laced with imperceptibly minute machines. Alien, but hers—hers by purchase. She pictured the nano particles, the shimmering tails they made as the Tiisii swam through them and pictured herself feeding them Universal Currency and drawing them close. The behavior she purchased was simple: collect in place. She clustered them in a sludge near the latch on the sub's exterior, knowing she was misusing them. These infinitesimal machines were subtler tools than this—credit cards, Robert had said. You don't build a table with credit cards. Unless credit cards are the only thing you have.

She grouped them in a mass and crushed them, forming them the way Landerson made his swords and his fields and his machines of war. What she needed to make was stupid-simple, but she had no experience with it; she lacked his technology to magnify her efforts. What she did have, in explosive excess, was mankind's Golden Field.

So, she paid. *Whatever it takes*, she thought, gasping now, sweat pouring down. *Whatever the cost*. A tiny pellet of solid matter began to coalesce in the floating sludge. She moved it up—paid to move it—to the clasp where the ballast hung above her on the fuselage. She *paid* to position her globule inside that clasp. She *paid* and her tiny ball grew, expanding and pushing as it did. The closed latch had only to bulge out a fraction of an inch, that was all she needed, so she *paid*. Her pinpoint of solid matter became an orb and she *paid*. It expanded under the latch the lock resisted, the nature of locks, but her ball was big and getting bigger. And the latch. At Last. Snapped.

A crack reverberated through the hull, then grinding and all three heavy, makeshift ballast nets slid from their cradles and dropped to the ocean floor. The Spear groaned and shifted, sliding Diana down the rounded wall. Unable to stop herself with only one arm and one leg, she rolled and spun like a child going down a grass hill.

The Spear settled upwards.

For a moment she lay and felt it rise. *Twenty minutes to the surface, she thought*. The pod shrouds had stopped moving. *Please*, she implored them, *stay with me*. Surely they'd last twenty minutes?

Beside her, netted to the console, rode the pericarp. She'd rolled to a stop just below it. The timer told her she had an hour and twenty-one minutes to spare. All she had to do was touch it and make the payment.

Her fingers closed the gap and hovered inches from the friction-less oblong. They trembled with cold. But also, with indecision.

The problem was it didn't make financial sense. The economics of the thing didn't add up, a problem that had been growing in her mind. If she initiated this payment, wasn't she just pointing humanity down a long path of ever-increasing debt? This was the minimum payment. In thirty years, another minimum would come due and after that, another. It was a game The Fund would surely win in the end, given enough time and with the ITC on their side. They would rig it, that's what lenders did. Mankind would end up embezzled, penalized, plundered, or would simply default. So, failure now, or failure in some distant future? The outcome was the same: foreclosure. She couldn't pass that problem down. She had to solve it. She had...

Some force slammed into the side of the Spear. Its upward trajectory was halted momentarily and Diana was thrown against the edge of the console. She fell back, striking her head and then felt an extraordinary acceleration pressing her into the capsule wall. She could hear water churning past the dome; the Spear was being forced to the surface. Something had hooked her, she realized. Was it Black Marlin? Were they reeling her in?

It was not the Black Marlin. The Spear rolled as it rose and she saw a platform below her, lifting. A gray platform, faintly glowing—someone manipulating nano particles. *So wasteful.*

Her speed was so great the current began stripping pieces of thruster housing away and then *everything* peeled off—batteries, harnesses, impellers—each component wailing tortured, hyper-metal shrieks as it torqued off, until all that remained was her transparent capsule. A giant gel cap holding a supine, elderly amputee.

Light blossomed above. Mere seconds after sighting the surface, Spear One crested, casting spray up a hundred feet to fall and bathe her capsule in a plunging shower, blurring everything but light. And then, all motion ceased.

The PressureGlass dripped clear and Diana found herself suspended twenty feet above the waves. She saw an island, half a mile in diameter, just a few hundred yards away. As flat as a dinner plate, it rose in the water from a bed of coral, ringed with bone white sand and peppered with palms. Fais Island, the closest of the Mariana Isles to their dive site. A vessel lay across the shore, its back broken and aft third pouring oily smoke. It arched sideways in a death spasm— the gleaming ebony wreck of the Black Marlin.

The remains of its graceful wings hung broken in the palms. Figures ran beneath the trees near the fire in the engine bay, some extinguishing the flames, others pulling crewmates from the wreckage. The Marlin was far from the water, so far up the beach that fully half the hull lay under palms, as if an exuberant leap from the sea had gone terribly wrong.

As if it had been lifted and dropped.

The platform beneath her shifted and moved toward the island, carrying her along like a daiquiri on tray. Only one man could be doing any of this.

As she swept forward, the deep water shallowed into gentle waves and sand and then she was over the beach. The carcass of the Marlin was a hundred feet away, but only a few feet from her she saw a different, though familiar sight—a Landerson Field. A half circle hollowed from the sand, its peculiar multicolored glitter distorted the sunlight. A figure was suspended there. A purple, floral, alien figure. Robert.

Tiisii swept up toward her and other beings too, shapes her mind couldn't categorize. It was all just so much smoke and destruction and tropical chaos. Too much.

The platform beneath her vaporized and the capsule fell. She saw the fine sand of the beach pressed beneath the dome and the heat from the sun grew instantly unbearable in the sealed chamber. The air barely breathable, she slid to the hatch and twisted, one-handed, frantic, until it spun and fell open and fruit-sweet, humid air blew across her face. She scanned the beach in both directions, the sky, the tree line. Somewhere, someone was responsible for all this.

The pod shrouds, she remembered.

She emerged like a chick through the porthole and fell to the sand, her cloak of wet jello making made her feel even more newly hatched. Her missing limbs made it hard to crawl the standard hands and knees method, but she could manage *hand* and *knee* and *stump* and started lurching toward Robert. She could see a lip hole in his cube. He was shouting and his purple stalks swayed in violent arcs, but no sound escaped the Field. She dragged, dragged until she lay beside the sheer edge in the sand where the Field sliced its curve, wet and oval and deep on Robert's side, flat and dry and white on hers.

She peered at the Field and saw something new, a layer beneath the oily surface, within the shimmer glints—the nano particles linking to *create* the Field

Diana lifted her hand and pressed. The Field bowed. Robert yelled, his lip hole wide, but she still couldn't hear. He was begging to be let out, she was sure, or for her to bring back the pod shrouds. She pushed harder, feeling the Landerson field begin to deform under her hand and watching it grow opaque.

But she needed *through*. Could she buy that? *Through?* Was she still connected to Earth's Obelisk? As soon as she had the thought her hand pierced it, so unexpectedly that the rest of her body tumbled after. Her head and shoulders passed inside and a pseudopod shot up from Robert's cube to keep her from plummeting. Suddenly she could hear him.

"LOOK THE FUCK BEHIND YOU!" he had been screaming.

She turned. A figure bounded up the beach in distance-eating leaps. A naked man, torso and arms thick as a rhino, gate as graceful as a ballet prince. Landerson. Tiisii and other alien forms swooped behind him as he ran. At his heels sped a phalanx of yellow, undulating cucumbers, each the size of a couch. Behind those a whole riotous cavalcade of exotic forms pinwheeled. Diana saw them all. Landerson did not.

She leaned further into the Field and reached for the flat of Robert's ectocube, hearing him gasp as she thrust her arm through it and into the plasm. No time for manners—this might be a breach of Neoooxcolu etiquette but they had only moments remaining and...

"Take them!" she yelled, as wet gel slid like another skin from her body; a score of pseudopods reached up after a second and began pulling shrouds in, sucking and massaging and urging them off Diana's body and back into his.

"I could feel you connect to your account!" he yelled as he gripped—*stop yelling Robert I'm right here*—and pulled, "Like a fucking gong. Every Appraiser on the planet heard it. Landerson must have felt it. No way he knows what it meant. But suddenly he was here—fucker pulled the Marlin up and smashed it on the beach, screaming for you!"

"Are they ok?" she demanded. "Your shrouds?"

"Yes, Diana Roark. My pod shrouds survived. Thank you, may you live always in sunlight." He pushed her back gently until her hand pulled free of his side. "What about the pericarp? You haven't made your payment. Is there a problem?"

"No, but..."

And that's as far as she got, as the Landerson Field, with Robert in it, suddenly rose from its hole and launched down the beach spraying sand, rolling toward the Marlin, knocking down trees and wreaking havoc. A pack of pony-sized lettuces fluttered wildly out of its path. Diana was left to teeter on the edge of a sandpit that began crumbling and sucking her down.

But only for a moment, before she felt herself clamped around the waist. She writhed but was lifted into the air and spun to face the other direction, then shaken like a magic eight ball. It left her cross-eyed. When they uncrossed she was staring into Terrance Landerson's own fixed, gray gaze.

"Terrance!" she coughed, spitting sand from her mouth. "Let me go! Look around you! The aliens are here!"

His arms were stretched out to his sides, shoulder height, with his hands cupped forward like a man reaching out two windows of a moving car. He flicked his eyes past her, down the beach and she looked to see Robert still rolling.

"I've seen your aliens!" he snarled.

His voice was a guttural mess, as though writhing rage shredded the flesh in his throat. His phrasing was different too, not chopped up and absent like it had been. It was drawn out. Like he was, for this moment, at last fully in his body. He dropped her to the ground with a gesture and walked to where she lay, his arms still extended, his shoulders hunched forward. He peered at her missing limbs.

"I'd hoped the Field would slice your arm off when I threw it. But I see someone beat me to it. You're chopped up like a garden salad."

There wasn't anything she could add to that. He described her exactly the way she felt. There was irony to the observation though, because, invisible to him, real vegetables had begun gathering around them in a circle. Behind him she saw the cucumber slugs. They'd hopped into a pyramid to see what Landerson would do next. She wondered what their species designation was. Tier 4 Circus Acrobats? A ball of brown twigs rolled up beside them and thrust bark tendrils into the sand, then rose like a stick house. From up and down the beach the aliens streamed.

Robert had not been exaggerating—Earth was overrun. Diana was astonished. Untold hundreds of species crawled this beach, a tide of intergalactic life, ninety-nine point nine out of a hundred of them plants, according to Robert, a figure she found easy to believe if this was a representative sample. Some plumose seed umbrellas swooped, flapped and landed beside the slugs and a herd of lima beans, beige with fur, rolled in beside them. A beaked, color-changing kale leaf spun up and seemed to sit, as if in a beach chair. All of them faced Landerson and Diana.

"You and your philanthropist patrons made a mistake," Landerson growled at her. "Whatever your plan, you revealed yourself and I came. And what I did to your ship is *nothing* compared to what I will do to you."

"Look, Terrance!" she said, her eyes going to the Spear, her thoughts to the pericarp. "Open your eyes! Let me go, they're all around you!"

"So," the words tore from his throat like spit blood, "now you can transgress my Field. They are training you!"

"Jesus Christ, you fool," she gestured everywhere, pointing one armed at the ring of wild figures which continued to grow, spectators at a cockfight, "these things are here to steal the planet from us!"

He opened his mouth and he might have been trying to laugh, but nothing came out. The whites of his eyes flashed, riding his lunatic face like froth on terrible waves.

"Invisible philanthropists everywhere, scheming to steal us blind —what kind of imbecile do you take me for?" Sweat flew from his jowls. *But Augmented bodies aren't supposed to sweat,* she complained. She could see a nimbus of micro particles sweeping his body and now that he was close she felt his heat; it was like squatting before a forest fire.

"The Obelisks are going to fall, capitalism will return!" he cried. He was all wild spittle and heat and rage and she watched his Nano Sphere churn. "Neither you nor your philanthropic handlers can stop it!"

"They'll never let you tear the Obies down you idiot! They're making too much money from them!"

In an instant he was holding a gray sword; it grew in his hand, fast and sharp. This time she saw it, saw the particles that made it, saw them gather from the air. He swung it, testing its heft and raised it high, up over her body.

"You will tell me their plans!" he raged, "Tell me or I will cleave your remaining limbs from your body!"

"I just told you their goddamn plans," she screamed back, "they want to take the planet! Open your eyes!"

The audience around them was huge now, pressing forward in ranks, smaller plants in front, larger ones to the rear—a grade school class arranged for picture day. They chittered and howled a chlorophyllic symphony. A section of the ring opened and an inverted beet stalked forward on fronds, stopping at the edge of the circle, imposing and priestly. The Swandeen Pracis.

Landerson bellowed, swinging his sword toward her leg. She thought—*the pericarp! The debt! If he kills me I won't be able to...*

"STOP!" she shouted.

And the plunging sword stopped, mid-air. Surprising both Landerson and Diana herself, and stunning their rapt audience to silence, Diana now wore an arm where her empty socket had been. A gray arm.

Its hand held his falling blade.

She met his eyes, and in them she saw a surprise and a touch of fear.

"Look, Landerson! Look around!"

But both their eyes flew to the junction of blade and palm. He howled, pushing and on instinct Diana resisted, her nano arm absorbing his weight. His sword twisted, becoming a hook, then a spear, then a brutal, studded mace as he levered her down. But her arm held him.

His eyes bulged. He brought his other hand to the hilt and ground against her, but she held. Heat off his looming chest blasted her and he cried in fury; but she held. Pounds of hate bore down upon her and she, crippled and dying but somehow unbroken upon the beach, held him, while his conflagration went hellfire wide.

What is this costing us, she wondered? *This has to stop.*

She *paid.* From her gray hand grew a sheath that rose up his mace and froze it. He pulled, but she was locked to him now. Like a skin her sheath grew up his weapon, over his hand and up his arm. When he saw what was happening his eyes went wide and he desperately heaved, pulling her up. And then he was stumbling back, but there was nowhere to go. She enveloped him. Slowly. She watched his face as across his shoulders, down his chest, she bound him— bound his arms, bound his waist and stitched his legs. He pulled away, trying to burst out with surges of pure formed nano force. But she was rich and he was indebted. *No contest.*

Until at last he stood, motionless and enwrapped in a scabbard of gray, only the pommel of his head free.

She separated her gray arm and fell to the beach. It was so hard to move now, and she was so tired. She looked up, raised her leg and tapped him over. He fell to the sand. She crawled to his face and lay beside him. *So exhausted.*

"I'm putting a stop to this, to you and your plan, Terrance. It's a bad plan."

Landerson watched her. Lunatic rage still stretched his mouth, but a canny glint rode his eyes. He struggled, but he was caught.

"We took the wrong daughter," he said. "I see that now."

She closed her eyes. *And then what?*

"You what?"

"You were the one," he breathed. "We thought your sister was the dangerous one. Maybe we should have taken you both. How could we have known?"

"What are you…"

He smiled, cruelty dripping from him. At least he could do this, that was the thought she saw. Hurt her. One final pleasure.

"We kidnapped her. She knew what we planned with Ebola 3. I couldn't let her interfere, although we hadn't necessarily planned for her to die. At first." He watched her face and she could almost see the words forming in his mind. *Yes. Oh yes, he saw her pain. So nice.* "It was just so much more efficient to end it." He smiled. "But now it's you who stopped our plans. I'm your prisoner, all trussed up. Will you kill me now, like I *killed your sister?*"

She looked up at the sky, the plants around her motionless. The denouement of their long-play drained it all from her. She was spent.

Spent empty.

His scabbard dissipated and in a bound Landerson was up, heaving blow after blow of concussive force at her, gouts of sand and soil exploding around her. She fended him back with feeble sweeps of her gray arm, but it was only a moment before he had her pinned to the sand. A triumphant cry broke from his lips.

Spent. She was spent.

He spread his arms and around them a hundred naked Economists rained down, their Fields coruscating in the tropical sun. They dropped to the beach like balloons from a championship ceiling.

And however much she was willing to pay it could never be enough, not now. There were too many and she was too empty. They ringed her, grounding her lower with the debt they summoned, spinning her like a doll of bones until they ripped her only shield, the gray and foreign arm, from her socket in a brilliant spray of particles. It was clear in the way they were so coordinated, so calm, they had practiced this. But not to battle her, surely? In preparation for some campaign Landerson had planned against The 27. It had to be that.

She didn't even struggle. She was fixed to the beach with translucent cords on her limbs and stumps and throat, pinioned, though she had no strength to even try to rise. *Overwhelmed.* She knew, if she reached further, if she found the will, there might be more to spend, but why? She had paid. Paid and paid, but every blow she dealt, every blast she slipped or took or threw back, just buried humanity in greater debt, because it urged him to respond. She was finished.

Terrance knelt beside her.

He shook his head.-Diana could tell by looking at him that he was about to say something tragic, or dramatic, or both. She took a breath to cut him short.

And then the audience ringing them exploded apart, panic seeming to scatter the alien botanical garden. The cucumber slugs sprayed sand and fled down the beach, bumping some of the Economists and knocking them over so they gazed wildly around. It was as if the island had tilted, so all the aliens on one end were shaken down to the other. A nightmare parade flooded over Diana and the Economists, a safari-land tour in reverse where the creatures drive past you; the walking sticks and the flying seeds and the tubers and leaves, leaves of every variety, they all charged away, past the smoking Marlin, to crowd at the far end of the island. All of them. Until the beach was empty.

"What are you doing you philanthropist *bitch?*" Landerson screamed at her as his Economists staggered. And then the ground shuddered and a shadow fell over her, and she looked up and thought, *running away. Totally away.*

The Wuln Vuln Drongplo had come, falling upon the atoll and spanning it from one side to the other, towering two hundred feet in the sky. It cast a dark shadow over everything and spread the reek of breeding oil from its loins, an alien *animal*. It had eyes, dozens or hundreds, pressed in haphazard groups on a mouthless snout. Titanic legs flexed, six of them with severing claws. Its chest rippled sinew beneath brown waves of peeling skin, stiff with hair. Three cruel mouths lined its neck and flashed pike walls of yellow teeth and from somewhere down its throat its lungs sprayed train engine fetor across the beach.

Reptile. Wolf. Horror—it heaved above and blocked the sun.

This was what The Fund had set loose to hunt. It screamed through all its mouths and the sound shook her and left her deafened. Landerson and his battalions were protected by the mesh and heard nothing like what really shook the island. But they heard something and felt the ground move.

"What do you see?" she screamed at him as he turned toward the interior of the island.

"There is no volcanic vent on this island!" He pointed. "What is this? How is it possible? You! You are doing this!"

He raised his hand, venting gray fire. He would pulverize her now, unless the Wuln Vuln Drongplo did it first.

"Look!" she screamed, bouncing her head and pointing her chin. "Open your *eyes!*" But he was caught in the mesh—*the god damn mesh!* "God damn you, Landerson, *SEE!*" she screamed. And *paid*.

Straight through his optic disc, down his optic tract, she blasted money. Pure, hot, fierce, she bid her Golden Field. *I want this*, she screamed. *I'm buying THIS!* She felt the mesh respond. Then from somewhere another bidder stepped in, came in above her and control jumped back. Someone wanted this scene erased, she saw. But if it was a bidding war they wanted... *be careful what you ask for, fuckers*, she thought.

Diana opened up. She blasted. She held a supernova behind her mind, and she used it. *SEE!* It was overwhelming. For a fraction of a second her adversary tried to keep up, but she washed them away. They ceded their hold on the machinery of Landerson's vision. *No, all these economists!* And then, as Diana wanted, Landerson and his minions were confronted with reality.

He saw the beast bent toward him—death and hell and Armageddon all rolled into one.

"The 27!" he screamed. *"The 27 are here!"*

They all saw the beast, how it blocked the sun; they smelled the stench and were deafened by its roars, and it was a testament to their preparation that they remained frozen for only a moment and didn't flee. It took one beat to process the most horrific animal presence ever conceived and then they were airborne.

"To me!" Terrance cried. *"To me, my agents of change!"* He formed his Field and surged up, diving straight for the oily belly above him.

Others split into coordinated and precise groups, communicating with one another. Or somehow Landerson was controlling them himself. Six separate companies of airborne warriors split and raced above the island, Fields flashing in spectral bursts. The beast paid them no attention; it didn't realize it had been exposed and it was so fixed on Diana's destruction that it might not have cared if it had known. It bent toward her, three mouths agape, saliva cascading past great teeth like snow melt off a precipice.

Landerson thought she had called the Wuln Vuln Drongplo, Diana saw. *Of course.* And he'd left her fixed to the sand. Maybe he thought the creature was only bending down to receive instructions, or to free her. He seemed determined to deal with the beast before he dealt with her.

Landerson swept beneath its oily stomach with a handful of followers, while the other groups took positions, each company to a leg. The snout, a three story pine cone covered with black, lidded eyes, swung down ten feet from Diana and roared. And then Landerson struck from below.

His cohort lashed scintillating quantum whips against the flaking belly and the Wuln Vuln Drongplo screamed. Lizard like and unbelievably quick, it scampered back and looked to see what had pierced it. But Terrance and his corps stayed below, moving along with it and continuing to flay, though from Diana's perspective they seemed to do little damage.

Damage was not their plan, however. When the creature reared away from them on its hind set of limbs to paw at its stomach, nearly four hundred feet in the air, Diana saw yet another of the wasteful, amazing tricks Landerson had learned; each of six groups threw a loop of throbbing gray rope to circle a limb of the beast and then backed off, until those cords were strung tight—and then, to her amazement, they flipped the beast onto its back.

Or almost. The Wuln Vuln Drongplo had been surprised when they'd first appeared, but that changed fast and it focused on its new enemies. It twisted as it fell and lashed with its tail to shatter three of the six groups on one side. It flipped forward, regained its feet and dug the now free left limbs into the island to *pull*. It hauled, vicious and strong, and the three remaining cables and their handlers were ripped from the sky like party balloons. Then it bent to its belly, where Terrance and his group remained.

The battle had moved to the other side of the island and it was difficult for Diana to see. She struggled to sit up but was still bound to the sand. Fifty feet away she saw the Spear, and inside, webbed to the console, the pericarp. She didn't have a favorite in the current clash. Either side would quickly return and kill her if it won. All she wanted was the briefest respite, a moment of distraction, to get to her sub. But she was caught.

The atoll shook like a carpet-bombed trampoline. The screams of the Wuln Vuln Drongplo were sonic blasts, launching trees sideways. She turned back to see the creature flip onto its haunches and she watched it open its lowest mouth to spray clouds of oily glitter over a phalanx of fliers. They burst into flame, their fields dissolved, and plunged from the sky.

Only Landerson at the belly and two airborne groups remained.

The beast cast its vomitus spray again, but one of the remaining groups swept close from behind, trailing pulsing cord. Rodeo cowboy fast, they flipped it around the neck, below the snout where a brain might be.

As they did it, Landerson, still astride the belly whipping the beast to distract it from his corps, was caught in one of its claws. His field was pinned to the beast's chest, first by one clawed foot, then by another. The beast lifted Terrance toward its mouths. All the remaining had Economists joined the group on the line around the creature's neck, and now, suddenly, they pulled it taut and backward.

The Wuln Vuln Drongplo was dragged into the air.

It hung, screaming and flailed. And then slowly, methodically, those corps of fliers began tightening, foot by foot closing the loop, to cut the thick flesh of its neck. Black and ichorous blood flew, some landing on pilots in their fields; those who were hit fell from the sky like insects. But Diana saw what was happening and gasped.

They were going to cut off its head. The only sure way to kill the Augmented. *So brilliant.*

Landerson was still in its grip directing his fliers and the creature, frenzied, began pounding its paws together upon Landerson in his Field, brutalizing him with force, again and again, smashing with thunderous claws and brutish, inconceivable power. Landerson rocked like a snow globe clapped by an elephant; at each blow a thundercrack echoed over the sea, the land shivered and the waves frothed. And Landerson's warriors pulled the rope slowly, tightening, the rope digging deeper and deeper, the blood running thicker.

And then there was a bright pop.

Landerson's field shattered. He crouched in one claw, exposed, without armor. At the same time, the loop around the scaled neck cinched closed. The mountainous head was shorn from the great body.

The head and the other parts fell from the sky and as they did, the beast clapped one last time. Diana couldn't see it, but she knew— Landerson was dead. Every one of the skyborne Economists faltered, their fields flickering out. They moved in the air for a moment like a handful of pale sand tossed toward the sun. And when momentum failed, they fell into the sea after the beast, rising a wave that threatened to wash across the island.

Diana's restraints vanished.

Despite the terrible urgency, it took her a moment and then she sat up.-When she did, there was Robert, released from his own field. He sped past her on his extraordinary pseudopods, upending the Spear and reaching in for the pericarp.

He returned to her side, so fast he was a blur, or maybe it was simply her exhausted eyes.

"Diana Roark," he said, "you've only got a few minutes. Touch the pericarp. Make the fucking payment."

She took him in, so less alien now even in his broccoli form, almost conventional compared with the other things she'd seen.

"Are you ok?" she croaked. "All your jello good? Your fronds?"

"What? Yes, I'm fucking fine. Do this! Before they think of something else to stop you!"

He held the pericarp out to her, imploring.

"Just touch...*fucking touch it!*"

But she didn't. Instead, she looked up at him, where she had decided his eyes were.

"I'm not making this payment."

"What. The fuck. Are you saying?"

"Robert, I need your help." She looked up at the sky, where, now that she had bought her way clear of erasure, she saw ships pressing down through the blue of the atmosphere, just as they had been when they'd come thirty years before. There were hundreds. How long had they been there? Years? They spanned the sky from horizon to horizon. She shrugged and turned back to Robert. Her friend. Her doughty, Consumer Protection agent.

"I want to re-negotiate my loan," she said.

13

The Known Economy is eternal in nature, increases and supports our knowledge of truth and reality, and creates balance and harmony in and among all sentient Stakeholders. But do not be deceived by its seeming indisputability: it is only the *Known* Economy. There have been others. There will be others. There likely are others now. We are simply blinded by the brilliance of what is Known, and cannot see.

—From *The Book of* Ω64, of the Swandeen Pracis

It was a moment before Robert spoke.

"There is no re-negotiate," he told her. "Nobody negotiates anything with The Fund."

"I'd like to meet them." Her voice sounded thick, as though grated by concert screams, leaving her just the dregs.

"Just make the fucking payment Diana Roark!"

"It's a trap! We're just going to go deeper into debt. Make an interest payment every thirty years for the next million until they bleed us dry? No."

"You don't have a fucking choice. This is what they do." His tone was quiet, sympathetic. "Mankind went on a spending spree. It agreed to a set of terms and now you're fucked and you have to pay. Or they take everything. You've got fifteen minutes."

She shook her head. It made her dizzy and she reached to catch herself. *Crap, missing arm,* she thought and fell to her side like a toddler. Robert did nothing. He would have helped her up a moment before, but she'd used up his goodwill. Or this was his way of making a point about her helplessness.

"I just want to talk to them," she said from the sand. "Can you make that happen, or not?"

"No, Diana Roark, I can't. All my funding's been pulled."

"Could I loan you Universal Currency?"

"You could, but I can't obligate the ITC to pay back a fucking loan."

"What if I *gave* it to you? A charitable contribution?"

Several seconds passed. She assumed it was him jumping back on his choice tree, the only reason he ever paused. Finally, he sighed.

"We could do that. The government will always take free money. But Diana Roark, you'll never be able to budge The Fund."

"We'll just see," she rasped.

***

SHE TRANSFERRED Currency to him with the pericarp and a moment later they rose off the Earth in a gray, boxy ship. The cheapest he could find, he told her. She looked down at the damage the Wuln Vuln Drongplo had done to the island—black pits sunk where blood had spilled, flame spreading where the thing had sprayed and the hull of the Black Marlin, shattered, never to sail again. A battlefield. She wondered why it felt like a battle she had lost.

Landerson had stolen her sister. The secret decoder ring of the universe had turned another gear and now everything meant something new, *yet again.* She'd always wondered *why. Why hadn't Phoebe come* back? As a child she'd asked everyone. Phoebe had promised she would come back. Little Diana had wondered why her sister hadn't kept that promise; big Diana understood now and she wanted it to feel horrible, but it didn't. *So long ago,* she thought. So little left to work with now.

At least she had the truth.

She turned away from the twisted boat broken on the beach, and the fires and the bodies, back to the present. The walls of the ship were white and the interior was...commonplace. Shelves and pillows. A photo of a sunset on one wall. There were no spaceship controls anywhere she could see and when she wanted a seat, one formed, specially shaped to accommodate her asymmetrical body. When she wanted to look outside at the sky, a wall became transparent. It was absolutely silent in flight, with no sensation of acceleration or direction and no straps or belts to protect against the possibility of turbulence. She was going to space in a spare, modernist living room.

"Like flying in one of Terrance's Fields," she said, just a burble of noise to humanize the room. She'd tried talking to Robert but he hadn't said a word since leaving Fais Island. He'd used some of her donated funds to assume a human body for her; just being polite, she supposed. That human face was obviously worried now. He stared at her and looked away when she turned to him. *Maybe just fed up with me,* she thought, *me and my ridiculous account.*

"I don't know what Landerson was doing with those Fields, but it wasn't this," Robert said finally. He looked at the walls. "This ship is quantum inertia-less. Landerson was..." He trailed off. She waited. There was more, she could see.

"Just, Diana Roark, you told me your species was nothing special."

"I don't know, I mean, how would I know? I *doubt* we're special. Unless idiocy is special in outer space."

"You people... you just killed a fucking Wuln Vuln Drongplo! That's not done. I mean, it doesn't happen. No one has ever even tried. Not even other animals kill Wuln Vuln Drongplo."

She shrugged. Killing things, the power of humanity to kill, was old news to her. Her father was a past master. She had more important things to talk about, now that he was talking But he wasn't finished.

"You should be fucking amazed about that," he snapped. "Or afraid. You would be, if you knew…"

She was afraid she'd lost him, but then abruptly he transformed to Neoooxcolu form, and extended the pericarp to her, still hung in the webbing they had used to stow it in the Spear.

"Take it," he said. "You'll need it to pay."

She held it by the net, careful not to touch the surface. It slipped and rolled in there, like an angry, deep-water fish. It grew lighter after she held it a moment, adjusting its mass to her strength. She held it as far away as she could.

Robert had turned off the autopay feature. She'd insisted. Otherwise, a single touch on the gray oval could have initiated their installment payment. She didn't want any more tricks, not even with her best interests at heart.

"Can I use this when I re-negotiate?" she asked.

He spread his fronds, the equivalent of a shrug; she had begun to parse untranslated Neoooxcolu. Greg would have been proud.. "If you could change your terms with The Fund—which you won't—but if you did, you'd use that to make a transfer. Diana Roark…"

"What?" she asked, after she'd waited another moment for him to continue speaking. She wished he'd just finish a sentence.

"I've been thinking about what's happening on your planet."

"Good. Keep it up. Do some Consumer Protection."

"You don't know how things are supposed to work, so there's no way you can understand how *unbelievably* fucked up this is. But it is. The Fund is so, *so* far out of compliance, there's only one explanation I can think of. Only one reason they'd be taking these risks by themselves, or for whoever's providing them leverage to buy all this."

She waited. He didn't want to say it, whatever it was.

"Do you know what a hardfork is?" he asked. "On a blockchain?"

"Of course. On earth a hardfork happens when the blockchain

gets forked in two. The old fork is abandoned and the new fork goes forward. Basically, the old one dies and the new one takes its place."

"I think someone, somewhere, wants to hardfork the Metaspatial Blockchain." His voice was just loud enough to be heard. "And I think mankind's Golden Field is right the fuck in the middle of their plans."

"How could you hardfork the universe?"

"Who the fuck knows?"

More frond spreads and then a series of anxious and random pseudopods stuck out in various directions. "Some people think our current Metachain is already a fork; the universe has been forked before. They say the Sentient One gave us this Metachain, which is fucking bullshit. I mean, I'm *pretty sure* it's fucking bullshit—the Obelisks and the Metachain did come from *somewhere*. And maybe whoever set them up wants them back. But listen to me, Diana Roark. I'm a forensic accountant. And I'm telling you, the numbers do not add up. You're in grave danger. We might all be."

"So, are they going to kill me when I get up there?"

"Fuck no, they're cowards. They're not going to harm you directly. The Wuln Vuln Drongplo was a private contractor, so they had plausible deniability. They'll probably claim it went rogue, legal firewall and all that." Diana thought about Atticus and his shell companies, about how Immpenta never touched Roark Pharma. How the rich so seldom had to pay. Was the whole universe just a table where the same bread got served, over and over, regardless of whether anyone wanted to eat it?

"You requested a mediated conference," Robert continued, "or I requested it for you. There's a whole layer of ITC oversight for mediation. They're not going to come right out and kill you."

The ship had escaped the atmosphere and she could see her planet below, a shining globe of water. It had taken no time at all to get here. And now what had been a string of cloudy smudges from the surface had grown into a flotilla of vessels, ponderous and watchful.

"We're heading for the mediation ship." He pointed through the suddenly transparent roof at a rapidly nearing white craft.

"What are the rest of these ships?"

"You don't want to know. It would fucking terrify you."

We're about to crash into a spaceship, she wanted to point out. But before she got the words out their small boat pierced the bright side of the mediation ship and all visual evidence of motion disappeared. They might have been standing still, or they might have been launched at a million miles an hour toward the sun. Her inner ear was no reliable instrument.

"We're here," he said.

He tilted the net where the pericarp nestled, so both of them could see the timer still fastened to the strands. "You have twelve minutes. Fucking please, Diana Roark, don't fuck around. They won't be able to keep you from touching this if you want to. So, when whatever your plan is *doesn't work,* then *make the payment.* Otherwise, they're going to rip your planet to pieces and steal all your shit and there's going to be nothing left."

She nodded. *Agreed, no planetary ripping permitted.* She didn't know what would happen next, but inside she felt something stirring, the same feeling she'd had while escaping the mission. The same thing she'd felt before she broke the ballast lock. Hope. She allowed herself to admit the possibility that if she could do this thing, she could be free.

The wall behind Robert swelled and then, like a sail filling, it ballooned back to become a much larger space, a floor and a desk materializing. The desk was white, because everything was white up here and in front of the desk was a white chair. On the desk was a white pen, a small notepad and an elegant vase with a single white flower.

Against the rounded wall beyond the desk another white chair materialized and then another and another until fourteen empty seats sat in a semicircle. And then people materialized—incorporated—into them. They alternated in appearance between human male and human female and all wore carefully tailored suits. The men looked exactly alike, as did the women—coiffed and smooth and half smiling.

The Fund.

"Welcome, Ms. Roark," they said in unison. Their mouths moved in perfect synchrony when they spoke, but she heard only one voice, an extraordinarily well modulated and polite voice, which issued from a spot in the air in front of the desk.

"You are right on time," they mouthed. "Come in."

"Diana Roark," Robert said behind her, "it has been an extraordinary honor to be your Account Representative. I wish you the best of luck. May you face upward to brightest sun all your days."

And when she turned to say thank you, he was no longer in her spaceship living room. He was no longer anywhere.

"Where's my Account Representative?" she asked. The semicircle did not change their expression.

"He has been processed to his next engagement, we presume. That, of course, is out of our purview. If you would like more information, we suggest you contact the Interstellar Trade Commission. May we get you a glass of water, Ms. Roark?"

A tall glass of water materialized on the desk beside the pen and the pad and the flower.

"Thank you." She was very thirsty.

"It is our pleasure to make you comfortable. Please come forward and take your seat." As one, they raised their arms and gestured to the seat at the desk.

For many reasons, Diana wished she still had Robert beside her. She wanted to know about his next assignment. She wanted to know more about The Fund, who they were and how they operated. But mostly she wanted someone to help her stand up and walk. If Robert had been here she would have leaned on him to limp those ten long feet to the desk. Her only choices now seemed to be to crawl, or to try some precarious, one legged hopping. She really had no energy for either.

She leaned forward in her chair and pushed, managing to get

vertical; her single hand swung the pericarp in its webbed satchel and her single leg shook beneath her. The distance to the desk looked endless.

"Ms. Roark, may we be of some assistance getting you seated?"

The Fund remained expressionless, but something about the tone of the voice—solicitous, concerned, warm and formal—reminded her of someone. Or something. She didn't know how to get to that desk without help. It was an age-old negotiating ploy; create a feeling of helplessness and dependency in your adversary. In her case they didn't even have to create that feeling. It already existed.

She nodded.

"Would you be so kind as to vocalize your answers while in mediation, Ms. Roark?" they mouthed. "All responses are being recorded to the Metachain."

"I'd like assistance getting to the chair," she said. The clock was ticking.

Invisible hands lifted her, the most considerate and powerful butler in the universe, polite and precise and flew her into the mediation room and seated her. Her pericarp swung and bumped the leg of the desk. She lifted it and set it beside the pen and the flower.

"You've brought your own pericarp," said their voice. There was still something familiar in the tone. *What was it?* "Wonderfully efficient. We really are deeply concerned with resolving our differences in the most economical fashion possible. Is there anything we can do to make you more comfortable? May we bring you a cup of coffee or tea?"

She sat up, started to answer and groaned. A small sound. It just came out. The moment she'd been whisked into the room she'd felt the tiniest flicker of pain light up her leg, and there was no mystery about that sensation. *Let it come,* she thought. *I have seven minutes left. Can't get much worse in seven minutes.*

But as she straightened at the desk she was forced to stifle a gasp. It came fast. In her hip a Wuln Vuln Drongplo of pain began ravaging up her nerves, rushing straight up her body to her throat. Too fast. The knife sharp heat forced tears to her eyes.

"We are confident we can resolve this situation efficiently, Ms. Roark," The Fund nattered on, taking up time. Diana knew she should be paying attention, but the pain was a claw in her side now. Rising, it bent bones back one atop the next. It never came this fast. This forcefully. Ever.

"We feel as though, in you, we have a negotiating partner who shares our interest in minimizing waste."

"Yes," she squeezed out. "Not a fan of waste."

"Then together, let us arrive at the most economical solution."

She nodded but hardly heard them, whatever these opening platitudes were. Her head was helium light, her skin brazier hot. She reached for the water on the desk and saw the timer on the pericarp: six and a half minutes. She had to hurry. But instead, her mind wandered. Beside the time she saw the date: 3/13/77. The Anniversary of the Great Augmentation. Thirty years—minus six and a half minutes—since the Obelisks had fallen from heaven. Thirty years since she'd taken Greg to the bottom of the sea and killed him.

"Would you prefer to do this another time, Ms. Roark? We would be happy to postpone."

That's when she realized who the polite, considerate voice of The Fund reminded her of. All she had to do was append one clause to the end of anything the voice said:

'Would you like some tea or coffee, Ms. Roark, *before we cut off your head?*'

'Would you like assistance getting to your chair, Ms. Roark, *before we cut off your head?*'

It could be Jianguo Tsou she was talking to, or any earthly banker she had ever met. The Fund were bankers. Polite, solicitous, serene in their cocoon of currency. Murderers.

The room was sliding, the pain fogging her memory and squeezing the breath from body. But bankers. She could handle bankers.

So, she smiled a negotiator's smile.

"Thank you, I'm fine." She paused, gathering a handful of forward momentum. Once she began, it would go quickly. It had to. "I'm here because I would like to renegotiate the terms of our loan."

"Oh. Would you like to increase your credit limit?"

"No." Did she detect just the slightest tone of mockery in that voice? *A weakness like arrogance? That would be fantastic.* But still no change in their appearance; lined up in their chairs like a clutch of perfect ducklings, they showed no physical signs of weakness.

"Then how can we better serve you, our valued client?"

"I would like to request a complete forgiveness of the debt," she announced, her own tone conversational and warm despite the numbing, brittle cold spreading through her back. The blood in her neck. The length of her hand and arm.

"We are sorry," said the voice, sounding plausibly sorry. "We are not able to forgive your debt at this time."

"At this time? Or ever?"

"We are not able to forgive your debt. That would be wasteful. We know you understand."

In fact, she did. Every ten year old knew this strategy and she was sure she wasn't fooling The Fund. Ask for the ridiculous to begin and after that, everything else appears just a little more palatable.

Time to try running the stakes up. She spread out her smile again, despite a thousand tiny hooks trying to tear it from her face.

"We are prepared to register a formal complaint with the Interstellar Trade Commission," she said, "due to irregularities in the documentation and execution of our contract, if accommodations are not made to redress our grievances."

"Perhaps you have an accommodation to suggest other than the complete elimination of your legally binding debt?"

The formalities were out of the way. Just three minutes left.

"I do. We would accept a reduction of the interest rate on our account."

"The interest rate is not a negotiable item. Twenty seven percent is the legal and appropriate rate for an applicant with humanity's credit history. It is the very best we can do."

Two minutes left. Diana reached for the water, her hand trembling; she knew she would spill it if she tried to drink, as she was a single muscle twitch away from convulsing in dry heaves. Suddenly everything inside her was going wrong. She felt something drop in her stomach and then something expanded and refused to tighten back. Something wet spread down her leg and looking at her lap Diana saw a stain. She was pissing, unable to control it. She was about to lose her body.

Why? Why was this happening so fast?

"In..." she took a shuddering breath, forcing herself to smile. "In that case, we would... we would like to request a change in the payment schedule... the payment schedule for the loan. From thirty years to something more reasonable."

"The payment schedule is not a negotiable item."

Of course. Her vision blurred, then cleared. A minute and a half. It was very, very difficult to remain seated in this chair. She leaned farther forward, and something in her spine cracked.

She felt it, a small wet pop, like a rotten stick snapping and then could no longer feel her legs. Some festering, consumptive force had eaten through her core and now the only thing keeping her erect was her forearm, propped on the table. She no longer had the ability to smile, or to pretend in any way to be something other than what she was: close to the end.

"Then we would like to prepay... the remainder of our debt," she said. The real offer, the one she had been saving, spoken through lips and tongue swollen thick and dry. She watched the white wall in front of her through burning eyes. "We would be willing to pay... a one hundred percent penalty... to discharge... what we owe."

She had seen humanity's Golden Field, and mankind's debt to The Fund amounted to an infinitesimal fraction of humanity's total reserve. This was an acceptable deal from her side. She didn't know how much a Neu was worth—what you could do with it, what you could buy. Probably not happiness. Probably not forgiveness for all the people you had killed. But if The Fund wanted to turn a profit, this was the way, by doubling their money in a single pass: a huge, zero risk profit, instantly deposited. There wasn't an investment banker in the universe who'd pass up a deal like that.

Including, it seemed, The Fund.

"That will be acceptable," said their voice smoothly. "That would be the most economical solution. If you would be so kind, please initiate the transfer quickly."

Which brought her up short. This was the first time The Fund had asked for something. Speed. The Fund wanted her to move quickly—because she was breaking? Did they know? Something about the rapidity with which they'd accepted the offer made her pause. It seemed off. Even so, she lowered her arm toward the pericarp. She had to press her elbow to the table to keep her body from sliding to the floor. The Fund was right about one thing. She needed to hurry.

"After this... we'll owe... nothing?" she probed, weak and numb, but still suspicious.

"That is correct, Ms. Roark. Debt free. Won't that be nice?"

Again, a slightly mocking tone. A sudden, shocking thought stopped her fingers, just inches from the pericarp.

"Is there... a prepayment... penalty?" she asked. All she had to do was lean. Lean across the table a hands breadth to touch and pay.

"Yes," came their reply.

"What is the penalty?"

The response was a slow admission.

"Forfeiture of your planet."

There it was. The contract had been written so that mankind, like so many unsophisticated borrowers before it, was doomed to failure. Absurdly, if she were to pay back the entire loan early, she would have to give up the collateral which backstopped the loan: their entire planet.

So. It was over then. The contract had been signed by others and she had no power to change it. Having tried everything, she had no options left, and now she had to pay. Despite her harrowing pain, she felt a flicker of something else. She'd done everything. Spent everything. No one could ask for more than she had given. So, it was here, finally, what she had been ready for on the beach. Just one last payment and she would be free.

Thirty seconds left.

Her body was draped forward over the desk, chest down, facing left. How had it gotten like that? With nerves to her leg severed, she had no way to lever the last few inches to the pericarp. She couldn't lift her head. Her neck had suffered the fate of her spine. Eaten through. At eye level she saw blood spread on the desk. She tasted it, flowing from her nose or mouth. It slid off the side of her face. *Oh,* she thought. *Dear god. I may not be able to reach.*

"Is there anything we can provide you, Ms. Roark?" The fund inquired, their mouths moving together—or at least the ones that remained in her view. Their faces still betrayed nothing. "You seem to be dying of cancer on the mediation table. Would you like a napkin?"

She saw it then. They knew. They had known the whole time.

"You... are killing me," she breathed as realization crystalized.

"No. That would not be legal. Worse, it would be a waste to devote currency to killing you when your body is so effectively killing itself. We abhor waste. We did, however, contribute a very tiny expenditure to your body's campaign of death. You want to die, so think of it as a donation, just to assure the timing. There are no laws against donations. Very economical. As a committed capitalist, you will understand. Waste is the enemy, isn't it, Ms. Roark? Goodbye, Ms. Roark."

She could no longer speak. She shuddered, straining, reaching, opened at every orifice, stretching for freedom. There was only an inch. She could still be free. She had the strength for that. An inch. *Just one inch.*

Two seconds.

Her arm stretched.

One second.

A crack. Her shoulder broke open. Her fingers pulled. Pulled her arm forward.

Zero seconds.

Contact. Too late. The end.

SHE WAS INSIDE HER CAPSULE, dying again. The phosphorescent jellies of the sea passed her, going the wrong direction. She floated from her harness, up to the top of the dome, wonder in her heart. *Look at it*, she thought. *Just look. I'm leaving.*

She passed the moon. It fell behind her, and the rest of the planets too. The sun shrank to the prick of a pin. And then above her were the stars. Greg's domain.

She had seen them from her planet over so many years. Scenes of life, death, struggle and triumph. Some stuck out in her memory: stars framed behind a tree on a stolen, romantic stroll, stars seen while laying on her back, fiercely focused, just a girl, her sister beside her. Her whole life they had been up there. But now she was really here, among them and she knew she had never *really* seen them. And she wanted to. She could go where she liked. The Milky Way pulled her, a bright score chalked into the dark, brilliant as a headlight in a candlelit church. She reached for it, her hand pressed against her capsule roof.

There the Southern Cross shone, the Coal Sack Nebula dark at its side and the Eta Carinae Nebula beside it, just a flutter in the celestial wind. She had them all in sight and rose toward them.

And *there*, the nebula she called her own, the Butterfly. *Let's go there*, she thought and so she did. The gauzy wings expanded. The too hot gas of a billion stars seemed to cool a degree in welcome for her. She was expected. She was accepted.

And there, what was that? Like the trail of a laser swung in a pitch-black room, an unexpected something—a glimmer, a diamond mystery. *Yes,* she thought. *Let's go THERE.*

Her mortal thoughts were still with her as she drew closer to the astonishing celestial surprise: Earth had been foreclosed. Its ownership transferred. Even now the bankers were beginning to drain it. Well, maybe not quite *now.* She was still caught in the moment between being and not being. As soon as this moment passed, when she was dead and this phantom capsule was gone, time would start again. Earth would be torn to pieces. Which was, so thankfully, no longer her worry.

Was it?

She came closer to her goal and then she *saw.*

Links. It was a chain. Dense, white-cloud soft, made of compact star gas and space dust and gravity and time. The link nearest her recorded the totality of everything. It was the biggest one. The End. And fading back behind, winding away through the stars and down through time to the beginning, were the other links, each one smaller than the one before. It was just the thing she'd studied and tried to build, so long ago. But it was so much more than that; it was a temporal database, built in the fabric of time.

And then up through the distant blackness from which the links emerged, up from the beginning, something swam toward her. *A ghost?* It billowed and moved with smooth sweeps of a tail, heading for the End, where Diana existed in her moment. It came fast, like a spectral train. A cloud leviathan.

It slowed, arriving in a veil of star bits and steam. She watched it from her capsule. Its eye, an enormous, gaseous, transparent portal in which the universe was faintly present, that eye imposed itself on her. It was a globe, massive as a temple door, imposing as time itself.

Inside Diana's capsule, inside Diana's mind, the scientist and the economist agreed; this thing was unlikely. Probably a mistake. Possibly a fraud. Most likely nothing. But the rest of her, which, as it turned out, comprised the much larger percentage of her being, had no such reservations. This was *something*. Science and economy didn't get a vote, not out here in space time.

Moments passed. Or years. Or seconds. A pain slowly grew in Diana. *That isn't right,* she thought. There should be no more pain. But the pain was sadness. It was hers. It was the leviathan's. The pain of things ending. The being reached out, turning Diana's capsule. She looked down at the moment she had left, at Earth floating in space.

She saw the beauty of what mankind's Golden Field had been, the ravishing, superabundant rondure of human choice that burned in its pocket of time and space. Their treasure. She could see other fields of Currency nearby, churning energetic concentrations of choice, built and maintained by other sentient species. None of those looked like humanity's Field. It was a different color than the rest, obscuring the others with brightness, like the noon sun eclipses a match.

She could see The Fund and their own Golden Field. Theirs was far away and a long and twisting cord had been tied from it to humanity's. The Fund's was very small in comparison, but a tremendous torrent of Universal Currency coursed through it from elsewhere. There was a contract, a tiny closed chain-link, around the cord from humanity's Field to The Fund's. The Fund was preparing to export mankind's Currency. She saw other cords with contract links attached to The Fund's Field, great rivers of currency pumping through them, feeding The Fund—Universal Currency The Fund was using, to buy and sell and loan and hire and hold and strip. To pay Private Equity and pay the hordes of Appraisers and Accountants and Human Resource contractors swarming Earth. Those pumping cords fed it debt, strung back to loans it had taken out. The Fund, Robert had said, was leveraged to the eyeballs and she could see that it was true.

Diana was forced to watch it all. Back wherever her body was, life blanched out. But as that had happened, her fingers had managed to push themselves against the pericarp, too late to make her payment, but just in time to transport her as she died. Pericarps are just transmitters. They transmit anything that wants to *go.*

She really did want to go. But here she stayed. The sadness was an unbearable pain now, rising behind her. She turned back, within her capsule, to face the leviathan.

"When can I go?" she asked. Her/Its/His sadness made it difficult to speak. But someone had to say something.

[*Paid are debts your when go can you.*]

"That's backwards," she said when she'd it figured out.

[*Polarity reversed. You can go when your debts are paid.*]

"I don't have any debts," she assured the thing. "I've never taken any debt."

[*Then why have you been paying?*]

"I'm not paying."

[*You have been. You are.*]

"I don't have anything to pay *with.*"

[*Because you have paid it all away. To clear your debts. You have paid out everything—yet still you have debt.*]

It was ridiculous. What was this giant fish saying? And what in the world was it so sad about—it really was distracting, all the sadness. It made it hard to feel.

"No, that's wrong, I didn't pay it. I gave everything away."

[*Your fortune.*]

"Yes. Gave it all."

[*To give is to become free. To purchase is to take debt.*]

"Ok. Well, one way or the other, it's gone."

[*And what of your limbs?*]

"I don't know what you mean. They're gone."

[*You bought your life with those. You paid.*]

"I suppose. Ok."

She didn't like the direction this was going. She pushed on the roof of the capsule. It looked so thin and she wanted out. The Leviathan watched her struggle, its portal orb unblinking.

[*You paid with your lovers, did you not? What did you buy with them?*]

"Not fair."

[*You paid with your pride. And your friends. And your family.*]

"Stop."

[*Any happiness.*]

"Stop. Please stop."

[*Bones.*]

"Stop!"

[*Hope.*]

"Please, *stop!*"

[*Everything.*]

"Yes! I did. Ok. It's all gone, just stop!"

[*All given? Or paid?*]

"Paid. I paid it, all of it *paid...*" How was it possible to be dead and still be out of breath? She panted. Would there never come a day when there was *always* air to breathe, when you didn't have to worry that the world would squeeze in and stopper you?

[*And what of your heart, little one? That is gone. Did you give that away?*]

She wished she had a different answer.

"No."

[*No.*]

It watched her.

[*You paid that too.*]

She was stuck, with nowhere to hide.

[*And yet.*]

"What?"

[*Despite everything. You have not discharged what you owe.*]

"I don't owe *anything!* To *anyone!* I'm free!"

[*Are you? If a river refuses to flow, there is debt to unwatered trees. If the sun refuses to shine a debt is owed, for flowers die.*]

"Stop. Stop this. I would like to die now." She thrust harder against the roof of her capsule. Pounded. *Out. She wanted out!*

[*You cannot leave. Not until your debts are paid. There are so many debts.*]

"*I don't HAVE debts!* How many times do I have to say it? And even if I did, how could I pay anything? You said it. I've got nothing left. I paid *everything!*" It was astonishing how painful that was. She had pain. She had pain everywhere. But that was all.

[*To begin, you must accept what I will give you.*]

"What?"

[*A loan.*]

And then, like an Olympic swimmer spinning at the end of a pool, the eye—and the whole leviathan behind it—turned and thrust away and Diana was caught in its wake. Down she went. Down the Blockchain. Down the ages. Down time, to the opposite end, which was the Beginning.

"What are you?" Diana asked as they dropped.

[*We were once the Sentient One.*]

"Not anymore?"

[*We dispersed myself. Now we are merely a formula.*]

"A formula for what?"

[*Choice.*]

The links around them grew tiny as she tumbled behind the great ghost and the medium through which they passed thinned, stretched and when it seemed it could not support them another moment, that they must collapse out of it, they stopped.

There where everything had begun, they hung, cold, dark, empty nothing all around them, where the smallest and first link in the Metaspatial Blockchain shimmered like thin milk. The Beginning.

Before them wavered a ball of Currency. A single ball. *Large or small?* It was hard to tell. Nothing else was here where the beginning started, nothing to compare to anything else. Size was an unsolvable mystery.

"What is this?" she asked of the pulsing ball.

[*The leftovers. After all the things were made, this was left over. We saved it. A rainy day fund. It is your leverage.*]

"What do you mean, all the things were made? What things?"

[*Choices.*]

"What am I supposed to do with this rainy day fund?"

[*Assume it. We are loaning it to you.*]

"For what? What am I supposed to do with a loan? I just died of cancer!"

[*All the paying you have done has not bought you freedom, little one. Do not fight this. The act of payment is not the act of becoming free. Not the same act at all. And some debts can never be repaid. What can you do with those? In the meantime, thermodynamics insists energy is recycled. My adversary persists and grows. So, you must take this loan, because in the financial crisis to come, you must have access to your own Currency. You must use this loan to take it back. Take back humanity's Currency. Own your Golden Field again. You think you have born all that you can bear, but you have not. Not yet.*]

"A loan? You want me to take a loan? What are the terms of this loan?" She spun in her capsule, staring into the dark. "Where's our contract?"

[*The terms are these: you will only be free after you have taken this loan and paid us back. And you cannot repay us as we are now, because we do not exist. You must find the Scattered Pieces of us and make us one again. Those are the terms of the contract.*]

"You exist. I see you."

[*Only in this moment with you, here. We were gone before you came. We will be gone after you leave.*]

"Please. I want to stay the way I am, debt free. Can't I stay debt free?"

More sadness. A whole universe of sadness.

[*None of us are debt free, little one. You can choose not to take this loan, that is the right of any sentient creature and then you will hang here, at the Beginning, until the end. Trapped in your capsule here where there are not even stars, a part of what was left over.*]

It was very cold, there at the Beginning. Not a place to stay for very long if you could help it. Not trapped in a capsule. Certainly not until the end.

She watched the ball of Currency, weighing the pros and cons. She did the math. And, finally, she chose. And just before she touched it, she thought, *for you, Phoebe. I'll fix it if I can. I'll try.* And then it suffused her—the leverage, the currency, the loan—and her lack of understanding was no hindrance at all.

It grew and she grew with it and as she grew her capsule was driven forward, away from the Beginning back toward the End, sliding up the Metaspatial Blockchain link after link as if climbing a ladder through stars and deepest space. She left the ghost of the Sentient One alone in its curve of hollow time, its little burrow. And she returned to her own frozen moment. The End. Where The Fund had possessed her Golden Field.

She could feel the leftover Currency within her. It yearned. Like a living thing it wanted to flex and pry. What was she supposed to do with all of it? The Sentient One had told her to get mankind's Golden Field back. But mankind had defaulted; The Fund owned their Golden Field and they'd never sell it back. No matter how much Currency she had to spend, there was no way she could buy what was not for sale. The Fund had worked too long and too hard— had stepped too far over too many boundaries—to give anything back now. They had their own obligations to repay.

She saw the lines of their debts and obligations stretching away from The Fund's Golden Field, the contract links tied to the Blockchain. She saw the lines of credit which supported all their efforts. The debt which bound them.

She saw her own loan contract and understood. Then, once more, she paid.

SHE RETURNED to herself from very far away, coming back into what she knew was her body, where she knew it rested in a white room on a wet chair with a hard table flattening her cheek. Her eyes were closed. The first impressions she had were a series of hollow sounds, the kinds of sounds you heard when you held a jar to your ear.

Alive. Apparently. Her death had been just a frozen moment. Some new mesh application had already begun to pull the cuts on her face closed.

"Mediation's not over," she wheezed.

The sounds in her jar stopped abruptly.

The sudden silence could have been due to what she'd just said. She puzzled it out, eyes closed, body like a hunting trophy on a hood —it must surely be a surprise to The Fund that she was not dead. It was certainly a surprise to Diana. But just as likely was that they'd stopped their talking. Their preparations for burning and chopping and selling, the delicate questions of who would get what and how much to ask and where to send it when they got it, all suddenly became moot.

Suddenly, she hoped with irritation, *shockingly* moot.

Her swollen tongue made it tough to swallow and her broken spine and separated neck made the simple act of breathing a monumental undertaking, talking a herculean task. It was going to take a few minutes to get herself back together. About her body flitted a deeply concerned swarm of nano fabricating alien specks, formed in an application and waiting for instructions. Where to start, they wondered?

Start at the ends, she told them. *And work in. And make it fast.*

They began to rebuild her.

"On my planet..." she said to The Fund, pausing to watch them and finding that she could now turn her head. *Yes. Better. Look them in the eyes.* They had expressions now, she saw. Oh, did they ever.

"...Ow. That hurts...On my planet we have a thing called a home mortgage."

It all came together quickly. Her spine strengthened and she could sit up.

"On my planet," she continued, stronger as the pain retreated, "you borrow your home mortgage from a bank. You make your payments every month until your debt is gone. But behind the scenes, your debt is just a product. It gets bought and sold to investors, other banks, funds. There's a huge market. And you know what the funny thing is? The funny thing is—the Known Economy works exactly the same way."

She watched their shocked faces, noticing that none of them were offering to get her any water now. That was nice.

"Loans get bought and sold all the time out in the Known Economy, I discovered. So, in case you hadn't already guessed where this was going: I'm your new investor. I just bought all your debt. I own all of it. Including my own line of credit. I own my own Golden Field."

She felt like she had taken a drug that was making her giddy and loquacious. A drug called all-the-pain-is-gone. For-now.

"I own *you*. I guess you could say I'm your new alien overlord."

"We do not accept this outcome."

"Tough titties."

"We will seek redress with the ITC."

"Yeah. Let's do that. In the meantime, I want my Account Representative back."

"We do not know where he has been assigned."

"Look, you little shits. We can do this the hard way if you want. But I'm warning you, I despise bad employees and I have a long memory. You have connections with the ITC. Use them."

It took only a moment and then Robert reevaporated right beside her. His fronds were splayed wildly and he scooted back and forth on his cube with pseudopods shooting out everywhere, like she had caught him in the middle of a fire drill.

"Diana Roark! I'm here! Diana Roark! *DIANA ROARK!*"

"Stop yelling! Where did they send you?"

He stopped.

"Nowhere! They just fucking erased me! I've been right here for ten fucking minutes!"

Diana turned, shot a low ominous look at The Fund. Together, as one, they raised their hands and shrugged. "We're getting off to a really bad start, people," she murmured.

"We apologize profusely, Ms. Roark. The Neoooxcolu is an ITC employee. There are certain lines we cannot cross."

"That'll have to change."

She turned back to Robert. She'd felt more cut off than she could describe after he was gone. She'd drunk his urine, suffocated in his ectoplasm—she needed him, for some reason. Suddenly, some unfathomable impulse made her lean to his cube and throw her arms, one flesh, one gray and stony, along the sides of him. After a moment he extended pseudopods and returned the embrace, stroking her head and holding her.

"Diana fucking Roark," his voice sounded a little bit awed. "You amazing fucking animal. You actually did it."

"So it seems." She leaned back. "Can you get us a ship, Robert? We need to get down to the surface."

"Us?"

"Yeah." She looked at his fronds very seriously. "I just bought a bunch of stuff and I'm going to need help. Someone to advise me about the Known Economy. Also, I don't like answering my own phone. Are you interested?"

He looked uncertain.

"I've already got a job..." he noted.

"Do you like it?"

"Well, I'm about to ask for a raise. And the benefits are universe class. I hope to have a family to think about soon, you know. Kids are expensive."

"I'm offering you a paying gig, Robert." She showed him the terms on the Metachain.

"Oh! Consider me hired!" He said, instantly, then continued, a sheepish note to his voice, "I would have taken it anyway, you know. I hate my fucking job. I was just negotiating."

"I know." She patted his ectoplasm fondly. "Very nice. Now we have a planet to run. And I don't know how much time we've got to get everything in order. There's a financial crisis coming."

He transformed back to a khaki clad human, drawing on his new, very substantial salary. The wall bowed away from them and assumed its spaceship living room shape and Robert helped her limp aboard. The wall resealed behind them.

Then they started back to the planet, or she presumed they did, anyway, but she didn't feel like looking out a window to check. She'd had enough of space travel for one day. Instead, she looked down at her single, ancient leg refreshing itself as 23-year-old flesh and bone. While she hadn't been looking, her missing leg had already been regrown. Very fancy, she thought, rotating her new ankle. Maybe I should get my nails painted to celebrate.

Then the little fabricators wanted to regrow her flesh arm, but she saw her gray, hard prosthetic and made them stop. She decided to keep it. As a memento. Plus, it was excellent at fighting and who knew how much more of that was coming? Plenty, she suspected. So the tiny fabs began to work their way down her other arm, turning it from 60 to 23, which was very satisfying until they reached her wrist. She stopped them again, looking at her butterfly star. She was keeping that too, she knew. Some people might think it was cutesy bullshit. But that was their opinion.

Robert was talking on the phone. *He can't possibly be talking on the phone*, she thought. But he was indeed on a phone, conferring with her new subordinates, getting things straightened out. She decided to take a quick stroll on her new bipeds. She got up—just like that—and walked to the wall. It was a small miracle. A much smaller miracle than a lot of other things that had already happened, but it could easily end up being her favorite.

She sat by the wall and leaned her shoulder to it and thought about the planet below. A transparent square opened to show her a deep blue, cloud scoured, half round planet, the sun settling over Asia. How was it going to work, getting that place integrated into the

Known Economy? How was she supposed to do all the things she now had to do? For a moment, all she could do was stare.

Penny for your thoughts, said the voice.

"What?" She turned to Robert. He was still on the... phone? *Yes, still a phone.* There was no one else in the room. Was something going wrong with her teeny tiny fabricators?

I think that was supposed to be a light, ironic introduction, said the voice. *Was it? Did it read?*

Diana twirled. The voice had come from inside her head; Robert had obviously not heard a thing. She stood, but did not move, and examined her body. A parasitic alien growth? Some kind of implant? Nothing seemed out of place or suspicious.

It is peculiar, isn't it?

who are you?

I believe my name is Crystal Clear.

She sucked in a breath. When the bottom had fallen out of the world, there *had* been that helpful presence. Could this be it? Had that been real?

Crystal Clear. I don't understand. are you real?

I don't know. Are you?

are you alive?

Now that's a very good question. I'm going to have to get back to you.

And then the voice was gone. Male? Female? She couldn't remember anything about the way it had sounded. It had just... been there. But she'd definitely heard it. Definitely. *Right?*

Robert approached her.

"I've got the fucking Fund on the phone," he said. "There are some documents we need to get registered on the Blockchain." He covered the mic with his hand and hissed. "Diana Roark, what the fuck? Are you fucking crazy? Do you know what you did?"

"Yes." She thought about it. "No. What?"

"The Fund controlled one tenth of the Known Economy. A fucking *tenth of the Known Economy!* You're, like, fucking in charge of... fucking... *fuck!* I don't even know. This is going to be a problem. I'm going to need a raise."

"Ok. Robert? In your new position as Earth's High... Councilor Appraiser? Please get in the habit of bringing me solutions, not problems. I have enough of those."

"Ok, well, The Fund needs to know what to call you. Chief operating officer? Director? President? We need a title to put on this form."

Diana thought about it. None of the official titles she'd ever had seemed right. Too big. Too small. All mostly without meaning. Although, when she thought about it, there was one. Before this, it had never really fit. But now the time for it might have come at last.

"Can I be anything I like?" she asked.

"You control one-fifteenth of the Known Economy. Pick any fucking title you want."

She rolled it around in her mind. *Yes.*

"Tell them to call me *The Seer of Sonoma*." she said.

THE END

Keep checking the Metaspatial Blockchain, where a sequel to *A Debt to the Stars* will someday become available, entitled *The Seer of Sonoma*.

About the Author

His name is Kevin Hincker. His website is kevinhincker.com. He sometimes emails short stories about the creatures of the Metaspacial Blockchain to everyone on his email list.

He's deeply appreciative of science fiction readers.

Also by Kevin Hincker